Beauty Is a Wound

Eka Kurniawan

Beauty Is a Wound

TRANSLATED BY ANNIE TUCKER

A New Directions Paperbook Original

Published by arrangement with the author. *Cantik ita luka* was originally published in 2002 by AKY Press and Penerbit Jendela, Yogyakart, and from 2004 by PT Gramedia Pustaka Utama, Jakarta.

Publication of this book was made possible with assistance from the Indonesian Translation Funding Program.

Manufactured in the United States of America
New Directions Books are printed on acid-free paper
First published by New Directions as New Directions Paperbook NDP1313 in 2015

Library of Congress Cataloging-in-Publication Data
Kurniawan, Eka, 1975– author.
[Cantik itu luka. English]
Beauty is a wound / Eka Kurniawan ; translated by Annie Tucker.
pages cm
Novel.
ISBN 978-0-8112-2363-8 (alk. paper)
I. Tucker, Annie, translator. II. Kurniawan, Eka, 1975– Cantik itu luka. Translation of: III. Title.
PL5089.K78C3613 2015
899'.22132—dc23 2015013461

10 9 8 7 6 5 4 3 2

New Directions Books are published for James Laughlin
by New Directions Publishing Corporation
80 Eighth Avenue, New York 10011

Having cleaned his armor and made a full helmet out of a simple headpiece, and having given a name to his horse and decided on one for himself, he realized that the only thing left for him to do was to find a lady to love, for the knight errant without a lady-love was a tree without leaves or fruit, a body without a soul.

– Miguel de Cervantes, *Don Quixote*

{1}

ONE AFTERNOON ON a weekend in March, Dewi Ayu rose from her grave after being dead for twenty-one years. A shepherd boy, awakened from his nap under a frangipani tree, peed in his shorts and screamed, and his four sheep ran off haphazardly in between stones and wooden grave markers as if a tiger had been thrown into their midst. It all started with a noise coming from an old gravesite with an unmarked tombstone covered in knee-high grass, but everybody knew it was Dewi Ayu's grave. She had passed away at fifty-two, rose again after being dead for twenty-one years, and from that point forward nobody knew exactly how to calculate her age.

People from the surrounding neighborhood came to the grave when the shepherd boy told them what was happening. Rolling up the edges of their sarongs, carrying children, clutching broomsticks, or stained with mud from the fields, they gathered behind cherry shrubs and jatropha trees and in the nearby banana orchards. No one dared approach, they just listened to the uproar coming from that old grave as if they were gathered around the medicine peddler who hawked his goods at the market every Monday morning. The crowd wholly enjoyed the unnerving spectacle, not caring that such a horror would have terrified them had they been all alone. They were even expecting some kind of miracle and not just a noisy old tomb, because the woman inside that plot of earth had been a prostitute for the Japanese during the war and the *kyai* always said that people tainted with sin were sure to be punished in the grave. The sound must have been coming from the whip of a tormenting angel, but they grew bored, hoping for some other small marvel.

When it came, it came in the most fantastical form. The grave shook and fractured, and the ground exploded as if blown up from underneath, triggering a small earthquake and a windstorm that sent grass and headstones flying, and behind the dirt raining down like a curtain the figure of an old woman stood looking annoyed and stiff, still wrapped in a shroud as if she'd only just been buried the night before. The people grew hysterical and ran away even more chaotically than the sheep, their synchronous screams echoing against the walls of the faraway hills. A woman tossed her baby into the bushes and its father hushed a banana stalk. Two men plunged into a ditch, others fell unconscious at the side of the road, and still others took off running for fifteen kilometers straight without stopping.

Witnessing all this, Dewi Ayu only coughed a little and cleared her throat, fascinated to find herself in the middle of a graveyard. She had already untied the two highest knots on her burial shroud, and then set to loosening the two lowest ones to free her feet so she could walk. Her hair had grown magically so that when she shook it loose from the calico wrap it fluttered in the afternoon breeze, sweeping the ground, and shimmering like black lichen in a riverbed. Her skin was wrinkled, but her face was gleaming white, and her eyes came alive inside their sockets to stare at onlookers abandoning their hiding places behind the shrubs—half of them ran away and the other half fainted. She complained, to no one in particular, that people were evil to have buried her alive.

The first thing she thought of was her baby, who of course was no longer a baby. Twenty-one years ago, she had died twelve days after giving birth to a hideous baby girl, so hideous that the midwife assisting her couldn't be sure whether it really was a baby and thought that maybe it was a pile of shit, since the holes where a baby comes out and where shit comes out are only two centimeters apart. But this baby squirmed, and smiled, and finally the midwife believed that it really was a human being and not shit, and said to the mother, who was lying weakly across her bed with no apparent desire to see her offspring, that the baby was born, was healthy, and seemed friendly.

"It's a girl, right?" asked Dewi Ayu.

"Yes," said the midwife, "just like the three babies before her."

"Four daughters, all of them beautiful," said Dewi Ayu in a tone of complete annoyance. "I should open my own whorehouse. Tell me, how pretty is this one?"

The baby wrapped up tight in a swaddling cloth began to squirm and cry in the midwife's arms. A woman was coming in and out of the room, taking away the dirty cloths full of blood, getting rid of the placenta, and for a moment the midwife did not answer because there was no way she was going to say that a baby who looked like a pile of black shit was pretty. Trying to ignore the question she said, "You're already an old woman, so I don't think you'll be able to nurse."

"That's true. I've been used up by the three previous kids."

"And hundreds of men."

"One hundred and seventy-two men. The oldest one was ninety years old, the youngest one was twelve, one week after his circumcision. I remember them all well."

The baby cried again. The midwife said that she had to find breast milk for the little one. If there was none, she'd have to look for cow's milk, or dog's milk, or maybe even rat's milk. Yeah, go, said Dewi Ayu. "Poor unfortunate little girl," said the midwife, gazing at the baby's upsetting face. She wasn't even able to describe it, but she thought it looked like a cursed monster from hell. The baby's entire body was jet black as if it had been burned alive, with a bizarre and unrecognizable form. For example, she wasn't sure whether the baby's nose was a nose, because it looked more like an electrical outlet than any nose she'd ever seen in her entire life. And the baby's mouth reminded her of a piggy-bank slot and her ears looked like pot handles. She was sure that there was no creature on earth more hideous than this wretched little one, and if she were God, she would probably kill the baby at once rather than let her live; the world would abuse her without mercy.

"Poor baby," said the midwife again, before going to look for someone to nurse her.

"Yeah, poor baby," said Dewi Ayu, tossing and turning in her bed. "I already did everything I could to try to kill you. I should have swallowed a grenade and detonated it inside my stomach. Oh wretched little one—just like evildoers, the wretched don't die easy."

At first the midwife tried to hide the baby's face from the neighbor women who arrived. But when she said that she needed milk for the baby, they pushed against each other to see it, since it was always fun for those who knew Dewi Ayu to see her adorable little girl babies. The midwife was unable to stave off the onslaught of people pushing aside the cloth hiding the baby's face, but once they'd seen it, and screamed from a horror unlike any they had ever experienced before, the midwife smiled and reminded them that she had tried her best not to show them the hellish countenance.

After that outburst, as the midwife left in a hurry, they just stood for a moment, with the faces of idiots whose memories had been suddenly erased.

"It should just be killed," said a woman, the first one freed from her sudden-onset amnesia.

"I already tried," said Dewi Ayu as she appeared, wearing only a rumpled housedress and a cloth tied around her waist. Her hair was a total mess, like someone staggering away from a bullfight.

People looked at her with pity.

"She's pretty, right?" asked Dewi Ayu.

"Um, yes."

"There's no curse more terrible than to give birth to a pretty female in a world of men as nasty as dogs in heat."

Not one person responded, they just kept looking at her with sympathy, knowing they were lying. Rosinah, the mute mountain girl who had been serving Dewi Ayu for years, led the woman into the bathroom, where she had prepared hot water in the tub. There Dewi Ayu soaked with fragrant sulfurous soap, attended by the mute girl who shampooed her hair with aloe vera oil. Only the mute seemed unfazed by any of this, even though she surely already knew about the hideous little girl, since no one else but Rosinah had accompanied the midwife while she worked. She rubbed her mistress's back with a pumice stone, wrapped her in a towel, and straightened up the bathroom as Dewi Ayu stepped out.

Someone tried to lighten the gloomy mood and said to Dewi Ayu, "You need to give her a good name."

"Yeah," said Dewi Ayu. "Her name is Beauty."

"Oh!" the people exclaimed, embarrassingly trying to dissuade her.

"Or how about Injury?"

"Or Wound?"

"For God's sake, don't name it that."

"Okay then, her name is Beauty."

They watched helplessly as Dewi Ayu walked back into her room to get dressed. They could only look at one another, sadly imagining a young girl black as soot with an electrical outlet in the middle of her face being called by the name of Beauty. It was a shameful scandal.

However, it was true that Dewi Ayu had tried to kill the baby back when she realized that, whether or not she had already lived for a whole half century, she was pregnant once again. Just as with her other children, she didn't know who the father was, but unlike the others she had absolutely no desire for the baby to survive. So she had taken five extra-strength paracetamol pills that she got from a village doctor and washed them down with half a liter of soda, which was almost enough to cause her own death but not quite, as it turned out, enough to kill that baby. She thought of another way, and called a midwife who was willing to kill the baby and take it out of her womb by inserting a small wooden stick into her belly. She experienced heavy bleeding for two days and two nights and the small piece of wood came back out in splinters, but the baby kept growing. She tried six other ways to get the better of that baby, but all were in vain, and she finally gave up and complained:

"This one is a real brawler, and she's clearly going to beat her mother in this fight."

So she let her stomach get bigger and bigger, held the *selamatan* ritual at seven months, and let the baby be born, even though she refused to look at her. She had already given birth to three girls before this and all of them were gorgeous, practically like triplets born one after another. She was bored with babies like that, who according to her were like mannequins in a storefront display, so she didn't want to see her youngest child, certain she would be no different from her three older sisters. She was wrong, of course, and didn't yet know how repulsive her youngest truly was. Even when the neighbor women furtively whispered that the baby was like the result of randomly breeding a monkey with a frog and a monitor lizard, she didn't think they were talking about her baby. And when they said that the previous night wild dogs had howled in the forest and owls had flown in to roost, she didn't in the least bit take those as bad omens.

After getting dressed, she lay down again, suddenly struck by how exhausting it all was, giving birth to four babies and living longer than half a century. And then she had the depressing realization that if the baby didn't want to die then maybe her mother should be the one to go, so that she would never have to see it grow into a young woman. She rose and staggered to the doorway, looking out at all the neighbor women who were still clustered together gossiping about the infant. Rosinah appeared from the bathroom and stood at Dewi Ayu's side, sensing that her mistress was about to give her an order.

"Buy me a burial shroud," said Dewi Ayu. "I have already given four girls to this accursed world. The time has come for my funeral procession to pass on by."

The women shrieked and gaped at Dewi Ayu with their idiot faces. To give birth to a hideous baby was an outrage, but to abandon it just like that was way more outrageous. But they didn't come right out and say so, they just tried to talk her out of dying so foolishly, saying that some people lived for more than one hundred years, and that Dewi Ayu was still much too young to die.

"If I live to be a hundred," she said with a measured calm, "then I will give birth to eight children. That's too many."

Rosinah went and bought Dewi Ayu a clean white calico cloth that she put on immediately—though that wasn't enough to make her die right away. And so, as the midwife was traversing the neighborhood looking for a lactating woman (although this was in vain and she ended up giving the baby water that had been used to rinse rice), Dewi Ayu was lying calmly on top of her bed wrapped in a burial shroud, waiting with an uncanny patience for the angel of death to come and carry her away.

When the time of rice-rinse water had passed and Rosinah was feeding the baby cow's milk (sold in the store as "Bear's Milk"), Dewi Ayu was still lying in bed, not allowing anyone to bring the baby named Beauty into her room. But the story of the hideous baby and its mother wrapped in a burial shroud quickly spread like a plague, dragging people in not just from the surrounding neighborhoods but also from the farthest-flung villages in the district, to come see what was said to be like the birth of a prophet, with people comparing the howls of the wild dogs to the star seen by the Magi when Jesus was born and comparing the mother wrapped in her burial shroud to an exhausted Mary—a pretty far-fetched metaphor.

With the terrified expression of a young girl petting a baby tiger in the zoo, the visitors posed with the hideous infant for a roving photographer. This was after they had done the same with Dewi Ayu, who was still lying in her mysterious peacefulness, not at all disturbed by the merciless clamor. A number of people with grave and incurable illnesses came hoping to touch the baby, something Rosinah was quick to forbid because she was worried that all the germs would infect the infant, but in exchange she prepared pails of Beauty's bath water. A number of others came hoping for a little luck at the betting table or sudden insight on how to make a business profit. For all of this mute Rosinah, who had quickly sprung into action as the baby's caretaker, had prepared donation boxes that were soon filled with the visitors' rupiah bills. The girl, wisely anticipating the possibility that Dewi Ayu might actually die in the end, acted in order to make some money from such a rare opportunity, so that she wouldn't have to worry about the Bear's Milk or their future alone together in the house, since Beauty's three older sisters could never be expected to turn up there at all.

But the ruckus quickly came to an end as soon as the police came with a *kyai* who considered the whole thing heresy. That *kyai* began to fume and ordered Dewi Ayu to stop her shameful behavior, even demanding that she remove the burial shroud.

"You are asking a prostitute to take off her clothes," said Dewi Ayu scornfully, "so you'd better have the money to pay me."

The *kyai* quickly prayed for mercy, moved along, and never came again.

Once again the only one left was young Rosinah, who was never troubled by Dewi Ayu's insanity no matter what form it took, and it became all the more evident that the girl was the only one who really understood that woman. Way before she tried to kill the baby inside her womb, Dewi Ayu had said that she was bored of having children, and so Rosinah had known that she was expecting. If Dewi Ayu had said such a thing to the neighborhood women, whose penchant for gossip beat the habit of yowling dogs, they would have smirked with contemptuous smiles and said that was just hot air—stop whoring yourself out and you'll never have to worry about getting knocked up, they would have said. But just between you and me: tell that to another prostitute, but not to Dewi Ayu. She had never thought of her three (and now four) children as a curse of prostitution, and if the girls didn't have fathers, she said, that was because they really and truly didn't have fathers, not because they didn't know who their fathers were, and certainly not because she had never stood next to some guy in front of a village headman. She believed them instead to be the children of demons.

"Because Satan loves to get his kicks as much as God or the gods," she said. "Like Mary gave birth to the Son of God and Pandu's two wives gave birth to their god children, my womb is a place where demons deposit their seed and so, I give birth to demon children. And I'm sick of it, Rosinah."

As often happened, Rosinah just smiled. She couldn't speak, except in an incoherent mumble, but she could smile and she liked to smile. Dewi Ayu was very fond of her, especially because of that smile. She had once called her an elephant child, because no matter how angry elephants get they always smile, just like the ones you can see in the circus that comes to town at the end of almost every year. With her sign language, that couldn't be learned in any school for mutes but had to be taught directly by Rosinah herself, the girl told Dewi Ayu that she shouldn't feel fed up—she didn't even have twenty children, meanwhile Gandari gave birth to a *hundred* of Kurawa's children. That made Dewi Ayu laugh out loud. She liked Rosinah's childish sense of humor and was still laughing as she retorted that Gandari didn't give birth to a hundred children a hundred separate times, she just gave birth to one big hunk of meat that then turned into one hundred children.

That was the cheerful way Rosinah kept working, not in the least bit put out. She took care of the baby, went into the kitchen twice a day and did the washing every morning, while Dewi Ayu lay almost without moving, truly looking like a corpse who was waiting for people to finish digging her grave. Of course if she was hungry, she got up and ate, and she went to the bathroom every morning and afternoon. But she would always return and wrap herself back up in her burial shroud to lie with her body stiff and straight, with her two hands placed on top of her stomach, her eyes closed, and her lips curved in a faint smile. There were a number of neighbors who tried to spy on her from the open window. Time after time Rosinah tried to shoo them away but she never succeeded and the people would ask, why didn't she just kill herself instead. Refraining from her usual sarcasm, Dewi Ayu remained silent and completely still.

The long-awaited death finally came on the afternoon of the twelfth day after the birth of hideous Beauty, or at least that was what everybody believed. The sign that death was near appeared that morning, when Dewi Ayu instructed Rosinah that she did not want her name on her grave marker; instead she wanted an epitaph with the sole sentence, "I gave birth to four children, and I died." Rosinah's hearing was excellent, and she could read and write, so she wrote down that message in its entirety, but the order was immediately refused by the mosque imam leading the burial ceremony, who thought that such a crazy request made the whole situation even more sinful, and decided himself that the woman wouldn't get anything at all inscribed on her headstone.

Dewi Ayu was found in the afternoon by one of the neighbors who was spying through the window, in the kind of tranquil sleep that is only seen in a person's last days. But there was something else too: there was the smell of borax in the air. Rosinah had bought it at the bakery and Dewi Ayu had sprinkled herself with the corpse preservative that others sometimes mixed in with their *mie bakso* meatballs. Rosinah had let the woman do whatever she wanted in her obsession with death, and even if she had been ordered to dig a grave and bury Dewi Ayu alive she would have done it and passed it all off as part of her mistress's unique sense of humor, but it wasn't that way with the ignorant snoop. This woman leapt in through the window, convinced that Dewi Ayu had gone too far.

"Listen up, you whore who slept with all of our men!" she said resentfully. "If you are going to die, then die, but don't preserve your body, because it's only your rotting corpse that nobody will envy." She shoved Dewi Ayu, but her body only rolled over without being awakened.

Rosinah came in and gave a signal that she must already be dead.

"That whore is dead?"

Rosinah nodded.

"Dead?!" She revealed her true character then, that whiny woman, crying as if her own mother had passed, and said between throaty sobs, "The eighth of January last year was the most beautiful day for our family. That was the day when my man found some money under the bridge and went to Mama Kalong's whorehouse and slept with this very prostitute who is now lying dead before me. He came home afterward, and that was the one and only day when he was kind to the family. He didn't even hit any of us."

Rosinah looked at her disdainfully as if to suggest one couldn't blame him for wanting to hit such a bellyacher, then got rid of that whiner by telling her to spread the news of Dewi Ayu's death. There was no need for a burial shroud because she'd already bought one twelve days ago; there was no need to bathe her, because she'd already bathed herself; she had even preserved her own body herself. "If she could have," Rosinah signed to the imam of the closest mosque, "she would have recited the prayers for herself." The imam, looking at the mute girl with hatred, said that he himself was not inclined to recite the prayers for that lump of a prostitute's corpse or what's more, to even bury her. "Since she is dead," said Rosinah (still with sign language), "then she's no longer a prostitute."

Kyai Jahro, that mosque imam, finally gave up and led Dewi Ayu's funeral.

Up until her death, which few had believed would come so quickly, she truly never saw the baby. People said that she was really lucky, because any mother would be unthinkably sad to see her baby born so hideous. Her death would not be tranquil, and she would never be able to rest in peace. Only Rosinah wasn't so sure that Dewi Ayu would have been sad to see the baby, because she knew that what that woman hated more than anything in the world was a pretty little baby girl. She would have been overjoyed if she knew how completely different her youngest one was from her older sisters; but she didn't know. Because this mute young girl was always obedient to her mistress, during the days before her death she didn't force the baby upon its mother, despite the fact that if she had known what the baby looked like, Dewi Ayu might have postponed her death, at least for a couple of years.

"That's nonsense, the moment of death is up to God," said Kyai Jahro.

"She was fixing to die for twelve days and then she died," Rosinah's gestures said, inheriting her mistress's stubbornness.

According to the will of the dead, Rosinah now became the guardian of the wretched baby. And it was she who then busied herself with the pointless task of sending telegrams to Dewi Ayu's three children saying that their mother had died and would be buried in the Budi Dharma public cemetery. Not one of them came, but the funeral was held the next day with a festivity that had not been rivaled in that city for many years before, nor would it be for many years to come. This was because almost all the men who had ever slept with the prostitute saw her off with tender kisses breathed into bouquets of jasmine blossoms that they then tossed all along the road as her casket passed. And their wives and lovers also crowded the length of road pressed up against their men's backsides looking on with a lingering jealousy, because they were sure that those horny men would still fight each other for the opportunity to sleep with Dewi Ayu again, not even caring that she was now just a corpse.

Rosinah walked behind the casket carried by four neighborhood men. The baby was fast asleep in her embrace, protected by the edge of the black veil she was wearing. A woman, the whiner, walked next to her with a basket of flower petals. Rosinah grabbed the flowers, throwing them into the air along with coins that were quickly fought over by the young children who ran underneath the casket to grab them, risking being tumbled into the irrigation channel or trampled by the mourners chanting the blessings of the prophet.

Dewi Ayu was buried in a far corner of the cemetery among the graves of other ill-fated people, because that was what Kyai Jahro and the gravedigger had agreed upon. Buried there was an evil thief from the colonial era, and a crazy killer, and a number of communists, and now a prostitute. It was believed that those unfortunate souls would be disturbed by ongoing tests and trials in the grave, and so it was wise to distance them from the graves of pious people who wanted to rest in peace, be invaded by worms and rot in peace, and make love to heavenly nymphs without any commotion.

Just as soon as that festive ceremony was done, people promptly forgot all about Dewi Ayu. Since that day, nobody came to visit the grave, not even Rosinah and Beauty. They let its ruins be pummeled by ocean storms, covered by piles of old frangipani leaves, and grown over with wild elephant grass. Only Rosinah had a convincing reason for why she didn't care for Dewi Ayu's grave. "It's because we only tend to the graves of the dead," she said to the hideous little baby (with her sign language that of course the baby didn't understand).

Maybe it was true that Rosinah had the ability to see the future, a modest skill that had been handed down by her wise old ancestors. She had first arrived in the city five years earlier with her father, a sand miner in the mountains who was old and suffering from severe rheumatism, when she was just fourteen years old. They had appeared in Dewi Ayu's room at Mama Kalong's whorehouse. At first the prostitute was not at all interested in this little girl, nor in her father, an old man with his nose in the shape of a parrot's beak, his silver curly hair, his wrinkled skin dark as copper, and above all his overly cautious way of walking as if every last one of his bones would collapse in a heap if she shoved him the tiniest little bit. Dewi Ayu immediately recognized him and said:

"You are addicted, old man. We made love two nights ago."

The man smiled shyly, like a young kid meeting his sweetheart, and nodded. "I want to die in your arms," he said. "I can't pay you, but I'll give you this mute child. She's my daughter."

Dewi Ayu looked at the little girl in confusion. Rosinah stood not very far from her, calm and smiling at her in a friendly way. At that time she was very skinny, wearing an embroidered dress that was way too big for her, barefoot, and with her wavy hair tied back by only a rubber band. Her skin was smooth, like most mountain girls, with a simple round face, intelligent eyes, a flat nose and wide lips, with which she was able to give everyone that pleasing smile. Dewi Ayu had no idea what use a girl like that would be to her and she looked back at the old man.

"I myself already have three daughters, so what would I do with this child?" she asked.

"She can read and write, even though she can't talk," said her father. "All my children can read and write *and* they can talk," said Dewi Ayu with a teasing laugh. But the old man was hell-bent to sleep with her and die in her arms and give her the mute young girl as payment. She could do whatever she wanted with the girl. "You can turn her into a prostitute and take the money she earns for as long as she lives," said the old man. "Or, if there's no man who wants to be with her, you can chop her up into bits and sell her flesh at the market."

"I'm not really sure that anyone would want to eat her flesh," said Dewi Ayu.

The old man refused to give up and after a while he started to resemble a little kid who can't hold in his pee any longer. It wasn't that Dewi Ayu didn't want to be kind and give the old man a few beautiful hours atop her mattress, but she was truly confused by this strange transaction, and over and over again she looked back and forth from the old man to the mute child, until the girl finally asked for a piece of paper and a pencil and wrote:

"Go ahead and sleep with him, any minute now he is going to die."

So she slept with the old man, not because she agreed to the deal, but because of the child's suggestion that he was about to expire. They wrestled on the bed while the mute girl sat on a chair outside the bedroom door, clutching a small bag filled with her clothes that had just a moment ago been carried by her father, waiting. As it turned out, Dewi Ayu didn't need that much time, and she admitted that truly she didn't feel much, just a little tickle in the middle of her crotch. "It was like a dragonfly scratching at my bellybutton," said the prostitute. The man attacked her fiercely, with almost no small talk, like a battalion of Dutch soldiers approaching with a mission to destroy, moving freely and forgetting his rheumatism. His haste quickly bore fruit when he let out a brief groan and his body spasmed; at first Dewi Ayu thought it was the spasm of a man spewing the contents of his balls, but it turned out it was more than that—the old man also spewed his soul. He died sprawled out in her embrace with his lance still wet and outstretched.

They buried him quietly in the same corner of the cemetery where later Dewi Ayu would also be buried. Even though she never cared for her mistress's grave, Rosinah always took the opportunity to visit her father's grave at the end of every fasting month, weeding the grass and praying without conviction. Dewi Ayu brought the mute young girl home, not as payment for the sad evening, but because the mute no longer had a father or mother or anybody else she could call family. At least, Dewi Ayu thought at the time, she could keep her company at home, search for lice in her hair every afternoon, and keep watch over the place when she went to the whorehouse.

Rosinah did not at all find the lively house that she had expected, but a simple home that was quiet and still. There were cream-colored walls that looked like they had not been painted for years, dusty mirrors, and moldy curtains. Even the kitchen looked like it was never used except to make an occasional pot of coffee. The only rooms that looked well taken care of were the bathroom, with its large Japanese-style bathtub, and the bedroom belonging to the lady of the house. In her first few days at the house, Rosinah proved herself to be a young girl worthy to be kept on. While Dewi Ayu took her afternoon nap, Rosinah painted the walls, cleaned the floors, scrubbed the window panes with some sawdust that she got from a woodcutter, changed the curtains, and started to organize the yard, which was soon filled with all kinds of flowers. When afternoon came, Dewi Ayu awoke and for the first time in a long time encountered the aroma of herbs and spices coming from the kitchen, and they ate dinner together before Dewi Ayu had to go out. Rosinah was not in the least bit disturbed by the ramshackle house that needed so much tending, but she was intrigued by the fact that only the two of them lived there. At that time Dewi Ayu had yet to learn the sign language of the mute girl, so Rosinah wrote again.

"You said you had three children?"

"That's right," said Dewi Ayu. "They left as soon as they learned how to unbutton a man's fly."

Rosinah immediately remembered that comment when a number of years later Dewi Ayu said that she didn't want to get pregnant again (despite the fact that she was already pregnant), and that she was sick of having children. They often chatted in the afternoon, sitting in the kitchen doorway while watching the chickens that Rosinah had started to raise claw at the dirt, and like a Scheherazade Dewi Ayu would tell many fantastical tales, mostly about her beautiful daughters. That was how they established a friendship that was full of understanding, so that when Dewi Ayu tried to kill the baby in her stomach in all those different ways, Rosinah did not try to stop her. Even when Dewi Ayu began to show signs of despair, Rosinah again proved herself to be a wise young girl and signed to the prostitute.

"Pray that the baby will be ugly."

Dewi Ayu turned to her and replied, "It's been years since I believed in prayer."

"Well, it depends on who you're praying to," Rosinah said and smiled. "Indeed some gods have proven to be quite stingy."

Tentatively, Dewi Ayu began to pray. She would pray whenever it crossed her mind; in the bathroom, in the kitchen, on the street, or even if an obese man was swimming on top of her body and she suddenly remembered, she would immediately say, whoever is listening to my prayer, god or demon, angel or Genie Iprit, make my child ugly. She even began to imagine all kinds of ugly things. She thought of a horned devil, with fangs sticking out like a boar, and how very pleasing it would be to have a baby like that. One day she saw an electrical outlet and imagined that as the baby's nose. She also imagined its ears as the handles of a pot, and its mouth as the mouth of a piggy-bank slot, and its hair that would look like the straw from a broom. She even jumped for joy when she found some truly disgusting shit sitting in the toilet and asked, couldn't she please have a baby like that; with skin like a komodo and legs like a turtle. Dewi Ayu ran with her imagination that grew wilder every day, and all the while the baby in her womb kept growing.

The height of it came on the night of the seventh full moon of her pregnancy when, accompanied by Rosinah, she bathed in flower water. This is the night when you make a wish for how your baby will be and draw their face on a coconut rind. Most mothers would have drawn the face of Drupadi, Shinta, or Kunti, or whichever *wayang* character was the prettiest, or if they were hoping for a boy they would have drawn Yudistira, Arjuna, or Bima. But Dewi Ayu—perhaps the first person in the world to do so, and because of that even up until the day she died she could not be sure of the outcome—used a piece of black charcoal to draw a hideous baby. She was hoping that her baby would not be like anyone or anything she had ever seen, except maybe a wild pig, or a monkey. So she drew the figure of a frightening monster such as she had never seen nor would ever see before the people buried her dead body.

But then finally she did see her, after those twenty-one years, on the day she rose again.

At that time, day was turning into night, and rain poured down in the cyclone storms that signaled the season was about to change. The wild *ajak* dogs howled in the hills with shrill voices that drowned out the *muadzin* who was calling people to Maghrib prayer at the mosque, and who was apparently failing, because people didn't like to go out when it was raining heavily at twilight and they could hear the sound of howling dogs, and especially not when there was a ghost in a burial shroud walking along the roads in a bedraggled condition and whimpering.

The distance from the public cemetery to her house wasn't a short distance, but *ojek* drivers preferred to crash their motorcycles into a ditch and run away as fast as they could rather than give Dewi Ayu a ride. No minibuses would stop. Even the food stalls and stores along the road chose to close down for the day, locking their doors and windows up tight. There was no one in the street, not even any homeless or crazy people, no one except this old woman who had risen from the dead. There were only the bats who flew with all their might, slamming against the storm, moving in the sky, and the curtains that occasionally parted to reveal faces pale with fright.

She shivered from the cold, and was hungry too. A few times she tried to knock on the doors of people who she thought might still remember her, but the inhabitants preferred to stay quiet, if they hadn't already fainted dead away. So she was overjoyed when from a distance she recognized her own house, which still looked just as it had before the people had laid her in the grave. Bougainvillea blossoms lined the length of the fence, with chrysanthemums along the perimeter looking peaceful under the sheets of rain, and there was a warm light coming from the veranda lamp. She missed Rosinah terribly and fervently hoped a plate of dinner was waiting for her. The image made her hurry a little, like people in train stations and bus terminals, which in turn made her burial shroud come loose as it was tossed by the storm, revealing her naked body, but her hand quickly grabbed the calico cloth and wrapped it back around herself like a young girl in a towel after a bath. She missed her child, the fourth one, and hoped to see what she was like. It's true what people say, a good deep sleep can bring a change of heart, especially if it lasts for twenty-one years.

A young girl was sitting on a chair on the veranda alone underneath the ghostly halo of light, right where Dewi Ayu and Rosinah used to spend the afternoon hunting lice in each other's hair. She was sitting as if expecting someone. At first Dewi Ayu thought it was Rosinah, but as soon as she stood in front of her, she realized that the girl was unfamiliar. She almost shrieked when she saw the horrifying figure, who looked as if she had suffered severe burns, and a malicious voice inside her head said that she had not returned to earth, but was instead wandering through hell. But she was sensible enough to quickly realize that the hideous monster was nothing more than a wretched young girl; she even gave thanks that she had finally met someone who did not run away at the sight of an old woman wrapped in a burial shroud passing by in the middle of a downpour. Of course she didn't yet realize that it was her daughter, since she didn't yet realize that twenty-one years had passed, and so to clear up all of the confusion, Dewi Ayu tried to greet the girl.

"This is my house," she said in explanation. "What is your name?"

"Beauty."

Dewi Ayu erupted into a truly impolite laugh, before quickly stopping herself and understanding everything. She sat in another chair, separated by a table covered with a yellow tablecloth and a cup of coffee belonging to the girl.

"Like a cow who sees that her glazed calf already knows how to run," she said mystified, and then politely asked for the coffee on the table, which she drank. "I'm your mother," she added, full of pride that her daughter was exactly what she had hoped for. If the rain hadn't been coming down, and she hadn't been starving, and the moon had been shining brightly, she would have loved to run and climb up to the rooftop and dance in celebration.

The girl did not look at her and didn't even say anything.

"What are you doing out here on the veranda in the middle of the night?" Dewi Ayu asked her.

"I'm waiting for my prince to come," the girl said finally, even though she still did not turn her head. "To free me from the curse of this hideous face."

She had been obsessed with that handsome prince ever since she realized that other people were not as ugly as she was. Rosinah had tried to bring her to neighbors' houses back when she was only a babe in arms, but not one person received them, because their children would scream and cry for the rest of the afternoon and the old folks would instantly come down with fever and die two days later. They rejected her everywhere, and it was that way too when it was time to for her attend school; not one school accepted Beauty. Rosinah had even tried begging a principal, but he seemed more interested in the mute young woman than in the ugly young girl and had boorishly fondled her in the office once the door was closed. Wise Rosinah thought, where there's a will there's a way, and if she had to lose her virginity to get Beauty into school, she would give it up in any way possible. So that morning she found herself naked on the principal's swiveling office chair and they made love under the drone of the fan for twenty-three minutes, but it turned out that, even so, Beauty was still barred from admission, because if she attended the other children would refuse to enroll.

Without giving up, finally Rosinah planned to teach her herself at home, at the very least her numbers and letters. But before she had the chance to teach her anything, Rosinah was dumbfounded to realize the girl already knew how to correctly count the lizard calls. She was even more surprised when one afternoon Beauty pulled out a pile of books left by her mother and read them aloud at the top of her lungs without anyone ever even teaching her the alphabet. There was something not right about these astonishing events, which had actually started years before when, to Rosinah's amazement and without knowing who had taught her how, the girl had learned to speak. Rosinah tried to spy on the little one, but the child never went farther than the fence and not one single person appeared, and so she never met anyone except the mute servant, who spoke with her hands. And yet she knew the words for all visible and invisible things, for cats and lizards and the chickens and the ducks that roamed around their house.

Aside from all these marvels, she was still an unfortunate, ugly, and pathetic little girl. Rosinah often caught her standing behind the window curtain, peeking out at people in the street, or gazing at her when she had to go out to buy something, as if asking to be invited along. Of course Rosinah would have been happy to take her along, but the little girl herself would protest, saying in her pitiful voice, "No, it's better I don't come, because people will lose their appetites for the rest of their lives."

She would go out in the early morning when people had not yet awoken except for the vegetable sellers hurrying to market, or the farmers hurrying to the fields, or the fishermen hurrying home, walking or gliding by on their bicycles, but those people wouldn't see her in the dimness of the dawn. That was the time when she could get to know the world, with bats who went home to their nests, with sparrows who alighted on the buds of the almond trees, with chickens who cockadoodledooed loudly, with butterflies who hatched from caterpillars and flew to perch on hibiscus petals, with kittens who stretched out on their mats, with the aromas that wafted from neighbors' kitchens, with the clamor of engines being revved in the distance, with the sound of a radio sermon coming from somewhere, and above all with Venus incandescent in the east, all of which she would enjoy while sitting on her swing that hung from the branch of a starfruit tree. Rosinah didn't even know that the small gleam that glowed so brightly was called Venus, but Beauty knew it very well, as well as she had come to know the astrological portents of all the constellations in the sky.

As soon as day dawned, she would vanish inside the house, like the head of a turtle shying from those who disturb it, because schoolchildren always stopped in front of the fence gate, hoping to see her, staring at the door and the windows in their curiosity. The old folks had already told them the scary tales about terrifying Beauty, who lived in that house, ready to cut off their heads at the slightest disobedience, ready to gobble them alive for any whiny complaint: all these stories haunted them, and yet at the same time heightened their desire to meet her and determine whether such a frightening specter truly did exist. But they never met her, because Rosinah would quickly appear brandishing the handle of an upside-down broom, and they would run away screaming insults at the mute young woman. In truth, it wasn't only children who would stop in front of the fence gate hoping to see Beauty, because the women who passed by in *becak* rickshaws would also turn their heads for a moment, as would the people leaving for work and the shepherds leading their sheep.

But Beauty did go out at night, when children were forbidden to leave their houses and parents were busy taking care of their children, and the only people out were the fishermen hurrying to the sea, carrying oars and nets on their backs. She would sit on a chair on the veranda, kept company by a cup of coffee. When Rosinah would ask what she was doing late at night on the veranda, Beauty would reply just as she had to her mother, "Waiting for my prince to come, to release me from the curse of this hideous face."

"You poor girl," said her mother that night, the first night they met. "You really should dance for joy at such a blessing. Let's go inside."

ꕥ

Dewi Ayu once again experienced graciousness *à la* Rosinah, wherein the mute girl had almost instantly prepared warm water in her old bathtub, complete with sulfur and a pumice stone and pieces of sandalwood and betel leaves that made her appear refreshed at the dinner table. Rosinah and Beauty gaped at her ravenous appetite, eating as if she was making up for the years upon years that had gone by without food. She finished two whole tuna fish, including their bones and spines, and a bowl of soup and two plates of rice. Her beverage was a clear broth with bits of birds' nests floating in it. She ate faster than the two women accompanying her. After finishing the food, her stomach gurgled continuously, and after emitting a rumbling sound out of her asshole, the kind of fart that can't be held in, she asked while wiping her mouth with a napkin:

"So, how long have I been dead?"

"Twenty-one years," said Beauty.

"I'm sorry, that was way too long," she said regretfully, "but there are no alarm clocks in the grave."

"Don't forget to bring one the next time," said Beauty attentively, then added, "and don't forget a mosquito net."

Dewi Ayu ignored Beauty's words, which were said in a small shrill lilting soprano, and continued, "It must be confusing that I rose again after twenty-one years, because even that long-hair who died on the cross was only dead for three days before he rose again."

"It *is* very confusing," said Beauty. "Next time, do send a telegram before you come."

Somehow, Dewi Ayu just couldn't ignore that voice. After thinking about it for a while, she began to sense a tone of hostility in the young girl's comments. She looked in her direction, but the hideous girl just gave her a smile, as if to imply that she was merely reminding her not to act so carelessly. Dewi Ayu looked at Rosinah, as if hoping for a clue, but even the mute woman just smiled, seemingly without any double meaning at all.

"Just like that, Rosinah, you are already forty. In just a little while longer you'll be old and wrinkled." While saying that, Dewi Ayu laughed softly, trying to lighten the dinner table atmosphere.

"Like a frog," said Rosinah with sign language.

"Like a komodo," joked Dewi Ayu.

They both looked at Beauty, waiting for her to say something, and they didn't have to wait long.

"Like me," she said. Short and dreadful.

For a number of days, Dewi Ayu, busy with the visits of old friends who wanted to hear stories about the world of the dead, could ignore the presence of the annoying monster in her house. Even the *kyai*, who years ago had led her funeral with reluctance and looked at her with the disgust a young girl feels for earthworms, came to visit her with the virtuous manners of the pious in front of a saint, and with sincerity said that her rising again was like a miracle, and surely no one would be granted such a miracle if she wasn't pure.

"Of course I am pure," said Dewi Ayu lightly. "Because not a single person has touched me for twenty-one years."

"What does it feel like to be dead?" asked Kyai Jahro.

"Actually, it's pretty fun. That's the main reason why, out of everyone who dies, not one person chooses to come back to life again."

"But you came back to life," said the *kyai*.

"I came back just so I could tell you that."

That would be really good for the Friday midday sermon, and the *kyai* left with a radiant face. He didn't need to feel embarrassed about visiting Dewi Ayu (even though many years ago he had shouted that it was a sin to visit that prostitute's house and that you could roast in hell from just opening her gate), because as the woman had said, she was no longer a prostitute after twenty-one years of not being touched by a soul, and you'd better believe it that now and forever nobody would ever want to touch her again.

Who suffered the most from all the fuss over this old woman come back to life was none other than Beauty, who had to lock herself in her room. Luckily, no one ever stayed longer than a few minutes, because the visitors would soon sense an awful terror coming from behind Beauty's closed bedroom door. With a strange nauseating smell, an evil wind, black and heinous, would sweep past them, sliding out from under the door and through the keyhole, with a penetrating chill that reached the very marrow of their bones. Most people had never seen Beauty, except for when she was a little baby and the midwife had circled the village looking for a wet nurse. But the idea of her was enough to make the hair on the napes of their necks stand up and their whole bodies tremble as they gazed at the monster's door, when the evil aroma carried by the wind reached their noses and the sound of silence clamored in their ears. That was when their mouths would let out some nonsense small talk, and forgetting their desire to hear whatever amazing things Dewi Ayu had to say, they'd quickly stand up after forcing down half a glass of bitter tea and excuse themselves to go home and tell their story.

"However strong your curiosity about Dewi Ayu who rose from the dead," they would say to anyone who asked after their terror-filled visit, "I advise you not to go into her house."

"Why?"

"Because you'll be scared half to death."

When people no longer came to visit, Dewi Ayu began to notice Beauty's peculiarities, aside from her habit of sitting on the veranda waiting for a handsome prince and predicting her fate by the stars. In the middle of the night, she heard a scuffle coming from Beauty's bedroom, which made her climb down from her own bed and walk in the darkness and stand in front of the girl's door apprehensively, growing more and more confused by the sounds emerging from that hideous young girl. She was still standing there when Rosinah appeared with a flashlight, passing it over her mistress's face.

"I know these sounds," said Dewi Ayu in a half whisper to Rosinah, "from the rooms of the whorehouse."

Rosinah nodded in agreement.

"It's the sound of people making love," Dewi Ayu continued.

Rosinah nodded again.

"The question is, who is she making love to, or rather, who would want to make love to her?"

Rosinah shook her head. She wasn't making love to anyone. Or, she was making love to someone, but you would never know who it was, because you wouldn't *see* anyone.

Dewi Ayu stood there in awe of the mute girl's equanimity, which reminded her of the time of her own insanity when it was only that girl who understood her. They sat together in the kitchen that night, in front of the same old stove, heating up some water for a cup of coffee and waiting for it to boil. Illuminated only by the glowing flame that licked the edges of the dry burnt kindling made of broken cocoa twigs and palm tree branches and the fibers of coconut rinds, they chatted just as they often used to do.

"Did you teach her how?" asked Dewi Ayu.

"How to what?" asked Rosinah, just the shape of her mouth without a sound.

"Masturbate."

Rosinah shook her head. Beauty isn't masturbating, she is making love to someone but you just won't know who.

"Why not?"

Because I don't know either. Rosinah shook her head.

She told Dewi Ayu about all the miraculous events, how when Beauty was still little the girl could speak without anybody teaching her how, and how she even began reading and writing when she was six years old and how, in the end, Rosinah didn't teach her a thing, because the girl had already been able to do things that Rosinah herself couldn't yet do. Embroidery at the age of nine, sewing at the age of eleven, and don't even ask, she could cook whatever food you wanted.

"Someone must have taught her," said Dewi Ayu in confusion.

"But no one comes to this house," Rosinah signed.

"I don't care how he came, or how he came without you or me knowing. But he must have come and taught her everything, even how to make love."

"Yes, it's true, he comes and they make love."

"This house is haunted."

Rosinah had never believed that the house was haunted, but Dewi Ayu had her reasons. Still, that was another matter, and Dewi Ayu didn't want to say anything about all that to Rosinah, at least not that evening. She stood up and quickly went back to bed, forgetting about the boiling water and the cup of coffee.

In the following days, the old woman tried to spy on the ugly young girl, to discover the most sensible explanation for all of these miracles, because she didn't want to believe a ghost was responsible, even if a ghost was truly present in the house.

One morning, she and Rosinah found an ancient man sitting in front of the blazing stove, shivering from the cold in the morning air. He looked like a guerrilla, with hair that was going every which way, matted and tied back with a wilted yellow leaf. The impression was reinforced by his face, sunken as if he had been starving for years, and by his dark clothing, covered in mud stains and dried blood. There was even a small dagger swinging on his hip, tied to his leather belt. He was wearing shoes like the ones the Gurkha forces wore during the war, way too big for his feet.

"Who are you?" asked Dewi Ayu.

"Call me Shodancho," said the old man. "I'm freezing, let me spend a moment in front of your stove."

Rosinah tried to size him up rationally. Maybe in the past he really had led a *shodan*, maybe he had been in a battalion in Halimunda and rebelled against the Japanese before running away into the forest. Maybe he had been trapped there for years, not knowing that Holland and Japan were already long gone and we now had a republic with our own flag and our own national anthem. Rosinah gave him some breakfast with a tender gaze and a show of respect that was just a little bit excessive.

But Dewi Ayu looked at him with some suspicion, wondering whether he was the prince her daughter waited for every evening, and whether it could be him who had taught her how to make love. But the man looked like he was more than seventy years old and should've been impotent for years, and with that Dewi Ayu's unpleasant thoughts began to fade. She even invited him to live in the house, because there was still an empty room, and the man appeared to have lost all connection to the outside world.

Shodancho, who was indeed in a confused and sorry state, agreed. That was Tuesday, three months after Dewi Ayu rose from the dead, the day when they found Beauty sprawled out across her bedroom floor in a pitiful condition. Her mother tried to help her stand and with Rosinah's help laid her across the bed. Shodancho suddenly appeared behind them, saying:

"Look at her stomach, she's pregnant, almost three months along."

In disbelief, Dewi Ayu looked at Beauty with a gaze that no longer showed confusion but only an anger not at all tempered by any ignorance and then demanded, "How did you get pregnant?!"

"The same way *you* got pregnant four times," said Beauty. "I took off my clothes and made love to a man."

{2}

SOMETHING STRANGE MUST have been going on, because one night the old man was forced into marrying the teenage Dewi Ayu. He was fast asleep and snoring when a Colibri car stopped in front of his house, but the sound of its engine coughing in the middle of the pitch-black night startled him awake. The old man, Ma Gedik, had not yet recovered from that shock when the next came like a hurricane: a tough guy got out of the car with a machete swinging at his hip and kicked the old man's pet mongrel who was sleeping in front of the door. The dog barked stridently and sprung up ready to fight, but its efforts were in vain because the Colibri's driver swiftly shot him with a rifle. The dog let out a howl before he died, just as the tough guy kicked in the plywood door of the old man's hut, leaving it drooping from one hinge.

The hut was very dark, more like a house for bats and lizards than for a human being. Its two small rooms were faintly visible in moonlight: a bedroom where the old man sat in confusion at the edge of his cot and a kitchen where the stove sat filled with ash. Cobwebs crisscrossed everywhere, except for the path the old man followed from his bed to the stove and the door. The tough guy, gagging from a stench of piss far stronger than any pigsty, grabbed a handful of dried palm fronds from a pile near the stove, folded them, and lit their tips on fire, turning them into a torch. Immediately the room came ablaze with swaying and trembling shadows of all different shapes and sizes. The bats began to scatter. The old man still sat on the edge of his cot, looking at the uninvited guest with unabated confusion.

The next surprise: the tough guy showed him a chalkboard that was written on with a young girl's neat penmanship. He couldn't read it, nor could the tough guy, but the tough guy knew what was written there.

"Dewi Ayu wants to marry you," he said.

This must be a joke. He knew his place—he was an old man, he had already lived more than half a century, and even the old widows whose husbands had died in the Deli dirt or been thrown into Boven-Digoel preferred to stock up pious good works for the afterlife than to marry a cart-puller such as himself. He would be lucky if he even remembered how to support a woman, since he had practically forgotten how to sleep with one. The last time he had gone to the whorehouse had been many years ago, and the last time he had done it by himself, with his own hand, had been many years ago as well. So with the naïveté of a village boy, he said to the tough guy:

"I'm not even sure I *can* marry her."

"It doesn't matter whether it's you or a dog's dick that takes her virginity, she wants to marry you," the tough guy snarled. "If not, Lord Stammler will turn you into breakfast for the *ajak*."

That made him shiver. Many Dutch people raised wild dogs for hunting wild boar, and it was no lie that if they didn't like a native, he would be pitted against those *ajak* in a fight to the death. But even if that threat was true, marrying Dewi Ayu was no simple matter, and he just didn't understand why he had to marry her. And in any case he had already vowed not to marry anyone, out of his eternal love for Ma Iyang, a woman who had flown off into the sky one day and vanished.

That woman was another story, the kind of love that was too good to last. Ma Gedik and Ma Iyang grew up together in the fishing encampments, meeting every day, swimming in the same bay, and eating the same fish, and the only thing preventing them from marrying each other straight away was their age, because they were not quite a young man and a young woman yet. Unlike most kids his age, Ma Gedik carried a bamboo container filled with his mother's milk wherever he went, long after he could walk and leave his mother behind. One day Ma Iyang grew curious and asked why, at nineteen, he still drank that milk and didn't care that it was already long spoiled.

"Because my father drank my mother's milk all the time, until he was an old man."

Ma Iyang understood. Behind a clump of pandan shrubs, she took off her blouse and told the guy to suck on her adorable pert little nipple. No milk came out, but Ma Gedik finally stopped drinking his mother's milk and fell in love with that young girl for life. And that's how it all went, until one night Ma Iyang was picked up by a horse-drawn carriage, all made up like a *sintren* dancer, very beautiful to see but painful too. Ma Gedik, who was always the last to know anything, ran the length of the beach chasing that carriage, and when he reached the coachman he ran alongside, shouting out to the beautiful girl:

"Where are you going?"

"To the house of a Dutch lord."

"Why? You don't have to become a maid for the Dutch."

"I'm not," said the girl. "I'm going to become his concubine. You can call me Nyai Iyang."

"Shit!" screamed Ma Gedik. "Why do you want to become someone's concubine?"

"Because if I don't, Mother and Father will be made into breakfast for the *ajak*."

"But don't you know that I love you?"

"Yes, I know."

He was still running next to the carriage, and there they were, the youth and the young girl, crying over their painful separation, their tears witnessed only by the coachman, who tried to calm them down a little and think, saying:

"You don't need to belong to one another in order to love one another."

This was in no way comforting, and actually made Ma Gedik fall into the sand at the side of the road wailing and lamenting his wretchedness. The girl ordered the coachman to stop, and she climbed down to stand in front of the young man. Then, with the old coachman, the horse, the croaking frogs, the owls, the mosquitoes, and the moths as her witnesses, the girl made a vow.

"Sixteen years from now, that Dutch lord will be bored with me. Wait at the top of the rocky hill if you still love me, if you are still interested in some Dutchman's leftovers."

After that they never saw or heard of each other again. Ma Gedik never even knew who that Dutch lord was, a lord so full of lust that he wanted his very own sweetheart, in full flower at the age of fifteen. Ma Gedik, who himself was nineteen, swore he would love her even if she returned home chopped to pieces.

Still, losing one's sweetheart is no simple matter. He kicked off the years of waiting by becoming crazier than the crazies, more idiotic than the idiots, and more tragic than mourners in the throes of grief. His cart-puller friends and the coolies at the port tried to comfort him by telling him to marry another woman, but he preferred to spend his wages and time gambling and stumbling home drunk on *arak* wine. His friends then began to persuade him to go to the whorehouse, hoping that at least another woman's body could ease his lusty grief. At that time there was only one brothel, at the end of the pier. It had actually been built for the Dutch soldiers living in the barracks, but after syphilis spread most of them stopped going there, preferring to keep their own personal concubines, and then the port laborers began to visit.

"It would be just as much a betrayal to go to the whorehouse as to marry another woman," said Ma Gedik stubbornly. But one week later his friends dragged the man, drunk and only half-conscious, to that whorehouse and he spent one day's pay on a bed and an obese woman with a vagina as big as a mouse hole, and immediately awed by these charms, he corrected himself to say, "Doing it with a prostitute is not really a betrayal, because prostitutes are paid with money and not with love."

After that he became a faithful regular at the brothel at the end of the pier, sleeping with the women there while whispering Ma Iyang's name. He did that almost every weekend, with a group of friends who were just as good to him as ever. When their cash flow was ample each fellow slept with his own prostitute, but sometimes when they needed to be thrifty, five of them would share one woman. It continued that way for years, until one by one the men got married. That was hard for Ma Gedik, because his friends no longer had time to go to the brothel—and anyway, now they had wives who could be slept with for love, not money—but going to a whorehouse all by yourself was the most depressing thing in the world. When Ma Gedik felt lonely he would start off practicing with his hand, but that would soon grow intolerably frustrating, and he would be forced to slip out alone into the middle of the pitch-black night to the brothel again, returning home before the fishermen returned from the sea.

After a while he turned into a strange person, if not even an enemy of the people, because time after time there would be a ruckus in a neighbor's stable and he would be caught raping a cow, or even a chicken, until its intestines came spilling out. Sometimes he would punch a shepherd boy and then catch a sheep and work it in the middle of a field, once making a middle-aged woman with a basket full of yam leaves run the whole length of a rice field, shrieking in a hysterical panic at the sight of a lust so completely out of control. Everyone began to distance themselves from him, and he stopped bathing. He stopped eating rice or anything else except his own shit and the shit that he scavenged from the banana orchards. His family and his friends were deeply concerned and called in a *dukun* from a distant land, a mystical healer famous for being able to cure all kinds of illnesses. With his white robe and a streaming beard, he looked like a wise apostle. He examined Ma Gedik in a goat pen, because for the last nine months the man had been tied up there, surviving only on the excrement inside the cage. Calmly, the *dukun* told the worried onlookers:

"Only love can heal such a crazy person."

But that was a difficult matter, for the people could not return Ma Iyang to him, so they ultimately gave up and left Ma Gedik in shackles for the long wait.

"They made a promise to wait for sixteen years," said his mother crankily, "but surely he will rot before that day comes." She was the one who had decided to tie him up, after slaughtering the sixth chicken found writhing in agony with its intestines protruding from its asshole.

But he did not rot. In fact, he seemed quite healthy, his cheeks flushed as the days melted away, and the time he had been waiting for drew near. Barefoot schoolboys would gather outside his goat pen in the afternoon before they went home to herd their cattle, and joking around for a bit he would teach them how to fondle their own genitals, rubbing and using their own spit: and so the teachers at school forbid anyone to go near him. But the children must have tried what he had taught them, because a number of them visited the goat pen in secret in the middle of the night and whispered to him that they had discovered a new way to pee that felt way better than peeing the usual way.

"It will be even more enjoyable if you try it with the private parts of little girls."

When one afternoon a farmer found two nine-year-old children making love in the pandan shrubs, the villagers cruelly boarded up that goat pen. Ma Gedik was stuck inside with no one to talk to, and of course without any light at all.

Still, this punishment did not destroy his spirit. With his body shackled inside a boarded-up cage, his mouth began to sing lewd songs that made the *kyai*'s faces turn red and the people toss and turn in the middle of the night, shivering in their misery. This revenge continued for weeks, but just when the villagers had decided to stuff his mouth with a young coconut, a miracle came in the nick of time. That morning he no longer sang lewd songs, but quite the opposite; he sang beautiful love ballads, moving many people to tears. From one side of the neighborhood to the other people stopped their work, transfixed as if expecting heavenly nymphs to come down from the sky, until someone finally figured out: this was the last day of Ma Gedik's long wait. This was the day he would meet his sweetheart on top of the rocky hill.

Everyone who knew him quickly swarmed to dismantle the boards closing him in. When the rays of light illuminated the goat pen, stinking like an acrid rat's nest, they found the man still shackled, but still singing. They loosed his bonds and brought him to a trench, and bathed him all together, as if he was a newborn baby or an old man who had just passed away. They sprinkled his body with fragrances, from rose oil to lavender, and they gave him fine warm clothes, including a jacket and a pair of pantaloons discarded by a

Dutchman, and they made him up like the corpse of a Christian about to be laid inside a coffin. When all this was finished, one of his old friends commented in amazement,"You are so handsome I'm worried that my wife will fall in love with you!"

"Of course she will," Ma Gedik boasted. "Even the sheep and the crocodiles fall in love with me."

And it was true what the *dukun* had said, love could cure his illness, could cure any illness at all. No one worried about him anymore, and everyone forgot his past bad behavior. Even the young girls stood very close without fear that his hands would rudely wander, and pious people greeted him kindly without worry that their ears would be jammed full of profanity. His mother had a small party to celebrate his sudden recovery, with a yellow cone of *tumpengan* rice and a chicken that had been slaughtered the proper way, without its intestines protruding from its anus, and a *kyai* was invited to recite prayers of blessing and thanksgiving. That was a glorious morning in the fishing encampments, in one far corner of Halimunda still covered in fog, a morning that would be remembered for years to come whenever the people told their children and grandchildren the story of the sweethearts' passion, which for generations remained a tale of true and abiding love.

But ultimately, that long sixteen-year wait ended in tragedy. Not long after the sun began to sting, people came racing by in cars and on horseback, chasing a concubine who was running away to the rocky hill, no doubt Ma Iyang. Borrowing a donkey, Ma Gedik chased the Dutchmen and his sweetheart, and the people from the neighborhood ran behind him in a line, like the tail of a giant snake. They had reached the valley when the Dutchmen finally stopped, and Ma Gedik howled, calling and calling the name of his lover.

Ma Iyang looked so small on the peak of the rocky hill where cars, horses, and donkeys could not reach. The Dutchmen furiously vowed to drag her into the *ajak* cage if they could catch her. Ma

Gedik was trying to climb that rocky hill, but it was so mercilessly difficult that people wondered how the woman had ever managed to reach its peak. After a brutal struggle, Ma Gedik was standing next to his love, boiling over with longing.

"Do you still want me?" asked Ma Iyang. "My whole body has been licked and splattered with a Dutchman's spit, and he has stabbed my privates one thousand one hundred and ninety-two times."

"I have stabbed twenty-eight different women's privates as many as four hundred and sixty-two times, and I have stabbed my own hand countless times, and that's not even counting the privates of animals, so are we really all that different?"

As if a lewd god took possession of them, they embraced ever so tightly, kissing beneath the heat of the tropical sun. And to relieve the passion that had been building up for so long, they removed all the garments sticking to their bodies and tossed them away: the clothes floated down over the valley, twirling round and round like mahogany tree flowers blown by the wind. The people almost didn't believe their eyes and some of them screamed, and the Dutchmen's faces all turned red. Then, without hesitation the two made love on a flat rock, in plain view of the people who filled the valley as if they were watching a film at the movie theater. The virtuous women covered their faces with the edges of their veils and all the men got hard and did not dare look at one another, and the Dutchmen said:

"What have we always said, the natives are like monkeys."

The real tragedy occurred after they finished making love, when Ma Gedik invited his beloved to climb down the rocky hill and go home with him, so they could marry, live together, and love one another forever. That would be impossible, said Ma Iyang. Before they set one foot in the valley, the Dutchmen would throw them into a cage of *ajak.*

"So I prefer to fly."

"That's impossible," said Ma Gedik, "you don't have wings."

"If you believe you can fly, you can fly."

To prove what she said Ma Iyang, with her naked body covered in drops of sweat that reflected the rays of the sun like beads of pearl, jumped and flew toward the valley, disappearing behind a descending fog. People only heard the sound of Ma Gedik's pitiful screams, as he ran down the slope looking for his love. Everyone searched for her, even the Dutchmen and the wild dogs. They scoured every corner of the valley, but Ma Iyang was never found, dead or alive, and finally everyone believed that the woman had truly just flown away. The Dutchmen believed it, and so did Ma Gedik. Now that all that was left was that rocky hill, the people named it after the woman who had flown off it into the sky: Ma Iyang Hill.

After that day Ma Gedik went to the swamps, where the Dutch couldn't withstand the malaria in the wet season, and built a hut there. During the day he hauled a cart filled with coffee, cocoa beans, and sometimes copra and yams to the port, and except for his brief exchanges with other cart pullers, he only talked to himself or to the surrounding spirits. People began to think that his insanity had relapsed, even though he was no longer raping cows and chickens or eating shit.

Almost immediately after the hut was first built, more people started to arrive in the swamps, and the huts that sprung up turned the place into a new encampment. The only Dutch person who ever went there was a controller tasked with carrying out a census, and one week later he was found in his rented room, dead from a malarial fever, the last and only person to visit Ma Gedik for many years until the night when the Colibri driver shot his mongrel dog and a tough guy kicked in the door of his house, with the shocking news that Dewi Ayu wanted to marry him. He didn't know why she wanted to marry him, so a dark story began to form in the back of his mind. Still shaking, he asked the tough guy:

"Is she pregnant?" She was probably being forced to marry him to hide the Dutch family's shame.

"Is who pregnant?"

"Dewi Ayu."

"If she wants to marry you," said the tough guy, "it must be because she doesn't *want* to get pregnant."

Dewi Ayu welcomed her fiancé with joy. She ordered him to bathe and gave him nice clothes to wear because, she told him, the village headman would arrive soon. But that didn't fill Ma Gedik with joy, just the opposite. He felt it was a complete catastrophe, and the closer the time of their marriage grew, the more morose he became.

"Smile, darling," said Dewi Ayu. "If you don't the *ajak* will eat you."

"Tell me, why to you want to marry me?"

"This whole morning you keep asking me the same thing," said Dewi Ayu, slightly annoyed. "You think other people have such a good reason for getting married?"

"It's usually because they love each other."

"And this is exactly the reverse, we don't love each other at all," said Dewi Ayu. "So that's a good reason, isn't it?"

Just sixteen years old, and like many mixed-blood girls, the girl was beautiful. She had gleaming black hair and bluish eyes. She was wearing a tulle wedding dress, with a small tiara that made her look like a fairy in a storybook. She was the only one in charge of the Stammler household now, ever since the rest of her family had packed their bags and flocked to the port with the other Dutch families to escape to Australia while they still had the chance. The Japanese army occupied Singapore, and although they hadn't reached Halimunda yet, they had quite possibly already arrived in Batavia.

Talk of war had actually arrived months before, when they heard on the radio that fighting had broken out in Europe. At that time

Dewi Ayu had already started at the Franciscan School, the school that years later became the middle school where her granddaughter Rengganis the Beautiful was raped by a dog in a toilet stall. She wanted to become a teacher for the very simple reason that she didn't want to become a nurse. She would leave for school with her aunt Hanneke, who taught kindergarten, in the same Colibri car that soon after would come to get Ma Gedik, and with the same driver who would shoot the old man's dog.

She had the best teachers in Halimunda: the nuns who taught her music, history, language, and psychology. Sometimes the Jesuit pastors from the seminary would visit to teach religious education, church history, and theology. They were impressed by her natural intelligence, but worried by her beauty, and a number of nuns tried to persuade her to take the vows of poverty, purity, and chastity. "There's no way," she said. "If every woman took a vow like that, humans would go extinct like the dinosaurs." Her shocking way of speaking was even more troubling than her beauty. In any case, the only thing she liked about religion was the fantastical stories, and the only thing she liked about church was the dulcet tones of the Angelus bells.

When she was in her first year at the Franciscan School, war broke out in Europe. The radio that Sister Maria had set in the front of the class reported with alarm that German troops had invaded the Netherlands and it had only taken them four days to occupy it. The children were enthralled and amazed that war was real and not just some mumbo-jumbo written in their history books. What's more, the war had broken out in their ancestral homeland, and Holland had lost.

"First France, now Germany is occupying it?!" said Dewi Ayu. "It's really a pathetic country."

"Why, Dewi Ayu, whatever do you mean?" asked Sister Maria.

"I mean we have too many merchants and not enough soldiers."

She was punished for her inappropriate comment, and forced to read psalms. However, among her classmates, Dewi Ayu was the only child who enjoyed the news of the war and she even went so far as to make a chilling prediction: the war would reach the East Indies, and would even reach Halimunda. Even though she still joined in the prayers the nuns led for the safety of their families in Europe, Dewi Ayu didn't care that much.

The anxiety about the war also engulfed her home however, especially because her grandfather and grandmother, Ted and Marietje Stammler, had a lot of family in the Netherlands. They continuously asked about letters from Holland, which never arrived. Above all, they worried about Dewi Ayu's father and mother, Henri and Aneu Stammler, who had run away. They had left all of a sudden one morning sixteen years ago, without saying goodbye, leaving Dewi Ayu, who was still an infant, behind. Even though this had truly infuriated the family, the truth was they were still worried.

"Wherever they are, I hope they are happy," said Ted Stammler.

"And if the Germans kill them, may they continue to live happily in heaven," said Dewi Ayu. She then answered herself: "Amen."

"After sixteen years, I am not angry anymore," said Marietje. "You should pray that you might meet them instead."

"Of course I hope to, Oma. They owe me sixteen Christmas gifts and sixteen birthday presents, and that's not even counting the sixteen Easter eggs."

She already knew about her parents, Henri and Aneu Stammler. Some kitchen servants had told her the story in whispers, because if Ted or Marietje Stammler knew that they had leaked the story, they most probably would have been whipped. But after a while Ted and Marietje understood that Dewi Ayu had heard everything, including the part that one morning they had found her lying in a basket on their doorstep. She was sleeping soundly, wrapped in a swaddling blanket, along with a short note with her name on it, explaining that her parents had sailed with the ship *Aurora,* bound for Europe.

She had always been amazed that she didn't have any parents, only a grandpa and grandma and auntie. But when she realized that her father and mother had disappeared one morning, she wasn't angry, in fact quite the opposite, she was in awe.

"They are real adventurers," she said to Ted Stammler.

"You read too many storybooks, child," replied her grandfather.

"They must be religious. The Holy Bible tells of a mother who left her child on the banks of the Nile River."

"That was different."

"Yes, of course. I was left on a doorstep."

Henri and Aneu were both Ted Stammler's children. They had lived in the same house since they were infants, but no one had realized that they had fallen in love—truly a shameful scandal. Born from the womb of Marietje, Henri was two years older than Aneu, who was Ted's child with a native concubine named Ma Iyang. Even though Ma Iyang lived in a different house guarded by two tough guys, Ted had decided to bring Aneu to live with them after she was born. At first Marietje put up a terrible fight but what could be done, after all most men had concubines and bastard children. She finally agreed to let the child live in their house and gave her the family name, to avoid any gossip at the club.

They grew up together, so they had plenty of time to fall in love. Henri was a pleasant youth, clever at hunting pigs with his borzoi dogs (sent straight from Russia), a good soccer player, swimmer, and dancer. Meanwhile Aneu grew into a beautiful young woman, playing the piano and singing in a sweet soprano. Ted and Marietje gave them permission to go to the night fairs and the dance hall, because now was their time to have fun, and maybe even find a good match. But that was the beginning of the whole catastrophe—after dancing until midnight and drinking a festive restaurant lemonade, they didn't come home. Ted was worried and took two tough guys out to look for them at the night fair. They only found a carousel dark and still, a haunted house locked up tight, an empty dance hall, food stalls that were already closed, and some sleeping clerks sprawled out exhausted in front of their kiosks. There was no sign of the teenagers there, and so Ted resorted at last to questioning their young friends about their whereabouts. Someone said:

"Henri and Aneu went to the bay."

There was nothing at the bay at night except for a few boarding houses. Ted searched them one by one and found the pair in a room, naked and taken by surprise. Ted didn't say a word, and they never came home again. No one knew where they went after that. Maybe they lived in one of the boarding houses, surviving by working odd jobs, if not by borrowing money or taking charity from their friends. It's also possible that they went into the forest and lived off fruit and boar meat. Someone else said they were in Batavia working for the train company. Ted and Marietje never knew their whereabouts or condition, and then one morning Ted found a baby in a basket outside his front door.

"And that baby was you," said Ted. "They named you Dewi Ayu."

"And then they made more babies on the *Aurora* ... there might be baskets in front of all the houses in Europe," said the girl.

"When she found out, your grandmother got hysterical. She ran from the house like a crazy person and couldn't be caught, not even by horses and cars. We found her on the peak of the rocky hill, but she never came down. She flew away instead."

"Grandma Marietje flew?" asked Dewi Ayu.

"No, Ma Iyang."

The concubine, her other grandmother. According to her grandfather, if she sat on the back veranda and looked north, she would see two small rocky hills. The western hill was where Ma Iyang flew away and disappeared into the sky, and the locals had named the hill after her: Ma Iyang. It was impressive, but also kind of sad. Dewi Ayu often sat alone in the afternoons and gazed out at that hill, hoping to see her grandmother still floating there like a dragonfly. Only the war redirected her attention, and then Dewi Ayu began to sit more often in front of the radio listening to the reports from the front lines.

Even though the war was still far away, its effects could be felt in Halimunda. Along with a few other Dutchmen, Ted Stammler co-owned a cocoa bean and coconut plantation, the biggest one in the district. Thanks to the war, global trade was in ruins. Their income fell and it seemed their businesses were doomed. The families grew thrifty. Marietje only bought food from the peddlers who traveled from house to house. Hanneke curbed her habits of going to the movies and buying records. Even Mr. Willie, the Indo man who worked for them as a guard and mechanic had to cut down on the bullets for his gun and gas for the Colibri. Meanwhile, Dewi Ayu had to evacuate to the school dormitory.

That was how the Franciscan nuns tried to help during the war; they opened the doors of the dormitory at no charge. Now all of the lessons at school were filled with anxious stories about the war that was finally right in their own front yards. Dewi Ayu, who was impatient with the endless speeches, stood up and asked loudly:

"Rather than sitting here talking, why don't we learn how to shoot rifles and cannons?"

The nuns expelled her for a week and it was only because there was a war on that her grandfather did not dole out any extra punishment. She returned to school just after the bomb fell on Pearl Harbor and Sister Maria, who usually taught history with a cheerful countenance, solemnly pronounced: "It's time for America to intervene."

They realized that the war was now very close, creeping like a lizard in the grass, slowly but surely covering the face of the earth with blood and bullet casings. Dewi Ayu's suggestion now looked prophetic, but it turned out it wasn't the German troops but the Japanese approaching. Like a tiger pissing on its expanding territory, the flag of the rising sun began to fly in the Philippines, and then all of a sudden it was flying in Singapore too.

At home, this caused bigger problems. Like all the adult men Ted Stammler, who wasn't old yet, received a summons to enter mandatory military service. This was a much more difficult situation than merely trying to save money. Hanneke tearfully gave him some protective amulets and Dewi Ayu gave him some good advice: "Getting captured by your enemies is way better than getting shot to death."

Ted went away without a soul knowing where he would be stationed, although most likely he would be sent to Sumatra to face the Japanese troops rapidly approaching Java. With the other men, mostly from plantation families, Ted left Halimunda and his family behind. "I swear on my life, he has never even shot a pig his aim is so off," said Marietje through her tears when parting with him in the town square. She now took her husband's place at the head of the household, looking so pitiful that her daughter and granddaughter tried to comfort her. Mr. Willie came almost every day—he hadn't been called to war because he was an Indo who had never registered as a Dutch citizen, and plus he had a lame leg after being rammed by a wild pig.

"Stay calm, Grandma, Japanese eyes are too narrow to see Halimunda on the map," said Dewi Ayu. Of course she was only trying to make Marietje feel better, but she didn't even show the hint of a smile.

Dejection spread through the city. The night market closed, and no one visited the club. There were no dances and the plantation offices were guarded by a handful of frail old folks. People only met at the swimming pool to soak in silence. Around that time, all the Japanese people who had been living in Halimunda disappeared. Some of them had been farmers and some of them had been merchants, one had been a photographer, and a couple of others had even been acrobats in the circus, but when they all suddenly vanished, everyone realized that they had been living among enemy spies the entire time.

It was only the natives who weren't bothered by any of this—they still just did whatever it was they did. The cart-pullers still headed toward the port in droves, because trade kept going and the freighters kept moving. The farmers still worked their fields and the fishermen went to sea every night.

The regular soldiers arrived in the port of Halimunda, now the largest port on the whole southern coast of Java and the likely gateway for a mass evacuation to Australia. At first it had only been a regular fishing port at the large mouth of the Rengganis River, and not part of the seafaring tradition. People from the coast and from further inland gathered there to barter goods. The fishermen exchanged fish, salt, and shrimp paste for rice, vegetables, and spices.

And long before that, Halimunda had been nothing but a swath of swampy forest, a foggy area belonging to nobody. A princess from the last generation of the Pajajaran had run away to that region and given it a name. Her descendants had then developed it into villages and townships. The Mataram Kingdom banished their dissident princes there and the Dutch were originally completely uninterested in the district—the swamps threatened malaria, the flooding was uncontrollable, and the roads were in terrible condition. The first large ship to dock there came in the middle of the eighteenth century, an English ship named *The Royal George*, which had come only to gather fresh water, not to trade. However, this made the Dutch administration a tad irate, suspicious that the English had in fact bought coffee and indigo, and maybe pearls, and maybe were smuggling weapons through Halimunda to store in Diponegoro. So finally the first Dutch expedition arrived, to have a look around and make a map.

A lieutenant, two sergeants, two corporals, and approximately sixty armed soldiers were the first Dutch to live there, and their small garrison opened a formal post in Halimunda. That was after the war of Diponegoro had ended, when the Cultivation System started. Before this garrison, and before the Dutch started planting their own cocoa, the harvest of the coffee and indigo that grew abundantly throughout inland Halimunda had been brought via the interior road cutting across Java toward Batavia. This route presented a lot of risks: the goods might spoil on the way, and there were thieves along the road. Now that Halimunda's garrison and seaport had opened, the harvests could be loaded directly onto ships and sent straight to Europe to be sold. Wider streets were built to accommodate the cart and wagon traffic. Canals were dug to avoid flooding, and warehouses were constructed all around the port. Even though it was never very significant compared to any of the ports in the north, Halimunda was noticed by the colonial government, and finally the port was opened to private businesses.

Of course the first business that operated in the city was *Nederlandsch Indisch Stoomvaartmaatshappij*, which had a number of sailing ships. Some warehousing businesses were also established, especially after the railway opened, traversing the island from east to west. As it turned out, however, trade there never really reached a golden age—instead, after establishing that first garrison, the colonial government developed Halimunda into a military stronghold. They saw a strategic opportunity; as the only big port on the southern coast, the city could act like a back door through which the Dutch could evacuate to Australia, without having to pass through the Sunda or Bali Strait, should war ever break out.

They began to build forts and install cannons on the beach to defend the port and the city. Watchtowers were built on the peaks of the hills in the jungle along the very same cape where many years ago the princess descended from the Pajajaran Kingdom had lived. One hundred artillery troops were brought in. Twenty years later, twenty-five massive Armstrong cannons were installed, and the defense plans reached their peak in the early twentieth century with the building of more military barracks. That was the start of several things in Halimunda: whorehouses, private clubs, hospitals, efforts to eradicate malaria, and the Dutch businessmen who began to spill into the city, some of whom established the cocoa plantations and stayed for many years.

When war broke out and Germany occupied Holland, all the military facilities were improved and even more soldiers were brought into the city. Then the radio announced that two English warships, *The Prince of Wales* and *Repulse*, had been sunk by Japan, and the Malay Peninsula had fallen to the enemy. The Japanese victory did not stop there. Not long after the Malay Peninsula was captured, Lieutenant General Arthur Percival, the commander of the English defense, signed the surrender of Singapore, long rumored to be the strongest British bastion. Everything was getting worse, leading up to the morning when a controller visited the houses of the Halimunda people and said something that really chilled them to the bone: "Surabaya has been bombed by Japan." The native laborers stopped working and all trade froze. "You have to evacuate, Miss," they said to Marietje Stammler, who along with Hanneke and Dewi Ayu said nothing in reply.

The city was quickly crowded with refugees who came by train or private cars that sprawled out beyond the city limits, filling the ditches as their owners waited in line night after night for the opportunity to board a ship. About fifty military ships came to the port to help with the evacuation. Everything was in chaos, and an East Indies defeat seemed guaranteed. After obtaining assurance as to when they could leave, the remaining members of the Stammler family hastily started to pack, but were surprised by Dewi Ayu's sudden pronouncement: "I'm not going."

"Don't be foolish, child," said Hanneke. "Japan will not just pass you by."

"Whatever the case may be, a Stammler must stay here," she said stubbornly. "You know as well as I do who we must wait for."

Brought to tears by her hardheadedness, Marietje wailed, "They will make you a prisoner of war!"

"Grandma, my name is Dewi Ayu and everyone knows that's the name of a native."

After the Japanese battered Surabaya with their bombs, they continued toward their objective, Tanjung Priok. A number of high-ranking officials in the colonial government were the first people to evacuate. Marietje and Hanneke Stammler finally boarded the mammoth steamship *Zaandam* without knowing Ted's fate on the battlefield and leaving Dewi Ayu behind, as she insisted. The ship had hauled loads of passengers back and forth many times, but this was its last voyage: the *Zaandam* and another ship crossed paths with a Japanese cruiser and the two were sunk without a fight. Dewi Ayu and Mr. Willie and the servants and the tough guys began their days of mourning.

A Japanese infantry from the forty-eighth division landed in Kragan after a battle in Bataan, in the Philippines. Half of them moved to Malang via Surabaya, and the other half arrived in Halimunda, naming themselves the Sakaguchi Brigade. Japanese planes were already flying in the sky and dropping bombs on Mexolie Olvado's oil refineries belonging to Bataafse Petroleum Maatschappij, on the workmen's housing, and on the cocoa and coconut plantation offices. The Sakaguchi Brigade had been battling with the Dutch KNIL army that was holding strong outside the city for only two days when General P. Meijer received the news that Holland had surrendered in Kalijati. All of the East Indies had been toppled and occupied. General P. Meijer surrendered control of Halimunda to Japan in City Hall.

Dewi Ayu saw and heard all of these events with her own eyes and ears, and yet during her period of mourning she didn't speak to anyone, she just sat on the veranda behind their house, looking out at the hill that Ted had said was named after Ma Iyang. One afternoon she saw Mr. Willie appear in the backyard, accompanied by a borzoi dog that supposedly used to belong to her father, Henri. For the first time since the mourning period had begun, she spoke.

"One flew away, the other drowned."

"What happened, Miss?" asked Mr. Willie.

"Oh, I'm just remembering my grandmothers," she said.

"You have to do something, Miss, the servants are confused. Aren't you the head of this family now?"

She nodded. That evening as the sun went down she ordered Mr. Willie to gather all the household servants: the cooks, the maids, the garden staff, and the security guards. She told them that now she was the sole mistress of the household. All her orders must be carried out, and no one could refuse. She wasn't going to whip anyone, but if Ted Stammler came home, he would whip all dissidents, and throw them in the cages with the *ajak*. Her first order did not seem to bother anyone at all, but did surprise and confuse them:

"Tonight, someone has to kidnap an old man named Ma Gedik from the settlements in the swamp," she said. "Because tomorrow morning I am going to marry him."

"Don't joke around, Miss," said Mr. Willie.

"Go ahead and laugh if you think I'm joking."

"But the priest has disappeared and the church has been bombed to pieces!"

"There is still the village headman."

"Miss, you're not a Muslim are you?"

"No, but I haven't been Catholic either, not for quite a long time."

That was the beginning of Dewi Ayu's marriage to Ma Gedik. A pitiful old man marrying a beautiful young girl: the news quickly spread to every corner of the city—even the arriving Japanese heard the gossip. Meanwhile those Dutch who had not been able to escape sent letters via their servants asking whether the story was true, and some began to resurrect the shameful scandal of her mother and father.

"What will happen if I don't marry you?" asked Ma Gedik finally, a short while after the headman arrived.

"You'll be supper for the *ajak*."

"Then let them have me."

"And Ma Iyang Hill will be flattened."

With that terrifying threat, he helplessly married Dewi Ayu around nine o'clock that morning, just as the Japanese soldiers began the ceremony marking their occupation of the city. No one was invited to celebrate their marriage except the servants and the security guards. Mr. Willie served as witness and the whole time Ma Gedik trembled and stammered and couldn't say his vows properly. He finally collapsed, unconscious, and the headman formalized their union.

"The poor man," said Dewi Ayu. "He would have been my grandfather, if Ted had not made Ma Iyang his concubine."

When Ma Gedik regained consciousness later that afternoon, he found himself Dewi Ayu's husband without understanding how it had happened, gaping at her as if she were a she-devil. He refused to touch her, shrieking whenever she forced herself near him, and hurling whatever he could grab at her. When Dewi Ayu relented, he curled up in the corner of the room shivering and crying like a baby in its cradle. Dewi Ayu waited patiently, sitting not far from him, still in her wedding clothes. Once in a while she would try to coax him to approach her and caress her, and even make love to her, since she was now his wife. But whenever Ma Gedik began to scream again, she would stop her seduction, and return to sitting there quietly, flashing him a smile now and then in her patient efforts.

"Why are you afraid of me? I just want you to touch me, and of course sleep with me, because you are my husband."

Ma Gedik didn't respond.

"Think about it, let's say we are married and you don't sleep with me," she continued. "I will never get pregnant and everyone will say that your dick doesn't work anymore."

"You are a she-devil seductress," stammered Ma Gedik finally.

"I'm a beautiful temptress," Dewi Ayu added.

"You are not a virgin."

"Of course that's not true!" said Dewi Ayu, a little hurt. "Sleep with me and you will know that you're wrong."

"You're not a virgin, and you're pregnant, and you want to make me into the black sheep."

"That's not true."

Their debate continued until the middle of the night, and then until the early morning, and neither of them changed their mind. When the new day came and the light streamed into their bridal chamber, Dewi Ayu was exhausted by the man's electrifying screams and gave up on approaching him. She took off all of her clothes, her wedding dress and her tiara, and threw them on top of the bed. Stark naked, she stood in front of the still hysterical old man, and said loudly in his ear:

"Do it, and you'll *know* that I'm a virgin!"

"I swear to Satan, I am not going to do it, because I know you are *not* a virgin!"

Then Dewi Ayu inserted her middle finger into her vagina, deep inside, right in front of Ma Gedik's nose. The girl whimpered a little at the pain, and trembled every time her finger moved in between her legs, until she pulled it out and showed it to Ma Gedik. A drop of blood hovered on her fingertip, which she then smeared in a straight line from the tip of Ma Gedik's forehead to the edge of his quivering chin.

"Well I guess you're right," said Dewi Ayu. "Now I am no longer a virgin."

She left to bathe and after that she slept atop her wedding bed, as if she didn't care about the old man who was still shivering in the corner of the room. She hadn't had any rest for a whole day and night, and so she slept quite soundly, not responding when the servants tried to rouse her for lunch. She awoke in the afternoon and without bothering about Ma Gedik went right to the table, eating with gusto, and with no conversation as the servants looked on, waiting for her orders. When she returned to her room, she realized that the old man was gone. She looked for him in the bathroom, in the yard, and in the kitchen, but she didn't find him. Dewi Ayu finally asked one of the guards in front of the house.

"He ran away screaming like he'd seen the devil, Miss."

"You didn't catch him?"

"He was running so fast, just like Ma Iyang ran sixteen years ago," replied the guard. "But Mr. Willie chased him with the car."

"And was he caught?"

"No."

She ran to the stable and joined the chase on horseback. Dewi Ayu guessed, although she was slightly mistaken, that the man had run toward the peak of the rocky hill where Ma Iyang had flown down and was lost in the fog. It turned out Ma Gedik had not run to that hill, but to another hill located to the east. After questioning some people on the side of the road, they picked up some Colibri tire tracks, which led them to the foot of that hill. Dewi Ayu found Mr. Willie sitting on the back bumper of the car, looking like he couldn't drive up any farther.

"He's singing on the hilltop," said Mr. Willie.

Dewi Ayu looked up and saw Ma Gedik, standing on a boulder and singing like an opera star on stage. She could hear him faintly, but she didn't know that it was the same song that he had sung years ago on the last day of his sixteen year wait for Ma Iyang.

"He's definitely going to jump, just like his beloved," continued Mr. Willie. "And he'll fly up into the sky and disappear behind the fog."

“No,” said Dewi Ayu, “He will crash on the rocks and be banged up like a pile of chopped beef.”

And that was what happened: right as he finished his song Ma Gedik jumped into the open air. He appeared to fly, overjoyed, as no one had seen him be for many years. His arms flapped like the wings of a bird, but they couldn't make his body fly any higher, and down he plummeted with ever-increasing speed. Even though he knew what was waiting at the end, he still smiled and whooped, full of excitement. He crashed onto the rocks, and his body was hacked to abysmal bits, exactly as Dewi Ayu had predicted.

They brought his remains, which looked more like broth or batter than a human corpse, home and buried him properly. Dewi Ayu named the hill Ma Gedik Hill, jutting up next to Ma Iyang Hill, and decided to mourn for a week. At the end of her mourning period she received word that Ted Stammler had fallen defending Batavia in the last battle before Holland's surrender. His corpse never arrived, but Dewi Ayu decided to mourn again for another week. At the end of her second mourning period, delighted that she hadn't received any more sorrowful news, she threw off all her mourning garments. She put on cheerful clothes, made herself up nicely, and went to the market as if nothing had happened. But upon her return home, she heard something way more surprising than news of another death.

Mr. Willie, wearing a jacket and tie and shiny leather shoes, approached her saying that he had some important business to discuss. Dewi Ayu thought the man was going to quit and go to Batavia to look for work, or maybe join the Japanese army. Neither of her guesses was even close. Mr. Willie's face, red with embarrassment, did not give anything away until the moment he spoke. He only a uttered few words but they made her catch her breath:

“Miss,” he said. “Marry me.”

{3}

DEWI AYU HAD forgotten that there was no way the Japanese soldiers could be winning the war without any information, such as the fact that she was the child of a Dutch family. It wasn't just her face and her skin that gave her away, but also the city's public records, the entire archive of which the Japanese now controlled, and so they weren't going to believe she was a native, whether or not her name was Dewi Ayu.

"I guess that's how it is," she said. "Just like everyone knows that guy Multatuli is a drunk and not really Javanese."

She was all by herself, feeling nostalgic and listening to the gramophone spin her grandfather's favorite songs, Schubert's *Unfinished Symphony* and Rimsky-Korsakov's *Scheherazade*, while thinking about how she should reply to Mr. Willie's proposal. She knew Mr. Willie was a very good man—she had even once hoped he might marry her Aunt Hanneke. Disappointing a good man like that was just as hard as recklessly marrying him, but whatever the circumstances, after her tumultuous marriage to Ma Gedik she would never even consider marrying anybody else.

Mr. Willie had come to Halimunda when her grandfather ordered their Colibri from the Velodrome store in Batavia to replace their ancient Fiat. The company belonged to a businessman named Brest van Kempen, a kind man who let people buy cars on installment plans. Her grandfather didn't need an installment plan, but his friends had told him about the great promotion that the Velodrome was offering—the car came complete with free accident insurance, access to a great repair shop, and they were throwing in a driver who was experienced in handling engines. He returned home with Mr. Willie, who became their driver and mechanic, especially useful because they needed someone to take care of the plantation equipment. He was of medium build, in his mid-thirties. His vest was always left unbuttoned, his clothes perpetually covered in grease, and he carried a pistol to shoot rats and pigs. That was back when Dewi Ayu was still just an eleven-year-old girl, five years before Mr. Willie proposed to her.

"Think about it, Mister," she said. "I'm sort of a crazy woman."

"When I look at you I don't see any signs of insanity," said Mr. Willie.

"When Ma Gedik died, I realized I had only married him because I was so angry that Ted had destroyed his love. So, clearly, I'm crazy."

"You're just a little irrational."

"And that's just another way of saying crazy, Mister."

But now her salvation came: she could run away and avoid having to reply to his proposal. It was still morning and the record had not yet finished playing its last song when she saw military trucks lined up on the beach, ready to round up all the remaining Dutch inhabitants and take them to a prison camp. The day before, the soldiers had come to their houses and ordered them to pack. That night, without saying anything to anyone, especially not to Mr. Willie, Dewi Ayu had gathered her things. She didn't take much, just one suitcase filled with clothes, a blanket, a thin sleeping pallet, and documents proving her family's holdings. She didn't take any money or jewelry, because she knew all that would just get stolen. Instead, she gathered up some necklaces and bracelets that had belonged to her grandmother and flushed the jewelry down the toilet into the waiting shelter of shit. She divvied up the remaining portion into a number of small envelopes to give to the household servants so that they could survive while looking for work someplace else. For herself, she swallowed six rings inset with jade, turquoise, and diamonds. They would be safe inside her, would come out along with her shit, and then she would swallow them again, for as long as she was imprisoned. But now it was time to go—one of the trucks had stopped outside her house and two soldiers had gotten out with bayonets in their hands and they were climbing the steps to the veranda where she was sitting waiting for them.

"I know you guys," said Dewi Ayu, "you're the photographers who used to work at the bend in the road!"

"Yeah, that was fun. We got photographs of every single Dutch person in Halimunda," answered one of the soldiers.

The other one spoke: "Prepare yourself, Miss."

"You mean Madam," said Dewi Ayu. "I'm a widow now."

She asked for a moment to say goodbye to the household servants. They seemed to know that their mistress would be leaving. She saw one of the cooks, Inah, crying. Inah truly owned the kitchen, and Dewi Ayu's grandmother had entrusted all the meals for family guests to her. Dewi Ayu would never again enjoy her tasty *rijsttafel*, maybe not for the rest of eternity—a good cook was an important part of any family's wealth, but now the family had disappeared and the last member was herself leaving, to become a prisoner of war. As she gave the woman a golden necklace, Dewi Ayu was flooded with memories. When she was little, Inah had taught her how to cook, had let her grind spices and fan the stove embers. She felt a shock of sadness more overpowering than when she had heard the news that her grandmother and grandfather had died.

Next to the cook stood a houseboy, Inah's son. Muin was his name. He always dressed sharper than anyone else, with his *blangkon* hat, impressing even the Dutch. His duty was to make rounds throughout the house, but he was busiest at mealtimes when he had to set and mind the table. Ted Stammler had taught him how to use the gramophone, often ordering him to change the record or search for a particular song. He was always happy to do it, turning the record and moving the needle as if he was the only man for the job. He had learned many classical pieces, and seemed to really enjoy them too.

"You can have all of that," Dewi Ayu said to him, pointing to the gramophone and the shelf of records.

"I couldn't!" said Muin. "They belong to our Master."

"Believe me, dead people don't listen to music."

Years later, after the war ended and the republic stood, she saw Muin again. At that time there were almost no Dutch families left, and no one was rich enough to have very many servants. She knew that Muin couldn't do anything much except set the table and work the gramophone; and there he was in front of the market playing the records inherited from her grandfather, while a clever little trained monkey passed back and forth pushing a little wagon or carrying an umbrella, dancing in time to the *Symphony No. 9 in D Minor*, and people threw small change into the *blangkon* that Muin now set out upside down. Dewi Ayu only watched him from afar, smiling at his good fortune.

Muin's only other job had been as a letter courier: there were no household telephones yet, and a "letter" was actually a double-sided chalkboard slate. She'd often exchange gossip with her school friends by writing on one side of the chalkboard. Muin would then run to her friend's house with the slate and wait for the reply to be written on the other side. Waiting, he would be treated to a cold drink and some small cakes, which he ate with gusto, and he would come home bringing the board, plus all the gossip from the other household servants. He enjoyed the work, and Dewi Ayu sent him out almost every day.

The only chalkboard she did not send with Muin was the last chalkboard she ever sent, her message to Ma Gedik, which Mr. Willie and a tough guy delivered to his shack.

"That chalkboard is also for you," she said.

Then she turned to Supi the washerwoman, the queen of the water pump and soap. When she was little the old woman had always kept her company as she slept, singing the lullaby *Nina Bobo*, and telling her the fairy tale of *Lutung Kasarung*. Her husband worked as the gardener. He always had a machete at his hip and a sickle in his hand, and often came home with surprise packages—a black kitten, snake eggs, a monitor lizard—or with delightful gifts like a bunch of king bananas, a half-ripe soursop, or a sack full of mangos.

There were a number of tough guys—the house guards, the garden security, and the goat-pen guards—and she hugged them all. For the first time in many years, Dewi Ayu wept. Leaving them behind felt like losing a piece of her own body. At last she stood looking at Mr. Willie. "I am crazy, and only a crazy person would marry a crazy person," she told him. "And I don't want to marry a crazy person." She kissed him before leaving with the two Japanese soldiers who would wait no longer.

"Take care of my house," she said to them for the last time, "unless these people seize it."

She climbed up into the back of the truck idling in front of the house. She almost didn't fit because it was already crowded with women and their crying and screaming children. She waved to the servants still standing on the house veranda. For sixteen years she had lived there, never going beyond the city limits except for a few short vacations to Bandung or Batavia. She saw the borzois running from behind the house and barking in the yard that was filled with the Japanese grass they loved to roll around in, with jasmine flowers creeping next to the house and sunflowers growing near the fence. That was their dominion, and Dewi Ayu hoped Mr. Willie would take good care of them. The truck began to move and Dewi Ayu struggled to breathe pressed up against the bodies of all the other women. She still waved in the direction of the barking borzoi dogs.

"It can't be believed, that we are leaving our own houses behind!" said the woman next to her. "I hope it won't be for long."

"*I* hope that our army can beat back the Japanese," said Dewi Ayu. "Otherwise we are going to be traded like sugar and rice."

Natives squatted along the sides of the road, watching the people jostling around in the back of the truck with impassive gazes. But then a number of them were brought to tears when they caught sight of the few Dutch women they knew, and handkerchiefs began to wave in between sobs. Dewi Ayu wiped away her own tears, smiling at the strange sight. The natives were kind and innocent, obedient, and a little bit lazy. Dewi Ayu recognized some of them; they had worked on her grandfather's cocoa plantation and she often had snuck away to their huts. She liked them because they told her many fantastic tales about *wayang* and *buta*, and they loved to laugh, and they would dress her up in their tight sarongs and *kebaya* lace blouses and pull her hair back in a bun. They were very poor, they were only allowed to watch movies from behind the screen so that the picture was backward, and they were never at the club or the dance hall unless it was to sweep up. "Look," she said to another woman next to her, "they must be confused by two foreign nations making war on their land."

The journey seemed to take forever as they headed toward the prison on the western shore on a small delta of the Rengganis River. Up until this point the prison had been filled only with serious criminals: killers and rapists, and political prisoners of the colonial government, most of them communists held there temporarily before being tossed into Boven-Digoel. The women baked beneath the blazing tropical sun, without a parasol or anything to drink. In the middle of the journey the truck came to a halt; its radiator got some water but the people got nothing.

Dewi Ayu, exhausted from crouching and looking out at the road, turned around and leaned back against the wall of the truck and realized that she actually knew some of the women quite well—they were her neighbors and her friends from school. The Dutch had a fairly close-knit social life. If you were a child, you would meet up almost every afternoon at the bay to swim. If you were a teenager, you would meet at the dance hall or the movie theater or the comedy shows. If you were an adult, you'd meet at the club. Dewi Ayu recognized some of her friends. They flashed each other bitter smiles, and one of them jokingly asked her, "So, how are you?"

With sincere conviction, Dewi Ayu answered, "I'm terrible. We're heading for a prison camp."

That was enough to make them laugh a little bit.

The girl who had started the joke was named Jenny. They used to go swimming together, floating on an old inner tube Dewi Ayu kept in the car. Those had been happy times, before the thunder of war. Young men would stand near the water, and old men would sit in the sand under umbrellas with tobacco pipes in their mouths, all there just to ogle the young women in their bathing suits. She also knew what they were up to in the changing room. What they called the changing room was really a natural spring at the edge of the beach, enclosed by woven bamboo. Even though the men's and women's sections were divided, she often caught eyes peeping through the cracks in the weaving. She would peep right back and shout, "Oh my God, yours is so small!" The men would usually flee, mortified.

From time to time the appearance of a shark fin would throw the swimmers into an uproar, but no one was ever attacked. Halimunda Beach was too shallow and they usually just swam back out to sea. Sometimes small sharks would get tangled in the fishermen's nets, but the fishermen always set them free, saying it was bad luck to keep them. Sharks were not the only animals to fear, since crocodiles lived near the mouth of the river and they liked to eat people too.

Now the bay, with all its gentle waves, must have been filled with only native kids, who always went barefoot and whose bodies were always crusted with dirt, and who always moved aside when the young ladies and gentlemen went swimming. Dewi Ayu wondered whether they would be allowed to go swimming in prison.

"Pray that we don't meet a crocodile," said a middle-aged woman with a baby in her lap.

She said this with good reason. To reach the prison in the middle of the delta, they would have to cross the water. After their unpleasant journey in the truck, they now stopped at the river. Japanese soldiers roamed the banks, screaming at the women in their own language, which no one understood.

The women were crammed into a ferryboat, which was way more frightening than the truck, because now there was the chance they could drown, and as the woman had said, a crocodile could appear at any time and none of them could outswim such a beast. The ship moved excruciatingly slowly, circling to avoid facing the current directly. Clumpy with black soot, smoke from the chimney pipe floated up into the sky. A group of herons was startled by the noise and took flight, coming to perch in the shallow water; yet this view did not feel beautiful as they arrived at an old building standing behind some bushes, looking as if it had been emptied out especially to hold prisoners of war. This was Bloedenkamp, a prison with a bloody history, feared even by criminals. Once inside, there was little chance for escape unless you could swim a mile across the wide river faster than a crocodile.

Once the boat docked the Japanese soldiers started screaming again, and the women jumped down as quickly as they could. Children began to cry, and there was some commotion: a suitcase was flung into the river and its owner got drenched trying to catch it, a sleeping pallet fell into the mud, and a mother was separated from her child who was trampled in the chaos. The group walked toward the prison, passing through three iron gates guarded by soldiers. Before entering, they lined up in front of a table where two Japanese men sat clutching a list. Next to them there was a basket for money and valuables. A number of women were already taking off their jewelry and tossing it in.

"Do it before we search you," ordered one of the soldiers in proper Malay.

You can go ahead and search my shit, Dewi Ayu thought to herself.

The prison was way more disgusting than a pigsty. The roof leaked, the walls were splattered with old blood, with moss and weeds growing through the cracks, and the floor was dirty, teeming with lice, cockroaches, and leeches. Sewer rats as big as a child's thigh ran around in a frenzy, startled by the newcomers, zigzagging in between the women's legs as they hopped up and down shrieking. The women scrambled to mark their own territory with their suitcases as quickly as possible, cleaning up and sobbing all the while. Dewi Ayu claimed a small spot in the middle of a hall, unfurled her mattress, and with her suitcase for a pillow, she lay down exhausted. She was lucky she didn't have a mother or a child who needed tending and that she hadn't forgotten the quinine tablets and other medicines, because there was the threat of malaria and dysentery: the toilet didn't work.

That evening there was no food. The small scraps that each of the women had brought had been finished by lunchtime. Someone asked the Japanese men about food, and they replied maybe tomorrow or the next day. That night they would have to go hungry. Dewi

Ayu went out of the hall toward the fields. The three prison gates were open and people could roam out of the fort to walk around. When she had arrived earlier, Dewi Ayu had spotted some cows. Maybe they belonged to the native wardens or the farmers who lived in the delta. She had gathered a bunch of leeches while cleaning her spot in the prison hall, stacking them inside a Blue Band margarine tin. She found one of the cows grazing, the fattest one, and plastered the leeches onto its hide. The cow only glanced up for a moment, undisturbed, and Dewi Ayu sat on a rock waiting. She knew the leeches were sucking the cow's blood, and when they were full, they would fall off like ripe apples. She plucked them off the ground and put them back inside the tin. Now they looked swollen and fat.

Making a small campfire, she boiled all the leeches in the tin with some water from the river. Without adding any seasoning, she quickly brought them back to the hall that was now her new home. "Dinner is served," she said to a number of women and children who were living near her, her new neighbors. No one was interested in eating leeches, and one woman practically retched at the very thought of such a meal. "We're not eating the leeches, but cow's blood," Dewi Ayu explained. She split open the leeches with a small knife, pulled out the clots of cow's blood inside them, stabbed them with the point of the knife, and swallowed them. Nobody moved to join in her savage meal, at least not until night fell and they could no longer bear their hunger. Then they tried it. It tasted bland, but sort of good.

"We won't starve," said Dewi Ayu. "In addition to leeches, there are geckos, lizards, and mice."

"Okay," the women said hurriedly, "great, thanks."

That first night was truly gruesome. Daylight disappeared quickly, as it does in the tropics. Though there was no electricity, almost everyone had brought candles, and their small flames crowded the walls with trembling shadows that terrified the small children. Stretched out on sleeping pallets, looking quite pitiful, no one could get any sleep. Mice skittered over them in the dark, mosquitoes buzzed from one ear to another, and flying foxes crisscrossed overhead. Even worse were the surprise inspections from the Japanese soldiers, looking for people who were still hiding money or jewelry. Morning came but promised nothing.

Bloedenkamp was filled with about five thousand women and children, gathered from who knows where. The only ray of hope came from a fortune-teller, who consulted her deck of cards and told them that American pilots were dropping bombs on the Japanese barracks. Dewi Ayu quickly rushed to the toilet, but a long line of people were already waiting so she took some water in her Blue Band margarine container, and went out to the fields. There, in between some yam trees, she dug a little hole and defecated like a cat. After she washed herself, saving a little bit of leftover water, she scraped at her own excrement looking for her six rings. A number of other women imitated her nasty routine at a safe distance, but they didn't know that Dewi Ayu was guarding treasure. She then washed the rings with the rest of the water and swallowed them down again. She didn't know what would happen after the war. Maybe she would lose her house and the plantation, but she vowed that she would not lose her rings. She returned to the hall not knowing if she'd be able to bathe that day or not.

That morning, the newcomers had to stand in the field baked by the sun, the children crying and the women about to faint, waiting for the camp commandant and his staff. The commandant then appeared with a thick mustache and a samurai sword swinging back and forth at his hip, his boots reflecting the blinding rays of the sun. He told the prisoners they had to bow down deeply, past their waist, to all the Japanese soldiers as soon as the order *Keirei!* was given, and they could only stand up straight again once they had heard the order *Naore!* "That is the sign of respect for the Japanese Empire," he explained through his translator. Those who did not obey would get a fitting punishment: they would be given extra work, be whipped, or even be killed.

Inside again, a few women, afraid of careless errors, quickly taught their children the orders. Their shouts of *Keirei!* and *Naore!* made Dewi Ayu double up with laughter.

"You are way more vicious than the Japanese!" she exclaimed.

And the mothers had to laugh too.

There wasn't much entertainment to be had. Dewi Ayu's instinct as a former teacher trainee emerged, and she gathered a number of small children, setting up a small school in an unused corner of the hall, and instructing the children in reading, writing, arithmetic, history, and geography. At night she recounted folk tales and Bible stories, and acted out the *wayang* episodes from the Ramayana and the Mahabharata that she had heard from the natives, as well as story lines from the many books she had read. The children liked her because her stories were never dry or boring. She'd regale them until it was time to return to their mothers and sleep.

The Japanese had demanded that the cells be kept clean, so the women organized themselves into small work groups, nominating a leader for each and developing a rotating schedule for the tasks to be done. They took turns cooking in the communal kitchen, filling the water troughs, washing tools and equipment, cleaning the yard, and carrying sacks of rice and potatoes and burnt wood and other things from the trucks to the warehouse. Despite her youth, Dewi Ayu was chosen as the head of her group. She was already mature enough to lead, and had nobody to distract her. In addition to her small school, she'd also found a doctor and they started a hospital without beds or medicine. A few women requested a pastor, but the men were in a different prison, so Dewi Ayu found a nun and for her that was good enough. "As long as nobody wants to get married, we don't need a pastor," she said confidently. "All we really need is someone to give sermons and lead the prayers."

But not everything went so smoothly. The little boys grew wild, ganging up with their friends from the same block and insulting one another. Fights between the children were easier to come across than an irate Japanese soldier. Their mothers felt forced to take an equally tough approach, hitting their children even though it seemed to make no difference. The Japanese had absolutely no intention of arbitrating or stopping these scuffles, quite the opposite; they instigated fights as if it was a new game for them.

Food was another problem. The rations they were given were not nearly enough for the thousands of prisoners. They were on a strict starvation diet, getting only salted rice porridge for breakfast. Lunch was whatever could be scavenged or later, the vegetables that they had planted themselves behind the cells. At night they got one slice of plain white bread. There was never any meat, and they had already hunted most of the animals in Bloedenkamp to extinction. First the mice—even though at the start nobody wanted to eat them, soon there were almost none left in the delta—and then the lizards and geckos disappeared. Then the frogs vanished. Sometimes the kids went fishing, but they weren't allowed to go too far and had to be satisfied with fish as small as a baby's pinky finger, or with tadpoles. The most luxurious thing was when they once found some bananas, but those were for the babies, and the women were left to fight over the peels.

Babies started to die, and then the old people. Sickness also killed young mothers, children, young girls—anyone might die at any moment. The field behind the cells turned into a cemetery.

Dewi Ayu was friendly with a young woman named Ola van Rijk. The girls had known each other for a long time. Ola's father also owned a cocoa plantation and they often visited one another's houses. Ola was two years younger than she was and was being held along with her mother and her younger sister. One afternoon, Dewi Ayu found her with tears streaming down her face.

"Mother is dying," she said.

Dewi Ayu went to see. Indeed it seemed to be true. Madam van Rijk was suffering from a severe fever, quite pale and shivering. It seemed that there was nothing to be done, but Dewi Ayu told Ola to go find the commandant and ask for medicine and food from the soldiers' rations. Ola quaked in fear at approaching the Japanese.

"Go, or your mother will die," said Dewi Ayu.

She finally left while Dewi Ayu applied cold compresses to the sick woman's forehead and tried to entertain Ola's little sister. After about ten minutes Ola returned without any medicine, just crying harder. "Let her die," she said sobbing. "What did you say?!" asked Dewi Ayu. Ola shook her head weakly while wiping away her tears with her sleeve. "There's no way," she said shortly. "The commandant would only give me medicine if I agreed to sleep with him."

"Let me talk to him," Dewi Ayu said, enraged. The commandant was in his office, sitting in his chair, staring absently at his iced coffee on the table and listening to radio static. She barged right in without knocking. The man turned, surprised by her nerve, his face showing the anger of someone who does not play around. But before he could explode, Dewi Ayu stepped forward, separated from him only by the width of the table. "I will take the place of the previous girl, Commandant. You can sleep with me, but give her mother medicine and a doctor. *And a doctor*!"

"Medicine and a doctor?" He already knew a few Malay phrases. This young girl was very pretty, no older than seventeen or eighteen, maybe still a virgin, and she was offering herself to him just for some fever medicine and a doctor. His anger evaporated at receiving such an extraordinary blessing on such a boring afternoon. He smiled, cunning and predatory, feeling like a lucky old man indeed, and walked around the table while Dewi Ayu waited with her typical composure. With one caress the commandant touched her whole face, his fingers creeping like a lizard over her nose and her lips, pausing at her chin to raise her face higher. His fingers continued their journey, traveling down her neck with rough hands that were too accustomed to holding a samurai sword, sweeping along the curve of her collarbone, and exploring the collar of her dress.

His hands pushed underneath the fabric and Dewi Ayu was a little startled, but the man was already grabbing her left breast, and after that he began to move much faster. The commandant opened Dewi Ayu's dress as efficiently as he examined his troops, and then he was squeezing her chest, and kissed her neck with a greedy lust, his hands moving this way and that as if he regretted being born with only two of them.

"Be quick, Commandant, if you're not, the woman will die."

The commandant seemed to agree with that analysis and without saying another word he yanked at Dewi Ayu, lifted her up, and after first setting aside his cup of coffee and the transistor radio, laid her out on top of the table. He quickly stripped the girl naked, undressed himself, and then pounced onto her body like a cat onto a fish. "Don't forget, Commandant, medicine and a doctor," she said for reassurance. "Yeah, yeah, medicine and a doctor," replied the commandant. Then, without beating around the bush, the Japanese man set upon her fiercely. Dewi Ayu closed her eyes, because whatever the circumstances, this was still the first time a man had taken her: she trembled a little bit, but she survived the horror. Then she couldn't really keep her eyes closed, the commandant was shaking her body so wildly, pounding her without pause, and rocking her from left to right. The one thing she managed was dodging if he tried to kiss her on the lips. The game ended in an explosion and the commandant rolled over next to Dewi Ayu, sprawled out heaving deep and ragged breaths.

"So, how about it Commandant?" asked Dewi Ayu.

"It was amazing, like an earthquake," he replied.

"I mean the medicine and the doctor."

Five minutes later Dewi Ayu was happy to get a native doctor, with round glasses and a kind demeanor, and gave thanks that she wouldn't have to do much business with the Japanese ever again. She brought him to the cell where the van Rijk family was staying and in the doorway she met Ola who immediately asked her, "You did it?"

"Yes."

"Oh my God!" screamed the girl, crying uncontrollably. As the doctor rushed to the sick woman, Dewi Ayu tried to comfort her. "It was nothing. Just think of it like I took a shit through the front hole."

Looking up the doctor pronounced, "This woman is already dead."

Ever since that they lived as a trio, like a little family: Dewi Ayu, Ola, and the young Gerda, who was just nine years old. Ola and Gerda's father had been drafted and had gone to war just like Ted, but they had not yet heard news as to whether he was still alive, captured, or dead. Their first Easter and Christmas in the camp passed, without eggs or a Christmas tree and without any candles, which had all been used up already. They tried to survive together, comforting one another and facing sickness and death. Dewi Ayu forbid little Gerda to steal anything from anybody, as the other children were doing. She wracked her brains trying to figure out what they were going to eat every day. The cows no longer grazed around the delta and the leeches were already gone.

One day Dewi Ayu saw a baby crocodile at the edge of the delta, and knowing that the only thing you really need to avoid with a crocodile on shore is its tail, she bludgeoned its head with a large stone. The unfortunate beast was wounded but it wasn't dead. It flicked its tail back and forth, and began moving toward the river. Taking a sharpened bamboo spike that was usually used to tether the ferryboat's ropes, with one reckless jab that she herself didn't imagine would be powerful enough, Dewi Ayu pierced the baby crocodile's eye and then its stomach. The creature died an agonizing death. Before its mother and friends could come for it, Dewi Ayu dragged the baby crocodile into the camp by its tail. Now they could really celebrate, with crocodile meat soup! Many people praised her bravery and shared their thanks.

"There are still lots of them in the river," she said casually, "if you guys want more."

Ever since she was little she had been taught to fear nothing. Her grandfather had taken her boar hunting with the tough guys a few times. She had even been at Mr. Willie's side when he was rammed by the wild boar that crippled him for life. She knew how to deal with a boar: zigzag, don't run in a straight line, because a boar doesn't know how to turn. The tough guys had taught her that, just as they had taught her how to face a crocodile, what to do if a python suddenly coiled around her or if a viper bit her, how to face down an *ajak*, and what to do if a leech was sucking her blood. She had never actually been threatened by any of those creatures until she had come to Bloedenkamp, but the lessons she learned from the tough guys were always in the back of her mind.

They also taught her mantras to get rid of evil spirits and to guard her safety. She never used them, but it made her happy to know that she could. She knew a Javanese merchant who came on foot from a mountain more than one hundred kilometers away just to sell the Dutch fruit from her garden. It took her four days to get there. She usually spent a night in the warehouse, and Dewi Ayu's grandmother would give her dinner and a cup of hot coffee, and the next day she would depart on another four-day journey home. In addition to money, sometimes she brought back some hand-me-down clothing. She was never afraid of any kind of jungle beast and Dewi Ayu knew why, it was because she recited mantras.

But Dewi Ayu also didn't really believe in them, just as she was always confused about the point of praying. Still, while she didn't believe in prayer, and never did it herself, she'd say to Gerda, "Pray that America wins the war."

The gossip about America's victory and Germany's defeat was spreading by word of mouth throughout the camp. It comforted them a bit, no matter how elusive that hope might be, but the days continued to follow one another, as did the weeks, and the months. Finally the second Christmas arrived, and Dewi Ayu celebrated it that year just to entertain Gerda. She broke a branch from a banyan tree growing in front of the camp's gate, decorated it with paper ornaments, sang *Jingle Bells*, and felt very happy to have Ola and Gerda, for a moment forgetting how miserable it was to spend all one's days in a prison camp.

They started to discuss their plans for when the war was over, however it might end, once they were finally free. Dewi Ayu said she would return to her home, set everything in order, and live just as she had before. Maybe not truly just like before, because maybe the natives would form their own republic and resist the old ways, but she would return to her home and live there. She would be pleased if Ola and Gerda could join her. But Ola thought rationally that maybe the Japanese had already stolen the house and sold it to someone. Or maybe the natives had, and now it belonged to them.

"We can buy it back," said Dewi Ayu. She told them the secret of the treasure she had left there, even though she didn't say exactly where it was stored. "Even if the Japanese have already bombed it and all that's left is a heap of tiles, we can buy it back." Gerda was really happy to hear such a tale. She was now eleven years old, but she had wasted away and her body hadn't developed at all in the past two years. But everyone was in the same boat, shrunken and skinny. Dewi Ayu was sure she had lost ten or fifteen kilos of flesh off her body.

"And that's enough for fifty bowls of soup," she said with a small laugh.

The real insanity began after almost two full years in the camp, when the Japanese soldiers began making a list of all the women who were between the ages of seventeen and twenty-eight. Dewi Ayu was already eighteen, almost nineteen. Ola was seventeen. At first they thought the list meant they'd be assigned to harder forced labor, until one morning a few military trucks arrived across the river and a handful of army officers boarded the ferry heading for Bloedenkamp. They had already come a number of times, for inspections or to give new rules and orders, and this time the order was to round up all those women between the ages of seventeen and twenty-eight years old. Chaos immediately descended, as the women realized that they were about to be separated from their friends and family.

A number of young girls, including Ola, tried to make themselves up to look like old women, which of course didn't work. Others ran, hiding in the toilets or climbing up onto the rooftop and crouching there, but the Japanese soldiers found them all. An old woman, who feared she was about to lose her daughter, tried to protest and said if the young women were to be taken then all should be taken. In response, two soldiers beat her black and blue.

Finally all the young women stood in rows in the middle of the yard, shaking in fear while their mothers huddled together in the distance. Dewi Ayu saw Gerda clinging to a post all alone gulping back tears, and beside her Ola didn't dare look anywhere except down toward her ugly tattered shoes. She heard a number of the girls crying and murmuring prayers. Then the officers came, examining them one by one. They stood in front of each woman, laughing quietly while scrutinizing her body, from the top of her head down to the tips of her toes. Sometimes, to get a better look at her face, they'd lift up her chin with their fingertips.

Then there was a selection. A number of women were separated off to the side and every time a young girl was released, it was like an arrow shooting from the group of girls to the group of mothers. Now only half of them were still standing in the middle of the yard, including Dewi Ayu and Ola, even after the second culling, they both were still in the middle of the yard, powerless pawns in the Japanese soldiers' ridiculous game. They were called one by one to face an official, who examined them much more minutely with small squinting eyes. That final selection left only twenty girls in the center of the yard clutching one another, but no one dared look at anyone else. These chosen girls—young, pretty, healthy, and strong—were ordered to pack all of their belongings immediately and gather in the camp office. The truck was already waiting to take them away.

"I have to bring Gerda," said Ola.

"No," said Dewi Ayu. "If we die, at least she will survive."

"Or the other way around?"

"Or the other way around."

They entrusted Gerda to a family that Dewi Ayu had known for a long time. But even so, Ola couldn't accept the situation and the sisters sat in a corner embracing for very a long time. Dewi Ayu packed their things and helped sort out what would be left behind for Gerda.

Then Dewi Ayu said to Gerda, "Ok, that's enough, after two years of this boring life, we are leaving for a while to go on a trip. I'll bring you back some souvenirs."

"Don't forget a guidebook," said Gerda.

"You're funny, kid," said Dewi Ayu.

The twenty women swarmed next to the gate, and from the look of it Dewi Ayu was the only one acting as though it would be a pleasant outing. The other young girls stood in confusion and fear, looking back at those they were leaving behind. The officers had gone on ahead, and the women were herded to the ferryboat by a number of soldiers, who pushed and shoved them forcefully. Once boarded, they could still see the prison gates and deep inside people crowded around watching their departure. There were some handkerchiefs waving, reminding everyone of when the Japanese had first taken them from their homes. Now another journey was waiting. But once the ferry began to move, the gate and the view inside vanished. That was when the girls began to wail, drowning out the ferry engine and the barks of the soldiers who were getting annoyed at their whining.

Then they were lifted onto a truck that was waiting across the river. Everyone crouched along the sides except Dewi Ayu, who stood leaning against the wall of the truck taking in the view along the familiar journey to Halimunda, next to two armed guards. After two years in the camps, almost all of the young women already knew each other well, but no one seemed to want to talk, and they were amazed by Dewi Ayu's calm demeanor. Even Ola didn't know what she was thinking, and presumptuously decided that Dewi Ayu didn't have anyone left to worry about—she wasn't leaving anyone behind.

"Where are we being taken, Sir?" Dewi Ayu asked a soldier, even though she knew that the truck was headed to the western edge of the city, or maybe beyond. The guards apparently had been given orders not to speak to the women, so he ignored Dewi Ayu's question, and instead kept talking to the others in Japanese.

The women were brought to a big house with a sweeping yard full of trees and bushes, a big banyan tree in the center, and alternating palm trees and Chinese coconut trees lining the fence. When the truck entered the grounds, Dewi Ayu guessed that there were more than twenty rooms in the two-storey house. The girls got down from the truck dumbfounded: from a vile and gloomy prison camp they had come all of a sudden to a comfortable and even luxurious mansion. It was so strange—the orders must have gotten mixed up or something.

In addition to the two guards, there were more soldiers patrolling the expansive grounds or sitting playing cards. A middle-aged native woman appeared from inside the house, wearing her hair in a bun and a loose-fitting gown with the belt untied at her waist. She smiled at the women standing in the yard like peasants too nervous to approach the king's palace.

"Is this your house, Miss?" asked Dewi Ayu politely.

"Call me Mama Kalong," she said. "Because like a *kalong*, a fruit bat, I'm much more often up and about at night than during the day." She came down off the veranda and approached the women, trying to lighten the bleak expressions on their faces with a joke and a smile. "This used to be a vacation house owned by a Dutch lemonade factory owner from Batavia. I forget his name, but it doesn't really matter because the house belongs to you all now."

"What for?" asked Dewi Ayu.

"I think you know what for. You are here to volunteer for soldiers who are sick."

"Like Red Cross volunteers?"

"You're smart, kid. What's your name?"

"Ola."

"All right, Ola, invite your friends inside."

The house interior was even more amazing. There were many paintings, most in the *Mooi Indie* style, hanging on the walls. The whole structure was still intact, made from intricately carved wood. Dewi Ayu saw a family portrait still hanging on the wall, a group of people from what looked like more than three generations all squeezed together on a sofa. Maybe they had successfully escaped, or maybe some were living in Bloedenkamp, or quite possibly they were all already dead. A large portrait of Queen Wilhelmina was leaning over in one corner; maybe the Japanese had taken it down. This all made Dewi Ayu realize that she herself must no longer have a home: probably the Japanese had it, or maybe it had been blown to smithereens by an off-target shell. But every little thing was diligently cared for, maybe by Mama Kalong, and when she walked into one of the bedrooms, she felt like she was entering a bridal chamber. The big bed had a soft, thick mattress and a mosquito net the color of a red apple, and the air was fragrant with roses. The armoires were still filled with clothes, some for young ladies, and Mama Kalong said that they could wear them. Ola remarked that after two years in the prison camp, it all seemed like a dream.

"What did I tell you," said Dewi Ayu. "We are on an excursion."

Each girl got her own room, and the luxury didn't end there. With the help of two servants, Mama Kalong served them a complete *rijsttafel* dinner, which, after starving for months on end, was the best thing they had ever tasted. Still, the memory of those they had left behind in the camp made it impossible for most of the girls to enjoy these indulgences.

"Gerda should be with us," said Ola.

Dewi Ayu tried to comfort her, "If we don't end up getting sent to do forced labor in a weapons factory, then we can go get her."

"The woman said we were going to be Red Cross volunteers."

"And so? What's the difference? You don't even know how to dress a wound, so what would Gerda do?"

It was true. But they were all already enchanted by the idea of becoming Red Cross volunteers, even if it meant working for the enemy. At the very least, it was better than dying of starvation in the prison camp. They became all abuzz discussing matters of first aid. One young girl said that she had been a member of the girl scouts, and knew how to staunch a wound, and not only that, she also knew how to treat less serious illnesses like diarrhea, fever and food poisoning, with wild plants.

"The problem is, the Japanese soldiers don't need diarrhea medicine," said Dewi Ayu. "They need someone to amputate them at the neck."

Dewi Ayu left the group and went into her room. Because she was the calmest among them, even though she wasn't the oldest, they had come to consider her their leader. So the nineteen other girls followed her and gathered in her room, some sitting on top of her bed, and resumed their conversation about how to amputate a Japanese soldier's neck, just in case their heads were wounded and no longer useful to them. Dewi Ayu paid no attention to their foolish chatter, and instead chose to enjoy her new bed, like a little child with a new toy. She massaged the mattress, stroked the blanket, rolled back and forth, and even jumped up and down to make the mattress jiggle and her friends bounce.

"What are you doing?" one of them asked.

"I just want to see whether this bed will collapse if it's given some hearty shakes," she replied while jumping.

"There's no way there will be an earthquake," said another girl.

"Who knows," she replied. "If I am going to end up falling onto the floor while I'm sleeping, I'd rather just lie down on the floor to begin with."

"Such a strange young girl," they said, and one by one they drifted off to their own bedrooms.

After they had all left, Dewi Ayu walked to the window and opened it. There were thick iron bars and she said to herself, "There is no way to escape." She closed the window, climbed into her bed, and pulled up the covers without changing her clothes. Before closing her eyes she prayed, "Well hell, you know that this is what war is like."

❧

When morning arrived, breakfast was already prepared: fried rice with eggs sunny-side up. All the girls had bathed but they were still wearing their old clothes, which resembled foul dishrags that had been used and washed and set out to dry one too many times. Their bloodshot eyes showed the traces of tears cried all night long. Only Dewi Ayu had brazenly taken the clothes from her armoire, and was wearing a short-sleeved cream-colored dress with white polka dots and a belt that cinched her waist with a round buckle. She had powdered her face, applied a thin layer of lipstick, and the faint scent of lavender perfume wafted off her body. She had found everything in the drawers of the vanity table. She looked elegant and bright, as if it was her birthday, quite out of place among the gloomy girls around her. They looked at her with accusatory gazes, as if they had caught a traitor red-handed, but after eating breakfast they all ran to their rooms, quickly changed their clothes, and admired one another.

It was near midday when the Japanese arrived, the sound of their boots filling the house. The girls immediately remembered that despite it all they were still prisoners, and it felt strange that they had just been so happy. They retreated until their backs were against the wall, once again overcome with gloom. Except Dewi Ayu, who quickly greeted one of the guests.

"How are you?"

He just looked at her for a moment, not bothering to speak, and then went to find Mama Kalong. They spoke for a moment, then he returned and counted the girls before going back out again. The house grew quiet with only the girls and Mama Kalong and a couple of soldiers patrolling outside.

"He was counting us as if we were a group of soldiers!" one of them complained.

"That's the job of a commandant," said Mama Kalong.

That whole day they didn't do anything except hang around in the living room or in one of their bedrooms, and boredom overcame them. After getting nostalgic about their happy childhoods before the war, they ran out of things to talk about. They didn't say anything more about the Red Cross, because there was no indication that they were really going to become volunteers. The Japanese didn't speak about it, but they didn't speak about anything at all. The women thought there really should be some kind of training if they were going to be volunteers, but it looked like they were just going to rot away inside the house, amid all that nonsensical luxury. What's more, if you think about it, said one of them, the front is far away from here, who knows where, maybe in the Pacific Ocean, maybe in India, but definitely not in Halimunda. There were no wounded soldiers in this city, and nobody needed the Red Cross.

"They still need neck amputators, though," said Dewi Ayu.

That joke no longer seemed funny, especially since the person telling it looked like she didn't have a care in the world. She seemed to be enjoying everything, eating the apples that had been set out, and then just as greedily eating the bananas and papayas.

"Are you starving to death, or just being greedy?" asked Ola.

"Both."

By the following day, nothing had happened yet, making them more and more confused. Ola tried to comfort herself, thinking that maybe they were going to be exchanged with other prisoners of war, and that's why they were being given good food, a house and clothing, so that they wouldn't appear to have been suffering. None of the girls believed that. The opportunity to ask questions came when a number of Japanese men appeared at the house, along with a photographer. But none of them could speak English, Dutch, or Malay. They just pantomimed to the girls to look stylish, because they were going to be photographed. Reluctantly the girls lined up in front of the camera, with forced smiles, hoping Ola was right that their portraits would be part of a campaign about the condition of the prisoners of war, and that there would be an exchange.

"Why don't you ask Mama Kalong what's going on?" suggested Dewi Ayu.

They found the woman and accosted her.

"You said we were going to be Red Cross volunteers!"

"Volunteers, yes," said Mama Kalong, "but maybe not Red Cross."

"So?"

She looked at the girls, who looked back at her expectantly. They waited, their innocent faces almost completely without sin, until Mama Kalong just shook her head weakly. She left them and they quickly followed her, demanding, "Say something!"

"All I know is that you are prisoners of war."

"Why are we being given all this food?"

"So that you don't die." Then she disappeared into the back yard. The girls didn't know where she was going and they could not pursue her because the Japanese soldiers intercepted them and let the woman go.

Their annoyance only grew when they returned to find their friend Dewi Ayu sitting in a rocking chair, humming softly and still eating her apples. She looked in their direction, and smiled to see their faces holding back rage. "You look funny," she said, "like a bunch of rag dolls." They stood around her in a circle, but Dewi Ayu stayed silent, until one of them finally spoke:

"Don't you feel like something strange is going on? Aren't you worried about anything?"

"Worry comes from ignorance," said Dewi Ayu.

"So you think you know what is going to happen to us?" asked Ola.

"Yes," she replied, "we are going to be made into prostitutes."

They all knew it, but only Dewi Ayu was brave enough to say it.

{4}

MAMA KALONG'S BROTHEL had been around since the opening of the massive Dutch colonial army barracks. Before that, she had just been a girl who helped out at the tavern owned by her evil aunt. They sold rice wine and cane sugar *tuak*, and the soldiers became their regular customers. Even though the influx of troops into the city made the tavern livelier than ever, the young girl still wasn't making enough to get by. Instead, she was ordered to work from five in the morning until eleven at night and all she was given in exchange was two meals a day. But then she discovered a way to take advantage of her limited free time and earn her own money.

After closing the tavern, she would go to the barracks. She knew what they needed and they knew what she wanted. The soldiers paid her to straddle their laps naked. Three or four of them would take turns screwing her before she went home with their money. After a while, she began to pull in way more than what her aunt was making. She had a good business instinct. One day, after getting scolded for falling asleep at work, she left her aunt and opened up her own tavern at the end of the wharf. She sold rice wine and cane sugar *tuak* and also her own body. She never went to the barracks anymore, the soldiers came to her tavern instead. By the end of the first month she had already found two young girls around twelve or thirteen years old to help her at the tavern, both as waitresses and as whores. She had begun her career as a madam.

After three months, there were six whores there, not including herself, enough for her to expand the tavern, building a few rooms with walls made from plaited bamboo. One day a colonel came to inspect the military post and visit the brothel, not to hire a prostitute for himself but to see whether the place was good enough for his soldiers.

"This is like a pigsty," he said. "They will die from such squalor before they even meet the enemy."

Mama Kalong, with a demeanor that was appropriately respectful for a colonel, quickly replied, "But they will die from sexual frustration if they are forced to wait for a better brothel."

The colonel came to believe that the brothel built up his men's morale and was good for their fighting spirit, so he wrote a favorable report and a month and a half after his visit the military decided to build more permanent facilities. They got rid of the bamboo walls and the sugar palm leaf roof, and installed cement floors and walls as strong as a defense fort. Almost all the beds were made from teak and the mattresses were stuffed with choice cotton batting. Mama Kalong, who received all of this at no cost, looked pleased and said to every soldier who came:

"Feel free to make love here as if you were in your very own home."

"That's ridiculous," said one soldier. "All I've got at home is my mom and my old granny."

And from then on, whoever came to that place would be pampered and doted upon. The whores dressed and did their makeup better than the most respectable Dutch women, and they were more beautiful than the queen.

When syphilis spread, Mama Kalong and the soldiers demanded that a hospital be built. It was actually a military hospital, but civilians came too. The brothel was threatened with bankruptcy, but she quickly came up with a number of good solutions. She tried to persuade some of the soldiers to take on their own private concubines, saying she could obtain such women for them for a fee. She traversed the villages and even ventured up the mountain to find young girls willing to become kept women for the Dutch troops.

She still cared for them all in her whorehouse, but they were each only used by one single soldier. She quickly got rich this way, with the guarantee that the women were not spreading foul disease. If the soldiers who felt choked by Mama Kalong's merciless tariff decided to marry their concubines instead, she would demand an even more expensive indemnity fee. Meanwhile, she still rented the old prostitutes out to whoever was interested. For these whores she even had new customers to take the place of the soldiers: the sailors and dockworkers.

During the last years of colonial power, it is fair to say that she was the richest woman in Halimunda. She bought land sold by farmers who had lost everything at the gambling table and rented it back to them, until her property extended almost the entire length of the foothills. Her holdings were exceeded perhaps only by the Dutch plantations.

She was like a small queen in that city: everyone respected her, the natives and the Dutch alike. She rode a horse-drawn carriage wherever she went to take care of her business matters, the most important of which remained the women who peddled their private parts. Her public presentation was incredibly proper, with a tight sarong and a *kebaya* blouse and her hair in a bun. Of course, she wasn't as skinny as she used to be, and this was when the people, following the habit of the young prostitutes, began calling her Mama. No one knows who started it, but her name then grew longer to become Mama Kalong. She liked that name and soon everyone, even she herself, had forgotten what her real name used to be.

"Now, after all the other kingdoms have collapsed, in Halimunda there is a new kingdom," said an intoxicated Dutch soldier at the tavern, "and that is the Kingdom of Mama Kalong."

Even though of course she was greedy, she never wanted to make her young prostitutes suffer. In fact quite the opposite, she tended to spoil them, like a granny taking care of a horde of grandchildren. She had servants who would heat warm water for them so that they could bathe after exhausting lovemaking sessions. On certain days, she gave them the day off and took them on outings to a nearby waterfall. She brought in the best tailors to make their clothes, and above all, their health was her highest priority.

"Because," she said, "the most exquisite pleasure is to be found in a healthy body."

Then the Dutch soldiers left and the Japanese soldiers came. But amid that era of change, Mama Kalong's whorehouse remained exactly the same. She served the Japanese soldiers just as graciously as she had served her previous customers, and even sought out fresher, younger girls. One day she was called in by the civil and military authorities for a brief interrogation. It was nothing too troubling; basically, a number of high-ranking Japanese military officials in the city wished to have their own private whores, separate from the prostitutes for the low-ranking officers and especially separate from those used by the dockworkers and the fishermen. They wanted new prostitutes, who were truly pristine and excellently cared for, and Mama Kalong had to find those girls as quickly as possible because, just as she herself had said before, the men were dying from sexual frustration.

"It's easy, Sir," she said, "to find girls like that."

"Tell me, where?"

"The prisoners of war," replied Mama Kalong shortly.

❧

When afternoon came and a number of Japanese men began to arrive, the girls began running frantically back and forth. They tried to find some crack through which to slip away, but every place was already guarded. The house's fairly large yard was surrounded by a high wall, with just one gate in front and a small door in the back, neither of which could possibly be breached. A number of girls tried to climb onto the roof of the house, as if they hoped they could fly away or find a rope there that they could climb up into the sky.

"I already tried everything," said Dewi Ayu. "There is no escape."

"We are going to become prostitutes!" shrieked Ola, collapsing and weeping.

"It's actually worse than that," said Dewi Ayu. "I don't think we're even going to get paid."

Another girl named Helena immediately accosted the Japanese officers who appeared and accused them of violating their human rights as outlined in the Geneva Convention. Not just the Japanese, but even Dewi Ayu laughed out loud.

"There are no conventions during wartime, honey," she said.

Out of all of them, that girl Helena appeared to be the most upset by the knowledge that they were going to be made into whores. The funny thing was, she had decided to become a nun before the war came and everything dissolved into chaos. She was the only girl who had brought a prayer book to this place, and now she began to recite a psalm in a loud voice, in front of the Japanese, perhaps hoping the soldiers would run away howling in fear, like evil spirits at an exorcism. But, unexpectedly, the Japanese soldiers were very polite to her and at the end of every prayer they would reply:

"Amen." While laughing, of course.

"Amen," she responded, before collapsing weakly into a chair.

An officer brought some sheets of paper, giving one to each of the girls. There was Malay writing on them, which turned out to be the names of different flowers. "These are your new names," said the officer. Dewi Ayu was excited to see her name: Rose. "Watch out," she said, "every rose has its thorn." Another girl got the name Orchid, and another got Dahlia. Ola got the name Alamanda.

They were ordered to go to their rooms while a number of Japanese men lined up at a table on the veranda to buy their tickets. The first night the prices were very expensive, because they believed that the girls were all still virgins. They didn't know that Dewi Ayu was no longer pure. Instead of each going to her own room, the girls gathered around Dewi Ayu, who was still testing out the strength of her mattress and commented, "So it turns out someone will make the earthquake on *top* of it."

Then the soldiers began to capture the girls one by one, in a battle they won with ease, gripping the girls in their hands like sick kittens thrashing about futilely as they were being taken away. That night Dewi Ayu heard hysterical screams coming from their rooms as the battle continued. A number of the girls even succeeded in running out into the hall stark naked, before the soldiers recaptured them and threw them back on top of their beds. They wailed all through those terrible unions, and she even heard Helena screaming out a number of psalm verses as a Japanese busted up her vagina. At the same time, she could hear the other Japanese men out on the veranda laughing at all of this uproar.

Only Dewi Ayu didn't grumble, or let out even a peep. She got a Japanese officer who was tall and big, stocky like a sumo wrestler, with a samurai sword at his waist. Dewi Ayu lay down on top of the bed and looked up toward the heavens, not looking at him at all and certainly not smiling. She appeared to be much more focused on the sounds of the commotion outside her room than to whatever was going on inside it. She lay down like a corpse ready for burial.

When the Japanese officer barked at her to take her clothes off, she remained perfectly still, as if she wasn't even breathing.

Annoyed, the Japanese took out his samurai sword and brandished it until the flat of its blade touched Dewi Ayu's face, and he repeated his orders. But Dewi Ayu remained immobile, even as the tip of the sword inscribed a mark upon her cheek. Her eyes still looked up to the heavens and it was still as if her ears were attuned to a faraway sound. Now, growing angry, the Japanese threw down his sword and slapped Dewi Ayu's face twice, which left behind a red welt and caused her body to sway for a moment, but she maintained her demeanor of infuriating indifference.

Surrendering to his bad luck, the stocky soldier finally tore off the clothes of the woman in front of him, threw them to the floor, and now she was naked. He parted the woman's two arms and two legs until she was spread-eagled. After appraising the still and silent chunk of flesh before him, he quickly got naked himself, jumped onto the bed, and lay face down on top of Dewi Ayu's body, assaulting her. For the whole cold coupling Dewi Ayu stayed in the same position that the Japanese soldier had placed her in, not responding with any heat or warmth or putting up any unnecessary struggle. She didn't close her eyes, she didn't smile, she just looked up to the heavens.

Her chilly demeanor had an extraordinary effect: the man didn't take even three minutes. Two minutes and twenty-three seconds, according to Dewi Ayu's count as she peered at the grandfather clock in the corner of the room. The Japanese guy rolled to her side and then quickly stood up, grumbling. He hastily got dressed, and left without saying another word, slamming the door on his way out. Only then did Dewi Ayu move, and smiling quite sweetly, she stretched her body and said:

"What a boring night."

She got dressed and went to the bathroom. There she found a

number of girls washing themselves, as if they could clean off all the feelings of filth and shame and sin with some scoopfuls of water. They didn't speak to one another. It wasn't over yet, because the night was still young and a number of Japanese were still waiting. After bathing, they were forced to go back to their rooms and then there was more struggle and more wailing, except from Dewi Ayu who returned to her frigid bearing.

That night they were taken by four or five men each. What made Dewi Ayu suffer was not the crazy tireless screwing that froze her body in a quiet and mysterious paralysis, but the screams and sobs of her friends. *You poor women*, she thought. *Fighting against the inevitable hurts worse than anything else.* Then the next day came.

That morning there was work to do. In despair, Helena had chopped off her hair in jagged chunks and Dewi Ayu had to neaten it out. On the third night, they found Ola almost dead in the bathroom, having tried to slit her wrists. Dewi Ayu quickly carried her to her bedroom, unconscious and soaked to the bone, while Mama Kalong looked for a doctor. She didn't die, but nevertheless Dewi Ayu realized that what Ola had experienced was even more gruesome and dire than she had first thought. When Ola had emerged from her crisis, Dewi Ayu said to her:

"'Ola was raped and she died.' That is not the souvenir that I want to bring back to Gerda."

Even though life had already gone on like this for days, a number of girls still could not accept their miserable fate, and Dewi Ayu still heard screams in the middle of the night. Two of the girls still often hid in the hallways or climbed the sapodilla tree behind the house. She then advised them to do what she did every night.

"Lie down like a corpse, until they get bored," she said. But the girls found that to be even more dreadful. To lie quiet while someone assaulted their body and fucked them, none of them could imagine it. "Or try to find one guy out of all of them who you like a little, and service him with your full attention, and make him addicted to you so that he will come back every evening and pay you for the entire night. Servicing the same person over and over is way better than sleeping with lots of different men."

That seemed like a better idea, but it was still too awful for her friends to imagine.

"Or tell them tales like Scheherazade," she said.

Not one of them was good at telling stories.

"Invite them to play cards."

Not one of them could play cards.

"If that's how it is, then flip the scales," said Dewi Ayu, giving up. "*You* rape *them*."

Despite everything, in time, during the day they could truly be quite happy, without any disturbances. The first week they were too ashamed to talk to one another, and they locked themselves up in their rooms, passing their time crying alone. But after a week had passed, they began to gather after breakfast, trying to comfort and entertain one another and talk about things that had no relationship whatsoever to their tragic nights.

Dewi Ayu spent some time with that middle-aged native woman, Mama Kalong, and the two developed an odd friendship, which was only possible because Dewi Ayu maintained a calm demeanor that betrayed no desire to rebel, and she didn't give Mama Kalong any problems about her relationship with the Japanese. Mama Kalong told Dewi Ayu that in all honesty she owned a brothel at the end of the wharf. Now many women were being brought there by force, to service the low-ranking Japanese officers. All her women were natives, except the ones in this house.

"You all are lucky not to be doing it day *and* night," said Mama Kalong. "Plus the low-ranking officers are way bigger assholes."

"There's no difference between low-level officers and the Emperor of Japan," said Dewi Ayu. "They all target female genitalia."

Mama Kalong provided a half-blind old native woman as a masseuse. Every morning the girls all got their routine massage, believing Mama Kalong when she said that was how they could avoid getting pregnant. The exception was Dewi Ayu, who usually spent the morning sleeping before breakfast and only wanted a massage every once in a while, when she was feeling especially worn out.

"You get pregnant from getting screwed, not from *not* getting a massage," she said lightly.

She took the risk, and after one month in that whorehouse, she was the first woman to get pregnant. Mama Kalong advised her to abort her fetus. "Think of your family," the woman said. Dewi Ayu then replied, "Just as you are telling me to do, Mama, I *am* thinking of my family, and the only family I have is this kid inside me." So Dewi Ayu let her stomach stick out, puff up, and get bigger day by day. Her pregnancy had its benefits: Mama Kalong told her to stay in a back room and announced to all the Japanese that she was pregnant and no one was allowed to sleep with her. No Japanese even wanted to sleep with her in that condition, and so she urged the other girls to follow her lead.

"It's true what they say, each child brings its own good fortune."

But not one other girl dared to take the same risk as Dewi Ayu.

Three months later, not even one person had abandoned their daily routine of morning massages, and nobody else got pregnant. They continued to face the same terror every night, choosing that over being sent home to their mothers with round bellies. "What would I say to Gerda?" said Ola.

"Just say, 'Gerda, your souvenir is inside my stomach.'"

As always, during the middle of the day they had a lot of free time. The girls would gather to gossip and chat. Some played cards and others helped Dewi Ayu sew small clothes for her baby. They were thrilled that one of them was going to give birth, and their hearts pounded in anticipation as they waited for the baby's entrance into this vicious world.

Sometimes they also talked about the war. There was gossip that the Allied troops would attack certain pockets of the Japanese military and the girls hoped that Halimunda would be one of them.

"I hope all the Japanese are murdered and their guts come spewing out," said Helena.

"Don't be so crass, my child can hear you," said Dewi Ayu.

"So what?"

"So, her father is Japanese."

They all laughed at her bitter humor.

But the hope that the Allied troops might come really lifted their spirits. So when a lost carrier pigeon flew into their house and one of the girls caught it, they sent messages for the Allied soldiers. *Help us*; *We have been forced into prostitution*; *Twenty young women are awaiting their warrior saviors*. The idea was silly, and they could not imagine how the bird would ever find the Allied troops. Still, they released it one afternoon.

There was no indication that the pigeon had returned to the Allied troops. But when the bird reappeared again without their letters, the girls believed that at least someone, who knows where, had read them. So with excitement they sent new messages. They did this over and over for almost three weeks straight.

No Allied troops came; who came instead was a Japanese general none of the girls had seen before. Upon his sudden arrival the soldiers who guarded the farthest corners of the property tried to block him from entering as best they could. The two soldiers he questioned trembled, their knees knocking together.

"What kind of place is this?" asked the general.

"A place of prostitution," Dewi Ayu called out before any of the soldiers could reply.

He was a soldier with a tall and sturdy build, maybe a descendent of the old-fashioned samurai, with a sword hanging from either hip. He cultivated two bushy sideburns on his cold and serious face.

"Are you all prostitutes?" he asked.

Dewi Ayu nodded. "We are caring for the souls of sick soldiers," she said. "This is how we have been made into whores, by force and without pay."

"Are you pregnant?"

"You sound like you don't believe that a Japanese soldier could knock a girl up, General."

He disregarded Dewi Ayu's commentary and began to scold all of the Japanese men at the house, and when nightfall came and a number of the regular customers appeared, his anger grew all the more impassioned. He called a number of officers and held a private meeting in one of the rooms. It was clear that no one dared disobey him.

In the meantime the girls in the house looked at their savior with joyful gratitude, as if he was a wonderful victory they had won with the letters that they had tirelessly sent. "I almost don't believe it, that an angel could have a Japanese face," said Helena. Before he returned to his military headquarters, he approached the girls who were gathered in the dining room. He stood in front of them, removed his hat and bowed, down as low as his waist.

"*Naore*!" cried Dewi Ayu.

The general stood up straight again and for the first time they saw him smile. "Send me another letter if these demented men so much as lay a hand on any of you."

"Why did it take you so long to come, General?"

"Well if I had come too soon," he said in a deep and gentle voice, "I would have found nothing but an empty house."

"May I know your name, General?" asked Dewi Ayu.

"Musashi."

"If my child is a boy, I will name him Musashi."

"Pray that you have a girl," said the general. "I have never heard of a woman raping a man." Then he left, getting into the truck waiting out front, as the girls waved. As soon as he was gone, the officers who had been standing and wiping their cold sweat off with their handkerchiefs, promptly hurried after him. That was the first night that no one came to rape them. It was so peaceful, and the girls celebrated with a small party. Mama Kalong gave them three bottles of wine and Helena poured it into small glasses like a priest at Holy Communion.

"To the safety of the general," she said. "He is so handsome."

"If he ravished me, I would not resist," said Ola.

"If my daughter is a girl, I will name her Alamanda, after Ola," said Dewi Ayu.

All of it came to an end quite suddenly—there was no more whoring and no more Japanese officers coming around at nightfall to buy their bodies. One thing that made some of the girls nervous was that they were going to have to meet their mothers, and they didn't know how to speak about what they had experienced. Some tried standing in front of the mirror, building their courage, saying to their own images, "Mama, now I am a whore." Of course they couldn't say it like that, so they would try again, "Mama, I used to be a whore." But that also sounded wrong, so they would say, "Mama, I was forced into prostitution."

But they knew that saying that to their mothers would be much harder than saying it to a mirror. The only slightly fortunate thing was that it seemed like the Japanese did not plan to take them back to Bloedenkamp any time soon, and instead would continue to hold them there at the house. Not as prostitutes, but as prisoners of war just like they had been before. The soldiers still guarded them vigilantly, and Mama Kalong still invited the girls to take advantage of the excellent care she could provide them.

"I treat all my whores like queens," she said with pride. "I don't care if they are already retired."

They filled their days, weeks, and months entertaining themselves with Dewi Ayu, who continued to sew for her baby. With the help of her friends, she already had almost one full basket of small articles of clothing, made from the fabric they had found in the household closets. At least it spared them the boredom of waiting for the war to end, until finally Mama Kalong came with a midwife.

"All of my prostitutes who have ever gotten pregnant have given birth with her help," said Mama Kalong.

"But I sure hope that all the women she has helped give birth have not all been prostitutes," said Dewi Ayu.

On a Tuesday of the same year that had begun with her being taken from Bloedenkamp prison and brought to the whorehouse, she gave birth to a baby girl she promptly named Alamanda, just as she had promised. The child was lovely, inheriting all of her mother's beauty. The only indication that her father was Japanese could be found in her small eyes. "A white girl with squinty eyes," said Ola. "Only in the Dutch East Indies."

"It's just too bad that she's not the general's daughter," said Helena.

That small baby quickly became lavish entertainment for the house's inhabitants, and even the Japanese soldiers bought her dolls and threw a party for her good fortune. "They have to respect her," Ola said, "because no matter what, Alamanda is the child of their superior." Dewi Ayu was pleased that little by little Ola had been able to forget her troubled past, and seemed to be her happy self again. Her days were spent helping out with the little baby, alongside the others, who all called themselves Aunties.

Early one morning, a Japanese soldier entered Helena's room and tried to rape her. Helena screamed so loudly she woke everyone up and the soldier ran out into the darkness. They didn't know which soldier had attempted the rape, until morning came and the general appeared. He grabbed one soldier, dragged him out into the middle of the yard, and gave him a pistol. The soldier shot himself in the mouth, exploding his own brains. After that no one dared approach the women.

Meanwhile, the war wasn't over yet. They heard through the grapevine, from Mama Kalong and from a number of the servants who came to help her, that the Japanese troops had finished building defense trenches along the southern coast. In secret Mama Kalong had given the girls a radio, so they heard that two bombs had fallen on Japan and a third bomb had not yet been dropped, which was enough to electrify the house. It seemed as though the Japanese soldiers had also already heard the news. In the following days they just sat underneath the trees listlessly, and one by one they began to disappear, sent who knows where. By the time the Allied planes finally began to fly across the Halimunda skies, releasing small pamphlets proclaiming that the war would soon be over, there were only two Japanese soldiers left guarding the house.

If the girls didn't try to escape, even though they were only guarded by those two soldiers, it was because the situation was so unpredictable. What's more, they had heard on the radio that British troops now controlled the cities, so it seemed that staying in the house was much safer than being out in the streets. Japan had lost and they were waiting for the Allied forces to save them. But it turned out those troops took their sweet time coming to Halimunda, as if they had forgotten that the city even existed on the face of the earth, but then the airplanes returned, throwing down biscuits and penicillin, and the emergency forces appeared. Who came first were the second tier Royal Netherlands East Indies Army troops, founded from the Dutch brigades. Calling themselves the *Koninklijk Nederlands Indisch Leger*, the KNIL, they quickly replaced the Japanese flag in front of the house with their own flag. The two remaining Japanese soldiers surrendered helplessly.

But what really surprised Dewi Ayu was that Mr. Willie was embedded in one of those brigades.

"I joined the KNIL," he said.

"Well that's better than joining the Japanese," said Dewi Ayu. She showed him her baby girl. "This is all that is left of them," she said, laughing softly.

The families of the twenty girls were then brought from Bloedenkamp. Gerda looked emaciated, and when she asked them what had happened while they were gone, Ola replied evasively, "We took a trip." But Gerda realized what had really happened as soon as she saw little Alamanda. They lived there in the house with the Dutch soldiers who took turns guarding them. Those were trying times for Dewi Ayu because Mr. Willie still professed his deep love for her, and even though he had come up against her rejection before, he seemed ready to come up against it once again.

But once again misfortune came to save Dewi Ayu.

One night, Mr. Willie and three other soldiers were taking their turn guarding the house, when a guerrilla raid of native troops attacked them, armed with weapons stolen from the Japanese troops, machetes and knives and hand grenades. Their sudden ambush was quite effective and they killed all four Dutch soldiers. Mr. Willie was beheaded from behind while chatting with Dewi Ayu in the front room, his head thrown toward the table and his blood splattering on little Alamanda. Another soldier was shot in the toilet while taking a crap, and the other two were killed in the yard.

There were more than ten guerrillas, and they gathered all the prisoners. When they discovered that all of them were women and all of them were Dutch, the men grew even more violent. They tied up some of the women in the kitchen, and the others were dragged off to the bedrooms to be raped. Their cries were even more heartbreaking than when the Japanese had turned them into whores, and even Dewi Ayu had to fight more than ever before, fending off a guerrilla who seized her baby and slashed her arm with a knife.

Help came so slowly and the guerrillas disappeared so quickly. The women buried the four dead soldiers in the backyard.

"If you had joined the guerrillas," said Dewi Ayu while placing a flower on top of Mr. Willie's grave, "at least you could have raped me." And she wept for him.

But things like that happened more than once. The four soldiers assigned to guard the house were always outnumbered by the guerrillas, who appeared fully armed for ambush. The local commandant couldn't provide any more guards because they themselves were still short on personnel. The women only felt safe once the British troops came to reinforce the security of the entire city. The troops were a part of the Twenty-Third Indian Division that came to Java, and a number of them were Gurkhas. They installed their machine guns everywhere, and some set up a post in the house's backyard. When the native guerrillas came again, they were confronted quite fiercely, couldn't enter the yard, and one of them was killed. After that they never targeted the house again.

For as long as they were guarded by the English troops, life was quite peaceful and pleasant. They threw small parties in order to forget all the bad times. Sometimes the young women would go to the beach in a military jeep, guarded by a few officers with full weaponry. A number of officers even fell in love with some of the girls, and some of the girls fell in love with them. It was difficult for the girls to have to talk about what had happened to them, but once all that had been taken care of, things just got better and better. A native music group was invited and they had another small celebration, with wine and cake.

The rescue of the prisoners continued: the International Red Cross arrived and all of the prisoners were to be immediately flown to Europe. This country wasn't safe for civilians, especially after they had been held in prison camps for three years. The natives had declared their independence, and armed militias were everywhere. A number of them claimed to be the National Army, others called themselves the Soldiers of the People, and all of them were guerrillas from outside the city. Most of these militias had been trained by Japan during the occupation, and they faced off with natives who had been taught by the Dutch military and had joined with the KNIL in a chaotic war. The battle was not over, in fact it had just begun, and the natives were calling it a revolutionary war.

All of the young women and their families in that house of captives prepared to leave on a flight arranged by the Red Cross, except for one girl who always had her own ideas: Dewi Ayu. "I don't have anyone in Europe," she said. "I only have Alamanda and this other baby who is now growing in my stomach."

"Well, you have me and Gerda, at least," said Ola.

"But this is my home."

She had already told Mama Kalong that she didn't want to leave Halimunda. She would remain in the city, even if it meant she had to be a prostitute. Mama Kalong said to her, "Live in the house just as before. It belongs to me now and there's no way the Dutch family will ask for it back."

So while everybody else was leaving, Dewi Ayu stayed behind with Mama Kalong and a number of servants. She awaited the birth of her second child, who she was sure was fathered by one of the guerrillas, while reading the copy of *Max Havelaar* that Ola had left behind. She had read it before, but she read it again because there was nothing else to do, and Mama Kalong forbid her to do anything anyway. The baby was finally born when Alamanda was almost two years old, and Dewi Ayu named her Adinda, after the girl in the novel she was reading.

After living in Mama Kalong's house for a number of months, she started to think about her treasure buried in the shit inside the sewer pipes in her old house, and she especially started to think that it was about time she got the house back. The house where she was presently living had already become a new brothel, filled with women who had been comfort women for the Japanese during the war. Mama Kalong had been able to find plenty of girls who didn't dare go home and instead decided to stay with her, flocking to fill her rooms and live as princesses in Mama Kalong's kingdom. The KNIL soldiers were their faithful customers. Mama Kalong let Dewi Ayu stay in one of the rooms with her two children for as long as they needed, without making her whore herself out in return. Dewi Ayu gratefully accepted Mama Kalong's kindness, but she still believed that a house of prostitution was not a good place for her two young girls to grow up, and was determined to return to her old home.

She didn't actually need to be a prostitute, because she still had the six rings that she had been swallowing for the duration of the war. She sold one of them, set with a jade stone, to Mama Kalong, and lived off that money for a while. She even bought a used baby carriage from the junk shop, which she used to walk her two children along the street leading back to Halimunda for the first time. Little Adinda lay under its awning, while Alamanda sat behind her little sister in a sweater and a cap. Dewi Ayu wore her hair in a topknot and a long dress tied at the waist, her two pockets stuffed with burp cloths and diapers and bottles of milk, calmly strolling and pushing the perambulator.

The road was desolate and abandoned. She had heard that most adult men had gone to the jungle to join the guerrillas. She only saw one old barber on the corner, about to die from boredom waiting for a customer. The only other people she saw were some KNIL soldiers guarding the city while reading old newspapers, looking sleepy and just as bored. Some sat behind the steering wheels of their trucks and jeeps while others perched on a tank. They greeted her warmly, after realizing that she was a white woman, and offered to escort her because it wasn't safe for a Dutch woman to be out walking by herself. A guerrilla could appear at any time, they said.

"No thank you," she said. "I am on a treasure hunt and I don't want to share."

She followed a path that was burned into her memory, heading toward the neighborhood that had belonged to the Dutch plantation owners. The houses were pressed up against the beach, with their front verandas facing a narrow road that extended the length of the shore and their back porches facing two hills that rose up in the distance behind the lush greenery of the plantations and farmland. She arrived there after a peaceful journey, following the beach path, feeling confident that no guerrillas would suddenly emerge out of the sea. Everything looked exactly as it always had. The fence still overflowed with chrysanthemum blooms, and the starfruit tree still stood next to the house with a swing hanging from its lowest branch. The flowerpots that her grandmother had lined up along the veranda were still there, even though all the aloe had died from dehydration and the elephant ears were a tangled mess. Clearly no one was tending to the wild grass or the orchids growing on the front arbor, which dangled down to the ground. She quickly realized that the servants and guards had left the house behind, and apparently not even the borzois lived here anymore.

She pushed the baby carriage into the front yard, and was confused by the clean veranda floor. Someone must have swept away all the dust, she thought. When she tried the door, she found it unlocked. She went in, still pushing the carriage even though the babies were starting to fuss. The sitting room was dark and she turned on a light. The electricity still worked, and in an instant everything was illuminated. Everything was still in its place: the tables, chairs, and cupboards, everything except the gramophone that Muin had taken with him. She found her own portrait still hanging on the wall, a young girl of fifteen years who was about to enroll at the Franciscan School.

"Look, that's Mommy," she said to Alamanda. "Photographed by a Japanese guy, and shortly after that raped by another Japanese guy, who might even be your Japanese daddy."

The three of them continued their tour around the house, and went up to the second floor. Dewi Ayu shared all her memories, telling them where grandpa and grandma used to sleep, and showing them the photograph of Henri and Aneu Stammler, taken when they were still quite young and had not yet fallen in love. Of course the little ones didn't understand any of it yet, but Dewi Ayu still enjoyed her role as a tour guide until she remembered her treasure in the sewer pipes. She invited her two children to inspect the toilet with her, relieved to see that it even still existed. All she needed to do was dismantle the plumbing and find her treasure.

"A Dutch woman wandering about in the era of the new republic." She suddenly heard a voice coming from behind her back. "What are you doing here, Missy?"

She turned around and there was the owner of that voice: an old native woman who looked quite fierce. She was wearing a sarong and a tattered *kebaya*, with a cane supporting her leg. Her mouth was filled with clumps of betel leaf. She stood looking at Dewi Ayu resentfully, as if she would strike Dewi Ayu with her cane just as she would strike a stray dog, without hesitation.

"You can see for yourself that my photograph is still hanging on the wall," said Dewi Ayu, pointing to the portrait of that fifteen year-old girl. "I own this house."

"I just haven't had the time to exchange your photo with mine."

The old woman quickly ordered her to leave, but Dewi Ayu insisted that she held the deed. In response, the woman merely laughed, waving her hand. "Your house has been confiscated, Missy," she said. And it was clear, just as the old woman explained while seeing the uninvited guest to the door, that the house had been taken by the Japanese and at the end of the war, a guerrilla family stole it back. This was the old lady's family: her husband had lost half his arm to the slash of a samurai sword before going to the jungle with five of his sons, and not long after that he died, shot by a KNIL soldier, along with two of those sons. "So now I have inherited this house. But you can take your photos with you if you want, and I won't charge you for them."

Dewi Ayu realized that there was no way to fight the woman with words. She quickly left, pushing the baby carriage, but she remained determined to get her house back. She went to the temporary civil government and military offices, met a KNIL commandant, and asked his advice. His recommendation was quite disappointing, telling her to swallow any hope of getting her house back any time soon. The situation did not yet allow it, he said, because guerrillas were still roaming about. If that house belonged to a guerrilla family, it was better to let it go, unless she had the money to buy it back.

But she didn't have the money. Her five remaining rings would never be enough to buy a house. Her only hope, her treasure, was still in the toilet, and she would never be able to get at it without owning the house first. She met with Mama Kalong straightaway, knowing that the woman was always quick to help anyone in need, and spoke as frankly as possible. "Mama, loan me some money. I want to buy my house back."

Mama Kalong looked at everything from a financial angle, and could always spot a good business opportunity. "And how will you repay me?"

"I have family treasure," replied Dewi Ayu. "Before the war I buried all of my grandmother's jewelry in a secret place and no one knows about it except me and God."

"And what if God stole it?"

"Then I'll come back and whore for you to pay off my debt."

They agreed on this as the best possible idea. Mama Kalong even offered to become the mediator for the repurchasing of the house, because if Dewi Ayu did it herself, there was the possibility that old guerrilla woman would refuse to sell. A native would never trust her, with her Dutch appearance, and in any case Mama Kalong was very experienced in buying properties from people like them, who needed money. She promised Dewi Ayu she would bargain for the lowest possible price.

The whole business took almost a week. Mama Kalong went back and forth every day to meet with this fierce old woman before finishing the transaction. The guerrilla granny agreed to sell the house if she could get another house and some cash in exchange. Mama Kalong handled it well, so that Dewi Ayu could finally order the woman to leave the house and never set foot there again. Accompanied by Mama Kalong, Dewi Ayu quickly moved in with her two small children, using a military jeep that belonged to a KNIL customer at the whorehouse. How happy she was to return to her home, with the assurance that it now belonged to her.

"So when will you pay me back?" asked Mama Kalong finally.

"Give me one month's time."

"Yes, that's enough for an excavation," she said. "If someone disturbs your house, you just come to me. I have good friends who are guerrillas and of course I know KNIL soldiers. They are all my customers."

Dewi Ayu did not immediately begin the dig. She first looked for a baby nurse, and she found her in the encampments in the foothills, an old woman named Mirah who used to be a Dutchman's servant before the war. Dewi Ayu told her firmly that she was not Dutch, she was a native woman named Dewi Ayu. Through Mirah, she found a gardener who could get the unkempt grounds in order. It was a week before she could relax and see everything returning to how it used to be, with a clean yard and fresh-looking plants.

"We are lucky that neither the Japanese nor the Allied troops destroyed it," she said to herself.

That was when she got word from Ola and Gerda. They had reunited with their grandmother and grandfather, and it even turned out that their father was safe after having been held in a POW camp in Sumatra. Ola was engaged to an English soldier and they were going to be married later that year, on the 17th of March, in the Church of Saint Mary. Dewi Ayu could not attend their celebration, but she sent some photos of her little girls, and received their wedding photo in return. She hung it on the wall, so that Ola could see it if she ever came to visit.

After most of the household duties were taken care of, she began to think about digging up the treasure. She already trusted the gardener, who was named Sapri, so she called him and told him about her plan to dig up the sewer pipes. She said that if she didn't, she would never be able to pay his wages. And so the gardener brought in a crowbar and a hoe, and Dewi Ayu rolled up her jacket sleeves, put on her grandfather's pantaloons, and helped Sapri dismantle the floor and dig up the dirt along the water pipe that was heading for the septic tank. Their work was made easier thanks to the fact that the toilet hadn't been used since the war began. They didn't find warm stinky shit, only crumbling loose dirt teeming with angrily writhing earthworms.

They worked all day while Mirah watched the two little kids, only stopping for a moment to eat and rest before continuing to dismantle the concrete and stir what was left of the shit that had already turned into dirt. But they didn't find anything. Dewi Ayu was sure that they had already removed all the excrement and soil from the pipes, but she still hadn't found any of the jewelry that she had stashed there. There were no necklaces or golden bracelets—there were only mounds of rotting earth, brown and humid. She didn't believe that the jewelry could have rotted away with the shit, so she abandoned her work and gave up, grumbling:

"God stole it."

In the revolutionary era, people boldly shouted flashy slogans and wrote them on the walls alongside the street, waved them on banners, and even scrawled them in school notebooks. Mama Kalong decided to rename her whorehouse in the same spirit, with a new title to represent the very essence of her soul. She'd already used "Make Love or Die," and then "Make Love Once, Make Love Forever," but finally decided on "Make Love to the Death."

Alas, that came true—a KNIL soldier died while making love, his throat slit by a guerrilla soldier, and a guerrilla died while making love, shot by a KNIL soldier, and a prostitute also died in the middle of a lovemaking session, after she'd been kissed so long she couldn't breathe.

And so it was there, in "Make Love To the Death," that Dewi Ayu became a prostitute. She didn't live there, because she had a house. She just went there when dusk fell, and returned home when morning came. Now she had three young girls to take care of: Alamanda, Adinda, and Maya Dewi, born three years after Adinda. At night, the children were cared for by Mirah, but during the day she took care of them herself just like any regular mom. She sent the kids to the best schools, and to the mosque to recite prayers with Kyai Jahro.

"They won't become prostitutes," she said to Mirah, "unless that's really truly what they want."

She herself had never honestly admitted that she was a prostitute because that was what she truly wanted, in fact just the opposite; she always said that she had been forced into prostitution due to circumstance. "Just like circumstance makes somebody a prophet or a king," is what she told her three children.

She was the city's favorite whore. Almost every man who had ever been to the brothel had slept with her at least once, not caring how much he had to pay. It wasn't because they had some long-standing obsession to sleep with a Dutch woman, it was because they knew that Dewi Ayu was an expert lovemaker. No one handled her roughly, as the other prostitutes were handled, because if someone did so all the other men would go nuts as if the woman was their own wife. Not one night passed without her entertaining a guest, but she strictly limited herself to just one man per evening. For this apparent exclusivity, Mama Kalong charged a high price and the extra profit went to her, that bat queen who never slept at night.

Yes, Mama Kalong was the queen in that city and Dewi Ayu was the princess. They had the same tastes, the kind of women who took good care of themselves and wore clothes way more modest than those of the virtuous ladies. Mama Kalong liked handmade batik that she bought straight from Solo, Yogyakarta, and Pekalongan, with a *kebaya* and her hair in a traditional bun. She even dressed that way at the whorehouse, and only when she was relaxing did she wear a loose housedress. Meanwhile Dewi Ayu copied everything she wanted exactly from the pages of women's fashion magazines and even the virtuous ladies furtively copied her.

The two were the city's source of joy. There was not one important event that they were not invited to. Every Independence Day Mama Kalong and Dewi Ayu sat with Mayor Sadrah, the regents, and of course Shodancho when he finally emerged from the jungle. Even though the virtuous and proper ladies really hated them, knowing that their husbands disappeared in the middle of the night to patronize "Make Love to the Death," they were polite to their faces (and bitched behind their backs).

Then one day a man got the idea in his head that he had to have the princess all to himself—he even wanted to marry her. No one dared cross him, because it was said he was invincible. That man was called Crazy Maman, or Maman Gendeng.

And so the happiness of the men in Halimunda came to an end, and wide smiles spread across the faces of their wives and sweethearts.

{5}

TO THIS DAY, people clearly remember how that man arrived one stormy morning when Dewi Ayu was still alive and how he fought on the beach with some fishermen. Yes, the people of Halimunda know all his exploits by heart, as well as they know all the parables in the Holy Book.

When he was still very young, Maman Gendeng was already a warrior in the last generation of grandmasters, the sole student of Master Chisel from Great Mountain. At the end of the colonial era he left to wander and seek his fortune but encountered not a soul, neither friend nor foe, until the Japanese came. Then he fought for The People's Army, and during the revolutionary war he awarded himself the rank of colonel. But during a restructuring of the troops he was one of the thousands of soldiers who got sacked, and was left with nothing except the glory of having fought in the struggle. Yet Maman Gendeng was not upset at all. He returned to his wandering and spent the rest of the war earning a new reputation: that of a bandit thief.

His thieving instinct came from his hatred of rich people, and his hatred of rich people was completely understandable. He was the bastard son of a Regent. His mother had worked in the Regent's house as a kitchen maid, as had generations of her family before her. No one knew when they began their secret affair, but everyone knew that the Regent's hearty sexual appetite meant that his wife and concubines and mistresses alone could never satisfy him. On certain nights he would still drag one of the servants into his quarters. Maman Gendeng's mother was one of the women who met that unfortunate fate, and ultimately she got knocked up. The Regent's wife found out about it, and to preserve the family's good name she banished the kitchen maid. She didn't care that the maid's family, from her mother and father to her grandmothers on both sides, to both her grandmothers' mothers and fathers, had served in that household. Without anything except the baby growing in her stomach, the unfortunate woman hacked her way through the jungle and was soon lost on Great Mountain. She was found by Master Chisel, an old guru who helped her give birth under a sugar palm tree.

On the verge of death the woman said, "Name him Maman like his father. He is that Regent's misbegotten bastard son." She passed away before she could gaze upon her child again. The old master, deeply saddened, brought the child home.

"You will become the ultimate warrior," he told the baby.

He cared for him well, gave him plenty of food and started to toughen and train him before he could walk. He dunked the infant in freezing cold water and roasted him under the noonday sun. When he was still just a toddler, the old man threw him into the river and forced him to swim. By the time he was five years old, believe it or not, he was the strongest little kid on the face of the earth. Maman Gendeng, which was by then his name, could already pulverize a stone into teeny soft grains of sand with only his bare hands. Unlike the other gurus, Master Chisel taught the kid everything he knew, holding nothing back. He taught him all the good fighting moves, gave him all the talismans and amulets, and even taught him how to read and write ancient Sundanese, Dutch, Malay, and Latin. He taught him how to meditate, and with the same seriousness of purpose he taught him how to cook.

When Maman Gendeng was twelve years old, Master Chisel died. After burying the old man and mourning for a week, he came down off the mountain and began his odyssey to get revenge on his biological father. But this happened at about the same time that the Japanese troops arrived and he did not find his father in his house, because the family was already in ruins, devastated by the war. The Regent had run away as an accomplice of the Dutch, and so Maman Gendeng had to search for his enemy, who had banished his mother and was responsible for her death, for three years. But even after those three years he was still unable to exact his revenge, because when he found his father the man had just been executed by a firing squad. He saw his father's corpse but did not deign to bury him.

After the Japanese left and independence was declared and the revolutionary war began, he joined a group of guerrillas. They stayed in fishermen's huts on the northern coast during the day and fought at night, but the KNIL troops usually won the skirmishes. Nothing much interesting happened during this time, except for one thing: he became infatuated with a very young fisherwoman named Nasiah. She was a dainty girl with dimples in her cheeks and lovely dark skin. Maman Gendeng would see her when he went walking along the beach gathering fish for his afternoon snack. She was friendly, and would sneak out to bring the guerrillas whatever food she had, smiling the sweetest possible smile.

He didn't know much about her, except her name. But she made him feel so alive that he vowed to quit his wanderings and win every battle so they could be together. His friends became aware of his secret passion, and encouraged him to properly request the young girl's hand. Maman Gendeng had never spoken directly to any woman except to the prostitutes during the Japanese occupation, and suddenly he realized that facing this dainty young Nasiah would be way more terrifying than facing a Dutch firing squad. But when the opportunity arose and he saw Nasiah walking alone, hugging a basket of fresh fish and heading for home, Maman Gendeng caught up with her. Seeing the girl's sweet smile, which brought out her dimples, he gathered his courage and asked her if she wanted to be his wife.

Nasiah had just turned thirteen. Who knows whether it was her young age or something else that made her gasp and choke, drop her basket, and run home without saying goodbye, like a child terrified by a crazy man. Standing among the flying fish, Maman Gendeng watched her go and wished that he were dead. But he did not retreat, not in the slightest. Love gave him the kind of courage that nothing else can give. He gathered up the fish and, walking with determined steps, carried the basket toward the young girl's home. He would propose to her properly, and ask her father for her hand.

He found Nasiah standing in front of her house next to a puny guy with a crippled leg. All he'd heard about Nasiah was that her two older brothers had died in guerrilla warfare and her father was an old fisherman. He had never heard anything about this starving one-legged youth. Maman Gendeng stood in front of them, trying to smile, and set the basket at Nasiah's feet. His heart pounded, agitated and on fire with jealousy. Only his courage, or his stupidity, made him repeat himself.

"Nasiah, would you like to be my wife?" he asked with a pleading face. "When the war is over, I will marry you."

The girl shook her head and started to cry.

"Mister Guerrilla," she stammered. "Don't you see the man at my side? He is weak, it's true. He will never be able to go to the ocean to fish, and he will certainly never be able to fight wars like you, Sir.

I know you could kill him quite easily and then you could catch me as easily as a flying fish. But if you do, then at least permit me to die by his side, because we love each other and cannot bear to be apart."

The skinny youth just stayed quiet with his head bowed, not once lifting his face. Maman Gendeng's heart was broken in an instant. He nodded slowly and walked away, without saying goodbye and without looking back. He could see it: they were completely in love. He didn't want to destroy their happiness, even though he would have to nurse his wounded heart for a very long time.

For the rest of the war he was plagued by terrifying hallucinations, triggered by this tragic refusal of his love. Sometimes he stayed behind in no-man's-land hoping to be shot by the enemy. He made himself a target for rifles and cannons but he was fated to survive. That whole time he never saw the girl again, and avoided any chance that they might meet. But when the war ended and he heard about her marriage to her sweetheart, as a wedding present he sent her a beautiful red sash that he bought from a local weaver.

The guerrillas were disbanded, and Maman Gendeng felt more happy than sad, as once again he was free to go wandering, even though he now carried the wound in his heart with him. He roamed the whole northern coast, following the old guerrilla trails, and he survived by raiding the houses of the rich, telling them, "If you weren't accomplices of the Dutch, then you must have been minions of the Japanese, because only collaborators get rich during a revolution."

With a dozen men, he terrorized the cities along the coast, with the police and the military in hot pursuit. With his band he lived like Robin Hood, stealing from the rich and redistributing the spoils to the poor, taking care of the widows and orphaned children whose husbands and fathers had died in the war. But his reputation, intimidating to friend as well as foe, did not make him happy. Wherever he went he still carried his old wound, which none of the pretty girls he saw and certainly not any of the prostitutes he found in the palm wine shacks could heal. When night fell and he started to feel crazy, he'd order his men to go find dainty young girls with luscious dark skin and dimples. He described Nasiah in great detail, and the girls who'd come to his hideout all looked like replicas, one indistinguishable from the next. He made love to them night after night, but no one could take Nasiah's place.

His zest for life only returned after a very long while, when he overheard a legend often told by the fishermen's children about a princess named Rengganis, so beautiful that everyone was ready to die for her. Maman Gendeng awoke one night ready to battle anyone to obtain such a woman and shook his men awake one by one to ask them where the Princess Rengganis lived. They replied, in Halimunda of course. Maman Gendeng had never heard of that town before, but one of his friends told him that if he canoed along the coast, paddling west, he would arrive in Halimunda. Full of conviction and above all determined to heal his old wound, he handed control of his territory over to his band and told them that he was setting out on a voyage in a dugout canoe to find his true love. He had finally fallen in love for the second time, even though all he knew about Rengganis was what he had heard from the fishermen's children.

They said that the princess was extremely beautiful, the last descendant of the Pajajaran royal bloodline, who had inherited the loveliness of all the princesses in the Pakuan Kingdom. People said that the princess herself had realized that her beauty brought misfortune. When she was still a child and free to wander about outside the palace walls, she caused turmoil and disruptions, big and small. Wherever she went people would gaze at her face, shrouded in a thin mist of melancholy, with blank idiotic stares. Frozen like absurd human statues, only their eyeballs moved, following her every step. Her appearances caused the civil servants to daydream and neglect state affairs, so that swaths of the kingdom were captured by bands of robbers before they could be reclaimed at great effort and cost, sacrificing the lives of half the royal army.

"A woman like that," said Maman Gendeng, "is truly worth seeking."

"I just hope your heart isn't broken for the second time," replied a friend.

Even the father of this princess, who they say was the last monarch before the kingdom was attacked by Demak, was prematurely aged by his obsession with his own daughter's beauty. Even though no one can bed his own daughter, falling in love is still falling in love. His feelings of desire and impropriety clashed and gnawed away everything inside him, until he came to think only death could free him from his suffering. And the queen, who of course was envious, came to think that the only way out of the situation was to kill the little girl. She would often steal away to the kitchen and take a knife and tiptoe toward her child's room, preparing to stab her right in her beating heart. But every time she saw her daughter, even she would be charmed and fall in love, and forget all about her murderous intent. She would drop the knife, walk toward her child, caress her skin and kiss her, before coming to her senses. Feeling ashamed she would then leave the young girl, suffering but not saying a word.

All along Maman Gendeng's journey fishermen kept on telling him tales about Princess Rengganis. He was paddling due west in his small dugout canoe, and when dusk fell he would dock in the fishing villages. He would ask how far it was to Halimunda, and the people would tell him to continue west before circling south and then turning once again toward to the east. They'd tell him to be cautious in the waves of the South Seas. And then they would tell him about the princess, which made the lonely wanderer grow ever more smitten.

"I will marry her," he vowed.

⁂

Princess Rengganis herself suffered greatly from her own growing beauty, locking herself up in her room. Her only contact with the outside world was by a small slot in the door, through which servant girls would pass clothes and plates of food. She vowed never to put her beauty on display, and hoped to marry a man who would love her for other reasons. So, sewing her bridal gown and trousseau, she kept herself constantly hidden but she could not hide the news of her beauty, which had been spread by storytellers and roving wanderers. Her father, plagued by his forbidden feelings, and her mother, blinded by jealousy, decided to marry her off. They sent ninety-nine messengers to the farthest reaches of the kingdom and even to neighboring countries to announce a contest for princes and knights and whoever else. The first prize was the right to marry the most beautiful woman in the world, Princess Rengganis.

Handsome men arrived and the contest began. There was no archery competition, like the one in which Arjuna won Drupadi. Each man was simply asked to describe his ideal woman—how tall she was, how much she weighed, her favorite foods, the way she combed her hair, the color of her clothing, the smell of her body, everything—and afterward he was told to sit in front of Princess Rengganis' bedroom door and to let her question him. The king promised that if the man wanted someone exactly like the princess and the princess wanted someone exactly like the man in front of her door, then they could marry. It was highly unusual for people to find their match in such a manner and indeed, by the end, the contest had not turned up one suitable man.

The fact is, obtaining such a woman was no easy matter. When Maman Gendeng passed through the Sunda Strait, a band of pirates tried to steal his riches, so he vented his pent-up desires by drowning them. But they weren't the only obstacle. Entering the southern seas, he was intercepted not only by fierce storms but also by a pair of sharks that endlessly circled the boat. He had to land in the swamps and hunt a deer, which he then gave to the sharks so that they could be comrades on the journey.

All of this for that rare specimen named Rengganis.

After the fruitless contest, the kingdom returned to the same despair, the same terrorizing beauty. Until one day a dissatisfied prince plotted to take the princess by force, accompanied by three hundred troops on horseback. Although truly overcome with joy at the idea of someone kidnapping the princess and marrying her, out of chivalry the king was forced to let his soldiers go to war with the marauders. Another prince from another kingdom came with three hundred more troops on horseback to help, in hopes of being granted the princess in thanks, and so a great war broke out. Sooner or later, other knights and other princes were swept up in this war, and by the end of a year it was no longer clear who was fighting whom, just that they were all warring over the woman who for years now had been Halimunda's goddess of beauty. The curse of beauty became even more extreme: thousands of soldiers were wounded and dead, the whole nation was in ruins, sickness and starvation struck without mercy, and all of this was thanks to that infernal beauty.

"That was the most terrible time," said an old fisherman at the boarding house where Maman Gendeng was spending the night. "Worse than the Bubat War when the Majapahit attacked us with such cunning, and after all, as you know, we don't like to make war."

"I myself am a veteran of the revolutionary war," said Maman Gendeng.

"Oh, that was nothing compared to the war over Princess Rengganis."

It wasn't that the girl herself didn't know about all this. Her ladies-in-waiting whispered all the news through the keyhole, just as the blind Destarata heard about the fate of her children on the Kuruserta battlefield. The little beauty suffered greatly, she couldn't eat and couldn't sleep, tortured by the fact that she herself was the source of all this misfortune. She could not atone with mere sobbing, perhaps not even with death, and suddenly she remembered her wedding dress and decided the only way to free herself from all of this was to marry someone right away—then the war, and all of its misfortune, would surely end.

At this point she'd locked herself inside her dark room for years, kept company only by a dim oil lamp and her wedding dress. She had already sewed the whole thing with her own hands, and her handiwork had rendered it the most beautiful wedding dress on the face of the earth, unrivaled by the work of any seamstress or tailor. One morning, the gown was finally finished. The princess didn't know whom she would marry so she said to herself that she would simply open the window, and whoever appeared in front of it would become her life partner.

Before following through on her vow, she bathed with flower-scented water for one hundred nights. Then, one unforgettable morning, she put on her wedding dress. She was not the kind of girl to go back on a promise: she would keep her word. She would open that window, for the first time in years, and she would marry the first man she saw. If she could see more than one man, she would take the closest one. She vowed she would not take another woman's husband, or a man who already had a lover, because she didn't want to hurt anyone.

Wearing that wedding gown, she was more beautiful than ever. Her beauty shone, even in that dim chamber, enthralling the young ladies-in-waiting spying on her, who wondered what she was about to do. With graceful steps, Princess Rengganis approached the window, stood for a moment, and let out an anxious breath. Her vow had been taken and her will would be done. Her hands were shaking violently as she touched the shutter, and suddenly she was weeping, caught somewhere in between a deep sadness and an overflowing joy. With a light touch of her fingertips she opened the window latch. The shutter creaked open. She said: "Whoever is there, marry me."

"It's too bad I wasn't there," said Maman Gendeng to another fisherman on another morning. "Tell me, how far away am I from Halimunda?"

"Not far."

Many people had already said "not far," and those words now brought him no comfort because he never seemed to arrive. He voyaged on, stopping at every fisherman's encampment and every port to ask: Is this Halimunda? Oh no, keep going east, they'd say. Everyone said the same thing, and it was making him lose confidence. All of a sudden he felt that the whole thing was one big conspiracy and everyone was lying to him and Halimunda was nothing more than an invention. He decided that if he asked one more time and the person said that he had to keep going east, he would punch him in the face to stop the dumb jokes and conniving.

Just then he saw a fishing port and a row of fishermen's encampments. He quickly turned toward land, saying a small goodbye to the pair of sharks who had kept him company all the while and with whom he had developed an unusual friendship. He trembled with fatigue and defeat, losing hope that he would ever meet the amazing Princess Rengganis. He disembarked and met a fisherman who was pulling a net along the beach. His fists were clenched as he asked, "Is this Halimunda?"

"Yeah, this is Halimunda."

That fisherman was a lucky guy because if Maman Gendeng, whose own teacher had called him the ultimate fighter, had unleashed all of his anger the man would never have been able to stave him off. But Maman Gendeng was truly overjoyed after his long journey, Halimunda was not just some phony-baloney; he had finally arrived, was smelling its fishy air, and was talking to one of its inhabitants. He dropped his knees to the ground he was so full of gratitude, while the fisherman looked at him perplexed.

"Everything looks so beautiful here," he murmured.

"Yeah," said the fisherman getting ready to leave, "even the shit here comes out looking pretty." But Maman Gendeng detained him.

"Where can I meet Rengganis?" he asked.

"Which Rengganis? Tons of ladies go by that name. Even streets and rivers are named Rengganis."

"The Princess Rengganis, of course."

"She died hundreds of years ago."

"What did you say?"

"I said she died hundreds of years ago."

Everything abruptly came to an end. This can't be true, Maman Gendeng told himself. But that did not soothe him, and his anger erupted ferociously. He threatened the poor fisherman, screaming that he was a liar. A number of other fishermen came with wooden oars in their hands to help, and Maman Gendeng destroyed those oars and left their owners sprawled out unconscious on the wet sand. Then three men, *preman,* tough guys, approached him. They ordered him to leave, the beach was their turf. Maman Gendeng didn't leave, and instead attacked them mercilessly, overpowering all three at once and laying them out, flat and half-dead, on top of the bodies of the fishermen.

That was the chaotic morning when Maman Gendeng arrived in Halimunda and caused such an uproar. Those five fishermen and three *preman* thugs were his first victims. His next was an old veteran who came with a rifle and shot him from a distance. He didn't know that the stranger was impervious to bullets. When he realized it he ran, but Maman Gendeng chased him down, snatched the veteran's rifle and shot him in the calf, making him fall down in the street.

"Who else wants to fight?" he demanded.

He had to punish at least some of the people in that city, who had tricked him with a centuries-old story. There were a few more bouts that day and he won them all, and no one left on the beach wanted to challenge him. But by now he was starting to look worn out. With a pale face, he went to a food stall and the owner served him whatever he had. The people even plied him with *arak* palm wine, hoping he would get drunk and not cause any more trouble. Full and spent, Maman Gendeng grew sleepy. He stumbled back to the beach and stretched out on his boat, which he'd pulled up on the sand. He mulled over the whole journey and all of his disappointment, and before falling asleep he said clearly and distinctly, "If I have a daughter, I will name her Rengganis." Then he slept.

It's true that Princess Rengganis had died many years before, but only after she got married and retreated into seclusion in Halimunda. When she'd opened the window, closed for so many years, the warm rays of the morning sun burst into the room, so that for a moment she was blinded. It was as if the universe had paused to witness this awesome beauty return to the world from a shuttered darkness. The birds stopped twittering, the wind stopped blowing, and the princess stood there like a painting, with the window around her like a picture frame. It took a while for her eyes to adjust, but then she began to look around. Her gaze was nervous and her cheeks blushed red, because she was about to meet the person who would become her lover. But there was no one as far as the eye could see, no one except a dog who was looking back over his shoulder in her direction after hearing the sound of the window creaking open. The princess was stunned for a moment but, remember, she never went back on her word, so from the bottom of her heart she promised she would marry that dog.

No one would accept such a marriage, so the two snuck away to a foggy forest at the edge of the South Seas. It was the princess herself who named it Halimunda, The Land of Fog. They lived there for many years, and of course had children. Most of the people who lived in Halimunda believed they were the descendants of the princess and that dog, whose name nobody ever knew. Even the princess herself seemed not to know, and she never gave him a nickname either. When she saw him that first time from the window, all she knew was that she had to quickly descend to meet her groom, not caring what people would say. "Because," she stated, "a dog could not care less whether I am beautiful or not."

Word of Maman Gendeng's arrival in Halimunda spread quickly. After his brief nap, he had decided to make his home in that city and join the descendants of Princess Rengganis. He was happy with the lively fishing encampments, which reminded him of the old days, with the drinking stalls and taverns that lined the length of the beach, the stores along Jalan Merdeka, and of course, Mama Kalong's whorehouse, the best in the city.

He found himself there on the recommendation of some random passerby. He thought to himself that if he wanted to live in that city, he would have to control it, and the best way to do that was to go start with the whorehouse. He entered the tavern and the old woman herself, who had already heard about the reputation he had built since landing on the beach, was waiting there with a number of her whores and *preman*. Mama Kalong herself served him a glass of beer, and after draining it he stood in the middle of the tavern and asked who was the strongest man in the city. A number of *preman* working as whorehouse bodyguards were annoyed by that question, and the umpteenth fight broke out in the tavern yard. Maman Gendeng disregarded their machetes, sickles, and leftover samurai swords, and it didn't take him long to turn the men black and blue.

Brushing his hands together in satisfaction, he went back inside hoping to find someone else to beat up, but instead he saw a beautiful woman sitting in a corner with a cigarette between her lips. "I want to sleep with that woman, whether she is a prostitute or not," he whispered to Mama Kalong.

"That's Dewi Ayu, and she's the best whore here," said Mama Kalong.

"Kind of like a mascot?" asked Maman Gendeng.

"Kind of like a mascot."

"I am going to live in this city," continued Maman Gendeng, "and I am going to piss on her privates like a tiger marking his territory."

Dewi Ayu sat in the corner looking indifferent. Under the glow of the lamp her skin gleamed clean and white, showing off her Dutch heritage. Her eyes were a shade of blue, her dark black hair was gathered in a long French twist, and she held a cigarette between her svelte fingers, her fingernails painted blood red. She wore an ivory-colored gown with a belt tied at her willowy waist. She heard what Maman Gendeng said to Mama Kalong, and she turned to him. For a moment they looked at one another and Dewi Ayu smiled tantalizingly without moving a muscle.

"Well be quick then, darling, before you pee in your pants," she said.

Dewi Ayu let him know that she had a special room, a pavilion just behind the tavern, and that she had never walked there on her own two feet because whoever wanted her had to carry her like a newlywed carrying his bride. Maman Gendeng had absolutely no problem with that, so he approached, stopped in front of this beautiful whore, and bent down. When he picked her up Maman Gendeng estimated she weighed about sixty kilos. He then walked to the back of the tavern, passing through a door, tromping through a fragrant orange grove, and heading for a small and dimly lit building in between a number of other buildings. Maman Gendeng said to her: "I came here to marry the Princess Rengganis, but I was more than a hundred years late. Would you care to take her place?"

Dewi Ayu kissed her suitor's cheek and said, "A wife has sex on a voluntary basis, but a prostitute is a commercial sex worker. The thing is, I don't like to have sex without getting paid for it."

They made love almost all night long, filled with heat and passion like lovers reunited after a long separation. When morning came they were still naked and, wrapped in the same blanket, they sat in front of the pavilion enjoying the cool air. Sparrows were noisily hopping about in the branches of the orange trees and taking short flights to the edge of the roof. The sun emerged with all its warmth from the cleft between Ma Iyang and Ma Gedik Hills to the north of the city.

Halimunda began to awaken. The lovers prepared for the day, threw off their blanket, soaked in hot water in a large tub left over by the Japanese, and got dressed. Just like every morning, Dewi Ayu rode a *becak* rickshaw home to her three daughters. Maman Gendeng prepared to start a new day in the city.

Mama Kalong served him breakfast, yellow rice with straw mushrooms and quail eggs that she had ordered from the market earlier that morning. Maman Gendeng asked again about the strongest man, truly the most powerful man, in that city. "Because there cannot be two hotshots in the same place," he said. That's true, said Mama Kalong. She mentioned a man, Edi Idiot, the most feared *preman* at the bus terminal, and summed up his reputation: soldiers and policemen were terrified of him, he had killed more people than any legendary warrior, and all the bandits and thieves and pirates in the city were his minions. What's more, it was quite likely that he already knew about Maman Gendeng, because surely all the *preman* in the whorehouse had reported on him by now. When midday came, Maman Gendeng headed to the bus terminal, finding the man relaxing in a mahogany rocking chair.

"Give your power to me," Maman Gendeng said to him, "or we will fight to the death."

Edi Idiot had been expecting him. He accepted the challenge, and the good news spread quickly. It had been many years since the city's inhabitants had had any really fantastic entertainment, and enthusiastic droves headed for the beach, where the two men had decided to fight. No one could predict who would kill whom. A military commandant from the city sent one company of troops led by a skinny man everybody knew by his nickname, Shodancho, but no one thought he would be able to stop the fight.

Shodancho controlled a small segment of the city from his headquarters hung with a nameplate proclaiming him "Commander of the Halimunda Military District." Because the brutal fight fell within his jurisdiction, he had volunteered himself to the city military as the one to take care of it. In reality, one company of armed forces couldn't do much except maintain a semblance of order among the bystanders. Actually, he was secretly hoping both men would die, because there was no way one region could have three guys in charge, and Shodancho thought he should be the only one. But he waited along with all the others, unable to predict the outcome.

It turned out that they had to wait one whole week for the end of the fight. It had lasted seven days and seven nights without a break, when Shodancho said to one of his soldiers, "It's clear that Edi Idiot is going to die."

"Well it makes no difference to us," replied the soldier mournfully. "This city is full of bandits and robbers and guerrillas and revolutionary soldiers and leftover communists. We are stuck with cleaning up after all their commotion, and we'll never put a stop to it."

Shodancho nodded. "We're just exchanging Edi Idiot for Maman Gendeng."

The soldier smiled bitterly and whispered, "Let's just hope he'll keep his nose out of military business."

Even though he only had control over the local military district in one corner of Halimunda, Shodancho was quite respected throughout the entire city. Even a number of his superior commanders gave him their formal respect, because everyone knew he had been the leader of the Halimunda *daidan* mutiny during the Japanese occupation, and that no one had been braver during that mutiny. The city inhabitants were pretty sure that if Sukarno and Hatta hadn't proclaimed independence, Shodancho would have done it himself. The people really liked him, even though they knew he wasn't a model soldier; his district mostly concerned itself with smuggling textiles to Australia and bringing in vehicles and electronic goods on the black market. This was an excellent business in those years, and none of the superior commanders wanted to disrupt a trade pulling in so much money for the generals. Taking care of somc petty skirmish was the least of their concerns.

Exhausted at last, Edi Idiot finally did indeed die, after being held down and drowned in the shallow ocean water. His opponent threw his corpse into the sea, where Maman Gendeng's friends the sharks rejoiced at the unexpected afternoon snack. Maman Gendeng returned to the beach and gazed at all of the city's inhabitants, still looking as fresh as if he could fight seven more men in exactly the same fashion. "Now," he announced, "all the power is mine," adding: "And no one can sleep with Dewi Ayu except for me."

Surprised by Maman Gendeng's edict, Dewi Ayu proceeded cautiously, and sent a courier inviting the new *preman* to pay her a visit. Maman Gendeng politely accepted the invitation and promised he would come as quickly as he could.

She really was the best whore in the city, still a very beautiful woman, only thirty-five years old. Every morning she scrubbed her body with sulfuric soap, and once a month she soaked in a hot bath filled with herbs. The legend of her beauty rivaled that of the city's founder, and the only reason there had never been a war over her was because she was a whore, so anyone could sleep with her as long as he had the money, and Maman Gendeng's proclaimed monopoly would have to be discussed.

She almost never appeared in public, but was only occasionally glimpsed passing by inside a rickshaw at dusk, heading for Mama Kalong's, or returning home in the morning. Aside from that, she might be sighted taking her young girls to the movies, to the fair, or dropping them off at school. Sometimes she went to the market, but that was very rare. Strangers to the city would never have guessed that she was a whore, dressed more modestly than anyone else and walking as daintily as a palace maiden, with her shopping basket in one hand and her parasol in the other. Even in the whorehouse she wore a thick warm gown that covered everything up, and preferred to sit reading travel books in a corner of the tavern. She never tempted men in public: that was not her way.

Her old family home was in the colonial section of the city, right at the foot of a small mountain facing the sea, behind the remaining cocoa and coconut plantations. She had bought it back out of a longing for the past, but now the nostalgia was killing her. A new housing complex was being built on the banks of the Rengganis River and she had already reserved a house there, hoping to move in the following year.

That afternoon the *preman* came to call, not long after the lady of the house had woken up and bathed, and he was greeted by a little girl, about eleven years old. She introduced herself as Maya Dewi and told Maman Gendeng to wait in the front room because her mother was drying her hair. The child would be as beautiful as her mother, that was already obvious, and she brought him a glass of iced lemonade, and when the *preman* took out a cigarette, the girl rushed to place an ashtray on the table. Maman Gendeng decided the house's neat and orderly appearance must be the young girl's handiwork. He had heard from Mama Kalong that Dewi Ayu had three daughters, and he was curious to see how beautiful the girl's sisters were. But it appeared that Alamanda and Adinda were not at home.

Dewi Ayu emerged with her hair left loose and shining in the afternoon sunlight. She told her daughter to leave them, woke up a kitten that was curled up sleeping on her chair, and sat down. All of her movements were slow, graceful, and deliberate. She leaned back, crossing her legs, in a long gown with large pockets on both sides and a ribbon that tied at her throat. Maman Gendeng could smell soft lavender and aloe vera in her hair. Even though he had already slept with her and seen her naked, he was still struck by her intoxicating beauty. Her slender hand was as white as milk, reaching for a packet of cigarettes in one of her pockets, and then she joined him smoking. For a moment Maman Gendeng could only bumble awkwardly, unable to look anywhere except at her feet and her pair of deep green velvet slippers slowly rocking back and forth.

"Thank you for coming," said Dewi Ayu. "Welcome to my home."

The *preman* already knew why he had been invited, or at least he could guess. He realized that he couldn't justify his claim, but he had fallen in love with the woman. He had finally been able to forget all his pain, forget Nasiah and forget the Princess Rengganis, enraptured by this incredible whore. He did not want to be hurt again, so if he could not marry her then at least he would be the only man to sleep with her.

The whore's composure, surely due to her intelligence, was truly extraordinary. She exhaled evenly, and her eyes followed the floating smoke like a thinker mulling something over. Her imported cigarette smelled crisp and light, without cloves. She had emerged carrying her own glass of lemonade and after she had finished her cigarette she drank a little and gestured for the thug to drink from the cold glass set before him, and awkwardly he did so. In a distant mosque a child beat a drum, so it must have been around three in the afternoon.

"It's sad," said the whore. "You are actually the thirty-second man to try and own me."

That didn't surprise the *preman*, he already knew what she was going to say. "I will either marry you," he said, "or pay you every day for your exclusive services."

"The problem is that I can't have sex every single day, so I'd often be receiving money for nothing," she said with a little laugh. "But I would like it because, at least I'll know who the father is if I get pregnant."

"So you agree to become my private whore for the rest of your life?"

Dewi Ayu shook her head. "Not for quite that long," she said, "but for as long as your dick and your finances allow."

"If you're not satisfied, I can use my finger or a cow's hoof in place of my dick."

"I'm sure your finger will be just fine, as long as you know how to use it," said Dewi Ayu chuckling. She fell silent for a moment and then murmured, "So this is the end of my career as a public prostitute."

She said it almost nostalgically. Over the years there had been so much sadness, but there had been some good times too. "Really every woman is a whore, because even the most proper wife sells herself for a dowry and a shopping allowance … or love, if it exists," she said. "It's not that I don't believe in love, actually it's the complete opposite, I do all of this with the utmost love. I was born into a Dutch family and was a Catholic until I recited my *syahadat* and became a Muslim on my wedding day. I was married once and I was once a religious person. Just because I have lost all of that doesn't mean I have lost love. I feel like I have become a Sufi and a saint. To be a whore you have to love everybody, everything, all of it: penises, fingers, and cow's hooves."

"Love has only made me suffer excruciating pain," said the *preman.*

"Well, you are free to love me," said Dewi Ayu. "But don't expect too much in return, because expectation has nothing to do with love."

"But how can I love someone who doesn't love me back?"

"You'll learn, Tough Guy."

To seal their agreement, Dewi Ayu extended her hand and Maman Gendeng kissed her fingertips. The arrangement pleased them both, and even though they did not live in the same house, they began to seem more and more like newlyweds. When Maman Gendeng met the prostitute's other daughters, who had inherited their mother's perfect beauty, Alamanda was sixteen and Adinda was fourteen. He proclaimed, "I will kill anybody who bothers those girls."

They began to be spotted out and about as a family, going to the movies together and spending Sundays at the beach, fishing or swimming. The rest of the time the *preman* met Dewi Ayu at night at the pavilion behind Mama Kalong's tavern. When morning came she no longer hurried home, and they would relax in the orange grove chatting.

But one night, weeks after Maman Gendeng's arrival, he didn't visit Mama Kalong's whorehouse. No one else dared touch Dewi Ayu, so she was passing the time reading travel guides when, flanked by his bodyguards, another man showed up: Shodancho.

This was his first visit to the brothel. Overjoyed, Mama Kalong came rushing out to greet him herself, ready to serve him anything he wanted. Shodancho didn't want anything except the most beautiful whore in the place. He turned toward Dewi Ayu and without hesitation he pointed straight at her. Onlookers trembled at his choice, and no one dared say a thing when Dewi Ayu shook her head no. This was the first time Dewi Ayu had ever refused a customer, but Shodancho was not a man to be defeated by a mere shake of the head. Brandishing his pistol he walked toward the prostitute and ordered her to toss her travel guide aside and come along to bed. For the first time ever, she was forced to walk to her room without being coddled and carried, and this filled her with resentment. Shodancho followed her to the pavilion while his bodyguards sat in the tavern.

"You point that pistol like a coward."

"It's a bad habit, please forgive me Miss," said Shodancho. "I really just want to ask, may I marry your oldest daughter, Alamanda?"

Dewi Ayu sneered disdainfully. She first reminded him that his harsh treatment of her certainly didn't help his chances, but then said rationally: "Alamanda is in charge of her own brain and her own body, so why don't you just ask her whether she wants to marry you or not." To herself she thought, *this skinny soldier is so pathetic, proposing like this.*

"Everyone in the city knows that she has already disappointed many men, and I'm afraid the same thing will happen to me."

Dewi Ayu knew young men and old geezers were crazy for Alamanda. They'd all tried to win her love and never won anything because, as her mother well knew, Alamanda only loved one man. He had gone and she was waiting for his return.

"You still have to ask Alamanda," said Dewi Ayu. "If it turns out she wants to marry you, I'll throw you both a fantastic party. But if it turns out she doesn't, I suggest you commit suicide."

In the orange grove, an owl hooted, and swept down to snatch a gopher. Dewi Ayu tried to stall for time, hoping that her thug would come at last and the two men could settle the affair. Shodancho approached her, stroked her chin that was as smooth as wax, and asked, "And what exactly do you suggest I do now, Madam?"

"Find another girl," Dewi Ayu advised. There were many beautiful young women in this city, all the descendants of Princess Rengganis and her infamous beauty. Still he didn't leave, roughly pushing Dewi Ayu into the bedroom, pulling off her clothes instead. He fucked that whore with urgency and after his dick spewed, he rested for a moment and then left without saying another word.

Dewi Ayu lay there, unable to believe what had just happened. It wasn't just that someone had slept with her after Maman Gendeng had explicitly forbidden it; it was also that this was the first time she had ever been taken so rudely. Men in Halimunda treated her better than they treated their own wives. She looked at her gown that had lost two buttons in being ripped open, and prayed that Shodancho would get struck by lightning. Her anger steadily increased as she thought about how he had only slept with her as if she was just a hunk of flesh, as if that man had been fucking a toilet hole for a few short minutes, as if the entire city wasn't in awe of her. The whole thing was enough to make her curse and even cry a little bit, and she hurried home.

Maman Gendeng heard the news as soon as the new day came. He didn't know Shodancho, but he knew where to find him. From the bus terminal where he lived he marched to the Halimunda military command headquarters. At the entrance gate, from inside the "monkey cage," a security guard stopped him. Maman Gendeng said that he wanted to see Shodancho. The soldier did not have a real weapon, just a dagger and a bludgeon, and he knew he could never fight the man, so he just saluted and pointed to a door and Maman Gendeng pushed past.

In jeans and a short-sleeved t-shirt that showed off the dragon tattoo on his right bicep from his guerrilla days, Maman Gendeng barged right into Shodancho's office without knocking. The commandant was in the middle of a radio conference with central command, and looked up, surprised. When he recognized the fighter from the beach standing there so cocky and presumptuous, he abruptly ended his discussion and rose to his feet with a fury contained in the fierce glint of his eye. Before Shodancho could say anything Maman Gendeng beat him to it: "Listen up! No one can sleep with Dewi Ayu except me, and if you dare return to her bed, I will show you no mercy."

Shodancho was infuriated to be threatened like this: here, in his own office. He asked whether the guy knew that he could be hung, executed by the state, if Shodancho so much as said the word. What's more, he knew that Dewi Ayu was a whore, so if the problem was that he had slept with a whore without paying, then he would pay her more than anyone had ever paid her before. Enraged by the high and mighty demeanor of the thug standing before him, Shodancho grabbed his pistol from his waist, released the safety and aimed at that man as if to say I am not afraid of your threats and you'd better move your feet unless you want to get shot.

"Well then," said the *preman,* "it seems as though you don't know who I am."

Shodancho didn't really intend to shoot, he just wanted to scare the guy. But when he saw Maman Gendeng was brandishing a dagger, he had no choice but to pull the trigger. As the pistol blasted, he saw Maman Gendeng lurch backward but then realized with a shock that the man suffered not a single wound. The bullet was spinning on the floor.

Shodancho was sure that he hadn't been even slightly off target, and his shock grew greater when he saw Maman Gendeng smiling in his direction.

"Listen up, Shodancho. I took out this dagger not to attack you, but to show that I am not afraid of you. I am invincible. Your bullets can't hurt me, and neither can this blade," said Maman Gendeng, plunging the dagger into his own stomach with full force. The blade broke and its tip rattled to the floor without even a scratch. He grabbed the bullet and the piece of the dagger from the floor and, holding them in the palm of his hand, showed them to Shodancho.

Shodancho, who was now standing still as a statue with his pistol dangling from his limp and powerless hand and his face the color of pale ash, had heard of people like this; but this was the first time he had ever seen one with his own eyes.

Before leaving, Maman Gendeng said, "For the last time, Shodancho, don't touch Dewi Ayu. If you do, I won't just tear this place to pieces—I'll kill you."

{6}

SHODANCHO WAS MEDITATING, buried in the hot sand with only his head poking out, when one of his men approached him. The soldier, Tino Sidiq, didn't dare disturb him—in fact he wasn't even sure if he *could* disturb him. Although Shodancho's eyes were as wide open as those of a decapitated head, his soul was wandering in a realm of light, or at least that was how Shodancho often described his ecstatic experiences. "Meditation saves me from having to look at this rotten world," he'd say and then continue, "or at least from having to look at your ugly face."

After a while his eyes blinked and his body slowly began to move, which Tino Sidiq knew signalled the end of his meditation. Shodancho emerged from the sand in one elegant gesture, scattering some grains of sand before coming to sit next to the soldier like a bird alighting. His naked body was skinny due to his strict regimen of alternate-day *Daud* fasting, even though everyone knew he was not a religious person.

"Here are your clothes," said Tino Sidiq, giving him his dark green uniform.

"Every outfit gives you a new clown role to play," said Shodancho, putting on his uniform. "Now I am Shodancho, the pig hunter."

Tino Sidiq knew that Shodancho didn't like this role, but at the same time he had agreed to play it. A number of days before they had received a direct order from Major Sadrah, the military commander of the City of Halimunda, to emerge from the jungle and help the people exterminate pigs. Shodancho hated getting orders from That Idiot Sadrah, as he always called him. This message was filled with respect and praise: Sadrah said that only Shodancho knew Halimunda like the palm of his own hand, and therefore he was the only one the people trusted to help them hunt pigs.

"This is what happens when the world is without war, soldiers are reduced to hunting pigs," Shodancho continued. "Sadrah is so stupid, he wouldn't even recognize his own asshole."

He was on the same jungle beach where so many years ago the Princess Rengganis had sought refuge after running away, a wide cape that was shaped like an elephant's ear, surrounded by more shell-strewn beaches and steep ravines, with only a few sandy stretches. The area was almost completely unspoiled by humans, because ever since the colonial era it had been maintained as a forest preserve, with leopards and *ajak*. This was where Shodancho had been living for more than ten years, in a small hut just like the one he'd built during his guerrilla years. He had thirty-two soldiers under his command, and civilians sometimes came to help them, and all the men took turns riding into the city on a truck to take care of their needs, but not Shodancho. His longest journey in those ten years had only been as far as the caves, where he meditated, and he only returned to the hut to go fishing and cook for his soldiers and take care of the *ajak* he had domesticated. This peaceful life had been disturbed by Sadrah's message. In the jungle there were no pigs, the animals only lived in the hills to the north of Halimunda, and so he would have to go down to the city. For him, to obey that order was to betray his devotion to solitude.

"This pitiful country," he said. "Not even its soldiers know how to hunt pigs."

He had last visited the city almost eleven years ago. The KNIL troops were to be disbanded, and he had gone to the city to oversee their departure. "Sayonara," he'd said with disappointment. "I'm like a fisherman who waits patiently for his catch only to have someone else hand him a basket full of fish." And then he'd returned to the jungle, along with his thirty-two faithful soldiers, and thus they began their boring duties that would continue for more than ten years. Keeping busy, they protected some smuggling trucks managed by a merchant he had met when they fought the Japanese together. Of course he himself never truly oversaw anything, because his thirty-two soldiers took care of everything. He was usually either out exploring the jungle looking for caves to meditate in, fishing for parrotfish, or practicing his combat moves. He could vanish all of a sudden, a guerrilla technique he had developed himself, and could reappear just as suddenly.

He had developed that technique back when he was still a real *shodancho* in the Halimunda *daidan*, when Japan's Sixteenth Army still occupied the island of Java. He was twenty-years old when a brilliant idea suddenly flashed into his brain: rebellion. The first person he invited to join him was Sadrah, a *shodancho* in the same *daidan*, his friend since childhood. They'd began their military careers at the same time in the Seinendan, a youth regiment established by Japan. They'd gone to Bogor together for their military training after Peta was founded, and graduated as *shodancho* before returning to Halimunda, each to lead their own *shodan*. Now he hoped to invite his friend to rebel together as well.

"You are asking for the grave," said Sadrah.

"Yes, the Japanese came from far far away just to bury me," he said with a chuckle. "Now that'll be a great story for my children and grandchildren."

He was the youngest *shodancho* in Halimunda, and had the puniest physique. But only he had obtained the nickname Shodancho, and when the plans for rebellion were finally in place, he himself led the movement. There were eight *shodancho*, each with their own *budancho*, who said they would join, and two *chudancho* became the guerrilla advisors. The *daidancho* found out about the plan, but chose to stay out of it and washed his hands of the affair. "I am not a grave-digger," he said, "especially not for my very own grave."

"Oh, I'll dig a grave for you, Daidancho," said Shodancho, then saw him out of their secret meeting. Once he was gone, Shodancho said to the others: "He prefers to rot to death behind a desk."

He unfolded a crude map of Halimunda, marking certain Japanese areas with the symbol for Kurawa's troops, and their own with the symbol for Pandawa, reminding his men: "There is no Bhisma who cannot die and no Yudistira who cannot lie; everyone can die and everyone must fight to survive, even if by lying." When he was little his grandfather had entertained him with tales of warriors from the Mahabharata, and he lived with such an exuberant passion for war that people often commented, "He should have been the commander of the Sixteenth Army."

As it turned out, those secret meetings went on for six months before they were confident enough to carry out the rebellion. They counted their weapons and ammunition, reviewed their plans for escape if they failed, and identified their targets if they were able to capture Halimunda. Couriers were sent to get the much-needed support of other *daidan*. In early February everything was finally ready: the rebellion would be carried out on the fourteenth.

"Maybe I will never return," Shodancho said when he said good-bye to his grandfather. "Or maybe I'll come home a carcass."

As the day of the rebellion approached, he gathered his pistol and ammunition, and double-checked that medicine had been distributed among everyone's survival packs, in case they became fugitives. He contacted a merchant named Bendo, who he had helped smuggle teak, to prepare food supplies for the guerrillas. He also met directly with the regent, the mayor, and the chief of police, saying that on February 14 there would be a "war simulation exercise," that all the Peta soldiers in Halimunda would be participating, and no one should disturb them, his code for rebellion. He was alert to the potential of a betrayal.

"Today," he said at half past two on the day of the mutiny, "will be quite a busy day for the gravedigger."

The mutiny began by shooting up the headquarters of the Kempeitai, the Japanese army, at Hotel Sakura. Thirty men were executed in the soccer field: twenty-one soldiers and Japanese civil servants, five mixed-blood Dutch Indonesians, and four Chinese collaborators. Their corpses were quickly dragged to the cemetery and tossed without ceremony in front of the gravedigger's house.

The public was not at all supportive. They locked themselves inside their houses, certain that this was the beginning of an even worse terror: back-up Japanese troops would surely be sent to the city and would leave no survivors. However, the rebels exulted. They took down the Hinomaru, the Japanese flag, and put their own flag back up in its place. They circled the city in a truck, shouting out slogans of freedom and independence and singing songs of struggle. When dusk fell, they disappeared as if swallowed by the night. They knew that the Japanese would hear about the rebellion—maybe all of Java had already heard about it—and as soon as morning came the backup troops would have arrived.

"After all that has happened," said Shodancho, "we must leave Halimunda until Japan is defeated." Now they were true guerrillas.

They divided the rebel troops into three groups and split up. The first group, under the command of *shodancho* Bagong and his *chodancho* adviser, moved to the western territory to face the Japanese entering Halimunda from that direction. They would push into the no-man's-land on the perimeter of the district, full of roving thieves. The second group, led by *shodancho* Sadrah and his *chodancho* adviser, moved to the dense jungles in the northern hills. The last group moved east, taking control of the river delta and, led by Shodancho, they readied themselves for a battle in the swamps and for attacks of malaria and dysentery. To the south, nature was already on their side in the form of the malicious South Seas. They all moved out before midnight, just as the *ajak* began to howl in the distance.

So it began. There was excitement and there was fear. Two soldiers started crying for their mothers, but when the commander threatened to send them home their bravery resurfaced and they swore they would win every battle or die trying. The troops moved into their designated positions, carrying the short-muzzled carbine pistols and Steyer rifles they had stolen from the KNIL, and a small cannon and an eight-millimeter mortar stolen from the *daidan*. Only the *shodancho* and *budancho* carried guns, while the enlisted men, who the Japanese called *giyukei*, carried bayonets or simple sharpened bamboo spears. Two scouts walked slightly ahead of the group while two more guarded the rear. With whatever weapons they had, they intended to win the battle against the most impressive troops in Asia, troops who had beaten Russia and China and chased out the French, the British, and the Dutch from their colonies, troops who were now making war against almost half the world, troops who had taught them how to hold their weapons properly.

"The hero always wins," said Shodancho in encouragement. "Even though it always takes a while."

On the first day of the guerrilla war, Shodancho's group attacked a truck heading for the delta, where Bloedenkamp prison was located. They detonated a mortar right underneath the truck and the gas tank exploded, killing all the Japanese soldiers inside. A courier next reported that the western troops had engaged in open fighting with Japanese soldiers on the outskirts of the jungle, and after a fierce battle Bagong and his men had managed to slip away and it seemed as though the Japanese troops would not pursue them. The northern group attacked the Japanese all along the main road but then were ambushed by a large battalion. They received an order to return to the *daidan*, and so *shodancho* Sadrah and all his soldiers returned to the city in surrender.

"Even a donkey remembers to forget the way home," said Shodancho. "He's dumber than an ass."

On the second day they were intercepted by Japanese troops and fought in skirmishes all along the riverbank. They were able to kill two Japanese soldiers, but they paid too high a price—five rebel soldiers perished, and then they were besieged. In an attempt to save themselves, they jumped into the river and became targets for enemy fire. After a rescue operation resulted in the death of another of their men, Shodancho and a number of his soldiers escaped.

He quickly changed his route and plans. They would return, but not to surrender, the greatest tactic his men had ever heard. To the south of the city there was a protected forest, and they walked in a circle through the mangrove swamps before climbing up the cliffs from a shell-strewn beach and entering the jungle. The Japanese and Peta soldiers chasing them were tricked, thinking they would continue east in order to reconnoiter with the rebels from other *daidan*, as they had originally planned. Shodancho had quickly calculated: the rebellion had failed. Japan had found them out, and the other *daidan* hadn't helped, so the best plan was to escape into the forest closest to the city, and from there prepare for a *real* guerrilla war.

They hid in a cave for a number of days, because the fishermen could see them from their boats out on the ocean. A scout was sent to determine the condition of the western battalion, and of the city in general. He returned with bad news: the Japanese and Peta soldiers had ransacked the forest where the western battalion had been hiding. Bandits and thieves had been allowed to escape, but the rebels had been taken alive. With nothing left but bayonets and bamboo spears, the battalion did not surrender and so the sixty remaining soldiers, including Shodancho Bagong and his *chudancho* adviser, would be executed on the 24th of February in the yard in front of the *daidan*.

Shodancho came down off the mountain disguised as a skinny hobo covered in scabies, with his clothes in tatters. The disguise wasn't too difficult to pull off, because after ten days as a guerrilla he was practically indistinguishable from an actual beggar. With his dirty stiff hair, he entered the city and not a soul recognized him. He walked along the pavement, his hands clutching a tin can with a stone inside, which he rattled softly. In front of the *daidan* headquarters, he stopped under a flame tree at the side of the road, and witnessed the execution. One by one the sixty men were shot, their corpses thrown into a truck and dumped in front of the gravedigger's house.

"Don't ever hope to die just to be remembered," he said to his remaining soldiers as they raised the flag in mourning back at the guerrilla stronghold. "Believe me, not many people are prepared to remember anything that isn't their immediate concern."

He plotted an act of vicious revenge. One night, he led an ambush against a military post and stole some ammunition before killing six Japanese soldiers and throwing their corpses into the street. They blew up a truck and then disappeared before the morning cock crowed. The six Japanese corpses strewn in the street threw the city into an uproar the next day, and the people wondered who had done such a thing. But the Japanese and the *daidan*, including Sadrah, quickly realized: Shodancho was still alive, and he had declared a never-ending war.

The Japanese from the Kempeitai retaliated in a blind rampage, and soon lost the trace. Soldiers ransacked people's houses, looking for Shodancho and his men, but got no answers. On the third day after the murder of the six Japanese, a warehouse worth of food and a truck were stolen, and the two Japanese guarding it were killed. The truck was found plunged into the river but all of the food was gone. The Japanese combed the length of the river and found nothing.

Two days later, a courier came one night to Shodancho's guerrilla hut and told him that news of their insurgence had reached almost everyone on Java. Their uprising had already inspired a number of other small rebellions in a number of *daidan*, and even though all had failed, the Japanese were gravely concerned and it had even been rumored that Peta was going to be dispersed and all their weapons stripped.

"That's the risk of keeping a hungry tiger as a pet," said Shodancho.

Four days later they blew up a bridge just as five Japanese trucks loaded with soldiers were driving over it. That isolated Halimunda for months, and the guerrillas were safe in their hideouts.

On one bright unforgettable morning, Shodancho had just finished taking a shit in a coral reef when he came across a man's corpse, tossed ashore by the waves. The corpse, already so swollen that it looked like it was about to explode, was wearing nothing but a loincloth. Shodancho and his men pulled the corpse of this drowned man onto the beach and inspected it. There was a deep wound in his stomach.

"That's the slash of a bayonet," said Shodancho. "He was killed by the Japanese."

"He's a rebel from another *daidan*," said a soldier.

"Or maybe he slept with Kaiser Hirohito's mistress."

All of a sudden Shodancho fell silent, looking at the corpse's face. He was obviously a native—his face was gaunt as if he hadn't had enough to eat, like most of the natives, and looked slippery without a mustache or beard. But that wasn't what interested him, it was the odd shape of the man's mouth. He finally came to the conclusion, "This man is sucking on something." With significant effort and the help of another soldier, he pried open the corpse's stiff jaws with his fingers.

"There's nothing there," said the soldier.

"No," replied Shodancho, and he groped around in the corpse's mouth and removed a scrap of paper that had almost completely disintegrated. "He was killed for this," said Shodancho. He spread out the paper on top of a warm piece of coral. It looked like a leaflet, printed by a mimeograph machine. The seawater that had leaked into the corpse's mouth had caused the ink to fade and run, but Shodancho could still make it out. Everyone's heart was pounding, expecting an important message, because no one would be killed for carrying some meaningless old wadded-up leaflet. With his fingers trembling (and not from the frigid air or from hunger), Shodancho held the piece of paper with tears streaming down his face. Before his confused soldiers had the chance to ask him anything he spoke first, asking them, "What date is it today?"

"The 23rd of September."

"So we are more than a month late."

"For what?"

"For the celebration." Then he read them what was printed on the dead man's leaflet. "PROCLAMATION: WITH THIS WE THE PEOPLE OF INDONESIA DECLARE OUR INDEPENDENCE . . . AUGUST 17, 1945. IN THE NAME OF THE INDONESIAN PEOPLE, SUKARNO & HATTA."

There was a moment of silence, before they broke out into a cacophony of whoops and shouts. Except for Shodancho, they all ran and danced in front of their guerrilla huts as if possessed, singing victory songs. Without one order, they gathered up their things and started packing, as if everything had come to an end. They were ready to run out of the jungle and burst into the city to bring the joyful news, but Shodancho quickly headed them off before the insanity spread any further.

"We have to have a meeting," he said.

They complied and gathered in front of the hut.

"There are still many Japanese in Halimunda," said Shodancho, "and they must already know about this, but they have chosen to remain silent." He quickly came up with a strategy. Half of them had to carry out a lightning attack on the post office, taking hostages if necessary, which wouldn't be too dangerous because all the post office employees were natives. There was a mimeograph machine there and they had to print up the dead man's note and disseminate it to the entire city as quickly as possible. "Use the mailmen!" he said confidently. The other half of them had to infiltrate the *daidan* and tell them what had happened, disarm the Japanese, mobilize the masses, and hold a huge gathering at the soccer field. After that quick and concise meeting, they emerged from the jungle.

The simple fact of their arrival in the city put everyone into a frenzy, even before the leaflet printed at the post office was swiftly shared. Shodancho was able to commandeer a truck and circle the city shouting, "Indonesia declared independence on August 17, Halimunda followed suit on the 23rd of September!" Everyone standing on the edge of the road froze, as if turned to stone. A barber almost snipped off his customer's ear, and a Chinese *bakpao* seller lost control of his bike and went rolling along with his steamed buns. They all looked at the passing truck in disbelief, and then snatched up the scattered leaflets and read them. Rejoicing broke out—the elementary school kids began dancing by the side of the road, and then all the grown ups joined in.

The Japanese came out of their offices, including the army commander Sidokan. They were helpless when they found out what had happened, and put up no protest when the Peta soldiers from the *daidan* appeared to strip them of their weapons. Without the proper ceremony the rebels lowered the Hinomaru while yelling in the faces of the Japanese, "Eat this accursed flag!" They then exchanged it for the Red and White in a solemn ceremony, singing the anthem *Indonesia Raya*.

People began to gather in the soccer field, emaciated and dressed in rags, but still looking radiant. Never in their lives, and never in their grandparents' or great-grandparents' lives, had there ever been independence. But that day they heard it for themselves: Indonesia was free, and so of course was Halimunda. Shodancho led another flag-raising ceremony in the afternoon, again reading the proclamation, while the people of the city sat cross-legged on the grass and the members of the military stood at attention, tall and stiff. Starting that year and for many years to come, only schoolchildren and the army commemorated the proclamation every August 17. The citizens still conducted their own private rituals on September 23, and after a while the schoolchildren and the military joined in. That day they did not just salute the flag and read the text of the proclamation while singing *Indonesia Raya*, but also sent each other gift baskets of food and held a street fair. And if a stranger asked, or if a teacher asked his pupils when Indonesia gained its independence, they would always say, "The 23rd of September." The central government made a number of attempts to clear up the confusion about the delay in information in the year 1945, but the citizens of Halimunda swore to the death that they would always celebrate Independence Day on September 23. After a while nobody made a big deal about it anymore.

A commotion broke out when a group of people came dragging the *daidancho* and it appeared that he was to be viciously executed on the grounds of committing treason during the rebellion. They were ready to hang him under a catappa tree that grew in a corner of the soccer field, but Shodancho put a stop to their proceedings. He released the *daidancho* and brought him to the center of the field. He already knew about the man's treason, and for that he gave him a revolver. Heard by all the people who swarmed around them, he said:

"We were both educated by the Japanese, so you know as well as I do what a traitor must do."

The *daidancho* put the pistol to his head and ended his own life. Even still, Shodancho ordered all the soldiers to conduct the ritual of the final salute, and the corpse was wrapped in a flag and buried in a plot of land not far from the city hospital, the precursor to their military cemetery. His was the only death that day. Shodancho took over all the *daidan*'s power, quickly sent a number of couriers to gather more information, and working with the city folk, he fixed the bridge that he himself had once destroyed. Two days later the couriers returned, saying that Peta had been disbanded and all the *daidan* had been turned into the Agency for the Safety of the People.

So they formed the Agency for the Safety of the People. But two days after that, another courier came and said that the Agency for the Safety of the People had already been disbanded and changed into the Army for the Safety of the People.

"If it gets changed again," Shodancho said annoyed, "Halimunda is going to go to war against Indonesia."

The central government made decisions about the distribution of rank. Shodancho, surpassing the commanders from the other *shodan*, was given the rank of lieutenant colonel and his dumb friend, Sadrah, felt satisfied as Major Sadrah. But Shodancho didn't pay too much attention to such matters, and told everyone, "I prefer to remain just Shodancho." A few weeks later, another courier came bringing a parcel containing a letter, which seemed to have been written many months ago and was only just now arriving at its destination, from the president of the Republic of Indonesia, addressed to Shodancho. Pretty soon everyone in the city knew what it said: the president had designated Shodancho as the great commander of the Army for the Safety of the People with the rank of general, in recognition of his heroism in leading the February 14 Rebellion.

While the city folk were celebrating his nomination as great commander, Shodancho disappeared to his old guerrilla hideout. That whole day he fished and swam in the ocean alone, meditating while floating on the surface of the water as if he himself was a drowned corpse. He didn't want to think about the nightmare of becoming the great commander of the Army for the Safety of the People. Before his departure, he said to Major Sadrah, "How sad to know that I was the first person to rebel, and because of that I was chosen to become the great commander. I have wondered what kind of army we have, to choose a man who hasn't ever even seen a woman's private parts up close as a great commander." As day turned into night, his friends discovered him and brought him home.

A while after that, he got news from another courier, which came as a welcome relief. Noting that the great commander's chair had not been sat upon by Shodancho even once, the division commander and the commander of the islands of Java and Sumatra held a powwow to look for his replacement. "The president of the republic has already chosen Colonel Sudirman as commander of the Army for the Safety of the People with the rank of general," announced the courier.

"Praise God," Shodancho said. "That position is only good for those who really want it."

While all the citizens of Halimunda were saddened to learn he'd been replaced, Shodancho was floating on unimaginable joy.

The Army for the Safety of the People was then renamed the Army for the Salvation of the People. They had just switched all of the nameplates when the news arrived: The Army for the Salvation of the People would now be called the Army of the Republic of Indonesia.

"Are we going to go to war against Indonesia?" asked Major Sadrah.

Shodancho laughed and shook his head. "There's no need," he said comfortingly. "As a new country, we're just now learning how to come up with names."

The Japanese army had not even left yet and the people had not yet had the chance to experience an era of peace when Allied planes began flying in the Halimunda sky. In just a few days, English and Dutch troops arrived. The KNIL prisoners of war were freed and rearmed themselves and began stripping the native army of their weapons. Shodancho immediately took emergency measures, calling all the soldiers back into the forest. This time he sent them out in the four compass directions, himself leading the troops that would fortify the jungles in the south. He decided to fight another guerrilla war, this time against the Allied troops and especially the NICA, the Netherlands Indies Civil Administration. But it wasn't just the guerrillas who went to the jungle; civilians, the majority of them young men, trailed after, swearing their loyalty to Shodancho. He split up all of his soldiers so that they could each lead a small unit of guerrillas, mostly made up of these civilians—some were the same men who raped Dewi Ayu and her friends before the English soldiers arrived.

This new guerrilla war lasted two years, and the guerrillas experienced the pain of defeat more often than victory. But even though they knew he was in the jungle on the cape, the KNIL soldiers never found the man they hunted: Shodancho. The jungle was filled with guerrillas, who knew the region better than anyone, sheltering in the old Japanese fort prisons. The KNIL soldiers, aided by the English, never had the courage to enter the jungle: they chose to hold their positions in the city. And for their part the guerrilla soldiers found it difficult to enter Halimunda. The KNIL soldiers blocked the flow of food and weapons, but that was pointless because the guerrilla soldiers planted their own rice fields in the middle of the jungle, and they were already accustomed to making war without ammunition. They tried conducting air raids, but the Japanese had taught the guerrillas how to evade those.

Shodancho further developed his guerrilla techniques, finding the best ways to camouflage and infiltrate; he could appear suddenly and disappear just as swiftly, sought even by his own men after he had disguised himself.

"It's different from a game of hide and seek," he said, "because the moment a guerrilla is found, he's dead."

This went on until Shodancho got news that stopped all the battles: the Netherlands had acknowledged the sovereignty of the Republic of Indonesia at the negotiating table. He found this quite annoying—the republic had already declared its independence four years before, but the Netherlands was only now acknowledging the fact, and for that they were simply being allowed to leave.

"It's as if this entire war was completely meaningless," he said dejectedly.

Even so, with his core guerrilla troops, Shodancho emerged from the forest. Their appearance was welcomed joyfully by the city folk, because he was still their hero. People waved colorful flags by the side of the road as Shodancho rode in on a mule, not paying any attention to the overenthusiastic welcome, and headed directly for the port. There the Dutch soldiers and civilians were preparing to board the ship that would carry them all home. Shodancho approached the KNIL commander, who was delighted that he could finally see his enemy. They shook hands warmly and they even hugged.

"At some point we will make war again," the commander said.

"Yes, if the queen of the Netherlands and the president of the Republic of Indonesia allow it."

They then parted at the gangway. Shodancho remained standing on the dock after the stairs had been hauled up and anchor lifted, while the commander stood at the railing. When the engine could be heard roaring and the ship began to sway, they both waved.

"Sayonara," Shodancho said finally.

❧

The end of the war brought a strange hush, the sort that falls over people when they retire. For a few days Shodahncho killed time in his old *shodan*'s headquarters, on Halimunda beach. During the day all he did was trim the grass and feed it to his mule, or fish in the little nearby stream, until finally he gathered his friends and told them he was going back into the jungle indefinitely.

"What are you going to do there?" asked Major Sadrah, who was now the head of the city military. "No one needs any more guerrillas."

Shodancho calmly replied, "There's nothing for a soldier to do in peacetime, so I'm going to conduct some business in the jungle."

And that's exactly what he did. He contacted Bendo, the merchant who'd smuggled teak under his protection in exchange for logistical support for the guerrillas. With a Chinese trader Bendo brought along, Shodancho began smuggling more goods through the headlands. After the trio had reached an agreement, he was ready to go back into the jungle, and selected thirty-two of his most faithful soldiers to join his new venture.

"Now, our only enemies are thieves," he told them.

Everyone in the city, civilian or soldier, knew about their smuggling. Everything came in and out through a small port built at the edge of the cape: TVs, wristwatches, copra, even flip-flops. People never complained, because Shodancho was still their hero—plus the surplus goods were sold in Halimunda at really cheap prices before most were sent off to other cities. And the military officials stayed mum too, in part because Major Sadrah was Shodancho's old friend, but mostly because Shodancho set aside half the profits for the general in the capital. Everyone soon realized that apart from his natural gift for warfare, he also had an extraordinary business instinct.

"There's no difference between war and business," said Shodancho. "Both must be conducted with extraordinary cunning."

In fact Shodancho was not too involved with day-to-day business matters, because everything was taken very good care of by his thirty-two men. He spent more than a decade living in a guerrilla hut, fishing, meditating, and domesticating *ajak*, the wild dogs. He even ordered his soldiers to get married, buy houses, live in the city, and take turns keeping him company in the otherwise deserted jungle. The men began to lose all their fighting instincts, as their bodies swelled from overeating and the enjoyable lives they were now living, but Shodancho stayed just as he had always been—his body was still lean, and he was as nimble as ever, without even the smallest hint of decline. He kept busy, even preparing meals for all the men, though he himself ate very little, and he began to enjoy this peaceful way of life, until Major Sadrah asked him to emerge from the jungle to exterminate the pigs on the slopes of the Ma Iyang and Ma Gedik hills.

"I don't know whether the soldiers can be convinced to hunt pigs," Tino Sidiq said to Shodancho. "They have just been sitting behind truck steering wheels for ten years now."

"That's okay, I already recruited new soldiers who are eager for combat," said Shodancho. Then he let out a piercing whistle, and all of his *ajak* came running—grey, agile, and ready to fight. There were almost one hundred of them, jostling each other at his feet.

"That's certainly enough to fight a pig invasion," replied Tino Sidiq, petting one of the dogs.

"Next week we will move to the front."

The pig extermination had begun four or five years ago, with a farmer named Sahudi and his five friends: their rice paddies and fields at the foot of Ma Iyang Hill had been ravaged by wild boars for a month. As harvest time approached, Sahudi's little child, who was only seven, spotted a pig in the yard behind the house. Sahudi had had it. He quickly gathered up his friends and prepared for an ambush.

They chose the night of the full moon. The six men sat in silent pairs in the guava, sapodilla, and ambarella trees, each one of them in their own corner of the field with an air rifle in their hands. They waited patiently, the tips of their cigarettes glowing in the dark, determined to shoot the first pig they saw. Right before dawn, they finally heard some snorts and snuffles. In a number of minutes the animal appeared under the light of the full moon—and not just one, but two of them set upon the fertile fields of beans and corn.

Sahudi quickly snatched up his rifle and aimed at one of the pigs, clearly visible in the light of the moon, and as he fired three more rifles simultaneously shot at the same pig, which collapsed in the dirt, three bullet holes right at its temple. The other men tried to shoot the second pig, but it escaped; at the sound of the rifle shots and the sight of its partner collapsed on the ground, the second pig ran away, crashing into everything in its path.

The six men leapt down from their perches in the trees, and seeing that the shot pig was not yet dead, Sahudi stabbed a wooden stake into its heart with all his might, releasing its soul for good. But something was happening to that carcass under the light of the moon: those six men could hardly believe their eyes—its black hairy body that was covered in mud suddenly turned into a human corpse, with three bullets wounds to his head and a stake stuck in his chest.

"Holy shit!" said Sahudi. "This pig turned into a person!"

The news quickly spread from one village to the next, until all of Halimunda had heard about it. No one recognized the dead man and no one claimed his corpse, so it rotted away in the city morgue before being buried in the public cemetery. Since then, no one had dared to kill any pigs, terrified of the same curse that had befallen Sahudi and his five friends: they all went insane. Four years had passed without anyone killing any pigs, even though the animals had now become the most vicious marauders. The farmers' only hope was the arrival of the military. Major Sadrah had already sent a number of soldiers to the forest; they had come home carrying wild fowl and rabbits to cook for their supper, but no pigs. Major Sadrah finally sent a courier to ask Shodancho for his help, knowing full well that the man was the only one he could rely on.

The people were looking forward to Shodancho's arrival. Just as they'd done ten years before, they lined up along the road waving handkerchiefs and little flags, hoping to see their long-absent hero. Little kids stood in front, intrigued by this figure their fathers and mothers and grandfathers and grandmothers had told them so many stories about. The revolutionary war veterans were also there, dressed in full uniform as if it were Independence Day. The regular soldiers gave him a salute by shooting off cannons over the beach, and schoolchildren celebrated with their drum bands.

Shodancho finally appeared, this time not riding a mule but walking on foot. He was wearing loose-fitting clothes with his hair in a buzz cut; his body was as skinny as ever, and he looked more like a Buddhist monk than a soldier. He was guarded by his thirty-two men, who remained faithful even after being tortured with heavy physical training for a week in his efforts to make them lose some weight for the occasion. Then there were ninety-six additional soldiers: some gray, some white, and some brown, the *ajak* trotted behind him, excited to get such an extraordinary welcome from the people of the city. Major Sadrah greeted his friend himself.

After embracing Sadrah, who had developed a sizable potbelly that made him look like a pregnant woman, Shodancho joked cruelly to the crowd, "It seems that I have already caught a pig! Believe me, these dogs are going to come in handy."

The group stayed in Shodancho's old headquarters, which since the Japanese era had been left unoccupied out of respect. The next day, just as he had promised, without very much rest, they began the epic hunt. Each soldier minded three dogs, while Shodancho led them all with a rifle and dagger. They didn't lie in wait, as Sahudi and his friends had done, but clambered through the jungle brush where the pigs were nesting. These large beasts, awoken from their naps, jumped up and ran this way and that.

That day they were able to catch twenty-six pigs, the next day twenty-one, and on the third day seventeen, making a noticeable dent in the swine population. Some were killed by rifle shots, while others were gathered alive in a very large makeshift pen in the soccer field near the *shodan* headquarters. The weird thing was that out of all of those pigs that were killed, not one of them turned into a human. They were truly just plain old pigs, with tusks and snouts and black-bristled skin covered in mud. This emboldened the farmers to join in the pig hunt on the fourth day, and from that point forward, hunting pigs from harvest time until planting time became an annual tradition.

Shodancho's men threw the slaughtered pigs into Chinese restaurant kitchens, while those kept alive were prepared for pig fights to be held in celebration of their triumphant victory. The pigs would be paired with *ajak* in an arena, and the entertainment-starved citizens of Halimunda eagerly anticipated the event. Shodancho had his soldiers create an arena in the soccer field, constructed out of boards about three-meters tall arranged into a large circle. On the outside perimeter, at a height of about two meters, they built a sturdy platform, buttressed by crisscrossed bamboo, where the spectators could stand. To reach the platform, the people had to climb up steps guarded by two soldiers who acted as the ticket collectors, and the tickets could be purchased from a pretty girl sitting behind a nearby table.

The pig fights started on a Sunday afternoon, two weeks after Shodancho had arrived. They lasted for six days, until every single pig had been killed and tossed into restaurant kitchens. From the farthest corners of the city and beyond, spectators came and lined up in front of the pretty ticket seller. Those who wanted to watch but couldn't afford to pay scrambled up the coconut trees that grew all around the soccer field, and sat in the branches. Their colorful clothes looked strange from a distance, as if coconuts no longer grew in the familiar shades of green and brown.

The pig fights were very entertaining. The *ajak* that Shodancho hadn't quite domesticated still showed a wild ferocity when ganging up on the wild pigs. One pig had to face five or six *ajak*, which of course wasn't fair, but everyone wanted to know for sure that the pig was going to die—they didn't want a battle, but a massacre. If the pig tried to take on one of the dogs, the rest of the pack attacked, biting into the swine's flesh and tearing it apart. When the pig began to look exhausted, a soldier would douse it with a bucketful of cold water, forcing it to perk up for the next onslaught. The outcome of each and every performance was obvious: the pig would die, and one or two of the *ajak* would have minor injuries. Then a new pig would be put into the arena, and six fresh *ajak* would be ready to tear it to pieces. All the spectators seemed content to watch this brutal show, except Shodancho, who was suddenly captivated by an entirely different sight.

There amid all the spectators he saw a very beautiful young girl, who was seemingly unperturbed by the fact that most of the other spectators were men. She was maybe just sixteen years old, and looked exactly like an angel who had fallen to earth. Her hair was gathered back in a dark green ribbon, and even from afar Shodancho could see her adorable piercing eyes, her shapely nose, and her rather cruel-seeming smile. Her skin was gleaming white, as if it were shining, and she was wrapped in an ivory dress that fluttered in the afternoon sea breeze. The girl took out a cigarette from her pocket, and with an extraordinary calm she smoked, her eyes all the while on the dogs and pigs in battle. Shodancho had been watching her ever since she came up the stairs, and it appeared that she was there alone. Intrigued, he asked Major Sadrah standing beside him, "Who is that girl?"

Tracking his gaze, Major Sadrah answered, "Her name is Alamanda. She's the daughter of the whore Dewi Ayu."

After the pig-hunting business was over, Shodancho divvied up his ninety-six *ajak* among the citizens of Halimunda. Most of them were given to the farmers to help them guard their paddies and fields, and the rest were given out randomly. Shodancho ordered those who did not yet receive one yet to wait patiently, because soon enough they would have puppies. Halimunda would become filled with dogs, who were all the descendants of those *ajak*.

Shodancho should have just returned to the jungle, as he had initially intended. When he had first arrived, he'd told Major Sadrah that he would stay in the city only until the pig business was settled. But since seeing Alamanda in the pig arena, he hadn't slept. "This must be love," he said to himself. And it was love that made him tremble and try to think of excuses to stay in the city longer, and maybe never leave it ever again.

A solution came when Major Sadrah said, "Don't go right away, we have more festivities to celebrate our victory. *Orkes melayu.*"

"Out of my love for this city, I will stay a little longer," Shodancho quickly agreed.

He saw her again, that girl, the night of the *orkes melayu* performance. It was held in the same soccer field, but this time there was no ticket required, so the place was way more crowded. A band of musicians came from the capital, bringing singers that no one had ever heard of, but nobody cared, it was still good music for dancing, and Halimunda's young men and women could rock and sway, thanks to the rhythm or maybe the booze.

The songs always had whiny lyrics about broken hearts, about unrequited love that was like one hand clapping, about cheating husbands, but no matter how tragically sad the song, the singers didn't cry—instead, smiling and laughing in their sexy makeup, they would turn their backs to the audience and shake their asses. After being applauded for their butts, they would then turn around and face forward, squatting a little bit, and the people would clap even more, because the girls were wearing miniskirts so that everyone could see what they were intended to see. That particular mingling of music, sentimentality, and lasciviousness was what made so many people feel so overjoyed that evening.

Shodancho saw Alamanda again, walking all by herself. This time she was wearing jeans and a leather jacket, and once again a cigarette was perched between her sweet lips. Shodancho gave wholehearted thanks that he had come out of the jungle and could meet a real live angel in his beloved city. The girl wasn't swaying in front of the stage. Instead she just stood next to one of the food stalls scattered around the soccer field, watching. Unable to resist the provocation of her beauty, Shodancho approached her. His popularity made the journey to the girl quite bothersome, because he had to field so many friendly greetings, but finally the girl was right in front of him, or he was standing right in front of the girl, and he could experience her stunning natural beauty from up close. He tried to smile, but Alamanda just gave him an indifferent glance.

"It's not good," Shodancho said, to start some small talk, "for a young woman to be roaming around at night all by herself."

Alamanda looked straight into his eyes. "Don't be stupid, Shodancho, I'm roaming around with all the hundreds of other people here tonight."

And with that, Alamanda departed without another word. Shodancho was frozen in disbelief. That crazy exchange had been far more terrifying than any battle he had ever fought. He turned around and started walking, with a body and soul truly drained of all power.

Is there a guerrilla strategy to defeat love? he asked himself in a brief lament.

He tried to forget the girl's image, but the more he tried to forget it, the more that half-Japanese half-Dutch and a-little-bit-Indonesian face haunted him. He tried to come up with reasons for why he couldn't love that girl. Just think about it, he said in the moments before he fell asleep (even though he clearly would never be able to sleep well again), that girl had probably just been born the same year I became a *shodancho* and was plotting the rebellion. There was an age difference of twenty years—and now, a man who had been named a great commander and had received the rank of general from the first president of the Republic of Indonesia had to surrender to a sixteen-year-old girl. Thinking further about that made everything all the more painful, and he found himself even more mired in a bottomless love.

One morning he awoke, and swore that he would stay in Halimunda forever and Alamanda would be his wife.

But he didn't tell his thirty-two faithful soldiers, who awaited his orders, until finally Tino Sidiq asked, "When are we going to return, Shodancho?"

"Return where?"

"To the jungle," replied Tino Sidiq, "where we've been living for the past ten years."

"Going back to the jungle would not be a return," said Shodancho. "Me, and you, and everybody else was born here, in this city, Halimunda. Here we have returned."

"So you don't want to go back to the jungle?"

"No."

He proved this by putting up a nameplate in front of his old *shodan* headquarters: Military District of Halimunda. To Major Sadrah, who suddenly appeared after hearing about Shodancho's decision to stay in the city and about his impulsive establishment of a military district, he said shortly, "Here I am, the commander of the military district, faithful to my sworn soldiers and awaiting further orders."

"Don't be silly. You are a general and your place is next to the president."

"As long as I can stay in this city, next to the girl whose name you told me," he said in a heartbreaking tone of voice, "I'll become anyone or anything—even if it means I have to turn into a dog."

Sadrah looked at his friend with a gaze full of pity. After hesitating for a moment, Major Sadrah said, "That girl already has a sweetheart." He couldn't bear to look at Shodancho's face, so looking away he continued, "He is a young man named Kliwon."

He knew that he was saying something that pierced right to the heart.

{7}

NO ONE KNEW how Comrade Kliwon ended up becoming a communist youth, because even though he had never been rich, he'd always been a hedonist. His father of course had been quite the communist, and a master speechmaker. He had managed to avoid being sent to Boven-Digoel by the colonial government and so for a time survived, but he was finally executed by the Japanese after his endless meddling and pamphlet writing made the Kempeitai realize he was a communist rebel. Still, there had been no sign that Kliwon would follow in his father's footsteps. He was good at school and had even skipped two grades, and it seemed as if he could be anything he wanted when he grew up.

Really, Kliwon seemed more like a prodigal son than a disciplined young communist. He led a gang of marauding neighborhood kids, stealing whatever they could get their hands on for their own enjoyment: coconuts, logs, or a handful of cacao beans that could be eaten on the spot. On the night before Eid, they would steal a chicken and roast it, and then the next day they would find the chicken's owner to ask for forgiveness. They didn't bother anyone too much, so they were usually just left to do their thing, although one or two people complained. Once they reached their early teens, everyone knew that they'd been to the whorehouse. To earn some spending money they'd go to the sea or help out hauling nets, and after getting the cash those kids would look for a whore—but sometimes they were really broke and thanks to the brothel they were no longer accustomed to controlling their lust.

Kliwon was clever and sometimes his way of thinking could be surprising, if not borderline insane. He once brought three of his friends to the whorehouse, and they took turns sleeping with a prostitute. At first the whore encouraged them to climb up on the bed in pairs because, as she said, she had a hole in the front and in the back. But none of them wanted to share a hole with a piece of shit, so they just slept with her one by one. Kliwon showed himself to be a selfless leader, inviting his friends to sleep with the prostitute first, and taking the last turn. When the sex was over, the prostitute was met with the depressing sight of those three kids crashing through the door and vanishing without paying.

"I asked her whether she liked having sex with us," Kliwon said, recounting the story in the beer garden not long after, "and she said that she liked it. If she liked it and we also liked it, then why should we have to pay?" People often enjoyed hearing such stories from him.

His mother, Mina—not wanting the same thing to happen to him as had happened to his father—tried to distance him from crazy Marxist ideas and anything associated with them, and didn't care what he did as long as he didn't end up a communist. She sent him to the movies and music concerts, and let him get drunk at the beer garden and buy records, and was perfectly happy with him hanging out with a lot of young girls. She knew that her son had slept with many of them, and that many others had begged him to sleep with them, but she didn't care. From her point of view, that was better than someday having to see him stand in front of a firing squad, about to be executed. "Even if he does become a communist, I want him to be a happy communist," said his mother. Her marriage to a communist, which had lasted for some years, and her interactions with her husband's comrades had led her to the conclusion that communists were always gloomy and pensive and never had a good time. So throughout that difficult era, the entire Japanese occupation and the revolutionary war, she let Kliwon live in an endless hoorah.

In his seventeenth year, life was truly sparkling and bright for this young toast of the town. He wore slacks with wide-piped edges and a dark jacket and loafers shiny with polish. The girls came out of their houses to follow him wherever he went, trailing behind him like the train of a wedding gown, and all the young men would fall in step, tailing the girls. The girls fell in love with him, and they showered him with gifts that piled up until the house began to resemble a junkyard. Thinking of nothing else, they held parties almost every night. His male friends also adored him, because he never kept the girls to himself. And that was how they lived. In those years, Kliwon and his friends probably had the happiest lives of anyone in the city.

Kliwon had heard about the renowned prostitute Dewi Ayu, and if there was one thing that marred his happiness, it was the fact that up until the age of seventeen he had never slept with this whore everyone was always talking about. He had tried a couple of times, but Dewi Ayu only wanted to sleep with one man a night, and he always came too late, when men were already queued up ahead of him. Or, if he did succeed in getting there on time, someone would push him aside because they had more money: Mama Kalong always gave the opportunity to the man who could pay the most. All that time, he was obsessed with being able to enter her room and her bed, and that image so infernally haunted him that sometimes he would sleep with some other girl while imagining she was Dewi Ayu, whom he had caught sight of only a few times out and about in the city.

At the very least, Dewi Ayu made him realize that not every single woman on the face of the earth was crazy about him. Even married women and widows, although not quite as obsessed as the young girls who followed him wherever he went, were always stealing glances at him, and he knew that deep in their hearts they longed to bring him into their bedrooms. He had slept with some of them, and it seemed that he could sleep with whomever he wanted—anyone except Dewi Ayu. He was certain that only that woman was not infatuated with him, and in fact quite the opposite, he would have to pay if he wanted her. He began to think of how he could get an opportunity to sleep with her—it didn't have to be for long, even less than five minutes would be enough, even just touching her body would satisfy him. He decided to go visit the woman at her house, something he was sure no other man had ever done before.

Kliwon liked music and was a good guitar player, or at least he had a solid repertoire of *keroncong* and whiny love songs that he could sing for his friends. He went to Dewi Ayu's house all alone one Sunday dressed up like a busker, carrying a guitar, with the intention of conquering the woman with his songs and his bullshit seduction. He had already done this a number of times, making young girls crazy for him by singing songs for them outside their bedroom windows. Now that he was standing in front of the door to Dewi Ayu's house, he began to pluck the guitar strings and sing in his distinctive falsetto.

Apparently the whore wasn't at all intrigued and so he had to stand there, singing five whole songs without anyone opening the door. He had heard people say that the woman lived with her three teenage daughters and two servants, and that they were all quite gracious. With this notion of their kindness, he kept standing there until he had sung ten whole songs and his throat felt dry. Then, after one full hour had passed, he took out a handkerchief and wiped away the drops of sweat that were beginning to speckle his forehead and neck. His legs were practically no longer able to support his body, but there was no indication that the lady of the house would emerge. He finally set his guitar down on top of a table and sat himself down in a chair to rest for a moment, practically seeing stars but determined not to give up.

It turned out that the music stopping was more interesting to the mistress of the house than the music itself had been. Unexpectedly, the door opened and a young girl, about eight years old, appeared with a glass of cold lemonade and placed it on the table next to his guitar.

"You can keep singing in our yard for as long as you'd like," she said, "but you must be really thirsty by now."

Kliwon jumped up and stood there awkwardly. It was not in reaction to the girl's words or the cold lemonade he had been offered, but the sight of this adorable little nymph standing before him. He had never seen such a beautiful girl in his entire life, even though he had seen Dewi Ayu. He didn't know what material God had used to make a creature such as this, because he thought he could see light radiating from her entire body. This vision made him shiver more violently than standing and singing for an hour had without anyone paying him any mind. With trembling lips, he stuttered, "What's your name?"

"I'm Alamanda, Dewi Ayu's daughter."

That name struck his brain like a hammer. He walked away carrying his guitar, stunned and disoriented. A few times he turned back to look at this beautiful little one, but every time he looked away again quickly, as if he couldn't bear the sight. He had just arrived at the door of the gate to the house when the girl called to him and said:

"Drink before you go, you must be thirsty."

As if hypnotized, Kliwon turned around and returned to the veranda, taking the glass filled with cold lemonade while the girl stood smiling at him warmly.

"Just because you made it for me, Little Miss, I will drink it," said Kliwon.

"But you're wrong, I didn't. Our servant made it for you."

From then on, Kliwon forgot his desire to sleep with the whore Dewi Ayu. This little beauty had erased everything else, destroying his daily life and maybe his future. In the days after that brief encounter, everything changed. He chased away every girl who tried to get close to him, refused every party invitation, and preferred to stay at home mulling over his pathetic romantic fate: a Don Juan brought to his knees by an eight-year-old child. That was the reality, even though nobody else knew what had happened. None of his friends knew about his Sunday visit to Dewi Ayu's house, so no one dared venture a guess as to the cause of his recent introspection. His mother grew quite concerned, because in all of her years raising him, she had never seen Kliwon look this dejected.

"Have you become a communist?" asked his mother, almost in despair. "Only a communist would be so gloomy."

"I'm in love," said Kliwon to his mother.

"That's even worse!" She sat next to Kliwon and stroked his hair that was curly and growing long. "Well, go play your guitar under her bedroom window like you always do."

"I already went, to seduce her mother," said Kliwon, almost weeping. "I didn't get the mother but then all of a sudden I fell in love with her daughter, and I'll never be able to have her."

"Why not? You're telling me there's a girl out there who doesn't want you?"

"Maybe only this one girl," said Kliwon, throwing himself on his mother's lap like a spoiled little kitten. "Her name is Alamanda. And if I have to become a communist, and revolt, and face a firing squad just like father and Comrade Salim in order to get this girl, I will."

"Tell me what this girl is like," said Mina, chilled by her son's vow.

"There's no one in this city, and maybe in the entire universe, who is more beautiful. She is more beautiful than Princess Rengganis who married a dog, at least I think so. She's more beautiful than the queen of the South Seas. She's more beautiful than Helen, who caused the Trojan War. She's more beautiful than Diah Pitaloka who caused the war between the Majapahit and Pajajaran. She's more beautiful than Juliet who made Romeo want to kill himself. She's more beautiful than anyone. It's like her whole body shines, her hair glistens like freshly polished shoes, her face is as soft and smooth as if it had been made from wax, and her smile magnetizes everything around her."

"You would be a good match for a girl like that," said his mother, trying to comfort him.

"The problem is, her breasts haven't even started to grow, and she doesn't even have any pubic hair yet. She's only eight years old, Mama."

Oppressed by his suffering, Kliwon found some release in writing love letters that he never sent. For days he tried to compose the kind of love letter that he thought would be suitable for an eight-year-old girl, but the letters all ended up torn apart in the trash, because in trying to write a love letter fit for a child, he couldn't adequately express his passion. Then he tried to pour out the entire contents of his heart, but he wondered whether the girl would understand what he had written. Finally he gave up.

At that time Kliwon had already graduated from school, two years before his peers. So while everyone else was leaving for school or going to work, he entertained himself with his pursuit of love. Every morning he slipped out of the house and walked toward Dewi Ayu's house, but he never set foot on their front yard. He waited until Alamanda, with her school uniform and school bag, appeared with her younger sister Adinda. He would approach them and offer to walk them both to school.

"Be my guest," said Alamanda. "But don't blame me if you get tired."

He did that every morning. When it was recess, he would stand under a sapodilla tree in front of her classroom, just to watch her play with her friends. When it was time to go home, he was already waiting for her at the gate, and accompanied her back to her house. If the child was in class, or had already gone home, Kliwon would once again descend into a state of gloom. His body seemed to shrink, and he wandered about aimlessly.

"Don't you have anything better to do besides walk next to us?" asked Alamanda one day.

"You're just saying that because you don't yet understand what it means to fall in love," he replied.

"Toy sellers also follow little kids wherever they go," said Alamanda. "I guess I didn't know that was called 'falling in love.'"

The girl truly terrorized him, made him tremble more than if he had encountered a demon. At night Kliwon dreamt about her but his dreams were more like nightmares, because he would startle awake gasping for breath, with his body stiff and covered in sweat. After a while their tepid relationship, which was limited to the walk to and from school, reached a crisis. Kliwon truly could not go on living the rest of his life like this, and one day he collapsed in a fever, the first day he did not walk that girl to school—in fact, he tried to go, but he could only make it as far as his own front door. Mina dragged her son back to his bed, lay him down, and put a cold compress on his forehead while singing soothing hymns like she used to do when he had a fever as a child.

"Just be patient," said his mother. "Seven years from now she will be old enough to love you."

"The problem is," said Kliwon weakly, "I will surely die from unrequited love before that day comes."

His mother went to visit a number of *dukun* and they suggested some spells and mantras that could make someone fall in blind love. His mother didn't want those kinds of spells or mantras—Kliwon would lose his mind if he knew that he had obtained the girl's love with the help of a *dukun*. She was only looking for something that would be able to quell the passion that was tearing her son apart.

"There aren't any spells like that, and there have never been any," said the last *dukun*, after all the *dukun* before him had said the same exact thing.

"So what should I do?"

"Wait until the situation becomes clear: then, either he will get his love or he will die of a broken heart."

When Kliwon had almost recovered from his fever, Mina tried another traditional remedy to make him happy; she took him walking along the beach and they sat in a nearby park while feeding the monkeys and deer. She pampered Kliwon as if he was a six-year-old kid and tried to get him to talk about all kinds of things, anything except that girl named Alamanda.

Meanwhile, Mina also told his friends everything, hoping they could help her solve this complicated problem. They began inviting Kliwon to parties again, asking him to play the guitar and sing. They invited him to come along and steal chickens and fish from other people's ponds, take a trip to the mountains, and camp out at cheerful bonfire parties. The young girls even tried to seduce him again, to capture his heart or at least incite his desire—one even dragged Kliwon into a tent, stripped him naked, and got his dick hard. He wanted to make love to her, but that wouldn't bring back the old Kliwon. He had lost all of his spontaneous humor, lost the jovial cast to his face, and even lost the lust that used to rage atop any available mattress.

None of these efforts were helping, and Kliwon himself knew it. He had been cursed to suffer, and only the love of that little girl could possibly cure him. He wished he could kidnap her, carry her away to some secret place, maybe to the middle of the jungle. They could live together in a cave or in a valley and herd wild goats. He would take care of her himself, watch over her and tend to her needs, and raise her up into a young lady until the time came when he could win her love. He left his friends and once again waited for the little girl in front of her house every morning. The child was surprised to see him reappear after being gone for so long, and asked him, "How are you? I heard you were sick."

"Yeah, I'm sick with love."

"Is love like some kind of malaria?"

"Worse."

Alamanda shuddered, and then leading her little sister, she took off walking toward the school. Kliwon followed and walked next to her miserably, before he finally spoke.

"Listen up, little girl," he said. "Do you want to love me?"

Alamanda stopped and looked at him, and then shook her head.

"Why not?" asked Kliwon, disappointed.

"You yourself just said that love is worse than malaria." Alamanda once again took her little sister's hand and continued walking. For the second time she left Kliwon, who promptly collapsed in another fever and an even more excruciating suffering.

When Kliwon was thirteen, an old man had come to their house with a weird request: "Let me die here." His mother could not refuse such a request, so she invited him in and offered him a drink. Kliwon didn't know how the man would die inside their house; maybe he would die of hunger, because it looked like he hadn't eaten for days. But when his mother invited the man to eat, he ate so ravenously that it seemed as if he wasn't really ready to die. He ate everything put in front of him, even gnawing on the fish bones, leaving not a scrap behind. He let out a satisfied belch and then opened his mouth again to ask, "Where is Comrade?"

"He was shot dead by the Japanese," replied his mother tersely.

"And that kid," asked the guest, "that's the child you had with him?"

"Of course," replied his mother, still a little curt, "I certainly didn't have him with a wild pig."

The guest was named Salim. Even though Mina did not seem pleased by the man's arrival, the guest insisted on staying with them. "I can stay in the bathroom and eat only bran porridge fit for the chickens, as long as you please let me die here."

Kliwon tried to convince his mother that it was better to let the man die in their house than in a drainage ditch. Finally Salim was given the front room, a guest room that had never been used, and Kliwon promised he would keep bringing him food until the moment he died.

He was not a vagabond. As soon as he took off his shoes Kliwon could see that the skin on his feet was covered in blisters.

"Are you a fugitive?" asked Kliwon.

"Yeah, tomorrow they are coming to execute me."

"Why? Did you steal something from someone?"

"From the Republic of Indonesia."

This exchange led them into a friendship. Salim even gave the kid his short-brimmed cap, saying that he had gotten it when he was still back in Russia, and explaining that all the Russian workers wore a cap just like that one. He had visited many countries, he said, ever since 1926.

"But it wasn't like you were on vacation," said Kliwon.

"You're right, I was a fugitive."

"Who did you steal from that time?"

"The Dutch East Indies."

The man was a rebel and a communist, an old-time kind of communist, one of the few people who had gotten their ideas directly from the Dutch communist named Sneevliet, and his nickname was Comrade Salim. He admitted that he knew Semaun well and had been a member of the Indonesian Communist Party ever since its inception. When they were in Semarang he had even brought warm milk to Tan Malaka, who was sick with tuberculosis, every morning. The *Partai Komunis Indonesia*, the PKI, was the first organization to use the name Indonesia, he said with pride. And, he added, it was the first to resist the colonial government. But the Dutch Indies administration had hated them, even before they rebelled. Sneevliet had been banished in 1919, and his compatriot Semaun was exiled four years later, one year after Tan Malaka. Other figures, including himself, packed their bags and prepared to be exiled or thrown in prison.

As it turned out, the colonial government decided to capture him in the month of January, 1926. Apparently they had heard about the stirrings of revolution, which had been discussed in Prambanan a month before. Salim was never thrown in prison, because he managed to escaped to Singapore along with some others. That was the first time he went wandering, even though he was not a wanderer.

"If someone says he is a communist but has no intention to rebel," he said to Kliwon, "don't believe he's really a communist."

He lay on top of the bed in a weird way: stark naked. He took off all of his dirty garments that stank of mud, and even though Kliwon generously offered to lend him his father's old clothes, Salim refused. At first Kliwon felt awkward but after a while he sat on the chair near the door, facing the bare old man as comfortably as he could.

"I want to die with nothing," said Comrade Salim. "I am afraid they are going to shoot me before I wake up."

"If that's how you feel, don't go to sleep," said Kliwon. "Once you are dead you can sleep for as long as you want. Forever."

It was true. So the man tried to keep his eyes open even though Kliwon knew he must be exhausted. To make sure he didn't fall asleep, Comrade Salim talked continuously, sometimes rambling incoherently, and sometimes sounding as if he were reciting a lamentation. Kliwon thought he was delirious. He said that he was very close with the president of the republic. They used to live in the same quarters in Surabaya, they studied under the same teacher, and sometimes they fell in love with the same woman. And later, when he came home for the first time after running away and spending a long time in Moscow, he had reunited with the president. They had embraced, their eyes welling up with tears of joy.

"Maybe you don't believe me now, but at some point you'll read all about it in the newspapers," he said. "And yet, now that very same man is sending soldiers to murder me."

"Why?" asked Kliwon.

"That's what happens when you steal something that belongs to someone else," replied Comrade Salim.

"Who else have you stolen from?"

"I already told you: the Republic of Indonesia."

Hesitation, he said, was the source of the Communist Party's failed revolution in 1926. He met with Tan Malaka in Singapore, after his first escape, to discuss their strategy. Tan Malaka strongly opposed the idea of revolution, because he felt the communists weren't ready. So he went to Moscow to get the input of the Comintern, but the Comintern forbade it even more vehemently.

"I was held by Stalin for three months," said Comrade Salim, "to be de-reindoctrinated."

But the idea of revolution had already filled his head. After he was allowed to leave Moscow, he returned to Singapore intending to carry it out—even if no one else supported him, even if he had to do it guerrilla-style. But it turned out that revolution had already erupted, and had failed. The colonial government had forced the

Party to disband, and all of its activities were forbidden. Most of its organizers were imprisoned, if not thrown into Boven-Digoel. What was even more frustrating was that the Comintern now supported the revolution, but it was a joke that came a little too late.

"I was yanked back to Moscow," he said, "for school."

He explained that there was still time for another revolution, at a future opportunity when it would be more likely to succeed. He had heard some bad news, that after being thrown into Boven-Digoel some communists had surrendered and chosen to collaborate with the colonial government. Those who persisted in their beliefs were exiled even farther, to places where malaria could kill them without mercy.

He stood up because he had to go to the toilet, and Kliwon rushed to wrap the man's body with a sarong, saying, "My mother will scream to high heaven if she sees you walking throughout the house stark naked."

Even though he let his body be covered, Comrade Salim retorted, "What's the difference, tomorrow she's going to see me stark naked *and* dead."

They continued their chat, now out on the verandah, with Comrade Salim still wearing only a sarong. From where they sat they could see the expanse of dark ocean flecked with lights from the fishermen's lanterns, and they could hear the sound of the peacefully pounding waves. The kid asked what the communists were looking for and Comrade Salim replied, "Heaven." At the stroke of midnight, they saw a truck pass by, filled with KNIL soldiers, but the soldiers didn't see the pair sitting on the unlit veranda.

"The world is changing," said Comrade Salim. For hundreds of years, more than half of the face of this earth has been controlled by European countries and turned into colonies, and the Europeans have sucked up whatever they could find, brought it all home, and made themselves rich. But not Germany and Japan; they didn't get anything. But now they have just as much power as any other developed country, and so they are demanding their share. That is the origin of this war, a war between greedy nations. (Comrade Salim asked if there were any cigarettes, and Kliwon went to fetch his tobacco from his room.) The natives are the most pathetic people, as wretched as can be. After so many years of living under rajas and being lied to by kings, all of a sudden the Europeans came, and they didn't even understand the excessive and crazy sense of respect that was still alive in the land of Java. Farmers, after they have been forced into labor and forced to hand over most of their harvest to the colonial government, still bow in the street whenever a young Dutch girl is passing by. Communism was born from a beautiful dream, the likes of which there will never be again on the face of this earth: that there would no longer be lazy men who eat their fill while others work hard and starve. Kliwon asked whether revolution was the way to achieve that beautiful dream.

"It's true," replied Comrade Salim, "that oppressed people only have one tool of resistance: run amok. And if I have to tell you, revolution is nothing more than a collective running amok, organized by one particular party."

His only reason for communist rebellion was the fact that the bourgeoisie would never negotiate peacefully. They would never surrender their power without a fight, they would never freely give away their riches, and they certainly would never agree to the loss of their comfortable lifestyle. They did not want to share, because then there would be nobody left to fetch and serve their coffee, nobody left to wash their clothes, nobody left to fix their engines, nobody left to pick their cocoa beans. In the communist world, everyone had the right to be lazy and everyone had the responsibility to work as well. "The bourgeoisie wouldn't want that, so the only option is to revolt."

Salim had returned home from abroad a few days before the Independence Day celebration. The republic had stood for three years, but the Dutch were still everywhere. Even more upsetting, the republic had lost in every war and at every negotiation table, so that it only controlled a small area of the interior. He met with the president of the republic, his old friend, who immediately said to him, "Help us fortify this country and launch a revolution."

"That indeed is my responsibility. *Ik kom hier om orde te scheppen*," he said. I came to get everything in order.

He believed the source of all the chaos ultimately originated from the president of the republic himself, and the vice president, and the officials and the party men. "They sold the people as little more than slaves during the Japanese occupation, now they are selling the territory to the Dutch," he said. The only group that he still trusted was the Indonesian Communist Party. He was openly received by the party, even though he quickly discovered that the PKI had made some crucial mistakes in the orientation of their struggle. He wanted to redirect it, and they handed over everything to him, this savior who had just come from Moscow. One month after his arrival, revolt finally erupted in Madiun—yes, of course it was the communists. He himself wasn't there when it started, but then he went to give some moral support. The revolution only lasted a week, and then he became a fugitive.

"So now, here I am, waiting for my grave to be dug."

"You have already walked a long road," said Kliwon. "There is still time if you want to escape."

"I have experienced revolution twice, and both times it failed, and that is enough to make me know what I am worth," the man said with a bitter sadness. "The time has come for me to die, so I'm sure that even if I do run away again I won't escape my fate."

Kliwon didn't understand this line of reasoning at all.

"But if you die, everything is over."

Comrade Salim closed his eyes, squinting against the night breeze that brushed across his face. "Now it's your turn, Comrade."

Comrade Salim admitted that he was not a good Marxist, that he didn't understand all that class theory yet, but he was fairly certain that injustice had to be fought in any way possible. There are no Marxists in this country, he said, but there are plenty of starving masses, who work more than what they get for it in return, who have to bend their knees every time a big man appears, who know nothing except that the one way to be free from all of that is to rebel. Think about it, he said, there are thousands of laborers in sugar factories all across the sugarcane plantations. They work for the whole year, while the plantation owners enjoy the comfort of their weekend and vacation homes in the foothills. The laborers only get enough compensation to live payday to payday, while the plantation owners reap their mammoth profits. The same thing happens in the tea plantations. That's the only reason we need to rebel, and the only Marxist phrase that we need to keep in our hearts is this: Workers of the world, unite!

When the cock's crow was heard in the distance, their conversation trailed off as if they had begun to smell the odor of death. Comrade Salim was silent in his chair, as if he had died before his time had come. He didn't sleep, in fact he was fully alert, waiting patiently for his last morning to begin. "Like the pious who believe they will get into heaven, I am a true communist and not afraid to die," he said in a quiet, almost inaudible voice.

"Do you believe in God?" asked Kliwon tentatively.

"That's irrelevant," Salim replied. "It's not man's job to think about whether God exists or not, especially when you know that right in front of your eyes one person is stepping on another's neck."

"So you are going to hell."

"I'd *rather* go to hell, because I have spent my whole life trying to eliminate any man's superiority over other men." He continued, "If I might share my opinion, this world is hell, and our task is to create our own heaven."

His last morning came, and just as Comrade Salim had predicted, a republican squad led by a captain suddenly appeared, coming to execute him. They came quietly, wearing civilian clothes, because Halimunda was in a KNIL-occupied area. The squad surrounded Salim while he was still sitting peacefully with Kliwon on the veranda.

"He wants to die naked, as pure as the day he was born," said Kliwon.

"That's impossible," said the Captain. "Nobody wants to see his privates dangling everywhere, especially since he's a communist."

"But it's his final request."

"No way."

"Well if that's how you feel, then do it in the bathroom," said Kliwon. "Let him stay naked. Maybe he wants to take a shit first, and then shoot him."

"Communist Number One dying in a bathroom," said the Captain while shaking his head. "Now that's a great story for the history books."

And that's how it ended. Comrade Salim threw off his sarong, smeared himself with earth while drawing in deep breaths of fresh air, as if to say goodbye to the world. Kliwon and the Captain and a number of soldiers followed him to the bathroom, with Kliwon hoping that the morning's fuss didn't wake his mother. In the bathroom, before being shot dead, he sang *The Blood of the People* and the *Internationale*, bringing Kliwon to tears. As soon as the second song was finished, the Captain pointed his pistol through the door, which was open a crack, and shot him three times, one shot right after another. Comrade Salim died naked in the bathroom: he was born with nothing, and when he died still had nothing. Mina was awakened by the pistol shots, ran to see what had happened, and found a couple of soldiers dragging out the man's corpse while her son looked on.

"You have seen your father executed by Japan," she said. "Now you are seeing this man dead at the hands of the republican army. Use your head, and don't even for one second consider becoming a communist."

"Many kings have been hanged to death," said Kliwon, "but that doesn't discourage people from wanting to become king."

"Did he influence you at all last night?" asked Mina with a twinge of worry.

"At the very least, he made me catch a cold in the night air."

The soldiers brought the corpse to a crossroads. They weren't worried about the KNIL patrol, because at such an hour they obviously wouldn't be awake yet. Kliwon followed them, and witnessed Comrade Salim's corpse sprawled out in the middle of the street. Standing amid the crowd who came to see the corpse adorned with three bullet holes, Kliwon was still wearing his newly-gifted cap, which he would wear for many years, and which he would still be wearing on the day the army came to execute him. Salim's blood was streaming out everywhere. A soldier poured gasoline over him, and another soldier tossed a match. As the corpse burned, it smelled like roasted boar.

"Who is that?" asked a man.

"Clearly not a pig," said Kliwon.

The kid stayed by his side until the flames died out and the soldiers disappeared. He gathered the ashes, put them into a small box, and brought them home. His mother was concerned by the excessive behavior her son was displaying, and said that the ashes would bring bad luck.

"And take off that cap."

He took off the cap and placed it on the table, then climbed into bed.

"Praise God," said his mother, "you are a sweet child."

"Don't misunderstand, Mama," said Kliwon. "I'm only taking off the cap because I've been awake for a long time and now I want to get some sleep."

Kliwon sat on the sidewalk in front of a store that was closed, ripping cigarette advertisement posters that he had torn haphazardly down from the walls to shreds. While ruminating over his pathetic love, he watched the cars going past, asking himself whether there was anyone else in the world more wretched than he was. His mother and his friends had already ordered him to make himself feel better, but he refused by saying that nothing could possibly make him feel better except having that young girl for his very own.

"Go look for someone else who is more unfortunate than you," said Mina finally, "and maybe that will make you feel just a little bit better."

The first people he thought of were his father and Comrade Salim, both executed. In her carelessness, Mina hadn't realized that her suggestion would remind Kliwon of those two men. For a whole week he just sat on the sidewalk to watch the wretched people Comrade Salim had told him about, the same people his father used to talk about when he was just a little boy. He wanted to see people passing by in their German or American cars while right next to him sat a beggar with a body covered in ulcers and boils. He wanted to see a young woman going to market, surrounded by servants who carried all of her baskets and even the very parasol that sheltered her. He wanted to see all of these social contradictions for himself, to distract himself more than anything else, thinking how depressing it was that a man could be destroyed by love while others were dying from starvation or being worked half to death.

He had been gone from his house for more than a month and was now living with the beggars. His body, that used to be strong and handsome, soon became emaciated and was now just a pile of bones, and his hair was turning a pale red and looked as stiff as the tip of a broom. He was in no way pretending; rather, he was trying to erase his suffering with another kind of suffering. He ate what others gave him, and if no one gave him anything he scavenged in garbage cans, fighting off other beggars, stray dogs, and rats.

There were no more girls following him wherever he went. In fact it was quite the opposite; if a girl met him, without realizing that he was the Kliwon that used to drive her crazy and maybe even used to take her to bed, she would pinch her nose, gag, shield her face, and quicken her pace. Even little children threw stones at him, so that he often found himself covered in wounds, and the stray dogs chased him as if he was a hedgehog ready to be devoured. Even when he went home, Mina didn't recognize him at all, and instead she said, "If you see a beggar named Kliwon, tell him to come home, his mother is dying and wants to see him one last time."

Kliwon accepted a plate of rice from his mother and replied, "You sure don't look like you are dying."

"It's no big deal to lie a little."

After a long time had passed, he began to lead this kind of life as if it was normal. He began to forget many things—his mother and his house, his friends and all the girls, and especially Alamanda (although this last memory still troubled his thoughts at certain times); everything was erased by his routine of bumming. Rather than thinking about these things, he thought about finding a handful of rice and a comfortable place to lie down, which came to seem way more important. The freedom from all his complicated thoughts turned him into a happy hobo, until the day trouble came to him in the form of a young beggar woman named Isah Betina.

He saw her twice. Once was while she was getting raped by five rampaging vagrants near the edge of the dump and it was obvious that he would be unable to fight off her attackers. But he had also seen her pass by before being ambushed by those five bums, looking pretty but also stinking to high heaven after weeks untouched by water or soap. Her wails were quite heartbreaking and so disturbed his afternoon nap inside his cardboard shanty that he came out carrying a machete and approached. Two of the men had just finished fucking her, and both were grinning while wiping off their genitals with the bottoms of their shirts. Another one was thrusting his spear, struggling in and out, but the girl was no longer putting up a fight. Another was squeezing her breasts, while the last guy was waiting impatiently, stroking his own dick with his hand.

"Give the girl to me," said Kliwon, clearly and firmly.

One of the men who was already done screwing the girl, and who looked like the leader of this group of bums, stood facing him while rolling up his sleeves.

"I said, give the girl to me," Kliwon repeated.

"You'll have to get by my dead body before you can have a go."

"Fine." And before any of them realized he had a machete hidden behind his back, Kliwon had drawn the weapon across the attacker's neck. The man's blood splattered out as his head drooped, his neck almost broken, and in a number of seconds he had collapsed on the ground, obviously dead. Kliwon kicked his corpse, and approached the four remaining men. "I got by his dead body, now give me the girl."

The man who was in the middle of screwing the girl quickly pulled out his dick with a disgusting splosh and ran away with a face as pale as rotten bread, followed by his three friends. They left the girl behind just like that, lying on her back on a tabletop that no longer had any legs attached to it, naked and unconscious. After wrapping the girl in his own shirt, Kliwon carried her on his back to his hut. He lay her down on his bed, which was an old sofa, and looked at her for a moment before he himself lay down on top of a pile of old newspapers and fell asleep.

When he awoke night had already fallen and he found the girl sitting on the sofa hugging her knees and shivering with hunger. She was still as bare as when he had laid her down, only slightly covered by the shirt draped across her shoulders. Kliwon gave her some corn porridge directly from the pot, nothing more than the cold and almost spoiled leftovers from breakfast, but the girl ate with gusto. The whole time Kliwon sat next to her, observing her with the diligent attention of a small child. The girl ate without acknowledging his presence. She didn't look traumatized in the least, or maybe she had already forgotten what had happened. Now Kliwon could see her light hair that looked like silk, her piercing eyes, her narrow nose, her thin lips.

"What's your name?" asked Kliwon.

She didn't respond, only placed the pan of porridge under the old sofa and sat down again looking at Kliwon with the shy demeanor of a young virgin. Her hand reached for Kliwon's hand, touching it with the tenderness of a lover. Kliwon shivered for a moment, and before he realized what was happening the girl had already jumped toward him, knocking the man backwards on top of the sofa with her on top of his body, hugging him tightly and kissing him in an almost violent attack. At first Kliwon tried to push her away with all his might, but then he hesitated, and stayed still with his hands up like a man surrendering in front of a firing squad. Then when the girl pulled off his shirt, and he felt the touch of her firm round breasts against his chest, everything dissolved into a mesmerizing warmth. He once again felt passionate blood voraciously pumping through his veins, returned the girl's embrace, returned her kisses, and took off his pants.

After such a brutal rampage of being raped by five homeless bums, the girl now showed herself to be a wild lover. Kliwon himself even forgot all about what had happened, holding the girl tight and reversing their position so that now he was on top, both of them naked and aroused. They overcame the limitations of the cramped sofa and made love with repetitive movements that were nevertheless full of lust, jolting and jarring and shuddering, like a boat blasted by a storm.

Then when their lovemaking was finished, Kliwon quickly remembered that he didn't know this girl at all, just as this girl didn't know him. They were still lying down together on top of the sofa, holding one another, exhausted. Kliwon asked her again, "What's your name?" But as before, the girl did not reply. She just smiled, muttered incoherently and perhaps deliriously, before closing her eyes and falling into a deep sleep, emitting gentle snores.

"Her name is Isah Betina," a bum told him not long after that, "because that's what everybody calls her."

"Where did she come from?" Kliwon pursued his line of questioning.

"They found her a week ago by the side of the road, and had been gang-raping her almost every day, before you came along and killed one of them," said the bum. "That girl's brain is scrambled."

So that's how it was. Kliwon couldn't imagine what his friends would say, if they knew that he had slept with a crazy girl. But outside of his own sound logic, or maybe because of some other urge, the first thing he did was bring the girl to the beach and clean her body, and get her some better clothes that he stole from his mother's clothesline. They lived in his cardboard hut, with the old sofa where sometimes they sat and relaxed while eating walnuts they had smashed open with stones, and where other times they slept or made love, next to a stove made from a heap of bricks and a pot to cook with. They never heard what happened to Isah Betina's vagrant rapists, even though for a while Kliwon had been worried they would return to seek revenge. And now that Isah Betina lived in the same house with Kliwon, everyone agreed that the two were officially a couple, and no one bothered the crazy girl any more.

Kliwon himself seemed to have forgotten his original reason for becoming a vagabond beggar. No longer seeking the unfortunate to distract him and no longer tormenting himself in an effort to forget his grief over the rejection of his love by the little girl Alamanda, he discovered the best way to forget the girl, which was another girl. And his chaotic life, without anything to eat or a proper place to live, didn't make him suffer—in fact, he was delighted with his current situation. He had rediscovered the ardor of love in full bloom, above all because Isah Betina received his love with an equal warmth, making them both immediately forget their squalid conditions. Intoxicated with love, no one would have guessed that Isah Betina was a crazy girl. And Kliwon didn't care about the fact that he didn't know her background, promising her, "I am going to marry you someday." They didn't do very much except caress one another almost all day and all night long, only stopping to eat when they were hungry or to sleep when they were tired. The sofa was their favorite place to make love, with moans that awoke and then aroused the neighbors in the middle of the night. Their behavior made people jealous but was understood as the honeymoon phase of a new pair of lovers, a phase that continued for weeks on end.

One night in the middle of one of their usual sessions, a snake slithered out from a pile of trash and entered their hut and bit the tip of Isah Betina's toe, which was lying in its path. The girl didn't cry out, absorbed in her lovemaking until they both reached the highest climax they had ever achieved. But their amazing good fortune would not last. After ejaculating, Kliwon collapsed on his side and heard the girl moan and writhe. He thought she still wanted him, but when he saw her leg turning blue he realized what had happened. It was too late; the snake that had bitten her was a poisonous cobra, and the girl died on that very same sofa, naked and still gleaming with the sweat of their lovemaking.

The neighbors, who were fed up with the nightly shrieking, interpreted this tragedy as retribution for the couple's casual relationship, which in their eyes was based on little more than fooling around. Kliwon brought the girl's corpse to Kamino the gravedigger, and asked for the kind of burial that was usually given to pious believers. Only Kliwon accompanied the gravedigger in the procession, arriving in some fine clothes he had stolen from someone's house. "She lived only to make me happy," he said, weeping.

He went off on the seventh day of mourning, burning their hut to the ground, and the flames had almost spread to the neighboring cardboard huts when the owners came running with sewer water as fast as they could to put out the fire. He went crazy, throwing dog shit at people and throwing rocks up at the streetlights. His grief couldn't be contained. He broke the windows in all the bakeries lining Jalan Merdeka with rocks as big as the palms of his hands, making the lady shopkeepers scream in panic. He hurt a mailman after stealing his bicycle, sending him rolling with his letters scattering in the street. He killed three dogs who appeared from rich people's yards, slashed the tires of cars that were parked in front of the movie theater, and burnt a security post. All of this provoked an aggressive response from the police, and he was quickly captured without a fight as he was trying to tear down the wall that marked the city limits.

He was captured without anyone caring whether he was to be taken to the courthouse or not. In his solitary cell, Kliwon found his peace returning, his old solemnity slowly reemerging and gathering force. The only disturbance he caused now was at night, when he would talk in his sleep, deliriously calling Isah Betina's name with earsplitting shrieks, drowning out the howls of the wild dogs and the yowls of mating cats. The news of the man imprisoned because he was suffering from lost love spread and reached his mother. Kliwon was held for seven months until Mina came and bailed him out. She dragged Kliwon home like an angry mother who finds her kid playing in the cow stables. "Is there nothing more important to you than the love of a woman?" she asked crankily, bathing him herself despite the fact that her son was now a grown man.

The house was still just as it had been when he left. All of the furniture and things were right where he had left them. He read pulp novels and love stories with happy endings, which girls had given him as gifts, in a fruitless attempt to make himself feel better. He also read the many love letters that those same girls had written him, but of course it all just made him more and more gloomy. It was as if everything had gone back to the beginning, to the same sadness, the same heartbreak. He tried to find his friends, a number of whom were now married with children, asking for just a little bit of their happiness. He also visited a number of his old girlfriends, a number of whom were also married, and some of whom were even already divorced, and he tried to sleep with three or four of them again, just to feel the warmth of love one more time. But it all made him miss Isah Betina all over again.

"Go back to living on the streets," said his mother. "Maybe you can find another love."

"That's what I'm going to do," he said.

He had already packed up all his things, with the hope that if he returned one day, they would be waiting for him nicely and neatly. He had taken the books that were previously scattered across his bed, table, and floor and had arranged them into cardboard boxes which he stacked in a corner of his room. He had also straightened up all the clothes in his closet, put away his old guitar, and stored all of his records. He had even neatly stashed his razor and his toothbrush in a drawer. There was only one thing that remained on top of the table, but he wasn't going to store it anywhere, because he chose to wear it instead: the cap Comrade Salim had given him. He stood in front of the mirror, looking at his reflection there. His body had become quite slender from his years of suffering, and he had a gaunt face and dull eyes. His hair still hung in inch-long ringlets. He stood there for a long time, peering at the cap and wondering whether it was true what the communist had told him, that all the laborers in Russia wore that kind of hat.

"Look at this gloomy person," he said to his reflection. "Gloomy enough to wear this hat."

Mina then appeared and stood in the doorway, looking at her son still standing in front of the mirror. She tried to guess where Kliwon was going wearing his neatly ironed pants, his cotton shirt, and that cap.

"You don't look like a beggar, child."

"Starting now and from this day forward," said Kliwon while turning to face his mother, "call me Comrade Kliwon, Mama."

{8}

ONE FOGGY MORNING, the throngs of people crowding the platform of Halimunda Station were astonished by a fantastic sight the likes of which they had never seen before. In front of the ticket counter, under an almond tree, two lovers were kissing passionately with no thought for the time or place. Their kisses were so full of heat that the people who witnessed the event and told the story for years to come would swear they saw a flame ignite between the couple's lips. And this became legend, because those two lovers were Kliwon and Alamanda. Both men and women would remember the event with a keen envy.

The couple's provocative behavior had indeed already become quite well known during those last weeks before Kliwon went to Jakarta, the capital city, to study at university.

Alamanda and Kliwon were dating and everyone thought they were the most beautiful couple that had ever existed on the face of the earth, except for Adinda. But Alamanda would shove her fingers in her ears when Adinda said you are a cheap slut who likes to break men's hearts, stop it right now, at least for the sake of this one man. Perhaps the girl still remembered how hard Kliwon had fallen for Alamanda when her older sister was only eight years old, and perhaps she felt it would be a shame for her sister to purposefully destroy a love as incredible as that. Adinda even swore that if Alamanda dared hurt the man, she would kill her. According to her, to flat out refuse his love would be way better than to accept it only to then toss it aside like trash. Alamanda didn't care about any of the threats that came out of her younger sister's mouth, and it became all the more evident that she was a stubborn young woman who couldn't be told what to do.

"Just admit that you are jealous, little girl," she said.

"If I was going to be jealous of someone it would be Mama, who has already slept with *hundreds* of men," said Adinda.

"You think I can't sleep with a man?"

"I'm sure you could sleep with every single man in this city, and be just as awesome as Mama," said Adinda, "but there's no way that you could properly love all of them."

Unlike her sister, who tended to be a homebody, Alamanda spent her days going to concerts with her sweetheart and their friends, and gathering in any place they could find to sing along to a guitar. They went out on the town and they went to the movies, so that sometimes she didn't come home until night was already turning into dawn. Even though her two little sisters would be waiting at the window with anxious faces, she would go straight to her room without saying a word, still humming some bars from one of those whiny love songs that were so popular at the time.

"You're worse than a prostitute," said Adinda crankily. "At least when prostitutes come home they bring some money with them."

"Just say it, Little Miss Grouch," said Alamanda from inside her room. "Or should I say it for you once again? You've fallen in love with Kliwon."

"Even if I was in love with him, I would never say it because if I did you would kill yourself."

It was not just a rumor, the youth was indeed quite popular with the ladies, not just in that house but throughout all of Halimunda. Actually, he had been that popular ever since he was a little boy, when people had been surprised by his brainpower because he could solve sixth-grade exam problems when he was still only in fifth grade and the principal decided to let him skip a grade. In middle school he won all the math competitions, and because he could also play the guitar and sing and his handsome face was so convincing, he began to go out at night, accompanied by the gangs of girls who had fallen in love with him.

That was when he would go out with whichever girl he wanted, before he fell in love with Alamanda who was only eight years old, became homeless, and had a relationship with a crazy girl named Isah Betina. Now everyone said that he and Alamanda were an extraordinary couple, a bright and handsome youth and a beautiful young girl heir to the most esteemed prostitute in the city. Everyone except Adinda, that is, who felt that it was nothing short of a complete catastrophe. So far Alamanda had already been with a lot of men, and had cast them each aside one by one. She had a bad reputation, and everyone knew it, including Adinda.

Alamanda had done this to a number of her classmates, provoking them with her beauty, her captivating smile, her coquettish sideways glances, her graceful steps, and other things like that, which induced insomnia in many of her peers. Some of these guys would try to pursue her and then she would begin to change, turning into a half-tamed turtledove who hops away every time you try to catch it.

But her pursuers wouldn't give up so easily, so they buried her under charming flirtations, drowned her in promises, and showered her with gifts, idle chatter, flowers, cards, letters, poetry, and songs. She would accept all of these and give an even more captivating smile in return, repay them with even more coquettish glances, with the sight of her steps that grew even more graceful, throwing in the extra bonus of a morsel of praise, saying you are a kind man, clever and handsome, with really good hair, and they would feel flattered, floating above the stars.

Each would grow ever more confident, feeling like the handsomest guy on earth, like the kindest man in the universe with the best hair on the planet, and convinced by all of this at the first opportunity that arose they would speak up or send a letter spewing their prehistoric pent-up desires: *Alamanda, I love you.* That was the best time to destroy a man, to shake him up, to tear his heart to pieces, the best opportunity to show a woman's superiority, so Alamanda would say, *I do not love you.*

"I like men," Alamanda said once, "but I like to see them cry from heartbreak even more."

She had played this game many times, and always enjoyed herself from one round to the next, even though it always turned out predictably in the end: she would be the winner and they would be the loser. And she would laugh heartily as a new suitor replaced the old suitor.

Imagine, she had already been doing this since she turned thirteen, two years ago. It cannot be denied that in fact she had inherited her mother's almost perfect beauty as well as the piercing eyes of the Japanese man who had fucked her mother. She first realized that she could capture a man's heart when Kliwon fell in love with her, back when she was eight years old. But then, when she was thirteen, two boys got into a fight just because they were debating the color of her underwear. The first one swore that he saw Alamanda wearing red underwear, but the other insisted she was wearing white underwear. They fought in the back of the classroom, beating each other to a pulp without a single person trying to step in—in fact, it served as free entertainment until the teacher realized what was going on. Once the two boys were both swollen and bloody from the tussle, Alamanda stepped in to mediate and said to the pair:

"I am wearing white underpants, but they are red too, because I have my period."

From that moment on she realized that her beauty was not just a sword that could cripple men, but also an instrument that could control them. Her mother grew worried and gave her a warning.

"Don't you know what men did to women during the war?"

"I know just what you have always told me," replied Alamanda. "And now you will see what women can do to men during a time of peace."

"What do you mean, child?"

"In times of peace, you have made many men line up and pay to sleep with you, and I've made many boys cry from a broken heart."

Dewi Ayu had long been concerned by her eldest daughter's stubborn nature, and followed her goings-on through the gossip that men brought to her bed about the number of young boys who had been driven insane by her beauty. "The only thing I can be thankful for is that she hasn't become a prostitute," said Dewi Ayu to her customers, "because if she had, maybe you wouldn't be here with me in this bed right now."

That was Alamanda. She had even succeeded in conquering Kliwon, the idol of so many girls in Halimunda; what made him different from all the other guys she conquered was that at the end of the game she didn't toss him aside, because it turned out she had fallen in love with him too. Alamanda had heard about the boy's reputation because the older neighbor girls were always whispering to each other about him, the handsomest guy in the world.

There were some nonsense rumors that he wasn't really the child of Mina the widow and her late husband the communist, who had been executed by the Japanese after the communists lost the rebellion at Madiun, when many people had had enough of anything associated with communism. One girl fabricated the story that he was discovered by that couple, curled up inside a large watermelon they found on the riverbank; he was the child of a nymph who took pity on their misfortune and entrusted her child to them for a time to alleviate them both from their eternal sin. Another girl said that he had descended from a rainbow when he was a baby, and another said he was found inside a gigantic cone-shaped flower, although, truth be told, not one of these girls had even been alive when Kliwon was born.

Such stories weren't just spread by the girls who had secretly fallen in love with him, but even the older folk swore that when he was born the stars shone a little brighter than usual in that city, as if the world was waiting for the birth of a new prophet, and the Dutch who were roaming around Halimunda at that time had taken it as a bad omen.

But whether all of that talk was true or not, Alamanda had been intrigued by that man ever since his sincere confession of love when she was eight years old, and for years after that she still heard stories about him, even though it was said that he had disappeared. The whole time that he was homeless and most people didn't know much about what had happened to him, the young girls still talked about him and missed him half to death. Many of them believed he might have been kidnapped by a band of robbers, who knows why, then taken somewhere and killed. Others believed that he had hidden himself away because he felt his soul was in peril. Whatever story they believed, Kliwon became a mythical hero to many young girls, almost rivaling the heroism of Shodancho in that city.

Alamanda was already fifteen years old when Kliwon finally reappeared. The man was now twenty-four, and he called himself Comrade Kliwon. When he returned from his life of vagrancy he became a tailor working beside his mother in their home, but that didn't mean very much because really he just shared the same old income that his mother had always made, only pulling in a little bit extra from the few girls who tried to get his attention by asking him to sew them a new dress. He soon left his undistinguished career as a tailor and joined one of his friends building boats. At that time fiberglass was still quite expensive, so they used black tar to patch the wooden boats and that was his job in the boat shop, along with some touch-up paint jobs, until he moved on to work at a mushroom farm belonging to Old Kuwu, with the primary tasks of keeping an eye on the barn thermometer to make sure it stayed at the right temperature and stirring the chaff. Other times he joined in spreading yeast, harvesting the mushrooms, wrapping them, hauling them, and doing whatever else he was asked to do. It was clear by that time that he had already become a cadre of the Communist Party, which had been one of the three main parties in the city election four years before (and it looked as though it could have become the majority party, were it not for the trauma the people of Halimunda had suffered during the revolution), and he was the youngest member to be found in the Party's headquarters, which was located on the corner of Jalan Belanda.

The Communist Party was using his reputation to lure the young girls into becoming their cadre, after it became evident that whenever they brought Comrade Kliwon to speak at the podium at public meetings the audience would be packed and the girls would be shrieking hysterically. Comrade Kliwon was indeed quite handsome and what's more, a skilled speaker. Alamanda went to see him speak once, at a labor day carnival, intrigued by her friends' hysteria. Many people were of the opinion that if the Communist Party obtained the majority vote in their city, it would be because of Comrade Kliwon.

When Alamanda was tempted to conquer the most handsome man in the city, she already had the distinguished reputation of being the only young girl to have disappointed twenty-three different men who had fallen in love with her, while Kliwon had already gone out with twelve girls in a fairly brief period of time and turned down the rest. It was to be a competition between the most formidable warriors, and it was not only the workers at the farm who were waiting for the outcome of the competition but also all of the members of the Communist Party, and all the city-dwellers' hearts were pounding in anticipation, wondering what was going to happen. A number of them even placed bets as to who would disappoint whom, and the young men and women prematurely prepared to be brokenhearted.

When the school ordered the students to start their job training, Alamanda convinced a number of her friends to intern at Old Kuwu's mushroom farm. And that was how the two met—on a mushroom farm, in the middle of the hot barn, surrounded by plastic tarps. Alamanda would come to the barn, pretending that she wanted to help with the daily morning mushroom harvest, and there she would meet that man, tempting him with her smile or teasing him by leaving the neck of her dress unbuttoned. The man watched her from the rack on the fourth level of the barn while she stood below, further tempting him with some inconsequential request. The man faced her with a measured calm, brashly admiring her magnificence as if he didn't care that a number of years ago he had been driven almost completely insane by that same wounding beauty.

They met every day during those weeks, stirring the chaff together, debating how high the temperature should be set, disputing how big the mushrooms had to be before they could be harvested, and arguing about whether the yeast should be sown on top of the chaff.

Standing there facing her among the bamboo poles propping up the racks of mushrooms Kliwon said finally, "Miss, you are pretty but you are so quarrelsome," before leaving Alamanda and going out to join the other laborers who were resting after their day's work.

Jerk, thought Alamanda. That guy wasn't meant to walk away and leave her just like that, he was meant to seduce her more fervently, pursue her, before she could then toss him aside as usual. Alamanda stood in the door of the barn, watching the man relaxing with his friends, sitting at the edge of the field, passing out cigarettes and lighting them, everyone exhaling the smoke into the open air, talking and laughing.

That was when she lost control of the situation, and for the first time ever she herself was struck by the insomnia of love, every night waiting for morning to come so she could return to the mushroom barn and be with that man, wondering whether the fever of love was still ravaging him or not. When she began to realize that she had truly fallen in love, she was horrified that she had been conquered and tried to kill those amorous feelings by thinking of the most appalling ways to make the man fall at her feet. And whether she cared about him or not she would still toss him aside just like that, in revenge for having made her love him. But every time they met, the man simply accepted the blessing of that beautiful girl's presence in the mushroom barn without exerting any further effort, as if he was overjoyed simply to have her keep him company.

Alamanda sunk even deeper into the feelings of love that she could not control, enraptured by her discovery of such an unusual man, who looked at her admiringly, who examined every curve of her body with desire, but who still didn't budge from his business of yeast and mushrooms. Alamanda began to dream about him seducing her, sending her flowers and love letters. She wanted to see him do all the embarrassing things he used to do when she was only eight years old, and she finally surrendered to the fact that she truly had fallen in love with him, no longer feeling the need to resist her heart. But this guy still did not change his attitude toward Alamanda one iota, despite the fact that she continued to make it obvious that she liked him by asking for a ride somewhere in a petulant voice or standing very close to him while he worked, until finally, scared that she was floundering even further, Alamanda convinced herself that her love was unrequited and she decided to give in and admit her defeat.

Okay, she told herself, *I am not going to try to get your attention.* But just when she had given up, and no longer hoped to have that man for her very own, out of the blue Kliwon plucked a rose and gave it to her. Alamanda's love once again ran wild.

"Sunday morning we are going to the beach," the man said. "If you would like to join us, I'll wait for you behind the barn."

He didn't even wait for her answer, just headed toward the group of workers to get a cigarette. Alamanda went home, placed the rose in a glass on the table, and left it there for days, even after the flower grew withered and rotten.

That Sunday morning she was not sure whether she should join the man on the outing or not. A war raged in her heart; her ego as a conqueror said that she had to play a little hard to get, but the other part of herself, which had been burned by the flame of love, ordered her to go because if she didn't the day would pass without her seeing the man at all. Her legs walked weakly toward the field behind the mushroom barn, and there she saw the man pumping a bike tire. She approached and asked where were the others.

"It's just going to be us two," replied Kliwon without turning to look at her.

"I don't want to go if no one else is going," said Alamanda.

"Well if that's how you feel, I'll go alone."

Damn it, said Alamanda to herself, and by the time Kliwon was finished with his tire pump, the girl was sitting on the back of the bike, as if the hands of the devil had sat her down there. Comrade Kliwon didn't say anything, just climbed onto the saddle, and together they headed to the beach.

As it turned out, that day was a very beautiful day for Alamanda. The man helped her relive all her pleasant memories from early childhood. First, like two little kids, they sat in the sand, building temples as high as they could. After those temples got knocked over by the waves, they had a competition to catch the dandelion fuzz that floated over the sand blown by the wind, and then they caught sea snails and had a little race where they each cheered for their own snail, and then tired of all that they threw themselves into the sea and swam joyfully. Lying on the wet sand as the ocean water swirled all around her, looking up at the sky turning pink, Alamanda wished the day would never end, but stretch out in an eternal dusk spent with the most handsome man in the world.

Comrade Kliwon then invited her to climb onto a boat that was docked in the sand. "It's okay," he said, "this boat belongs to a friend," and plus he could steer a boat through any tempest, no matter how fierce. In the belly of the boat there were a number of fishing rods and small fish to be used as bait. "Looks like we are ready to go fishing," said Comrade Kliwon. So they coasted toward the open sea that bright Sunday, without Alamanda realizing that they would not return home by nightfall. Comrade Kliwon steered the boat far from the beach, until they couldn't see any land, and there was only the ocean in the shape of a perfect circle all around them. Getting nervous, Alamanda asked, "Where are we?"

"A place where a man kidnapped a girl that he loved, many many years ago," replied Kliwon.

After that enigmatic statement, Comrade Kliwon lay down peacefully on a cross board, looking up at some seagulls flying in the blue sky. As the time passed Alamanda, who was not used to being in the middle of the ocean, began to shiver from the cold. Her clothes were still wet from their recent swim. Comrade Kliwon told her to take her clothes off and dry them on the roof of the boat, as long as there was still some sun left, because they were going to be at sea for a long time.

"Don't think you can just order me to strip naked," said Alamanda.

"It's up to you, Miss," said Comrade Kliwon. Indeed his own

clothes were also quite wet, and so he removed them piece by piece, spreading them out on the roof of the boat until not one stitch of fabric was left sticking to his body. Comrade Kliwon was now stark naked.

"What are you doing, you stupid man?!"

"You know exactly what I am doing."

He went back to lie in the same spot he had been before, his genitals drooping with no hint of lust, confusing Alamanda. After thinking for a few minutes, she thought that perhaps she *should* take off her clothes and lay them on the roof of the boat, just as he had done. She would be naked, and if that caused the man to become lustful and force himself upon her, well, whatever had to happen would happen.

"I'm not going to hurt you," said Comrade Kliwon as if he could read her mind. "I'm just kidnapping you."

The girl finally took off all her clothes. She sat with her back to Comrade Kliwon, clasping her knees. High up in the sky, maybe God and the angels were laughing down at them: stupid humans, naked but not doing anything except sitting silently as far away from one another as possible. They continued this standoff until sunset, when they both began to get hungry. Comrade Kliwon went fishing and caught a number of flying fish, which they had to eat raw because there was no fire. Comrade Kliwon had grown accustomed to this during his friendship with the fishermen, and had no trouble, but Alamanda refused and preferred to go hungry. When night fell, overcome by hunger, she too ate raw fish, and gagged.

"You'll only taste the fish for as long as it is in your mouth," said Comrade Kliwon. "After it goes into your stomach, you'll go back to feeling normal."

"Just like you are only going to be with me for as long as you kidnap me," countered Alamanda sharply, "and after we go home you are going to go back to being the same pathetic man as always."

"Maybe we won't be going home."

"That's even more pathetic," Alamanda continued to bait him, "because you are not even brave enough to come on to me in a place as quiet as this, without anyone to be a witness and with me here naked before you."

Comrade Kliwon just laughed, and returned to eating the raw fish. Not being able to stand his provocation, Alamanda finally emboldened herself to take another piece of fish and try again. She withstood her queasiness, chewing the fish as little as possible, and quickly swallowed it: and that was how she kept on doing it.

This drama lasted for two weeks as they drifted together out at sea, all alone. They never even encountered any other fishermen, because Kliwon had purposefully taken the boat to a very deep trough, which none of the fishermen liked because it was hard to catch fish there. The weather stayed clear the whole time, without any threat of a storm, but some changes did take place inside the boat.

Alamanda had finally gotten used to eating raw fish and even joined in the fishing on the second day. On the third day the two dove into the ocean together and went swimming around the boat, whooping and laughing. After that, they took off their clothes and lay them out to dry on the roof and sat at opposite ends of the boat: believe me, they did not make love, but at night Comrade Kliwon protected the girl from the cold wind by covering her with his own body, and they slept together peacefully. They were starting to get used to this strange life, and even starting to enjoy it, but on the fourteenth day Kliwon decided to row back to shore.

"Why do we have to go home?" asked Alamanda. "We can stay here quite happily."

"It wasn't my intention to kidnap you for the rest of our lives."

As he paddled, Comrade Kliwon sat next to the girl, but they both stayed mute. There was something they both were thinking about, even though it just spun around and around in their heads, and neither allowed it to come out during the entire journey home. Until finally, when they docked on the beach, Comrade Kliwon surprised the girl with his soft voice:

"Listen, Miss," the man said, "I care for you, but if you don't care for me, that's quite alright."

Oh my God, here is a man who always surprises me. Nothing he does can be predicted, even by the book of fate, thought Alamanda. She didn't say anything, even though her heart longed for her to say, yes, I love you too.

They maintained their silence for the journey back home on the bike. Alamanda interpreted the man's silence as heartbreak because she hadn't given him an answer, while Kliwon interpreted Alamanda's silence as a young girl's shy hesitance to respond to the love of a man. Alamanda was worried, and wanted to reassure the man that he didn't need to feel brokenhearted and that she loved him, so that when they arrived at the house, she started to speak. But before one word came out of her mouth, Kliwon cut her off and said:

"Don't answer me now, Miss. Think about it first!"

That week passed full of happy days. They worked in the mushroom barn together without debating anything, just talking about things that pleased them both. Wherever Kliwon went, Alamanda followed him and vice versa, until the people who saw them began to assume that they had become sweethearts.

The news of their relationship wasn't discussed only on the mushroom farm, but also by the rice farmers and the corn pickers, and then the talk began to creep past the city walls. Not liking to be the subject of all this gossip when they themselves hadn't even formally recognized their relationship, one day Alamanda finally said to Comrade Kliwon, "Don't you know that I love you?" and right then and there Kliwon replied with complete assurance, "Yes, everyone knows it." And that was enough to put an end to their reputations: Comrade Kliwon was no longer a womanizer and Alamanda was no longer a man-eater.

They continued their romantic relationship for about a year, until Comrade Kliwon got a scholarship from the Party to return to university, and to do that he had to go to Jakarta. The separation was so painful that Alamanda begged him:

"Please ravish me before you go."

"No."

"Why not? You have slept with almost all the girls in Halimunda but you won't ravish your own sweetheart?"

"No, because you are different."

Comrade Kliwon would not be swayed, and was determined to not even lay a hand on the girl. "Not until we are married," he said, like a pious youth. During the week before his departure they couldn't bear to be separated, together from morning until night. Then the day came. Alamanda took Kliwon to the train station. When the engineer was ready and the whistle blew, Alamanda couldn't keep herself from kissing the young man. They had never even brushed lips before, but now they were kissing each other in a smouldering embrace underneath the almond tree. It's true what people say, flames shot out of their lips. These were kisses of parting, a parting that proved to be excruciating.

The train began to move and the two reluctantly pulled their lips apart, while all the people at the station stood as still as statues, watching them.

"In five years," said Comrade Kliwon, "we will meet again under this almond tree."

Then he ran and leapt onto the train that was beginning to pick up speed, seen off by Alamanda's waving hand and her tears at his departure, as she stood in the same spot until the train's caboose was out of sight.

❧

And now on to the next game, with the most famous man in Halimunda as the contestant and victim, the head of the military district who once led the most infernal rebellion against the Japanese: Shodancho. Like an old fisherman who catches a big marlin on a tranquil day at sea, the girl's feelings were all in an uproar to think that she might capture such a big prey, perhaps the biggest of her entire life, and she would always remember her days of conquest, step by step, all the way back to the first offensive in the pig-fighting arena. She was aware that the man had been lured by her beauty the night of that event, and all she had left to do was yank on the snare to trap him.

One year had already passed since Alamanda had stopped being a young temptress who seduced men only to destroy them, just as Kliwon no longer had wandering eyes. They loved each other, and day by day that love had been planted deeper and deeper until they had vowed never to betray one another. But now Kliwon had gone to the capital to start university and Alamanda was getting bored. She had no intention of betraying her lover, because her love for him was still as high as the mountains and as deep as the ocean, she just wanted to have a little fun like she used to—flirting with men without having to love them.

What she didn't realize was that she was now facing a man who was truly in a class by himself, a man who had become a fugitive hiding from the Japanese army for months after a rebellion during the war, a man who had led five thousand troops in a battle against the Dutch, a man who in the time of military aggression had gained experience in many offensives, a man who had briefly been a great commander and was way more decorated than any other soldier, and the only man trusted to lead a city where large-scale smuggling operations were carried out on the hush-hush. Sooner or later, Alamanda might come to know about that man, but up until the era of her regret, she didn't realize that Shodancho was not the kind of prey to be casually toyed with.

Just as Alamanda had guessed he might, a few days after their meeting at the *orkes melayu* concert, Shodancho appeared at her house. He came alone, driving his jeep, and was greeted by her mother, which made him seem like a snot-nosed kid on his very first date. They got embroiled in a conversation about city matters, but Alamanda knew for sure that he hadn't really come for that, because he had brought a bouquet of flowers, which he gave to Alamanda and which she brought to her room and tossed out through the window right into the trash heap in the backyard before returning to join her mother and Shodancho with a charming smile.

That went on for days. Every time he came by, Shodancho brought flowers that were immediately tossed into the garbage heap, even though their bearer didn't know it. And it wasn't only flowers; on the third day he brought a stuffed panda bear that he had ordered directly from China, then he brought a ceramic vase, and the next day he brought a pile of American pop records, which Alamanda decided not to throw out.

She hadn't played a game like this in a whole year and, feeling proud that her ability to make men look stupid and foolish remained quite impressive, she played those records and danced alone in her room, imagining that she was dancing with her sweetheart. Dancing with Kliwon to the records that Shodancho had given her, now *that* was quite an amusing idea. She laughed at the idiocy of that city hero, but later that night she dreamed that Kliwon knew about everything and he got so angry that he wanted to murder her, and she woke up gasping for breath underneath a blanket drenched with cold sweat. She cursed that nightmare and reassured herself that she was not at all betraying her sweetheart, because her love for him hadn't changed one bit.

The next day she received a letter from her beloved. Alamanda was a little nervous about it and wondered whether it had any connection to her nightmare. She went into her room and lay down, at first not daring to open the envelope, worried that her bad dream would come true, but then feeling that she had to know what the letter said.

It turned out that her worries were totally groundless, there was no suspicion and no consequences at all. Kliwon said that he had started university, that his studies were not as difficult as he had imagined they would be, and that everything was going fine. Alamanda believed that the man would never have any difficulty with anything he put his mind to, and she felt proud to have such a clever lover. When Kliwon reported that he had become a roving photographer and was also working part-time in a laundry, tears trickled down her cheeks and she whispered that the future would be better for both of them. She kissed the paper the letter was written on, still crying, before falling asleep with the letter pressed against her cheek.

When she awoke two hours later, from a beautiful dream of a joyful wedding to her sweetheart, she realized that she hadn't yet read the letter through to the very end. In between the pages of the letter there was a photograph of her lover, and the explanation that he himself had taken it, so if the picture was crooked or his face looked ridiculous, he asked her forgiveness.

Alamanda laughed to see the photo and kissed it affectionately—eight times, plus three bonus kisses—clasped it to her chest, and then placed it to the side while she finished the rest of the letter, which wasn't very interesting, because Kliwon was just talking about Party matters. Alamanda wasn't interested in that kind of talk and she was thankful that Kliwon didn't write more than one paragraph before closing with a request for a picture of her. Alamanda smiled again, and said aloud, as if he were standing there before her: "I'll send you, the handsomest guy in the world, a picture of the most beautiful girl in the world."

That afternoon Alamanda made herself up to look lovely and was getting ready to go to see the photographer when she came upon Shodancho chatting with her mother in the front room as usual. Her man-eating instinct quickly reared its head and she smiled sweetly at Shodancho. Shodancho abruptly trailed off, thinking that the girl was all dressed up just for him, and he silently recited prayers of deepest gratitude to the king of the heavens when right at that moment Alamanda said she wouldn't be able to join them in their chat because she was going to see the photographer.

The girl saw Shodancho slump over in disappointment (realizing the makeup was for the photographer and not for him), but he quickly took control of the situation and offered to drive her there. Alamanda hadn't thought of this, but what was wrong with him driving her to the photographer, or with her taking advantage of the kindness of some sucker loser to make a portrait for her lover? She smiled again and glanced toward her mother, who was visibly upset by her daughter's bad behavior.

So Shodancho took Alamanda to the photography studio that had been around since the colonial era, at first belonging to a Japanese spy but now belonging to a Chinese couple. He sat in the waiting room facing the display window, and he told the photographer's wife to print two copies of each picture without telling the young girl he was with about it. The photographer's wife gave him an understanding nod.

Meanwhile Alamanda entered the studio with the photographer. She was first photographed standing gracefully in front of a screen with a picture of a lake with herons swimming across it and blue mountains in the background, then sitting on a fake rock that was there, and then the background screen was exchanged for a scene of a river with a footbridge and some trees, and exchanged again for a strange wintry scene from China. The photographer took her photo ten times, and when she went to pay, she discovered that Shodancho had already paid for all of them. She was thrilled to be sending her photograph to her lover on the man's dime, but Shodancho took her acceptance of the gift as a good omen for their relationship.

Shodancho himself delivered up the prints four days later, pretending that he just happened to be passing by the photography studio. Alamanda accepted them with pleasure and quickly retired to her room, enjoying the pictures of herself. She chose her four favorite ones, and began to write a letter to her sweetheart, telling him all about Shodancho and his foolishness, and frankly admitting that Shodancho seemed interested in her. She reassured her beloved that she was in no way interested, that she still felt just as before and her love was only for him alone, and that she had no intention whatsoever of betraying him. If she spoke of that man in her letter, it wasn't to make him jealous but to show him that there were no secrets between them. Alamanda was sure that Kliwon trusted her, so it was no problem to tell him about Shodancho. She sprinkled a little face powder on top of the letter so that her sweetheart could inhale the scent he used to smell on her body, and she even painted her lips with a thin layer of lipstick and plastered them on the bottom of the letter next to her signature, as a symbolic kiss of longing from afar. She put the letter and the photos into an envelope and smiled to imagine her man receiving it in a few days' time.

Meanwhile, Shodancho had returned to his house next to the military headquarters and was reclining with the photos of Alamanda in his hand, looking at them with a clammy gaze that seemed to penetrate the surface of the paper. One by one he placed the photos face down on his bare chest and then folded his hands behind his head.

He daydreamed about the girl's beauty, and her body, and he

found himself lost in a desire that was practically exploding with impatience, so that his hands again moved to clutch the photographs, caressing the paper as if it was the girl's very body, tracing the outline of her body with his fingers, and then he was even more dissolved in lust, like a dog in heat, his eyes clouded over with longing, and his lips began to mutter the girl's name. A half hour passed in this discomfort until the photos of the girl that he had obtained through the secret conspiracy with the photographer's wife began to look smudged and greasy, so finally he got up and placed all the photos in a drawer, put on his uniform, and walked out of his room toward the soldier who was tasked with being on duty in the "monkey cage" next to the entrance gate of the Halimunda Military District Command.

"Good afternoon, Shodancho," said the soldier.

"Where are the prostitutes in this city?"

The corporal laughed and said that there were many whores in Halimunda but there was only one who was any good, and he told him all about Mama Kalong's whorehouse. "I can take you there later tonight, if you would like."

Shodancho only laughed, not surprised that his underlings already knew about the brothels, and he quickly agreed: "We will go later tonight."

"If that's what you would like, Shodancho, of course we will go."

And that was when he visited Mama Kalong's whorehouse and slept with Dewi Ayu, and the next day Maman Gendeng was angry and came to his office to threaten him.

After that criminal paid his visit, Shodancho quickly realized that he now had an enemy in Halimunda. In the following days his men went out looking for information, and he soon learned the man's reputation and his name: Maman Gendeng. It seemed that there was no reason to return to the whorehouse and make love to Dewi Ayu again, because there was no good reason to get involved with that man. What's more, visiting a whorehouse was a really stupid thing for a man to do when he was trying to impress his potential future wife.

He was all the more determined to have Alamanda, the one woman he believed had been created just for him: a woman who would be warm in bed, elegant at parties, charming at public events, and imperious enough to stand beside him during military ceremonies. But he couldn't deny his uneasy feelings when the men who reported on Maman Gendeng's reputation also reported on Alamanda's: a young man-eater who laughed to see men brokenhearted and suffering in their unrequited love, plagued by her image. The only man who had ever won her heart was a communist youth named Comrade Kliwon.

"But that man went to the capital to study at university, so it seems as though their relationship is over."

At least the information revealed that the girl had once been vanquished and had once fallen in love, which made him feel a little bit relieved. And it was hard to believe that she would be so bold and uncouth as to play with a man who had absolute power in the city—unless of course it was the case that she had fallen in love for the second time, and Shodancho quite preferred this second possibility.

Shodancho's belief was only further confirmed when one afternoon during his visit, the girl noticed some stitching that had come unraveled in his uniform. Alamanda said, "A thread in your uniform has come loose, Shodancho. If it wouldn't be a bother, I'd like to mend it for you."

That sounded so incredibly sweet to his ears that his heart floated up to seventh heaven. He quickly took off his jacket, now wearing only a green undershirt, and gave the uniform to Alamanda, who brought it into the sewing room. Above all it was this incident that convinced him Alamanda returned his affections as she should. Now all he needed to do was speak more seriously about their relationship: Shodancho even hoped that they could discuss their wedding, and he complained to himself about how slowly the time seemed to pass.

The opportunity to speak his heart came one bright afternoon when they were walking together in the forest on an excursion to find the old guerrilla routes. The man showed the girl the hut where he had lived for many years, the caves where he had hidden and meditated, and the caches of leftover weapons, mortars, guns, and gunpowder. He also showed her the defense forts that the Japanese had built. Then the couple sat looking out at the sea, in the yard right in front of the guerrilla hut, on the very stone chairs and table where he once held meetings with his troops. The weather was warm and an eastern wind was blowing pleasantly.

"Would you like to drink some fruit juice here at the seaside? "asked Shodancho, and Alamanda replied, "Yes, that would be quite delightful." She had imagined that a guerrilla hideout would have been much scarier. Shodancho went back to the truck that had brought them both to that spot and returned with a thermos.

The scattered fishing boats that had headed out to sea that late afternoon bobbed softly out in the ocean, floating like lotus flowers on a pond. There were two or three fishermen on top of those boats and they all sat facing one another. They didn't wave or shout, they just sat there looking all around and chatting with their friends.

The fishermen wore thick clothes with long sleeves, sarongs tied around their shoulders, cone hats, gloves, and their feet in tennis shoes, all to protect them from the fierce cold ocean air which would gradually weaken them with rheumatism in their old age. Shodancho commented that in the future, individual fishermen would slowly go extinct; big fishing vessels that could match the catch of fifty fishermen would replace these boats that were so small and vulnerable against storms, and their captains would never have to worry about getting rheumatism. Alamanda only replied that the fishermen had been friends with the sea for too long to be frightened by storms or rheumatism, and maybe they didn't want to catch any more fish than they needed each day—she'd heard that from Kliwon.

Shodancho chuckled, and then they began talking about which kinds of fish were good to eat. Alamanda said that grouper was the most delicious and Shodancho said that he liked squid and then Alamanda protested because squid weren't really fish since they didn't have scales or fins. Hearing that, Shodancho laughed again. They both then fell silent for a moment, and then Shodancho poured some fruit juice from the cold thermos he had brought into Alamanda's empty glass. That was when Shodancho said what he wanted to say, or rather asked exactly what he wanted to ask:

"Alamanda, do you think you might like to be my wife?"

Alamanda was not at all surprised. She had heard that question asked by so many men, in so many different variations, that over time it had lost its power to shock her—she could even guess more or less when the man was going to pop the question. In her experience, there were always signs that a man was about to confess his love to a woman, even though the signs were different for each man. She felt that a woman just knew these things, especially if, like her, that woman had already refused twenty-three men and had accepted the twenty-fourth. Now Alamanda was scheming how to mire the twenty-fifth in a fever of unrequited love.

She stood and walked toward the edge of the cliffs, watching two fishermen slowly paddling their boat, and then said without looking at Shodancho, "A man and a woman must love each other if they are to get married, Shodancho."

"Well, don't you love me?"

"I already have a sweetheart."

Well then why do you get all dressed up every time we meet? Shodancho said to himself a bit indignantly. *And why did you want me to take you to the photography studio and let me look at the pictures of your body, and why did you mend my unraveled uniform, unless to show me that you cared?*

Shodancho replayed their courtship, made all the more irate by the realization that the girl had just been playing with him all along. He cursed himself for his carelessness, for letting himself forget that this girl was the same girl who had captured the hearts of so many men before tossing them aside like useless garbage. He had been a fool to think the girl wouldn't dare do the same thing to a *shodancho* who had led a rebellion and who was a city hero, but in fact she did dare, and apparently she had really enjoyed herself.

He was even more enraged to see her sitting there calmly across the table, having sat back down to drink her juice. And by the time she smiled at him he was blind with fury, but still completely composed. Finally he said, "Love is like a devil, more terrifying than satisfying. If you don't love me, fine, but at least make love to me."

This guy is pathetic, Alamanda thought. She looked at Shodancho's face, and for a minute she wondered why all of a sudden it was quivering and shaking all over and seemed as though it had split in two, and why each half seemed to rise and fall independently of the other. She wanted to ask Shodancho what was happening to his face but her mouth, just as inexplicably, couldn't be made to move. Suddenly she felt her own body begin to wobble, and she prayed that it had not split in two like Shodancho's face. But that was what had happened when she looked at her hand that was still holding the half-empty glass of fruit juice: now her hand had split into two, three, even four pieces.

She could still see but everything was starting to go blurry when Shodancho stood and walked around the table toward her, saying something that she could not hear at all. But she could feel it all right when Shodancho stood next to her and caressed her cheek softly, touching her chin and the tip of her nose. Alamanda wanted to stand up and strike the man for being so forward, but all of her strength was gone—she could only stagger, falling weakly against Shodancho.

She felt the man's hands holding her slender body tightly and then all of a sudden she felt as if she was flying in the air, wondering whether she had died and if her soul was heading for the kingdom in the heavens. But she could see, even with her evermore blurred vision, that she wasn't flying at all and was still just floating slightly because Shodancho had picked her up and placed her on his strong shoulder to carry her away. Hey, where are you taking me, she tried to protest, but not a sound emerged from her mouth. Shodancho brought her into the guerrilla hut, and Alamanda flew through the air once again when he threw her down onto the bed.

Now she was lying there, beginning to realize what was really going on. Frightened by what might befall her she began to fight back, but her strength had not yet returned. As time passed she felt all the weaker, until her body and her hands and even her feet stuck tightly to the surface of the bed, and she wasn't able to move them even the tiniest bit.

When Shodancho began to undo the buttons of her dress, Alamanda was completely powerless and she surrendered totally, in rage and ruin. She watched the man remove her dress and throw it to the edge of the bed. Shodancho continued to work with an eerie calm, and when she was totally naked, she felt Shodancho's fingers, with their rough fingertips calloused from carrying weapons during the war and scarred with old shrapnel wounds from the same era, begin to slither slowly across her body, nauseating her.

Shodancho said something she couldn't hear, and now it wasn't just his fingertips moving but the palms of his hands, which began to grip her body as if he aimed to destroy her. Shodancho wildly squeezed her breasts, making Alamanda want to howl, explored her whole body, pushed between her thighs, and he began to kiss Alamanda with his lips, leaving a trail of spit across her body. Alamanda now didn't just want to howl, she wanted to slit her own throat so that she would die before the man did anything else. She couldn't tell how long she was in this situation, maybe half an hour, maybe an hour, a day, seven years, or eight centuries, all she knew was that Shodancho then took off his own clothing to stand naked and cavalier next to the bed.

For a moment the man still kneaded her chest before throwing his body on top of her, kissing her lips with revolting little nibbles, and without wasting much more time he penetrated her. Alamanda could still see his face that looked like a white blob very close to her eyes, feeling her vagina torn apart by his savagery. She began to cry, but she didn't even know whether her body still had the capacity to make tears. It seemed to be going on endlessly, for an additional eight whole centuries. No longer having the strength to open her eyes, she only felt her body being treated so filthily. And then she lost consciousness, or that was what she thought happened because she could no longer feel anything at all, but maybe she didn't want to feel anything anymore. Finally Shodancho let her go and rolled to the side of her body, which since the beginning had remained in the same position: naked on her back, practically glued to the bed.

Shodancho lay beside her, with ever-deepening breath, so that Alamanda thought the man had fallen asleep. She swore that if she only had all of her power at that moment she would not have hesitated to take a knife and stab that man to death as he slept. Or to detonate a mortar in his mouth. Or to shoot him deep into the ocean with a cannon. But she was wrong to think the man had fallen asleep, because Shodancho now got up and said—and this time she could hear him—"If all you want to do is conquer men and throw them away like abject trash, well then it's too bad you met me, Alamanda. I win every war I fight, including the war against you."

She heard these cynical and contemptuous words that pierced like a thorn but couldn't say anything in reply, only look at Shodancho with a still-blurry gaze as he stood up and gathered his clothes.

After that, Shodancho dressed and put the girl's clothes back on her body piece by piece, saying it was time for them to leave the jungle and return home. Now Alamanda was dressed and it looked as though nothing had happened. But she was nowhere near as alert as she had been before, still anesthetized by the secret poison. She only remembered that everything had happened after drinking that fruit juice.

She again felt like she was flying when Shodancho picked her up from the bed. This time he did not throw her over his shoulder, but carried her against his waist with both of his strong arms, which in the olden days had carried a canon and had even carried one of his men, wounded in a battle against the Dutch, to safety. Now Alamanda lay in his arms while Shodancho walked away from the guerrilla hut toward the truck. He sat her down at his side and then he steered the truck along the dirt road through the dark and dense jungle.

He brought the girl back to her house. Alamanda could only recall the journey as a long dim tunnel of light. When they arrived at the house Shodancho came out of the truck carrying Alamanda's body and was greeted by Dewi Ayu, who helped Shodancho bring the girl to her room. She was laid out across her bed as Dewi Ayu asked what had happened. Shodancho replied calmly that it was nothing to worry about:

"She's just carsick."

"It's because you ravaged her body without permission, Shodancho," replied Dewi Ayu, whose life experience led her to understand what had happened without anyone having to say it. "But don't think you are a lucky man just because you won this battle."

Alamanda was left alone in her room, and for the first time she felt tears begin to wet her cheeks, as everything seemed to go black and then she truly lost consciousness.

{9}

WHEN ALAMANDA REGAINED consciousness the next day, the first thing she thought of was Kliwon and immediately she knew that everything was over for her and her sweetheart.

At that time, Alamanda felt she was a cursed woman; maybe she didn't regret what she had done, and maybe she accepted what had happened to her because of it, but she still felt cursed. She wanted to write a letter to her sweetheart to arrive right after the letter with the photographs, telling him what had happened, except not the part about how she been out of control and toyed with a man who should not be toyed with and also not the part about how Shodancho had raped her. She would only tell him that she had slept with Shodancho. She was ashamed of herself, but the only thing she truly regretted was that she was going to lose her beloved and despite the fact that she knew Kliwon would have her in any condition, she absolutely did not want to see him. She still loved him, but she would lie and say that she had fallen in love with Shodancho. She would say she was leaving her old lover to marry her new flame. And she would ask his forgiveness. She wrote the letter that very afternoon, and put it in the post box just as soon as she had slid it into a stamped envelope.

Now she had to reckon with Shodancho, get her revenge, and think about what she could do to satisfy her rage short of stabbing him with a stiletto knife. So, after she put the letter to Kliwon in the mail, she went to the military headquarters, receiving an uncharacteristic salute from the soldier standing guard in the monkey cage at the gate, and just as Maman Gendeng had once done upon his arrival, she went straight into Shodancho's office without knocking first. Shodancho was sitting behind his desk gazing at two photos of Alamanda that he held in his hand, with the eight other photos spread out across the table. When Alamanda barged in, he was taken off guard and tried to hide the photographs, but Alamanda gestured for him not to bother. Then the girl stood before Shodancho with one hand pressed against the table and the other shoved against her hip.

"So now I know what you men were up to during your guerrilla war," she said, as Shodancho stared at her with the look of a lovesick sinner. "And now you have to marry me, even though I will never love you. If you don't, I will kill myself right after I tell everyone in this city what you did to me."

"I will marry you, Alamanda."

"Fine. You will have to arrange for the celebration by yourself." Then she left without another word.

Within one week's time their marriage was a hot topic of discussion that came up whenever people met and talked, as they speculated about it, solemnly mulled it over, and joked about it too. Still, the citizens of Halimunda had become accustomed to just about anything, so they were not too surprised by the news. Some of them even said with an air of authority that Alamanda and Shodancho were the most well-matched couple that any human being on the face of this earth could ever imagine: a beautiful girl who was the daughter of a most well-respected prostitute married to an ex-rebel who had once been a great commander, there was nothing more fitting than that. Others said that Shodancho was in fact even more suitable than that rabble-rouser Kliwon, and Alamanda wasn't too stupid to realize it.

But Kliwon had many friends in that city: they were the fishermen, because when he had lived there Kliwon had gone to sea with them and helped them haul nets to shore, receiving one plastic bag full of the fish they had caught as payment, and he had helped them fix their leaky boats and their cranky outboard motors when he worked in the boat shop; they were the farm laborers, because many farmers on the outskirts of the city worked land belonging to others, just as Kliwon had done, and they had been on the sidelines when he had entertained his friends, talking about all kinds of things that sprung from his brilliant brain, things they had never known about or could have ever conceived; and they were the young girls who had fallen in love with him, or were still in love with him, and even though Kliwon had abandoned each of them when he went to find another girl, they held no grudge and loved him just as much as ever; they were those who had been his childhood playmates, his companions in swimming and bird-hunting, and in searching for firewood and grasses that could be sold to rich men, back when they were all still small; and all of them were upset that Alamanda had abandoned their friend to marry Shodancho. But they had no business getting mixed up in Alamanda's affairs and what's more, the issue of whether or not his heart was broken was only and completely Kliwon's own private business.

And so the news about the wedding celebration, that people were saying would be the most festive celebration that had ever occurred in the past or would ever occur in future of the city, quickly spread from one far-flung locale to another, all throughout the terrain of Halimunda's scattered villages. It was assured that the celebration would be enlivened by seven groups of *dalang*, master puppeteers who would perform the entire Mahabharata over the course of seven nights, and that every single inhabitant of the city would be invited to attend, and the people said the food to be served would be enough to feed the entire city for seven generations. There would also be performances of *sintren*, *kuda lumping* trance dancing, *orkes melayu*, films projected onto a screen, and of course, pig fighting.

Finally this news reached Kliwon, along with the letter that Alamanda had sent him. One day before the wedding, when the tents had already been set up in front of Dewi Ayu's house and Alamanda was primping and pampering and preparing her body with the help of a number of wedding planners, Kliwon returned home to Halimunda on the train with an anger smouldering throughout his entire body, not just because this was the first time he had ever been hurt or abandoned by a woman, but because he truly loved Alamanda with his whole heart.

In front of the station, the place where they had last met and kissed, Kliwon chopped down the almond tree as a crowd looked on. They didn't dare get in his way, partly because they saw his eyes blazing furiously in their sockets but mostly because he was carrying a machete, and so even the policemen who happened to be in the area didn't dare forbid him from chopping down that tree, which had originally been intended as a shade tree for people to rest under. When the tree collapsed, the crowd only moved back a couple of paces to protect themselves from being hit by the falling branches and twigs, all the while wondering why the man was taking out all of his passion and rage on a little almond tree that had never done anything wrong.

Meanwhile, Kliwon didn't seem bothered by the people gathered outside the front of the station watching him, and he began to hack off the twigs and branches and to tear off the tree's leaves until they blocked the whole path leading to the platform, and when the wind blew the leaves whirled about like a creepy tornado, but even the street sweepers didn't dare get in his way, they just looked at him trying to determine whether or not he had gone completely insane.

Only one guy, who was Kliwon's childhood friend, was bold enough to ask what he was doing with the tree. Kliwon replied tersely, "Chopping it down," and after that no one dared ask him anything else and he continued with his work.

After the tree was stripped of its branches and leaves, he began to chop it up into pieces of firewood. He split the largest branches into two or four so that in a matter of minutes the wood began to pile up on the side of the road. Kliwon walked to the baggage counter and there he took a length of coarse rope without asking for permission (although of course no one forbade him) and tied up the wood with it. After all this was finished, without speaking to any of the people who were still faithfully crowding around him, he put his machete back into his sarong, picked up the bundle of wood, and walked away from the station.

At first the people wanted to follow him, but the friend who had previously spoken and suddenly understood what was going to happen quickly said to them, "Let him go alone." And it turned out that what his friend suspected was exactly what came to pass: Kliwon went to Alamanda's house and found the girl overseeing the party preparations. Alamanda was surprised by his arrival and even more surprised to see the man she still loved so much hauling a stack of wood for who knows what purpose.

For a moment Alamanda wanted to leap toward him, embrace him and kiss him just as she had at the station, tell him that this was *their* wedding celebration, and that it was a lie that she was going to marry Shodancho. But she just as quickly came to her senses and tried to appear proud of her wedding to Shodancho, tried to look like a smug and self-satisfied girl. Kliwon let the wood fall from his shoulder to the earth, making Alamanda jump back to save her toes from getting squashed, and he finally opened his mouth to say, "This is that wretched almond tree, where we promised we would meet again. I am offering it to you, to be used as firewood on your wedding day."

Alamanda waved her hands as if ordering him to leave, and so Kliwon left, without telling her how he had been truly swept away by that gesture, tossed into a storm of hatred that erased everything in its wake. He probably didn't know that once he had gone and was completely out of sight, Alamanda ran to her room and wept, burning the remaining photographs of herself to ash. By the time she met Shodancho on their wedding dais the next morning, she had tried everything she could to hide the evidence of a night's worth of tears, but without success and so for months, even for years afterward, it remained gossip for the city folk.

Kliwon disappeared for months after that, or at least Alamanda didn't hear any more news of him, or maybe she just didn't want to hear anything about him anymore. She assumed that he had returned to the capital to finish his schooling at the university or to join the communist youth, who knows. But in truth Kliwon didn't go anywhere. He stayed in Halimunda, moving from one friend's house to the next or hiding at his mother's place. He even attended Alamanda's wedding in secret. He greeted Shodancho and Alamanda in disguise, without the couple realizing it, and Kliwon could see that Alamanda had been crying all night long, undeniable evidence that she was marrying against her will, and irrevocable proof that she had chosen a husband she didn't love. For his part Kliwon was no longer angry at Alamanda, just saddened by the tragic fate that had befallen the woman he loved.

But he kept wondering what had made Alamanda decide to marry Shodancho, whom she had only just met a few weeks before, until he heard a fisherman say that late one afternoon he had seen Shodancho driving a truck out of the jungle with Alamanda slumped unconscious beside him, and another fisherman swore that from the middle of the ocean he had seen Shodancho carrying Alamanda over his shoulder into the guerrilla hut. "I am saddened by what has come to pass between you and Alamanda," said the fisherman, "but don't act rashly. Or, if you plan to seek revenge, let us join with you and help."

"I won't seek my revenge," said Kliwon. "That man wins every war he fights."

For the time being Kliwon returned to the ocean with his friends as he used to do, and Alamanda went through the farce of a tense and anxious wedding night. She had drugged Shodancho with a sleeping pill so that the man straightaway fell snoring onto their wedding mattress, which was shining yellow with fragrant fresh flowers arranged prettily atop it. Exhausted, Alamanda unfurled a pallet on the floor and slept there, without the slightest inclination to lie down beside her husband the way most new brides do. But unpredictably, Shodancho awoke in the early morning hours and, looking all around, he was taken aback to find that his wedding night had almost passed him by and his new bride was lying on the floor on a thin pallet. Cursing himself at this unforgivable sight, Shodancho quickly bent down, scooped up his wife, and laid her down on the bed.

Alamanda awoke to see Shodancho smiling and saying how foolish it would be to pass their wedding night without doing anything, and when Shodancho took off all his clothes so that he was standing there naked, she turned her back on him and said, "How about I tell you a fairy tale before we make love?"

Shodancho laughed and said that was an interesting idea, then got into bed and cuddled up against his wife's back, inhaling the scent of her hair saying, "Quick, start your story, because I'm already really in the mood."

So as best as she could Alamanda began to spin a tale, inventing a story which circled endlessly with no resolution, so that there would be no time for them to make love—not until they died, or maybe not even until the end of the world. As Alamanda was telling her story, Shodancho was exploring Alamanda's whole body with his two hands, impatient to get to the end of the tale, even though he couldn't really tell where it was heading. He began to fumble with the buttons on Alamanda's gown, opening them one by one. Alamanda tried to hold out by curling up into a tight little ball, but Shodancho's strong hands turned her over easily and pinned her down as he rolled on top of her. Alamanda pushed Shodancho so that he rolled off again, and said, "Listen, Shodancho, we'll make love when my story is finished."

Shodancho shot a peevish look in her direction, detecting a whiff of antagonism in the game, and said that he could listen to the story *while* they were making love.

"But we already agreed, Shodancho," said Alamanda, "that you could marry me but I would never make love to you."

That angered Shodancho so that he didn't care about anything anymore and roughly yanked at his new bride's evening gown until it was torn. Alamanda let out a little scream but Shodancho quickly silenced her, pulling at her clothes. Just when it seemed that Alamanda was no longer really resisting and Shodancho had ripped off her gown, he cried out in surprise. "Damn it! What have you done to your crotch?" he asked, gaping down at a pair of underwear made out of metal, locked with a padlock that appeared to have no keyhole with which to open it.

Alamanda said with a mysterious calm, "This is an antiterror garment, Shodancho, I ordered it directly from a metalsmith and a sorcerer. It can only be opened with a mantra that only I know how to recite, and I will never ever open it for you, not even if the sky has fallen."

That night, Shodancho tried to break the padlock using a number of different tools: he tried prying at it with a screwdriver, he pounded it with a nail and axe, and he even shot it with a pistol, which made Alamanda practically faint with fear. But everything failed to open the lock on that metal underwear and, finally caught in between lust and anger, all he could do was have relations with his wife without being able to actually penetrate her. In the morning he sliced the tip of his finger just a little bit and dripped the blood on top of the sheet, in the time-honoured symbol that a newlywed couple had to show the laundress.

A week after the wedding, when all that was left of the festivities was garbage and rumors, the newlyweds moved to the house Shodancho had bought for them, a house left over from the colonial era which came with two servants and a gardener. It was Dewi Ayu who had told them to move, giving them the impression that they should come to visit her as rarely as possible, or maybe never come again. "A married woman doesn't associate with whores," she told Alamanda. Her mother was always right, and with a heavy heart Alamanda moved out.

That whole time, in accordance with her vow, Alamanda never removed her iron underwear. It was as if she was a soldier from the Middle Ages, forever wary of the enemy who could ambush at any time and come stabbing with his flabby but still quite fatal sword. Shodancho himself appeared to have given up all hope of opening them, especially after consulting with a number of sorcerers. All the sorcerers shrugged their shoulders and said there was no force, no kind of evil spirit, that could appease the vengeful power of a wronged woman. He paid a lot of money for those useless consultations—not for the advice per se, but to keep the sorcerers quiet so that the family shame would not leak out and spread. And it was that very shame that meant he couldn't ask anyone else for advice about his problems in the bedroom.

He had already tried to convince his wife to loosen up with her accursed hardheadedness, but then without ever surrendering or taking off her iron undies, Alamanda decided that she should sleep apart from Shodancho, like a couple waiting for the courts to finalize their divorce. This meant that Shodancho had to sleep alone, hugging his pillow and rolling about in a state of forlorn arousal. Alamanda said to him once—who knows, maybe out of pity or just because she wanted to show her magnanimity—"If you absolutely must spew the contents of your balls, feel free to visit a prostitute. I wouldn't be angry, in fact I would be happy for you."

But Shodancho refused to do what his wife advised. Not because he thought he could overcome his desire, and not because he wasn't interested in whores, but because he wanted to show her how deeply faithful he was, how selfless his love was for her, and he hoped that after a while his wife's heart would yield to his sweet and blameless manner.

But Alamanda showed no sign of giving in, and only took off her iron underwear during those brief moments when she was inside the locked bathroom in order to pee and wash herself, and after that she continued to clamp them up tight along with her secret mantra, which was safely hidden away inside her mouth wherever she went.

Shodancho hoped that his wife would carelessly say the mantra out loud and he would overhear it, but he waited in vain because she never even murmured it in her sleep. The only thing Shodancho could do now was surrender to his fate, and accept the fact that he would never again make love to a woman, forever confined to his emergency sessions with his pillow in his lonely bed. Other times, when he couldn't take the crazy game any longer, he would scurry to the bathroom and discharge the contents of his balls into the toilet.

During those days, he tried to distract himself by once again focusing on the smuggling business he had been running for years with his friend Bendo. Now they had acquired a large fishing vessel, their one legal operation. He also returned to his old hobby of breeding and domesticating wild dogs. After one year had passed, the dogs could help the farmers chase away trespassing pigs. But that whole year had passed without the newlyweds ever making love, and people started to gossip. They had the audacity to swear, full of certainty, that Shodancho and Alamanda had not had intercourse even once, which was proven by the fact that Alamanda still showed no signs of being pregnant.

A number of kids began to speculate that if Shodancho wasn't impotent then maybe he was sterile, and a number of others dared to say that he had been castrated by the Japanese during the war. That crazy story spread from the mouth of one kid to the ears of another and was soon overheard by some adults who believed it and spread the word even further.

No one thought to make any other speculations, like the couple's hasty marriage had not at all been based on love, because despite their secret bedroom woes, the pair always presented a congenial public face, looking just like a husband and wife who truly cared for each other. They attended parties together, and were often seen taking afternoon walks hand in hand and going to the movies on Saturday nights. It was easy for people to misunderstand when seeing the harmony of a couple like that. Alamanda always looked cheerful and Shodancho always doted on her, so the only reason why one year had passed and Alamanda wasn't pregnant yet *had* to be that either one or both of them was sterile. "It's such a shame, their wedding seemed so perfect," someone said finally.

The only person who didn't feel the slightest bit upset by all the gossip was Alamanda. As if she couldn't care less about the whole matter, or as if it amused her, when not accompanying Shodancho to ceremonies she spent her free time reading novels. It was in fact these books that had taught Alamanda how to play the role of a happy wife for the public. She didn't do so just to preserve her husband's image but also to preserve her own, because she didn't want anyone to know that she was married to a man she didn't love. She didn't want anyone to pity her.

Apparently Shodancho's were the last ears to hear the distasteful gossip about his impotence and potential castration, which had started in the mouths of those nosey little kids and had gone so far the kids had stopped playing war, under the mistaken assumption that soldiers were likely to be castrated. When he finally heard, Shodancho was completely distraught, stewing in a mix of humiliation and anger and helplessness. Outside the bedroom business with his wife he thought their marriage was going pretty well. Alamanda presented herself as the cordial wife she ought to be and so he didn't totally care that she was faking it. But he couldn't just keep shooting the seeds of their babies into the toilet forever, and it finally dawned on him that one whole year had passed and he still had not been able to break that fucking pair of iron underwear.

So one night, after many months of sleeping in separate beds, Shodancho entered the room where Alamanda slept and found his wife putting on her pajamas. He closed the door and locked it, then approached Alamanda who eyed him suspiciously while feeling for her crotch to ensure that her iron protection was still locked and set. Shodancho then said to his wife, "Make love to me, darling." His voice sounded miserable.

Alamanda shook her head and turned her back on him to get into bed. Shodancho grabbed her from behind and ripped her pajamas open. Before Alamanda could react, Shodancho had already pushed her down onto the bed, taken off his own clothes and quickly jumped on top of her. Alamanda resisted, pushing his body away with all her power, but Shodancho was holding her tightly, kissing her wildly, and squeezing her breasts, full of desire. "You are raping me, Shodancho!" screamed Alamanda, trying to roll away. But Shodancho kept after her, exploring and squeezing every region of her body. "Shodancho, you accursed satan, you devil, you asshole, try to rape me and your spear will break against my iron shield!" Alamanda said finally, no longer resisting and letting Shodancho fondle her in vain.

Now Shodancho could move more freely, fooling himself into thinking that he was really making love to his wife, until his weapon hurled sperm across the surface of the metal slab protecting her vagina. Shodancho rolled onto his side out of breath, drops of sweat decorating his entire body. He was completely silent for a moment as Alamanda enjoyed his foolishness, happy in her victory and her revenge. He glared over at her crotch in fury, his legs in excruciating pain after repeatedly colliding with the iron. Grimacing, he sat on the edge of the bed, and began to cry the pitiful tears of a pathetic and brokenhearted man, and he said, "No matter how many times I do this to you, you will never get pregnant. Your cunt and your womb are cursed." He got up, got dressed, and left his wife's room.

But Alamanda was wrong when she figured that Shodancho would give up and submit to the punishment that she had prepared for him. One day when she was in the carefully locked bathroom, completely naked with her iron underwear resting on the edge of the tub, something slammed against the door with tremendous force and Shodancho stampeded in through the gaping hole. Before Alamanda could even reach for her iron underwear, Shodancho was already clutching them in his grasp. She screamed like a wounded tigress, but Shodancho threw her over his shoulder just as he had carried her powerless body through the jungle where he fought his guerrilla war. He brought Alamanda out from the bathroom as she thrashed about pummeling his back. Two servants spied on this scene through a crack in the kitchen door, their bodies trembling in fear.

Shodancho brought Alamanda to his own room, the room that he had hoped would be their room, and threw her onto the bed before turning to lock the door. "You are cursed, Shodancho," said Alamanda, standing on the bed and shrinking back toward the wall. "How dare you rape your own wife!"

Shodancho didn't reply, just took off his clothes and faced Alamanda with the look of a horny dog. Seeing him like that, her instinct told her she was in danger and Alamanda squeezed herself even closer against the wall, but Shodancho quickly caught her, threw her down onto the bed, and then threw himself down on top of her.

Minute by minute they stayed locked in battle, the battle of a man who needs release for his lust and a woman who claws and screams to protect herself from a love that she in no way wants to consummate. Alamanda closed her thighs tightly, but Shodancho forcefully broke through her last defense with his mighty knee, and whatever was going to happen happened. Shodancho raped his own wife, until the end of the exhausting battle, when Alamanda sobbed, "Fuck you, you raping satan!" and fainted. Shodancho ended up with two scratches on his face and Alamanda with an extraordinary pain in her crotch.

She didn't know how long she lay there unconscious, but when she came to, she found herself still lying on her back naked. Her hands and feet were tied to the four corners of the bed. Alamanda pulled at the ropes binding her, but they were tied so tightly that whatever she did only made her wrists and ankles hurt all the more.

"Devil rapist, what have you done?" she asked angrily when she saw Shodancho standing beside the bed completely dressed. "If you are looking for a hole to stick your dick in, every cow and goat has one."

For the first time since he had kidnapped her from the bathroom, Shodancho smiled and said, "Now I can have sex with you whenever I want!" Hearing that, Alamanda hurled insults and spouted curses, still struggling against the cords as Shodancho left her.

That day Shodancho found a repairman to fix the destroyed bathroom door and threw Alamanda's iron underwear into the well. With a fearsome look he threatened the two servants never to tell anyone what they had seen. Meanwhile Alamanda grew weak after trying so hard to free herself, and wept continuously with piteous cries. Shodancho returned again and again to the room where Alamanda was held captive, making love to his wife as if they were real newlyweds, about once every two and a half hours without tiring. He was as delighted as a child with a new toy, and the longer this went on, the less Alamanda's resistance meant anything.

"Even if I died," Alamanda said in defeat, "believe me, this man would continue to fuck my grave."

So the whole day long Alamanda was tied up on top of the bed, raped over and over again. Then in the afternoon Shodancho came bringing a tub filled with warm water and a wet washcloth and he caressed his wife's body as tenderly and carefully as if he was handling an expensive and fragile ceramic vase. After that he had sex with her again, and then he bathed her again, and this went on for quite a while. Alamanda's heart was unmoved by Shodancho's gentle ministrations, and when he brought her some lunch, she closed her mouth up tight, and when Shodancho forced open her mouth and crammed rice inside, she spit it right out so that it splattered all over his face. "Eat, because I won't enjoy making love to a corpse," said Shodancho. Alamanda snapped, "It's way less enjoyable for me to make love to a living human being the likes of you."

This is crazy, thought Shodancho as he continued to cajole her. Alamanda refused to eat until she was released from her bondage and her iron underwear was returned to her, but Shodancho refused to honor that request. Trying to make himself feel better, Shodancho told himself that Alamanda's resolve would reach its limit. After being plagued by the painful twisting of her empty stomach all night long, by the next morning she would probably be ready to accept food.

Thinking this, Shodancho returned his wife's lunch to the kitchen and ate alone at the dining table. When afternoon came, he sat on the veranda enjoying the evening breeze and the turtledoves that had been given to them as a wedding present. The birds hopped up and down inside their cages, which hung from the ceiling. He also enjoyed the shining lamps and the clove cigarette that he sucked on with great pleasure, thinking back over his victorious day. Finally he knew what it felt like to make love to his wife, because even though he had raped Alamanda once before, that had been before they were married.

Usually he sat with Alamanda on the front terrace on afternoons like this. Many had noticed the habit, so when people passed by and greeted him, "Good afternoon, Shodancho," they also asked, "Where is the Lady of the house?" Shodancho replied good afternoon and explained that his wife wasn't feeling well and was lying down in bed. That made him miss Alamanda, so that when there was still a little bit of his cigarette left unsmoked, he threw the butt into the yard and went to see his wife.

He found her tied up flat on her back just as she had been the whole day, but it appeared she had fallen asleep. Whether Shodancho then momentarily changed into a good husband only God himself knows, because he covered his wife with a blanket to ward off the cold air and mosquitos, except it turned out that in the end he couldn't make it through the night without raping her again, twice: first at eleven-forty and then again at three in the morning, before the first cock had crowed.

Morning finally came and Shodancho reappeared in the room where his wife was still sprawled underneath a blanket with her hands and feet still tied to each corner of the bed. For breakfast he brought her some fried rice with a sunny-side up egg on top, some sliced tomato on the side, and a tall glass of chocolate milk. Alamanda awoke and stared dejectedly in his direction, with a mixture of nausea and hatred. "Here, let me feed you," said Shodancho with genuine friendliness, continuing with the sincere smile of a husband for his wife, "Making love always builds up a good appetite."

Alamanda returned his smile, not with her usual charming

grin but with a disgusted and contemptuous sneer. She looked at Shodancho as if she was looking at the devil incarnate she had imagined ever since she was a little girl. He didn't have any horns or tusks, and his eyes were just a little bit red from not having gotten enough sleep, but she was still positive her husband was the devil.

"Go to hell and take your fucking breakfast with you," said Alamanda.

"Come on, sweetheart, you will die if you don't eat," said Shodancho.

"Yes, I think that would be best."

And that was what started to happen: Alamanda developed a fever in the afternoon, with a deathly pale face and a climbing temperature and the shivers. Shodancho did not rape her even one more time that day, perhaps because he was exhausted, or because he was finally satisfied, or maybe to improve his relationship with his wife so that he could convince her to eat. Alamanda was now completely refusing everything, not just rice, she wouldn't even drink, and that was what finally made her fall ill, growing delirious but still hurling curses.

Shodancho started to panic at his wife's worsening condition, still trying to convince her to eat, now even just a bowl of porridge, and still he was met with refusal. What's more, Alamanda's body that had at first been trembling was now wracked with violent shudders, as if she was dying, but she endured it all with an extraordinary calm, as if she was ready to face even the most gruesome end. Shodancho tried to bring her fever down by putting a cold compress on her forehead. A vaporous mist rose from the wet cloth, but the heat of her fever didn't seem to subside.

Shodancho finally made the decision to untie his wife, but Alamanda just lay there, even though this meant that she was now free to get up and run away. Nor did she resist when her husband put on her clothes and carried her out of the room. Alamanda no longer understood what was happening so she didn't ask any questions, just hung there draped across Shodancho's shoulders. The man quickly told her, even though she was beyond being able to hear anything, "I truly don't want you to become a corpse, so we are going to the hospital."

Shodancho had thought that his wife just needed a vitamin shot and maybe a little infusion, but Alamanda ended up spending two weeks in the hospital. Every day he came to her room to say how much he regretted the way he had treated her. Alamanda no longer appeared hostile. She accepted the porridge the nurses spooned into her mouth (even though she still refused porridge from Shodancho), and nodded when Shodancho promised he would never do it again. But she didn't believe one word of his regret.

On the fourteenth day, after the doctor had called and said that Alamanda could be taken home, Shodancho met with the doctor in the hospital corridor. The doctor greeted him with small talk, "Good morning, Shodancho," and Shodancho said, "Good afternoon, Doctor." Then the doctor invited him to sit in the hospital canteen to discuss Alamanda. "Is there something seriously wrong with my wife, Doctor?" asked Shodancho, as the doctor ordered a simple lunch. Only when his meal arrived did the doctor shake his head and say, "There's no such thing as a serious illness, as long as you know the correct way to treat it."

Then he began to eat, as if to draw out whatever drama he was going to discuss, while Shodancho waited patiently. As he smoked a cigarette, because the canteen was the only place he was allowed to smoke in the entire hospital, he was still worrying about his wife and still worrying that he was to blame for everything, as he had been ever since the first day the doctor had given the diagnoses of dehydration and an ulcer, and had said that Alamanda was displaying the symptoms of typhus. The doctor had said that he didn't need to worry, Alamanda just needed to rest, eat only plain porridge, avoid all sour foods, drink a lot of fluids and take antibiotics, and the virus in her body would die of its own accord in no more than two weeks. But even though the doctor said there was nothing to worry about, Shodancho still worried, knowing he couldn't bear it if Alamanda were to die and leave him behind, even though he knew she had never loved him and never would.

"If I tell you the good news, though, will you buy my lunch, Shodancho?" asked the doctor as he finished his meal.

"Tell me doctor, what's going on with my wife?"

"I'm quite experienced in making this diagnosis so mark my words—you are going to have a child, Shodancho! Your wife is pregnant."

He was quiet for a moment. "The question is, who got her pregnant?" Of course he didn't actually say that. "How many months?" asked Shodancho, who did not look at all happy with his ashen face and his hands trembling on top of the table. Nasty images darted through his mind, as he imagined Alamanda having sex with whomever she wanted on the sly, with an old sweetheart or a new boyfriend, taking revenge for having been fated to marry a man she didn't love.

"What, Shodancho?"

"How many months is my wife pregnant, Doctor?"

"Two weeks."

Shodancho collapsed against the back of his chair while letting out a long breath, now quite relieved. He took a handkerchief and wiped away the beads of cold sweat that had begun to sparkle on his forehead. After remaining silent for a long moment he began to smile, then began to look truly overjoyed, and then finally he said, "I'm buying you lunch, Doctor."

So he was going to have a child, proving the gossip that he had never made love to his wife, that he was impotent, and that he had been castrated was all completely false. They both went to meet

Alamanda, who looked strong enough to be taken home. The doctor had told her she could eat something a little more substantial than rice porridge, whatever she wanted, and her face was slowly beginning to look refreshed. She even began to move about a bit on her sickbed.

When the doctor left them alone to arrange for Alamanda's return home, Shodancho said to his wife, "You have recovered, darling."

Alamanda replied without expression, "I guess now I'm healthy enough to turn you on."

Unmoved by her hard heart, Shodancho sat on the edge of the bed and put his hand on his wife's leg while she lay stock-still looking up at the ceiling. "The doctor told me that we are going to have a child. You're pregnant, darling," Shodancho continued, hoping to share his happiness.

But Alamanda surprised him by replying, "I know, and I'm going to abort it."

"Darling, don't!" Shodancho begged. "Save that child and I swear that I'll never do anything like that again."

"Okay, Shodancho," said Alamanda. "But if you ever dare to so much as lay a hand on me, I will not hesitate to kill this baby."

The speed with which Shodancho withdrew his hand from Alamanda's leg made her want to laugh at his ridiculousness. Shodancho reiterated his promise to never force himself on Alamanda again in any way, even if she wasn't wearing her iron underwear. And that was just how it came to pass: Alamanda stopped wearing her ironwear, not just because Shodancho had thrown them into the well but also because she trusted Shodancho would not go against his word. Having a child was more important than anything else for a man with an ego like Shodancho's and Alamanda said, even if she was seven or eight or even nine months pregnant, she would abort that baby if Shodancho forced her to service his base lust, even if she herself died because of it. So it should be clear that she didn't stop wearing the iron underwear because she had changed her mind. She had already sworn that she would never love him and so she would never give herself to him. And by God, she truly did not love him.

Alamanda's homecoming was joyfully celebrated by their friends and family and as soon as the happy news of her pregnancy had spread to the farthest reaches of the city, Shodancho held a small ceremony of thanksgiving. The people of the city discussed it in every canteen as if they were waiting for the birth of a crown prince, most of them in excited tones—except for Kliwon and his fishermen friends.

Kliwon even said brusquely, "She's a whore." His friends were shocked to hear him say such a thing about a woman he had once loved so dearly, but he calmly continued: "A whore makes love for money, so what else can be said about a woman who marries for money *and* social status? She's more than a whore, she's a princess of whores." There was no bitterness in his voice, as if he was merely voicing a commonly held truth.

And if there was some bitterness in Kliwon's heart toward that family, especially toward Shodancho, of course it wasn't because his lover had been unceremoniously taken from him. As a real man, he was always prepared to be abandoned by the woman he loved. What really made him bitter toward Shodancho in all of this were the man's two giant fishing vessels. Those two ships had changed the face of the Halimunda coast. They now floated in the sea and lowered their nets. Workers went back and forth on their decks and coolies hauled the catch to market. The two ships had also changed the faces of the fishermen, which were now crumpled in concern because the fish had grown scarce. They could not compete with the ships' equipment, and even if they did catch some fish, its price had fallen due to the oversaturation of the market that those ships had caused.

This was when Kliwon, at the instructions of the Communist

Party, decided to establish a Fishermen's Union and began to explain to his friends what was happening with the ships and their boats: "It's more than just unhealthy competition, they have stolen our fish." Many of his friends hoped they could fight back by burning the ships, but Comrade Kliwon (as he was now called) tried to calm them down, saying that there was nothing worse than anarchist action, and instead he told them, "Give me some time to talk to Shodancho, who owns those ships."

Comrade Kliwon chose the moment when the news of Alamanda's pregnancy had become an open secret in the city. He hoped that in his good mood Shodancho could be drawn into negotiations about the fishing business. He met him one afternoon in the military district office, purposefully not calling on him at home because he did not want to see Alamanda or in any way disturb the couple's happiness in welcoming their first child.

"Good afternoon, Shodancho," said Comrade Kliwon when they met and shook hands. Shodancho served him a cup of coffee, and indeed he looked very happy and displayed unusually cordial behavior.

"Good afternoon, Comrade. I have heard that you are now the head of the Fishermen's Union and I have heard that the fishermen are complaining about my boats."

"Yes, that's how it is Shodancho," said Comrade Kliwon, telling him about the fishermen's complaints regarding their meager catch and the falling prices. Shodancho told Kliwon about the progress of a new era, that the use of larger ships was inevitable. It was only with these ships that the fishermen would no longer be riddled with rheumatism in their old age. It was only with these ships that the fishermen's wives could be sure their husbands would not be swallowed up by the stormy sea. It was only with these ships that more fish could be caught in order to meet the needs of all people, not just the needs of the people living right here in Halimunda.

"For years, Shodancho, we have caught only as much fish as we need for the day, with just a little left over to stock up for when big storms come. And for years we have survived; we have never been very rich and yet neither have we been poor. But now you are plunging the fishermen into hopeless poverty; you and your ships have stolen the fish they usually catch, and if they do get some fish, it no longer has any value in the market so they are forced to turn it into salt fish they must eat themselves."

"I think you guys probably forgot to do the cow's head throwing ritual, and that's why the queen of the South Seas isn't sharing her fish with you anymore," said Shodancho with a chuckle, drinking his coffee and smoking his clove cigarette.

"That's right, Shodancho, we didn't do the ritual because we no longer have the money to buy even one cow! Don't make these poor people angry, because no one can win when pitted against a starving angry man."

"You're threatening me, Comrade," said Shodancho with another chuckle. "Okay then, I will pay for an ocean ceremony and we will throw a cow's head for the stingy queen, as a sign of my gratitude for my first child. But as for this business with the fishermen I only have one solution: I will add another boat and allow your fishermen to work on deck, with a salary and the guarantee they won't get rheumatism or be threatened by storms. How about it, Comrade?"

"It would better if you acted wisely, Shodancho," said Comrade Kliwon. He quickly took his leave of Shodancho, who only wanted to talk in circles and showed no intention of withdrawing his ships.

The new fishing vessel actually did arrive in the seventh month of Alamanda's pregnancy, but not one fisherman wanted to attend the cow's head throwing ceremony that was held by a handful of Shodancho's men. Even Comrade Kliwon grew upset and told Shodancho that he could no longer guarantee his ships' protection from the fishermen's anger, but Shodancho replied calmly that they should not act rashly. Shodancho didn't seem to care very much about the issue, because after that he didn't meet with anyone, he just stayed in his house awaiting the birth of his first child, who would be his pride and joy, his future, and whom he would clear his schedule to spend the afternoons with once it was born. He would even take the child to school himself once it was a little bit older, and give it whatever it asked for.

Because of this, he truly didn't care about the striking laborers on the fishing vessels, the majority of whom were fishermen from the villages along the coast. The men suffered blows from an army of policemen and soldiers from the military district, but remained unmoved. Without consulting Shodancho, the ship captain fired those laborers one by one, and replaced them with new workers who were willing to follow the rules of their contracts. The Fishermen's Union had succeeded in employing a couple of their men on the ship, but now they had all been fired.

This triggered widespread anger among the fishermen, who in their defeat were now planning to burn those ships down in earnest. But once again, Comrade Kliwon tried to restrain them and promised to go talk to Shodancho. This time he would have no choice but to go to his house, because Shodancho rarely went to the office in those last two months of waiting for his first child. So whether he wanted to or not, it looked as though Comrade Kliwon would have to see Alamanda.

And so it came to pass, because it was Alamanda who opened the door for him, waddling under the burden of her stomach, which puffed up under her white flower-print housedress. For a moment the two looked at one another with a rising longing, united in the same repressed wish to burst out and embrace, kiss, and cry together in their grief. They didn't even smile or say hello, just stood perfectly still and stared at each other. Comrade Kliwon marveled that Alamanda was even more radiant in her pregnancy, and he felt as if he was looking at one of those gorgeous mermaids the fishermen told tales about, or at the queen of the South Seas, who was so unbelievably captivating.

He looked down at Alamanda's pregnant belly, as if he could see the child inside. Alamanda was uncomfortable, thinking that the man was imagining that the child curled up in her womb should be his. She wanted to ask his forgiveness for everything, to say that she still loved him but ill fate had torn them apart. *Maybe someday, when I am a widow, I can marry you.* But apparently Comrade Kliwon wasn't thinking about that at all, because he then said to Alamanda, "Your stomach is like an empty pot."

"What do you mean?" asked Alamanda, as her desire to tell him everything she was thinking quickly vanished.

"There's neither a girl nor a boy inside, it's filled with nothing but air, like an empty pot."

Alamanda was offended and peeved, taking the comment as an insult from a brokenhearted man. She realized that the longer she stood before him, the more wounding words she would hear, so without saying anything else she spun around and almost collided with Shodancho, who had appeared in the doorway and who was just as surprised by what Comrade Kliwon had said. Alamanda withdrew into the house and the two men were left sitting on the veranda chairs, where the husband and wife usually sat together at dusk.

Unlike Alamanda, Shodancho took what came out of Comrade Kliwon's mouth quite seriously, and he became so worried that he asked the man again what he had meant by calling it an empty pot. Just as he had said to Alamanda, Comrade Kliwon repeated it was like an empty pot, there was neither a boy nor girl inside Alamanda's womb, there was *nothing* inside, except air and wind.

"That's impossible, the doctor has already confirmed my wife is pregnant. You can see her stomach yourself!" Shodancho protested anxiously.

"Yes, I have seen her stomach," said Comrade Kliwon. "So maybe this is just the grumbling of a jealous man."

{10}

ONCE UPON A time, the citizens of Halimunda were thrown into an uproar by the discovery of a baby, found lying in a garbage heap. It was a boy and he was still alive even though he was being dragged back and forth by dogs, so people knew he would grow up to be a strong man. For days they tried to find his mother, but she never came forward, so they couldn't begin to guess who his father might be.

The baby was cared for by an old spinster named Makojah, the most hated granny in the city, and yet the old lady everyone most depended on. She made her living by loaning money, because that was the only thing she could do. She couldn't farm, because no one would sell her any land and all she had was the tiny patch of earth she had inherited and on which she lived, and she couldn't work because nobody would give her a job. She couldn't even get a husband for as long as she lived, even though she had proposed to about sixteen men. Her life was lonely and full of misery, but she got her revenge by pretending to be charitable and loaning those city folk who had fallen into poverty money and then asphyxiating them with her high interest rates.

So, to repeat, everybody hated her, especially those drowning in their never-ending debt. Everyone avoided her, shunned her, and considered her worse than a demonic sinner. But if a hard-pressed time came and they had tried everything else to no avail, they would come knocking on her door, because they knew that just behind it temporary assistance could be found. Makojah knew all their polite bowing was just a charade, and their fake smiles masked their real plea, but she didn't care—it was all part of her business.

People sometimes wondered where all the money she collected went, because she never seemed to get any richer. Her house was just as it had always been, except for the occasional paint job or small repairs. She didn't live extravagantly, she didn't have any relatives, and they never saw her go to the bank to deposit the money she wrung out of them, so they began to think the old spinster must be stashing their money under her mattress. So one night, in a stealth operation, four men came to her house to rob her. Her neighbors, who knew all about it, watched from behind their curtains. Makojah calmly looked on as they searched every corner of her house. No matter where the thieves looked, they didn't find the money—there was nothing underneath her mattress, nothing in her stove, and nothing in the water jug. Her wardrobe held only clothes, and all her kitchen cupboard had inside it was a plate of rice and some carrot soup. Giving up, the four masked thieves called off their search and approached Makojah, who was still just standing there in her bedroom doorway.

"Where's your money?" asked one of them, annoyed.

"I would be more than happy to give it to you," said Makojah smiling, "at forty-percent interest, to be repaid in full by the end of the week."

They left her without saying another word.

No one tried to steal from her again, especially not after she took in the baby. Makojah cared for the little one mostly because she had always dreamed of having a child, but also because no one else was willing to take him from the trash heap. So the baby grew up with her. Makojah gave him a good name, Bima, after the strong prince in the Mahabharata, but everyone else called him Idiot, due to his truly annoying and aggravating behavior, and then the people forgot that his real name was Bima, including Makojah, and then the little kid himself forgot it too, so his full name became Edi Idiot.

An accursed fate was predicted to soon befall that child, because the old spinster brought misfortune—her mother had died giving birth to her and then, when she was five years old, her father died too, stung by a scorpion that had scuttled into the kitchen. Then Makojah was cared for by a childless widow auntie, who came to live with her. When Makojah was seven years old the auntie also died, struck on her head by a falling coconut. In any case, her father had owned a pawnshop and Makojah received a more than adequate inheritance, enough to hire a servant to take care of her daily needs, though her servant in turn died from a spiking fever when Makojah was twelve. After that, nobody wanted to live with her, thinking she brought bad luck.

When she was still young, she was honestly quite beautiful. Many men were secretly in love with her, but they knew everyone who had lived with her had died and preferred to marry other girls, who weren't as good looking but with whom they'd live long after their wedding day, as opposed to marrying Makojah and then dying right after. Nobody knew where all her bad luck came from, and nobody considered all those deaths to be mere coincidences. Everyone preferred a darker interpretation, and in fact she'd never be touched by a man up until the day she died.

Makojah had her business of money lending, but she was starting to get old and was sure that she wouldn't survive living all alone. She tried proposing to good men, but they refused her. She tried proposing to bad men, the gamblers and the drunks, but they refused her too. She even tried proposing to beggars, but they preferred to live in poverty rather than to live in luxury with her. Finally, when she was forty-two years old, she stopped trying to find a husband and tried to adopt a child, but this failed too, and she was all alone until the day she finally pulled that baby from the trash heap.

Edi Idiot grew up in her care with no sign of the curse. The only unlucky thing about him was that none of the other little kids wanted to play with him, infected by the prejudice toward the family. The children avoided Edi Idiot just as their parents avoided Makojah, except when they needed her money. This turned the boy into a difficult hothead who annoyed all the other kids. He'd tantrum anytime he didn't get his way. He berated people at the slightest perceived slight, and this made the other children withdraw from him even further.

He tried to develop friendships by spreading fear as the strongest kid in the city.

But in the end he found some real friends, in other outcast classmates. He noticed two crippled children made into the butt of other kids' jokes. He saw a starving and bone-skinny kid get teased, and another shunned because his parents were a coolie and a pickpocket. Edi Idiot was always there for them, coming whenever those kids were getting bullied, mercilessly attacking their tormenters. He became their protector and the group developed such a close friendship that the schoolchildren were divided into two groups: the good kids, and the delinquent kids led by Edi Idiot.

They began to grow into the city's public enemies. Unlike the other kids, who just caused small-time chaos and confusion, Edi Idiot did not hesitate to clean out all the chickens from someone's coop for a feast at the seashore. When he was just eleven years old, he had already robbed a tavern, wounding its owner and grabbing bottles and bottles of *arak* and beer, then getting drunk with his friends in a cocoa orchard. They had also started sampling almost all the prostitutes in the city. And they had the unique distinction of seeing the inside of a prison cell before they were teenagers. In such situations, Makojah would rescue them by bribing the police, not in the least bit upset by anything that Edi Idiot did. On the contrary, that old spinster was quite proud of him.

"He'll hurt the people of this city," Makojah said once, to the policemen guarding him, "just as they have hurt me for so many years."

And it was true. When parents threatened to withdraw their children unless the school got rid of Edi Idiot, the principal, who was powerless to refuse, finally expelled the kid, only to arrive one morning to find that all the windows and the door to the school had been smashed, all the legs of the desks and chairs broken, and the flagpole toppled over.

That was how Edi, just twelve years old, was running wild in the streets. He went to stores and demanded money from the owners, and if they didn't give it to him, well then their shop windows would be smashed. He went to the whorehouse and didn't pay, or watched movies without buying a ticket, and if someone had a problem with that he'd fight, and he always won.

To handle the kid, some shop owners finally hired a *preman* and Edi Idiot went up against him in a fight to the death. Edi Idiot went back to jail, but he started a melee in the prison, destroying all the cells and beating up the guards, and was quickly freed. Back on the streets he killed two or three other people who tried to fight him, but the police were no longer interested in trying to lock him up.

So he set up his regular post in the corner of the bus terminal, with a mahogany rocking chair left behind by the Japanese as his throne. He gathered followers one by one. He won some over by beating them in fights, but most joined voluntarily. They collected a "tax" from the shop owners, all the buses that entered the terminal and even those that didn't, all the kiosks in the market, all the fishing boats, all the brothels and beer gardens, all the ice and coconut oil factories, and even all the *becak* rickshaws and horse-drawn carriages.

Edi Idiot and his minions terrorized the city. Their posse would do whatever they wanted, drunk or sober: steal chickens, break windows, bother the girls whether they were walking alone or under the watchful eyes of their entire family, and even steal the sandals outside the mosque. The old folks' caged turtledoves, their fighting cocks, and their clothes hanging out on the line to dry also frequently disappeared.

Appearing at any moment to loot and pillage, the posse also became a serious bother to upstanding young men, taking their guitars, and in countless shakedowns forcing them to hand over their shoes while they were out taking a walk. Plus, don't even ask how many packs of cigarettes they demanded in the course of a day. Any protest only led to more fighting. It became even clearer that the posse could not be defeated, especially if Edi Idiot brought down his own fist. Most annoying of all was the attitude of the police, who treated this as little more than children's naughtiness.

"He'll surely die," someone said in an effort to make himself feel better, "because no matter what, he lives with Makojah."

"Yeah but the problem is *when* he will die."

His death didn't come for three more years. Instead, Makojah died first, without warning one morning while taking a shit in her bathroom. Edi Idiot himself discovered her. He awoke at nine o'clock and didn't find his breakfast waiting for him as usual. He looked everywhere, but he couldn't find that old maid anywhere, and then he became suspicious of the closed bathroom door. He tried to open it. It was locked from the inside. He broke it down and found her still squatting on the toilet, naked, with no life force left in her at all.

"Mama, are you dead?" asked Edi Idiot.

Makojah did not respond.

Edi Idiot touched Makojah's forehead with the tip of his finger, and her body immediately toppled over backwards.

Her death was joyful news for the city folk: most still owed her money. None of the neighbors wanted to take care of her body, so Edi Idiot himself carried her corpse to the house of the gravedigger, Kamino. At that time Kamino was still single, because no woman was willing to live in the middle of the graveyard with him, so the two men had to tend to Makojah's corpse all by themselves before a *kyai* who took pity on them arrived. The *kyai* ordered the corpse to be bathed, and then he said the last rites along with the gravedigger while Edi Idiot waited uncomfortably. Thus, Makojah, who was so well known by everyone in the city, and was always ready and available to help them in their time of need, was buried with only three people to witness her corpse being put into the ground.

Makojah didn't leave Edi Idiot any inheritance except the house and yard where they had been living all this time. No one knew where all the money she made from the interest on her loans went. Edi Idiot himself couldn't have cared less about the money, but the people of the city cared because they felt like it rightfully belonged to them. So for years afterward, people kept hunting for Makojah's money. It was said that she'd had an underground vault, so some people tried to dig a tunnel from a neighbor's house. They didn't find anything, but one of the diggers died from inhaling sulfurous smoke and they closed that tunnel right back up.

The people's joy didn't last long. They thought that now that Makojah had died, Edi Idiot would turn into a good kid, or at least make himself scarce for a couple of months to mourn. But it didn't turn out that way. Instead, he brought some girls home with him to sleep with, while their fathers went looking for them near and far and then gave up the search. He demanded food from any open kitchen, sitting down at the table and devouring whatever was there, before the cook could sample her own cuisine. And this isn't even counting the murders and bus stick-ups.

When Shodancho came down from his guerrilla post in the jungle, many of the city folk hoped that he wouldn't just take care of the pigs, but that he would also take care of all the *preman* in the city. But Shodancho declined.

"They are like turds," said Shodancho, "the more you stir them, the more they stink." He didn't explain any further, but the people quickly understood: if Edi Idiot and his posse were messed with, they would only become an even bigger bother to the city.

That was a time when many people in Halimunda sat on their verandas with exhausted faces. The occasional mischievous visitor might ask, "What are you guys doing?" And they would reply:

"Waiting for Edi Idiot's coffin to pass by."

Their prayers were never answered. Not because Edi Idiot didn't die, but because he didn't have a funeral, and he was never buried. He drowned, and his body was eaten by a pair of sharks.

Yes, a stranger arrived one morning, Maman Gendeng, and killed Edi after a legendary brawl that lasted seven days and seven nights. At first nobody believed that the hardheaded kid was truly dead, but then it was like they were awaking from a bad dream: Edi Idiot was mortal, just like anybody else. The city folk were incredibly thankful to that stranger, and Maman Gendeng was quickly accepted as one of their own.

To celebrate, the people threw a party, unrivaled by any celebration before or after. Even the 23rd of September celebration of Halimunda's independence had never been as festive. There was a night fair that lasted for an entire month, with a travelling circus full of elephants, tigers, lions, monkeys, snakes, little girl contortionists, and of course midget clowns. In every corner of the city people could enjoy *sintren* and *kuda lumping* trance performances for free. The young men and women went out together to enjoy their romances, without being afraid that Edi Idiot's posse would bother them. The chickens roamed about freely again in people's yards and kitchen doors were no longer locked up tight.

So when Maman Gendeng pronounced that no one except he himself could sleep with the whore Dewi Ayu, the people weren't all that upset, although clearly it was a huge loss. They thought it was an appropriate enough tribute to be given to the hero who had killed Edi Idiot, Makojah's infuriating son.

But then one day, in the tropical heat, Maman Gendeng got up from the mahogany rocking chair that he'd inherited from Edi Idiot and walked from the bus terminal to the closest store with a whooshing and buzzing sound in his ears. He demanded one crate of cold beer, because of the damned hot weather, but the shopkeeper only gave him one bottle. Maman Gendeng went nuts, smashed the shop window to smithereens, and took a whole crate of beer after berating the shop owner who, according to Maman Gendeng, was not one bit civilized. He returned to his rocking chair and killed that parched feeling with the hijacked beer.

With this event the realization hit home that, as far as the citizens of Halimunda were concerned, nothing had changed. Edi Idiot was dead, but a new scoundrel had arrived. His name was Maman Gendeng.

After Alamanda's festive wedding celebration, Dewi Ayu had ordered the newlyweds to move into their new house. She was quite upset by all the recent events, and by how they'd affected her oldest child. She had time and time again warned Alamanda about her horrible way of treating men, but Alamanda had inherited a certain stubbornness from who knows which family member, and now she was suffering the repercussions.

Dewi Ayu had never imagined that she would give birth to

beautiful but wild girls who would chase men only to toss them aside. But she had known about Alamanda's bad behavior ever since the girl had first discovered boys, and now it seemed that Adinda shared her sister's bad temperament. She used to be a total innocent, preferring to spend time at home rather than roaming about, but ever since Alamanda's sudden wedding, she was disappearing more and more often. Look at the girl, now to be found wherever the Communist Party was having one of its raucous celebrations. And Adinda began to chase the man who once belonged to Alamanda: Comrade Kliwon. Dewi Ayu didn't know what Adinda was thinking, but she suspected the girl wanted to get revenge on her sister through that man. It was really quite upsetting.

Men hunt my privates, she told herself, *and I gave birth to girls who hunt men's privates.*

So she worried even more about her youngest child, Maya Dewi, who was twelve years old. She was afraid the child would imitate her two delinquent older sisters. Right now she was a good and obedient child who didn't at all appear to be reckless. Her hands were busier than anyone else's in that household, making everything pleasant and comfortable. She picked roses and orchids to arrange in the flower vase that she placed on the front room table every morning. She swept away all the cobwebs from the ceiling of the house every Sunday afternoon. Her teachers reported on her good behavior and she opened her textbooks every night, finishing all her homework before going to bed. But all that could change, as had happened with Adinda, and this was what really worried Dewi Ayu.

"To marry someone you don't love is way worse than living as a whore," she instructed her youngest.

Dewi Ayu thought she should marry Maya Dewi off as quickly as possible, before she grew up and went wild. For years she had always solved her problems with quick thinking, and the first idea that popped into her head was always the very thing that she did next. She didn't want to see Maya Dewi grow up to face the same tragic fate that had befallen Alamanda and might yet befall Adinda. But she didn't know who to set up with her twelve-year-old, because she didn't intend to give her away to just anybody.

She wanted to talk it over with her lover, Maman Gendeng. One Sunday, the three of them went to a public park. They relaxed there all day, snacked all they wanted, fed the tame deer, and went on the swings. Dewi Ayu watched Maman Gendeng leading Maya Dewi here and there by the hand, pointing out the peacocks hiding in the shrubbery and throwing nuts to the gangs of monkeys. Dewi Ayu didn't even care that they seemed to have forgotten she was there. She watched them walk to the edge of the sea cliffs and try to count the seagulls flying.

After they had all returned home and Maya Dewi went off with her neighborhood pals, Dewi Ayu finally spoke to Maman Gendeng.

"Why don't you two get married?"

"Who?" asked Maman Gendeng. "Me and who?"

"You and Maya Dewi."

"You're crazy," said Maman Gendeng. "If there is any woman I want to marry, it's you."

Dewi Ayu explained her worries over a glass of cold lemonade. They sat together on the veranda in the warm afternoon air. They could hear the waves pounding in the distance and the sparrows making a din in their nest on the roof. The pair had been lovers for many months now, one a prostitute and the other the customer who held a monopoly on her. Dewi Ayu insisted that Maya Dewi had to be married off to somebody, and because there was no one else close to her, the only man she could be married off to was Maman Gendeng.

"Are you trying to tell me you don't want to sleep with me anymore?"

"Don't get me wrong," said Dewi Ayu. "You can still visit me at

Mama Kalong's whorehouse just like everyone else's husband, if you're not too embarrassed."

"I would have to think something like this over, maybe for many years," Maman Gendeng muttered.

"Try considering other people for once! The men of Halimunda are going insane. They are practically half-dead because they've been forbidden to touch my body, just because of some tough guy like you. If you let me go, you'll be their hero. And in exchange you'll get a girl who will never disappoint you, the youngest daughter of the most beautiful whore in the city."

"She's only twelve years old."

"Dogs get married at two years old and chickens get married at eight months."

"But she's not a dog or a chicken."

"You just think like that because you've never been to school. Every human is a mammal, just like a dog, and walks on two legs, just like a chicken."

Maman Gendeng already knew this woman's character, or at least he thought he did. He knew that Dewi Ayu would not give up on any idea, no matter how crazy. He drank his cold lemonade and felt himself shiver, as if he had to cross a bridge only seven strands of hair wide with all hell spread out below him.

"But I'll never be a good husband," he protested.

"So be a terrible husband if you want."

"And it's not yet certain that she will agree."

"She's an obedient young girl," said Dewi Ayu. "She listens to everything I say, and I truly don't believe that she will have any trouble with marrying you."

"There's no way I would sleep with such a young girl."

"You'd only have to wait about five years."

It was as if it were already decided. Even though he was a thuggish *preman*, Maman Gendeng trembled violently, imagining the gossip about such a marriage. They would say that he had raped the girl and was being forced to marry her.

"Marry her out of your love for me," said Dewi Ayu finally, "if for no other reason."

That was like a judge's sentence for Maman Gendeng. It was as if there was a bee buzzing inside his skull and dragonflies flitting around in his stomach. He finished his lemonade but couldn't rid his insides of all those creatures. Then he felt like there was a wild thicket growing in his chest, with thorns stabbing everywhere. Like a weakling loser, he collapsed against the chair with his eyes half-closed.

"Why'd you go and spring this on me all of a sudden?" he asked.

"Whenever I had said it, it would have felt just as surprising."

"Give me a place to sleep, I want to lie down for a minute."

"My bed is always open to you."

Maman Gendeng slept soundly for almost four hours, snoring softly. That was the only way to survive all of this bee and thicket and dragonfly nonsense. Dewi Ayu passed the afternoon freshening up in the bathroom and sitting in the front room with a cigarette and a cup of coffee, waiting for the man to wake up. At that moment Maya Dewi appeared, saying that she wanted to bathe, but her mother asked her to wait a moment and told her to sit down across from her.

"Child, you are going to be married soon, just like your older sister Alamanda," said Dewi Ayu.

"I've heard that getting married is easy," said Maya Dewi.

"That's quite true. What's difficult is getting divorced."

Then Maman Gendeng reappeared, coming out of the bedroom with the pale face of a sleepwalker, and sat in a chair, reluctant to look at the little girl sitting next to her mother. "I had a dream," he said. Neither Dewi Ayu nor Maya Dewi responded, because they were waiting for him to continue. "I dreamed I was bitten by a snake."

"That's a good omen," said Dewi Ayu. "You two will soon be married. I am going out to look for a village headman."

That was how Maman Gendeng, about thirty years old, married Maya Dewi, who was twelve, in the same year that Alamanda married Shodancho. Their brief and simple wedding ceremony was celebrated by cheerful gossip throughout the city about what had *really* happened. But at least the marriage made the Halimunda men quite happy, because they could once again visit Dewi Ayu at Mama Kalong's whorehouse.

Dewi Ayu left her house and two servants to the newlyweds, while she and Adinda moved to a complex of newly renovated homes left behind by the Japanese. Dewi Ayu liked those houses because the Japanese had big tubs, almost as big as swimming pools.

"If you want to get married too, just say the word," she told Adinda.

"Oh, I'm not in such a hurry," said Adinda. "The apocalypse is still quite a ways off."

Before they left for good, Dewi Ayu prepared a luxurious room for the newlyweds, with the scent of jasmine and orchids floating in the air. The new bed that she had ordered, the best mattress in the city with the latest spring-bed technology, had arrived directly from the store that afternoon and was surrounded by an elegantly pleated pink mosquito net. The walls of the room were decorated with crepe-paper flowers. But this was all sort of pointless, because those newlyweds didn't really spend their first night together then.

Instead, Maya Dewi, who was wearing her pajamas, jumped on the bed with the lightheartedness of a child. She wanted to test out its springs, just as her mother had done so many years ago at the brothel for the Japanese. When she tired of admiring the mattress and the splendorous room she lay down, hugging a bolster and waiting for her groom. Maman Gendeng appeared in a state of indescribable awkwardness. He did not jump into bed, embrace his wife's body and ravage her mercilessly like so many careless new husbands do. Instead he just pulled up a chair to the side of the bed and sat there looking at the little girl's face with the tortured gaze of a man watching his lover die. Her miniature beauty was really quite charming. Her black hair shone, unfurling beneath her atop the pillow. The eyes that returned his gaze were clear and innocent. Her nose and her lips and everything about her was marvelous. But see, everything was still so tiny and adorable. Her hands were still the hands of a young girl, as were her calves, and underneath her pajamas her breasts were not yet full grown. There was no way he could sleep with such a little girl.

"Why are you just sitting there so quietly?" asked Maya Dewi.

"Well what should I be doing?" Maman Gendeng retorted, in a complaining tone.

"You could at least tell me a story."

Maman Gendeng was not good at making up stories, so he told her the only story he had ever heard: the story about Princess Rengganis.

"If we have a daughter, let's name her Rengganis," said Maya Dewi.

"That's just what I was thinking."

And so every night passed in the same way: Maya Dewi would lie down first, in her pajamas, and then Maman Gendeng would appear in the same confused state. He would pull up a chair and look at his new bride with the same old dejected face, and Maya Dewi would ask him for a story. The story that he told was always the same, almost exactly word for word, about the Princess Rengganis who married a dog. But the two passed those evenings just as happily as most newlyweds, and there were no signs of boredom on their faces. Usually Maya Dewi had already fallen fast asleep before the tale was done. Maman Gendeng would cover her with a blanket, close the mosquito netting, turn off the lamp and turn on the night-light. After looking at her peaceful sleeping face, he would leave the room, close the door gently, and go up to the second floor to sleep in an empty room until morning, when his wife came to wake him up with a cup of hot coffee. Living in their new home, Dewi Ayu and Adinda laughed at such ridiculousness.

Maman Gendeng started a new routine. He woke up in the morning and drank the coffee his wife had made for him. A half hour later Mirah served breakfast, and the two of them would sit at the table just like most happy families. At first this was a miserable annoyance to Maman Gendeng, who was used to sleeping in. But after eating breakfast, his wife would allow him to return to his bed, and it turned out his sleep was even more restful with a full stomach. Maman Gendeng would wake up again around ten o'clock, to find his clothes neatly ironed and laid out next to his bed. He would go take a bath, something he rarely used to do, and put on those clothes. It felt strange to see himself in the mirror wearing a button-down shirt and slacks accented with a crisp pleat ironed straight down the front. Even though he only did it for Maya Dewi, he would put on those clothes and, after kissing his wife's forehead in the doorway, go to his faithful spot in the bus terminal.

After a while, none of it annoyed him anymore, even though his pals at the bus terminal looked askance at his strange new behavior. Feeling homesick all the time, and constantly longing for his wife, he never stayed at the terminal until evening anymore. Instead, the moment afternoon fell he would quickly head for home.

One night, after they had been married for a month, Maya Dewi asked him, "May I go back to school?"

That question was surprising. Of course, she was still of school age, and every girl of twelve belonged in school from morning until afternoon. But she was also somebody's wife and he had never heard of a married woman sitting on a school bench. That made him think for a while, until he realized that their marriage wasn't yet a true marriage like the kind other people had. He had not yet slept with his wife, and had no desire to. Maybe it was better if she went back to school.

But then there was a problem. The school wouldn't allow a married woman to register, worrying it would have a bad influence on the other students. Maman Gendeng was forced to pay a visit and negotiate with the principal so that his wife would be permitted to return to her studies. That negotiation ended badly, with him pinning that principal to the wall and knocking down the two teachers who tried to come to the man's aid. And many years later he had to do the same exact thing when the school refused to accept his daughter, Rengganis the Beautiful.

After that merciless intimidation, the school readmitted Maya Dewi.

Their marriage continued just as peacefully as before. In the morning, just as usual, Maya Dewi would waken Maman Gendeng with a glass of freshly ground Lampung coffee, only now she was wearing her school uniform. At the table, they would eat breakfast, looking to the servants like a father without a wife and a young girl without a mother. At quarter to seven, Maya Dewi was ready with her school bag. She would leave after Maman Gendeng kissed her forehead, and as she headed off to school Maman Gendeng would head back to sleep.

In the afternoon when she came home from school, Maman Gendeng wouldn't be there, so Maya Dewi would set everything in order to her utmost ability. In the evening, when they were together again after dinner, Maya Dewi would sit at her desk and finish the homework her teachers had assigned her. Maman Gendeng couldn't help her with it, all he could do was keep her company with the special patience of a dedicated lover. The routine would finish up around nine o'clock. That was bedtime, but there were no more tales about Rengganis the Beautiful who married a dog. Maya Dewi would put on her pajamas and lie in bed. Maman Gendeng would come to cover her with a blanket, pull the curtain closed, turn off the lamp and turn on the night-light, and then say, "Goodnight."

"Goodnight," Maya Dewi would reply, before closing her eyes.

There still was no lovemaking, even after one entire year had passed.

One night Maman Gendeng went to see Dewi Ayu in her chambers at Mama Kalong's whorehouse, just as he so often used to do. Dewi Ayu's only guest had already gone.

"Why have you come here?" asked Dewi Ayu.

"I can't hold back my desire."

"You have a wife."

"She is too adorable to be harmed. She is too pure to be touched. I want to sleep with my mother-in-law."

"You're a really screwed up son-in-law," said Dewi Ayu.

And they made love until morning.

The strange friendship between Maman Gendeng and Shodancho began at the card table in the middle of the market. The friendship was a strange one because ever since Shodancho had slept with Dewi Ayu and Maman Gendeng had come to the military headquarters, an eternal animosity had been planted deep inside them both. And this was exacerbated by the fact that Maman Gendeng's men always had problems with Shodancho's soldiers.

The soldiers didn't like to pay at the whorehouse, but the *preman* were there to take care of anyone who slept with the whores without paying. The soldiers also didn't like paying at the beer gardens and taverns—in fact, the owners didn't make a big deal out of that, because the soldiers never drank too much, but the *preman* had practically taken up residence in the beer gardens and felt it was a slap in their face. What's more, one of the *preman* was always getting caught by the military for something silly like being drunk and throwing stones through a shop window, then the soldiers would rough him up behind their headquarters before letting him go all black and blue. All of this provoked small scuffles between Shodancho's soldiers and Maman Gendeng's posse.

But up until this point, the problems could be easily solved. If a *preman* was captured by soldiers and beaten until he was black and blue, then the posse would capture a soldier passing by on the road and gang up on him in a cocoa plantation. If a criminal was captured and held, Maman Gendeng would come to free him with a little ransom money to shut those soldiers' mouths. In the middle of all these disputes were the police, but they preferred to sit at their posts and throw up their hands at the whole business.

Many people had hoped that Shodancho would quickly take care of these public enemies, but just as with Edi Idiot, this was nothing but wishful thinking, since Shodancho was busy dealing with his own family problems and the Fishermen's Union's demands and he had no time to think about Maman Gendeng and his friends. And so Shodancho's popularity as a city hero plummeted—in fact, the people actually began to distrust him and suspect that the military was conspiring with the *preman* to cause all of this chaos, especially when they remembered that the two men, Shodancho and Maman Gendeng, were both Dewi Ayu's sons-in-law.

So it got a little chaotic when one a day a soldier from the military headquarters tussled with one of the bodyguards at Mama Kalong's brothel. The dispute began over a village girl both men claimed for themselves. They fought in the street, and then their friends showed up. Their private scuffle became a heated brawl between a group of soldiers and a gang of thugs.

Who knows how it started, but in the end, after an hour of wild fighting, almost twenty shade trees had toppled over along the side of the road and shop windows stood shattered. Boulders and old scorched tires were lying in the street, two cars had been overturned, and the police station was burned.

The terrified people hid in their homes. The fight brought the usually bustling Jalan Merdeka to a standstill. On one side, a posse of *preman* stood watch with sabres, samurai swords, spears, iron clubs, machetes, stones, and Molotov cocktails. They even had hand grenades and weapons left over from the guerrilla army. Meanwhile, on the other side of the street soldiers, not just Shodancho's men but from all the military posts in the city, also stood guard with loaded weapons.

That day everything was quiet and still, as if the city had been abandoned for years. A tense silence crept across the land, along with the fear that a civil war would break out in that city, which had not known a time of peace ever since the war for independence. Many were fed up with the *preman*, and thought to themselves that if war broke out they would side with the soldiers. But many others were sick of the soldiers, who always seemed so full of themselves, and thought that if war broke out they would definitely help the *preman*.

But ultimately they would all kill each other, sparing no one.

That whole afternoon the sounds of exploding grenades and Molotov cocktails and pistol shots could be heard whistling in between shops and houses. Nobody knew if anyone had been killed yet. Wrapped up in his never-ending domestic problems, Shodancho was slow to hear about these dire conditions and once he did, he was annoyed that some village girl could lead to the destruction of the heart of the city. He decided he would put that wretched soldier in solitary confinement for seven days and seven nights without food or water, not caring if he died. But first he had to prevent widespread destruction. So he quickly sent his most trusted soldier,

Tino Sidiq, to talk to Maman Gendeng, to call for a cease-fire and make a peace treaty.

Maman Gendeng, who was enjoying the honeymoon period of his bizarre marriage, had also just heard about the fighting on Jalan Merdeka, but he didn't care that much either. He was just annoyed that people were still getting in the way of his efforts to build the happy life that could make up for all those years he had spent wandering, aimless and lonely. He felt sure the scuffle must have been started by some rude soldier.

But his twelve-year-old wife convinced him that he should take care of the chaos, and Maman Gendeng finally went out, after he and Tino Sidiq agreed that he would meet Shodancho in a neutral spot halfway between the bus terminal and the military headquarters. That spot was the marketplace.

They chased out the four men—a salt-fish seller, a rickshaw driver, a coolie, and the husband of one of the clothing merchants—who were sitting around a card table in the middle of the market betting with coins that jingled from one corner of the table to another. The card players withdrew and stood watching from the poultry seller's stall, as Shodancho finally appeared. All the market activities ground to a halt as the merchants and customers froze in their tracks, waiting for the two men to decide whether a horrible civil war would break out that afternoon or be postponed for years, maybe even centuries to come.

Shodancho said the *preman* should immediately retreat and surrender all their weapons, because only the military had the right to bear arms. But Maman Gendeng found that unsupportable, since the soldiers used their weapons with impunity. Shodancho spoke again:

"Oh my dear friend, we will not solve this problem by quarrelling like children." And then he continued, "All right then, for the time being there will be no disarmament, but order your men off the streets and tell them that there must be no more rioting crowds or broken shop windows."

"Oh my dear Shodancho," said Maman Gendeng, "then surely you agree that there must be no more disputes by armed soldiers over village girls or whomever. And, just like any other man in this city, the soldiers will have to pay for every visit to the whorehouse, and pay at the beer garden every time they drink, and pay the bus driver every time they take a ride. There are no more golden boys here, Shodancho."

Shodancho drew in a long breath, and complained that the soldiers weren't paid enough by the national government, and that his businesses with the military and the city forces lost most of their profits to the general in the capital. "So my dear friend, I am going to make you an offer that might not seem so enticing at first but will help us find a solution to this complicated problem," said Shodancho finally.

"Please tell me."

"Maybe my friend," said Shodancho, "it can be agreed upon that your thugs and goons surrender a portion of what you earn to the soldiers, so that they might pay their whores and get satisfactorily drunk."

Maman Gendeng thought for a moment and saw no problem with skimming a little bit off the top of whatever his minions obtained, if promised the soldiers wouldn't bother the *preman* no matter what happened, and would agree to live in a mutually profitable peace.

And so an accord was finally reached after whispers that no one in the market could hear, as the people looked on, full of curiosity. Maman Gendeng and Shodancho sent their most trusted men to spread the news that a cease-fire would begin at four o'clock that afternoon. The soldiers would return to their posts, and the *preman* would return to their old haunts. Now Maman Gendeng and

Shodancho were the only ones left, still sitting in the middle of the market, each breathing sighs of relief as if he had been freed from a tiger's mouth, leaning back in their chairs, until Shodancho asked:

"Do you know how to play trump?"

"I often play trump with my friends at the bus terminal," replied Maman Gendeng.

So they invited the salt-fish seller and the coolie back to play trump with them, and that was the beginning of their strange friendship at the card table. Many matters affecting the soldiers and the *preman* were taken care of quietly there by the two of them. They started a new routine of meeting at that same card table three times a week. It wasn't a secret that they always tried to trick one another and always wanted to win, but the cost wasn't too high, only a few coins difference whether they won or lost. Sometimes they played with the clothing seller's husband, and sometimes with medicine peddlers, coolies, *becak* drivers, butchers, salt-fish sellers, or couriers—anyone they could find in the market who knew how to play trump.

But if Shodancho was there at the table then Maman Gendeng would be there, and vice versa. A strange friendship, it's worth repeating, because in their hearts they didn't like each other. Maman Gendeng still held a grudge against Shodancho for his effrontery in fucking the whore he loved, and Shodancho still held a grudge against the impudent man across the table from him for daring to threaten him in his very own office not caring a whit that he was the local military district chief and had even been appointed great commander by the president of the republic.

Their friendship made the people's heads spin. They were thankful that all of the city's problems could be solved so easily at the card table, but they were also pretty annoyed once they understood that there was a cunning conspiracy between the soldiers and the *preman* to enjoy the money extorted from the city folk. They also realized, along those same lines, that now they didn't have anyone to whom they could complain. And don't think they could ask the police for help, because all the police ever did was blow their whistles at busy intersections.

That was when the Communist Party became the only place they could go, and they turned, above all, to Comrade Kliwon. At this time those two—Comrade Kliwon and the Communist Party—had the best reputation in Halimunda.

Meanwhile, the friendship between Shodancho and Maman Gendeng continued. As time went on, the trump table was no longer only used to discuss fighting between soldiers and the *preman* or the fairest way to share their spoils—Shodancho also began to lament his problems as if unburdening the contents of his heart to an old friend. That was what they usually talked about, after they'd finished their card game and after the merchants in the market began closing up their kiosk doors and heading home. Sometimes they talked about Comrade Kliwon too. Shodancho still believed the man wasn't a real communist, but was just avenging his beloved Alamanda. Maman Gendeng laughed, hearing of this drama (even though he actually already knew all about it) and he put forth the opinion that a man shouldn't steal someone else's sweetheart. That was why he'd been so hurt to hear that Shodancho had slept with Dewi Ayu. At that, Shodancho's face turned red and his eyes welled up like a little kid who has lost his mother.

"I'm the loneliest fucking person in this tumultuous world," he said. "I entered Japanese military training in the Seinendan troop when I was barely a teenager, before becoming a *shodancho*. I rebelled against them in a guerrilla war that lasted for months after they'd already surrendered. My life has been one war after another, including a war against pigs. I'm tired of all that." Maman Gendeng gave Shodancho the handkerchief that Maya Dewi always slipped into his pants pocket, and Shodancho dried his eyes. "I want to live like other people. I want to love and be loved."

"Your men love you very much," said Maman Gendeng.

"But you know full well there is no way I can marry them."

"Well, at least we both have beautiful wives now."

"Yeah, but it's my bad luck to marry a woman who loved another man first, with the kind of love that might never fade."

"That could be true," said Maman Gendeng. "I've seen Comrade Kliwon, in front of a group of fishermen. He is quite sympathetic and works hard to remedy the misfortunes of others. Sometimes I envy him. Sometimes I even think that he's the only person in this city who looks toward the future with hope."

"That's what communists are like," said Shodancho. "Pathetic people who don't realize this world is destined to be the most rotten place imaginable. That's the only reason God promised heaven, as a comfort to the wretched masses."

They would get so caught up in their conversation that they wouldn't notice day turning into night. Once they realized the time, they would quickly stand and give each other a hug and say see you later before heading home in opposite directions. Each to his own home and his own wife. One day some bad luck came: Mirah and Sapri decided to stop working in Maman Gendeng's house because all of a sudden they realized they were in love and now they wanted to get married and live in a village as farmers. Maman Gendeng was at a loss as to how he was going to get a new servant, and his wife was still just a snot-nosed kid. But it turned out differently than he expected. The first day without the servants, when he returned home after playing trump with Shodancho and it was already dark, he found dinner prepared.

"Who cooked all this?" he asked, confused.

"I did."

That's when he realized his wife's extraordinary talent for homemaking. She didn't just neatly iron and perfume his clothes, she also cooked all their food, and he found everything delicious and just to his liking. Dewi Ayu had been training her ever since she was a little girl, Maya Dewi explained. She was even an excellent baker, always trying out new recipes for cookies and cakes and sharing them with their neighbors. Maya Dewi had become the family ambassador, the one who maintained friendly relations with the neighbors, because Maman Gendeng could never hope to change his bad reputation. Those cookies and cakes brought the family a lot of good fortune, because the neighbors soon started ordering them for their sons' circumcision celebrations, and the orders kept on coming. Maya Dewi made them in the afternoon after school and so, whatever happened, the family would never have to worry about their economic situation.

Maman Gendeng began to regret all the times he had gone to Mama Kalong's whorehouse to sleep with his mother-in-law, when he had such an amazing wife. One evening, he returned to the brothel and met Dewi Ayu, who asked him with a chuckle, "Let me guess, you still haven't touched your wife and want to sleep with your mother-in-law?"

"I just came to say that I will never touch you again."

Now that surprised Dewi Ayu, and she asked him, "Why?"

"With a wife as wonderful as your youngest daughter, I don't want any other woman ever again."

And Maman Gendeng quickly left Dewi Ayu, longing for his wife who was waiting at home.

{11}

AFTER HE TOOK the chopped-up pieces of almond tree firewood to Alamanda's wedding, Comrade Kliwon gathered with his friends on the beach. Ever since he was little he had been quite fond of the ocean. He had lived among fishermen and went to sea just as often as the fishermen's sons did. He had nearly drowned as many times as a farmer's son accidentally cuts himself with his machete. He didn't want to go back to the mushroom farm—it reminded him too much of Alamanda and he didn't want to dwell on those bitter memories.

With two of his old friends, he built a small hut on the beach behind some pandan bushes. He would go night fishing with Karmin and Samiran and they'd split their catch with the guy whose boat they borrowed. At midday, after a short nap, he would study Marxist books and teach his two friends everything he learned. He often went to the Party headquarters on Jalan Belanda, and he struck up a correspondence with some communists in the capital. During his short time in Jakarta he had joined the Party school and made many new acquaintances there.

His pen pals sent him periodicals and magazines, and the Party sent their newspaper to his little hut. Books began to pile up in one corner, meaning he could study exactly what Marx and Engels and Lenin and Trotsky and Chairman Mao had said, and he could read pamphlets written by locals like Semaun and Tan Malaka. A number of these writers, like Trotsky and Tan Malaka, were in fact sort of forbidden, but someone in the Party obtained their books especially for Kliwon.

He wasn't truly a Party member yet, just a candidate. He studied all the material on his own, and diligently attended the political discussions the Party offered, appearing at the podium whenever the opportunity arose. He organized the fishermen and the plantation workers. Six months after Alamanda's wedding, the chairmen at the Party headquarters decided that he was the best cadre in his region and he was accepted as a full member of the Communist Party. He was assigned his first task, which was to gather the remaining guerrillas from the revolutionary army, the majority of whom had been communists, the men who had fought in the war alongside Shodancho's soldiers, scattered after the failed rebellion those many years ago. Now they were rejoining the Party with a romantic nostalgia for revolution.

The Fishermen's Union was founded then, with Samiran and Karmin as its first members and Comrade Kliwon as its chairman. Within two weeks there were fifty-three members, and soon almost all of the fishermen had joined the Union. Every Sunday, when they didn't have anything important to do, the fishermen would gather in the yard of the fish market, right next to the port. Comrade Kliwon would hand out Party propaganda and explain the threat that the large fishing vessels posed to their livelihood.

Now all the fishermen's ceremonies were taken care of by the Union. Comrade Kliwon would give a short speech that quoted a few sentences from the *Manifesto* before a cow's head would be tossed into the ocean as an offering to the queen of the South

Seas. He also did this at the funerals for fishermen who died under the pounding waves, and when the fishermen held their blessing ceremonies, giving thanks for the good weather with a *sintren* performance.

All the folk songs had been replaced with the *Internationale*, and all the closing prayers were offered with, "Workers of the world, unite!"

"I'm like a missionary spreading a new religion," said Comrade Kliwon, chuckling with his friends at the Party headquarters. "With the *Manifesto* as its holy book. That's the most important task for communists or religion—gathering followers."

Those were busy times for Comrade Kliwon. In addition to his organizing and his propaganda, he also began to teach in the Party school, offering political courses for new cadre. He still went to sea and took care of the Fishermen's Union, and seemed to enjoy it, so when the Party offered him the chance to continue his studies in Moscow, he demurred and chose to stay in Halimunda.

The only time he could relax was in the morning when he got home from the sea. He'd sit in front of his hut reading three newspapers that prided themselves on arriving in Halimunda before breakfast. He read the *People's Daily*, the Communist Party newspaper; the *Eastern Star*, which belonged to another party considered an "ally"; and a local Party newspaper published in Bandung. He read and drank his coffee before going off to bathe in the open air spring behind the hut, eating breakfast, and then sleeping until midday.

Once, in the middle of his morning routine he saw seven schoolgirls walking eastward on the sand. Comrade Kliwon glanced at them, but it was normal to see gangs of school kids bored with their studies playing hooky at the beach, so he didn't make much of their presence and returned to his coffee and his newspapers. He hadn't yet finished the lead article on the first page—to be continued on page eight—when he heard some commotion coming from those girls (there was no way it was coming from anywhere else because the beach was almost always deserted at nine in the morning). He heard them screaming shrilly—not the squeals of naughty kids, but cries of fear.

Comrade Kliwon set down his newspaper and walked toward the girls in the distance who were scattering, running back and forth, and all of a sudden one girl broke away from the group, chased by a dog. There were too many wild dogs in Halimunda, thought Comrade Kliwon, ever since Shodancho began breeding them.

He wanted to help the girl, but the girl was too far away and the dog was only ten feet behind her. When the girl saw him and realized he was witnessing her terror, she ran toward him with the dog in pursuit behind her, barking fiercely. Comrade Kliwon finally ran toward them, as the girl screamed in panic, "Help!" while her friends were shrieking far behind her.

Comrade Kliwon sped up his pace but what was extraordinary, and what he only realized after, was how fast the girl was going. Amid the screams and barks she was able to hold her distance from the dog's ferocious muzzle, and as he drew closer, Comrade Kliwon could see for himself that the distance the girl had covered was twice as long as the distance that he himself had, despite the fact that he had run as hard as he could to reach her. He could see the terror on the girl's face, and from a distance of five feet she leapt at him, grabbing tightly onto Comrade Kliwon just as the dog also leapt, thinking this was the perfect time to bite her. But Comrade Kliwon moved faster and right at that exact moment he struck the dog as hard as he could on its jaw, sending it flying back to howl for a moment before sprawling out motionless, with foam around its mouth. The dog had rabies, and he was dead.

Now Kliwon had a schoolgirl holding him tight, the first time since Alamanda's wild kisses in front of the train station. Even though a number of girls and young mothers still made eyes at him, he'd thrown off his reputation as a lady-killer and devoted most of his time to the Party and work, and didn't have any time for flirtation or seduction. But now this girl was clutching him close and without realizing it—just to protect her from the rabid dog—he found himself returning her embrace.

They were pressed together so tightly that Comrade Kliwon could feel the girl's breasts, so soft and warm, and strands of her hair, fluttering in the breeze, brushed across his face. When her friends arrived, relieved, Comrade Kliwon gently pushed the girl away, and that was when he saw her unique beauty, with that old-fashioned, gentle, and natural grace, her hair in two braids, her closed eyes with the tapering eyelashes of a nymph, her slim nose, her finely-carved ears, her lips curled in a small frown, her full cheeks, and then he realized the girl had fainted, and had perhaps been unconscious from the very first moment she'd leapt into his arms.

With the help of her friends, he set the unconscious girl down in a chair. After attempting to revive her, he stopped a horse-drawn cart making slow progress across the weeds and along the bathing springs near his hut and Comrade Kliwon told them to take the unconscious girl home and the girls then crowded together on top of the cart.

But even after they'd disappeared around the bend and the clopping hooves could no longer be heard, Comrade Kliwon could still smell the scent of the girl's hair, feel the soft touch of her breasts, and the effect of her mystical beauty. He tried to chase away those feelings, telling himself he had to work hard for the future of the Party, but that warmth simply would not go, even when he busied himself with burying the rabid dog in the thicket, and even after waking his friends because the rice was ready.

Bedtime made him suffer all the more. The morning's events haunted him, and he realized that the schoolgirl's face was somehow vaguely familiar—maybe he even knew her name. Still feeling the warmth of her body, he tried to remember how he knew her. The girl was about fifteen years old, so he definitely had never dated her. And then, once he remembered who the girl was, he suffered all the more—he indeed *had* seen her face, and he even knew her name, and *had* known it ever since she was six years old. In fact, in the year before he went to Jakarta, he'd seen her almost every day. He immediately tried to banish all memories of the girl's warmth from his body, to erase the soft touch of her breasts, but it was hopeless.

"Oh," he said quite pitifully, "her name is Adinda and she's Alamanda's younger sister."

He finally decided to get up. The fishermen had emerged from their houses and some were checking their nets, fixing any parts that had been torn by thrashing fish, and others were walking toward the city in search of entertainment. After ensuring the nets stretched out to dry next to their hut were in good condition, Comrade Kliwon went to bathe in the spring. The bathing spot had an open-air spigot protected only by pandan shrubs. There was just a big barrel with a small hole corked with an old rubber sandal. But indeed Comrade Kliwon didn't like bathing under a showerhead where the water dribbled down like piss, and he preferred to scoop and pour the water directly onto his body like this.

It turned out that he couldn't escape that girl, as if her family had been destined to hound him as long as he lived. Before he had finished bathing, Karmin shouted that two young girls were looking for him. After he had gotten dressed, with his hair still wet, he found two girls in the front room, looking at the portraits of Marx and Lenin and the hammer and sickle on the wall.

"Thank you for helping me," said Adinda with a small embarrassed bow. She wasn't at all like Alamanda—her face was calm and innocent and shy.

"You ran faster than the dog," said Comrade Kliwon. "You could have run him to death with such speed."

"He would have bitten me," said Adinda, "because I would have fainted."

For the time being, the disturbance that girl caused could be overcome by his Party duties. He had to attend to the complaints of the Fishermen's Union regarding the operation of Shodancho's fishing vessels. Comrade Kliwon tried to lead a group of fishermen in an action one morning. As the large boats were lining up in the port market to lower their catch, Comrade Kliwon and his group stood facing them. He told one of the captains that they would stand there until there was a guarantee the huge vessels would cease their operations in the traditional fishing grounds.

"I don't care if all your fish rot," he began, and of course ended with, "Workers of the world, unite!"

The workers on the large ships stood relaxed on the rails, with no intention of clashing with their fellow villagers, and without caring that the fish might rot, because after all they weren't paid in fish. Meanwhile the market buyers, who should have felt cheated, stayed quiet seeing how many fishermen were there, with their bodies as strong as baby whales. The truly bothered and infuriated ones were of course the captains and officials on Shodancho's ships, but even they didn't move to confront the Fishermen's Union men. One tense hour passed, with agitations and a choir singing the *Internationale*, and fishermen linking arms in a line to face whatever came down from the ship, man or fish.

Comrade Kliwon was fairly certain of victory. The fish would quickly begin to rot and, if the vessels did not comply, then in the following days they would continue to catch rotting fish. But before the blocks of ice on the vessels melted and the fish truly began to stink, some policemen and an army battalion arrived. After an anxious moment, the fishermen decided to fight, but then the soldiers began shooting their rifles into the sky and they ran away frantic. Comrade Kliwon was forced to order a retreat.

All this should have been enough to make him forget Adinda, but it was not. That girl appeared in the crowd of fishermen, and he saw her.

The hut where he lived with Karmin and Samiran served as the Fishermen's Union headquarters, so it was open to everyone. They held their frequent meetings, and talked on and on about anything and everything there, and he couldn't hardly just ask the girl to leave if, on her way home from school, Adinda showed up with a number of her friends.

Adinda was good at speaking English, which wasn't too unusual in Halimunda since so many foreigners came there to visit. Comrade Kliwon had a library that delighted book lovers; most of the volumes were philosophy and politics, but there were also English storybooks that Adinda enjoyed. When Comrade Kliwon awoke from his afternoon nap, he would quite often find the girl sitting at the large table, right under the photo of Lenin, solemnly reading. She would look up at him for a moment and smile as if to say, *Sorry I came in without asking*, and Kliwon would give her a cup of tea nervously, though the girl would say, *Thank you, I can get it myself*, but by then Comrade Kliwon would have quickly gone out back to the well to tremble.

Adinda read many books there. She read all the Gorky, Dostoevsky, and Tolstoy novels he had. All of them were published by the Foreign Languages Publishing House in Moscow, and sent through the Party. She read local novels too, and translated ones put out by Yayasan Pembaruan, the publisher of the Party, and the books of Balai Pustaka, which belonged to the government.

Comrade Kliwon never asked her to leave, but he did avoid her as best he could. Two things made him suffer when she was near: first, Adinda elicited a painful nostalgia for Alamanda, and second, seeing Adinda transported him back to their warm embrace that had so intoxicated him. He busied himself even further with the Fishermen's Union business, discussing the failure of their first action against Shodancho's ships. He organized Union cadres to infiltrate the ships and work there to win over the laborers. It would take some time, but he believed that communists were the most patient creatures on the face of the earth.

It wasn't easy, but he finally succeeded in placing two of his men on each vessel—nowhere near enough, but better than nothing. Most of the fishermen grew impatient waiting to provoke the ship laborers, and urged Comrade Kliwon to burn the ships. Comrade Kliwon tried to calm them down.

"Give me some time to talk to Shodancho," he said.

Comrade Kliwon's first negotiations with Shodancho had failed to produce results; instead, Shodancho had added one more fishing vessel. The fishermen then once again urged him to take the shortcut of burning the ships down. A second time, Kliwon asked to speak with Shodancho. That was when he went to the house and saw Alamanda's stomach, swollen but empty. And it wasn't just Shodancho who had taken his words that day as the curse of a jealous man—Adinda had felt the same.

She came one afternoon, begging him, practically in tears, "Don't hurt my older sister, she has already suffered enough, having to marry that Shodancho."

"I didn't do anything."

"You cursed her so that she would lose her child."

"That's not true," said Comrade Kliwon, defending himself, "I just saw your sister's stomach and told what I saw."

The girl didn't believe him one bit. She sat in the same spot where she usually read books, her feelings a mix of anger and confusion. Usually Comrade Kliwon would leave her be, but this time he weakly pulled up a chair and sat down. There was no one else around that afternoon except the lizards on the wall and the spiders hanging from the ceiling spinning their webs.

"I'm begging you, Comrade, forget Alamanda."

"I already forgot that was even her name."

Adinda ignored that lame joke. "If you're angry at her," she said, "take out all your anger on me."

"Alright then, I will squash you like a tomato," said Comrade Kliwon.

"You can kill me or rape me whenever you want, I won't put up even the tiniest bit of a fight," said Adinda, not drawn in by his jokes. "You can make me your slave, or whatever." She took a handkerchief from her skirt pocket, and wiped away the tears streaming down her cheeks. "You could even marry me if you wanted."

A gecko called out seven times in the distance, a sign that she was looking for a mate.

If that baby was truly going to disappear from his wife's stomach, Shodancho was sure it would be due to Comrade Kliwon's curse—the curse of a jealous lover. A problem like this couldn't be solved with weapons, nor with a seven-generation war; to save his first child he had to find a peaceful solution. He finally told Comrade Kliwon that he would order his captains to move their operations far away from the beach and the traditional fishing waters.

"But," Shodancho then said, "please remove your curse far from my wife's stomach." He desperately wanted a child to prove to the world that he and his wife loved each other, that their's was a happy marriage. Hearing that request, Comrade Kliwon smiled, not because he knew that Alamanda only loved him and didn't love Shodancho at all, but because, "There's no connection between an empty pot and those ships, Shodancho."

As if he hadn't heard what Comrade Kliwon said, Shodancho still moved his ships far back into the deep ocean.

The fishermen reveled in their victory—those ships no longer caught fish in their waters and no longer sold their fish in the local market, docking now in bigger cities that needed larger quantities of fish.

Comrade Kliwon tried to tell them as tangibly as possible, as his Marxist gurus instructed, what had happened and to discuss their new efforts, now that the big ships had been pushed into the distance and the fish had returned. But it turned out that as soon as the fishermen had some money, they bought a cow's head and after celebrating on the beach with some bottles of *tuak,* they threw it into the sea as an offering to the queen of the South Seas, still so superstitious. Comrade Kliwon couldn't do much about that, feeling sure that it would be difficult to teach them even the most basic logic, let alone instill the Marxist dialectic that he himself had only received in bits and pieces during his short stay in the capital. He was happy enough that they'd had the courage to fight back against the threat to their unity and their livelihood, but time and time again he told his friends that life wasn't as easy as all that, that they shouldn't let themselves get carried away by a small victory, and that the ties of their friendship must be knit even tighter, because even larger threats were sure to come.

The fishermen weren't the only ones to hold a cheerful *syukuran* ritual of thanks. Shodancho was so happy that he was constantly throwing these blessing celebrations. Perhaps because he had been so worried by Comrade Kliwon's curse, he also asked that a traditional ceremony be held for Alamanda's safety and the safety of the baby growing in her stomach. For that ceremony, Alamanda bathed in water filled with all kinds of flowers in the middle of the night as a traditional midwife recited mantras. This midwife reassured Shodancho that his wife's stomach was beautifully full, and the child was doing just fine in there, a baby girl who would be as beautiful as her mother.

Shodancho didn't care about the sex of the baby, just knowing that he was going to have a child was good enough for him. But when he heard the midwife's prediction that the baby was a girl, he jumped for joy, reassured that the curse was nothing but hot air from a man consumed with jealousy. He straightaway began to think of a name for the child and decided on Nurul Aini, not because it had any special meaning, but because it suddenly appeared in his mind, and yet it was for that reason precisely that he thought the child's name was a divine inspiration he had to follow. Meanwhile the midwife was dousing his wife with scoopful upon scoopful of flower water, and Alamanda was shivering in the chilly night air, sure that she'd wake up the next morning with the flu. And elsewhere, out at sea, Comrade Kliwon was hoping that he had been mistaken, wishing for the couple to have a real baby.

But Alamanda never gave birth to Nurul Aini because the baby vanished, just like that, from inside her stomach just a few days before her predicted date of birth.

Alamanda herself didn't know what had happened. Just as soon as she awoke she'd belched violently, pushing out a tremendous amount of air, and suddenly felt like a slim virgin, without any weight in her womb. She remembered quite clearly how Comrade Kliwon had said that her stomach was like an empty pot, filled with only air and wind, but she was still shocked, and she screamed out into the fresh and peaceful morning air. Shodancho, who was sleeping in another room, came scurrying in drawstring shorts and an undershirt, his face streaked with pillowcase creases and his arms covered in mosquito bites. He rushed to his wife's room and was stunned to see her slim and shapely once again.

First thinking that his wife had already given birth, he looked for puddles of blood and for the little one, on top of the bed or even underneath it, but he didn't find a newborn and he didn't hear its cries. He stared at his wife who stared back at him, her face ashen. She tried to speak but her mouth just hung open, her lips trembling like someone with the chills, and not one syllable came out.

Shodancho remembered Comrade Kliwon's words and in a rising panic he shook Alamanda violently, ordering her to tell him what had happened. But without saying word, Alamanda drooped weakly onto the bed just as the midwife arrived. The midwife, experienced in all manner of strange things, rearranged Alamanda into a more comfortable position, and said: "Sometimes this does happen, Shodancho—there's no baby inside, just air and wind."

In denial, Shodancho shouted, "But you yourself said I was going to have a girl!" His voice was high and full of anger, but when he saw the midwife's calm demeanor, he sat down on the edge of the bed and began to cry uncontrollably, not caring that he was a grown man—he had lost Nurul Aini, the little girl of his dreams. Shodancho immediately thought of Comrade Kliwon, this time not with the nagging worry that his curse *might* come true, but with an all-encompassing rage because the curse *had* come true. Comrade Kliwon had stolen his child and Shodancho would get his revenge.

The couple tried to hide what had really happened and announced that the baby had died. Only Comrade Kliwon really knew. To get back at Comrade Kliwon, after one week of mourning, Shodancho ordered his vessels back to the places they used to fish, and to sell the fish in the old market. The workers protested that the fishermen would burn the ships without a second thought. Shodancho didn't care and fired anyone who didn't comply.

Comrade Kliwon tried to talk to Shodancho, saying that he'd broken his promise, but Shodancho retorted that Comrade Kliwon had broken his promise too. Comrade Kliwon said he'd never promised anything except to protect the ships from the fishermen's wrath, but Shodancho kept on bringing up the curse, and how every woman in the world had the right to choose the man she'd marry.

Truly upset at this accusation of cursing an unborn child because he was jealous, Comrade Kliwon tried to remain calm and replied,

"There's only one explanation, Shodancho, which is that you had sex with your wife without love—the child that results from sex like that will either never be born, or be born a crazy child with a rat's tail growing from its ass." Shodancho swung at him but Comrade Kliwon dodged, saying, "Take those ships away at once, Shodancho, before we lose our patience."

Shodancho instead ordered the ships to operate as usual, now under the watch of soldiers who stood at the guard rails of the deck, looking down on the fishermen glaring up at them angrily. With a cunning smile, Shodancho watched as dusk fell and Kliwon and three other men approached the vessels in motorboats, followed by the other fishermen in their skiffs. The little boats tried to find some place in the wide ocean where there were still some fish, at the very least to supply their own kitchens.

Like Shodancho, Alamanda was completely shaken by the loss of her child, because no matter how or with whom the baby had been conceived, it was still hers. When the week of mourning had passed and Shodancho had returned to his business, Alamanda stayed locked in her room in a solemn grief, sometimes calling out Nurul Aini's name.

Shodancho tried to convince her that everything was fated by God and that they still had a second and a third and a fourth and basically an unlimited opportunity to have a child. "Come on, sweetheart," he said, "we can make love again, and have as many children as we want." Alamanda firmly shook her head, reminding Shodancho of the promise she'd made, that she would marry him but she would never love him. Shodancho tried to cajole her further, telling her that they might have another Nurul Aini, a little girl who would be real this time, but Alamanda said fiercely, "Losing a child is more horrifying than meeting a demon, but giving my love to you would be more horrifying than losing twenty children."

Just then, Shodancho remembered that his wife wasn't wearing her iron underwear, and just as soon as that foul idea started dancing inside his brain, and before Alamanda realized what he was thinking, Shodancho turned and closed the door and locked it. Alamanda, who hadn't gotten up from her bed since she lost Nurul Aini, immediately knew what the man aimed to do. She jumped up and looked at Shodancho with the stance of a woman ready to fight and said bitterly, "Are you horny, Shodancho? My earhole is still nice and tight if you want it."

"I still like your pussy, darling," her husband laughed.

Alamanda didn't have a chance to do anything else—Shodancho threw her back down onto the bed. With as much strength as she had, Alamanda tried once more to protect herself, but in an instant she was stripped naked with her clothes in shreds as if devoured by a pack of wolverines, and Shodancho fell upon her

During that copulation Alamanda no longer tried to resist because she knew it was useless, but if Shodancho approached her mouth she would bite his lips as hard as she could. Finally Shodancho was just tirelessly stabbing her again and again, in an unsettling union of pleasure and grief. Alamanda's spirit was now utterly destroyed—feeling humiliated, dirty, and so full of regret—as again she had failed to defend herself. When Shodancho finished, Alamanda kicked him onto the floor, saying, "You foul rotten rapist, you rape your own wife, and you probably raped your mother too!" She threw a pillow at Shodancho, adding, "If your dick was long enough, I bet you'd even rape your own asshole!"

This time, at least, her husband didn't tie her up and the next day, when he was out, Alamanda disappeared from the house. Shodancho panicked. He sent someone to look for her at Dewi Ayu's house, but they didn't find Alamanda there. Burned by the flames of jealousy, he also sent someone to Kliwon's house, but there was no evidence of her there either. He began to send people to the farthest reaches of the city, then to the station and the bus terminal to find out whether she'd left the city, but no one had seen her anywhere. Giving up, Shodancho collapsed into a chair on his veranda, so lost in his pitiful fate of being married to a woman he loved so much but who had never loved him that when passersby greeted him he didn't respond to a single one.

Dusk made him feel all the more empty, lonely, and abandoned, and he began to realize how pathetic he was. Even if Alamanda came back, he could see no joy in continuing to live with her as long as she gave no sign of returning his affection, not even a tiny bit. Maybe he had to start thinking like a warrior, like a real man, like an honest-to-God soldier, and offer to divorce her, and maybe that way Alamanda could be happy again. But even thinking about a divorce made him cry even harder, so he vowed to himself that if his wife was found, he would never to hurt her again and would be her slave so that she would stay. Maybe they could adopt other people's children.

Dusk had deepened and the veranda lamps had yet to be lit. When Alamanda's shadow fell on the gate Shodancho saw it immediately, praying that it wasn't just a hallucination, but the shadow approached and Shodancho quickly threw himself on his knees in front of Alamanda, begging her forgiveness.

Alamanda just wrinkled her forehead at this behavior. "You don't have to apologize, Shodancho. I am wearing new protection now, with even more complicated mantras. Even if I'm totally naked you won't be able to penetrate me."

In sincere amazement, Shodancho looked at his wife, astonished by the fact that she was showing no animosity toward him whatsoever.

"The night air is cold, Shodancho, come let's go in."

More laborers on the big ships were fired for striking—they hadn't unionized, but were so afraid of the threats to burn their ships they hadn't dared return to work. The big ships *did* return, and once again stole fish from the shallow waters and sold the catch in the local market. And the fishermen now said, "There is no other way, Comrade, we have to burn down Shodancho's ships."

Anxious and depressed, Comrade Kliwon was far from a vicious man who could easily just decide to burn down some ships. In fact, as his friends always pointed out, his eyes welled up just from watching a cheesy movie.

Secretly he tried talking to Shodancho again, but their discussions floundered on Alamanda and just like the fishermen, Comrade Kliwon finally thought to himself that indeed there was no other choice but to burn down those fucking ships. After all, the Russian Revolution might never have happened if Lenin hadn't ordered Stalin to rob a bank.

Shodancho had stationed a large number of soldiers on the decks of his ships, however, so it wasn't easy for the fishermen to carry out their plan. An exhausting six whole months passed, with the Fishermen's Union's secret meetings always coming to a dead end when they couldn't figure out exactly how they would do it, and the fishermen grew poorer and angrier every day.

In the past, when Comrade Kliwon was confronted with problems that made his head feel like it was about to explode, women had been his refuge. But now his only female companion was Alamanda's younger sister Adinda, whom he'd known for a year. So, as if he had no other choice, he left his hut and the men still discussing their difficulties and headed for Dewi Ayu's house like a pathetic refugee, exhausted by the endless revolutionary struggle. He wanted to share his feelings, his desires, but the Party had emphasized that the issue must not be discussed with anyone and so he passed a boring hour on the porch with Adinda, exchanging small talk that brought no relief to his worn-out spirit, and when he went home he collapsed in a chair outside his hut, looking out at the dusky sky over the ocean.

"Someone should put a pistol to your forehead," Adinda had said before he went home. "So that you're forced to think about yourself for a moment."

It was the same dusky sky he always saw, but that evening it felt different. It used to remind him of that beautiful evening he spent next to Alamanda in the sand, but that evening the cold sky was silent and sad, like a mirror for his arid and parched heart. Smoking his clove cigarette, he wondered whether the revolution could ever truly happen, whether it was possible for human beings not to oppress one another.

Long ago he had heard an imam in the mosque talk about heaven, about rivers of milk that flowed at your feet, about beautiful ever-available virgin nymphs, about everything being there for the taking and nothing forbidden. All of that seemed so beautiful, really too beautiful to be believed. He didn't need anything as grandiose as all that—it would be enough for him if everyone got the same amount of rice. Or maybe that wish was really the most grandiose wish of all.

Thinking like this always made him nostalgic for his past, before he knew that he needed revolution. He had always been a poor man, but he used to have a much simpler way of dealing with rich men: stealing whatever they had in their gardens, seducing their women, and letting them pay for the food he ate and the movies he watched at the theater, or accepting the invitations to their parties and drinking their beer for free, none of which required the Party or propaganda or the *Communist Manifesto*. He felt exhausted just looking out at the shining red dusk because his thoughts couldn't rest, and sinking even deeper into his chair before he knew it he had fallen asleep. That was how he was in the six months leading up to the burning of the ships, until he was awoken in his chair one night by a number of fishermen.

For two weeks now the soldiers hadn't been guarding the fishing vessels. Apparently they had grown bored. The ship captains, thinking that the fishermen had just been making empty threats, had decided to send the soldiers home so they wouldn't have to keep feeding them and supplying them with cigarettes and beer. The ship captains began going out to sea without any protection, and were only guarded by a few armed soldiers when they docked and lowered their catch. The Fishermen's Union's plan was to attack the ships in the middle of the night during a new moon—the very night they woke Comrade Kliwon, the night they had all been waiting for, the night that would settle the score.

"Wake up, Comrade," said one of his friends, "the revolution doesn't happen in your sleep."

And led by Comrade Kliwon himself, who'd shaken off his drowsiness and steeled himself, thirty small skiffs moved out under a clear sky studded with stars. That night was a turning point for Comrade Kliwon, the night he began to believe that a revolutionary had to have a cold and immovable heart, a stubborn boldness born of conviction. The dim porthole lights of the big ships were visible in the darkness, but the skiffs weren't equipped with any lights—the fishermen steered by instinct, knowing the ocean as well as they knew the villages where they were born. "Think of this as storming the Bastille," said their leader to himself, to give himself courage, "for the sake of the cursed and wretched masses."

The large ships were operating at slight distances from one another. Each small skiff had three to five fishermen, with ten skiffs aiming for each of the three ships. They moved slowly, like thirty slithering field snakes eyeing three ignorant mice. Through the flickering light from the ships they could see the laborers hauling up the nets and dumping the catch into the hull.

After leading the ten boats to the middle vessel, once he thought the other two ships were also surrounded, Comrade Kliwon blew the whistle shrilly, and the deckhands stopped their work in surprise. That surprise hadn't yet subsided when they realized that now thirty boatfuls of men were lighting torches. Spots of light suddenly encircled the ships like floating fireflies.

Comrade Kliwon called loudly to the men on the deck above, "My friends, jump down and swim to our boats, this ship is about to be burned!"

Even though the ship's captain shouted angry orders for his workers to fight back, he was the first one to leap down in panic and swim for the nearest skiff. He upbraided the fishermen, before someone clocked him and he sprawled out unconscious. Meanwhile the deckhands competed to see who could jump into the sea and swim to the boats the fastest, and the fishermen began cheering joyfully and someone even began to sing the *Internationale*—it was their most glorious celebration.

Plastic bags filled with gasoline sailed through the air to plunge down onto the ships' empty deck, and then torches began to fly ready to lick the gasoline. Three bonfires now shone awesomely in the middle of the ocean as the skiffs swiftly retreated, and when the three ships exploded in tremendous bursts, the fishermen whooped, shouting, "Long live the Fishermen's Union! Long live the Communist Party! Workers of the world, unite!"

Shodancho heard that the leader of the riot was Comrade Kliwon, that there had been no casualties, and that the three ships had been destroyed.

Hearing that report, Shodancho simply exhaled, thinking that he could get new fishing vessels with tighter security. He didn't appear angry, which could only be explained by the fact that Alamanda was six months pregnant. He was thankful their single episode of lovemaking had born fruit. He didn't want to be bothered by anything except preparing for the birth of a replacement Nurul Aini. He brought his wife to a bigger hospital in the provincial capital twice, to double check that there was a baby in her stomach, and paid powerful wizards to protect his child from any kind of curse.

But when Alamanda was nine months pregnant the second baby suddenly vanished from her stomach, just like the first. Shodancho exploded in an uncontrollable rage, grabbed his pistol, and stormed outside, charging back and forth wildly. People ran frantically out of his way, thinking he had gone insane as he screamed that Comrade Kliwon's curse had robbed him of his children, making them disappear before they could even be born. When Shodancho had finally had enough of shooting everything in sight, he ran toward the beach with one goal: to find Comrade Kliwon and kill him, and no one dared stand in his way.

{12}

COMRADE KLIWON CARRIED his cup of coffee to the veranda and sat waiting for his newspapers to arrive. The day before Shodancho tried to kill him, he had moved from the hut that also served as the headquarters for the Fishermen's Union to the Communist Party headquarters at the end of Jalan Belanda. Shodancho found nobody in the abandoned hut, so he went on a rampage, shooting at the hut before setting it on fire. Finally, exhausted and crying, he fell face-first onto the sand, and lay there until some passersby found him, unconscious. Part of Comrade Kliwon's good fortune: after years of dedicating himself to the Party, he had been named the leader of Halimunda's Communist Party.

It was the first of October, and he was feeling uneasy because his newspapers hadn't been delivered. Trembling with impatience, he picked up the previous day's newspapers and started to read the advertisements, because he'd already read everything else. There was nothing of interest, except two ads—one for a mustache growing tonic, and the other one for purchasing German cars on credit. He threw the newspapers under the table and drank a little coffee. He looked out at the street, hoping the newspaper boy would appear on his bike, but instead a young woman came down the street. It was Adinda.

"How are you, Comrade?" she asked.

"Terrible. My newspapers aren't here yet."

The girl wrinkled her forehead. "Haven't you heard about the bloody events in Jakarta?"

"How could I, without my newspapers?"

Adinda sat down next to Comrade Kliwon, and without asking first drank a little bit of his coffee, and said, "The radio is only talking about the Communist Party, saying they staged a coup and killed some generals."

"Well I'll find out about it when my newspapers come."

People started showing up, young and old, cadre and veteran, many of them the most important figures in the Party. Comrade Yono, who had been number one in the Party before Comrade Kliwon, appeared first, followed by Karmin and the others. They all reported the same thing: bloody things were happening in Jakarta.

"It looks like it's going to get really bad," said Karmin.

"You're right," replied Comrade Kliwon. "We have paid up all our subscriptions in full, and those newspapers still haven't arrived. I should box that newspaper boy's ears."

"What's wrong with you, Comrade?" asked Comrade Yono. "Are newspapers really all you can think about?"

Comrade Kliwon returned his glance crankily: "Those newspapers have never not arrived—and now what?"

"Listen to me, Comrade," said Adinda. "No newspapers have even been *published* today."

"Why not? Today's not Eid, it's not Christmas, and it's not New Year's Day."

"The army is occupying all the newsrooms," Karmin said. "So I'm sorry, Comrade, but today we won't be reading any newspapers."

"That's worse than a coup d'état," complained Comrade Kliwon, and drank the rest of his coffee down with one gulp.

In any case, many important Party men gathered for an emergency meeting. Reports were coming in from a number of cities, but most importantly from Jakarta: it was being said that all the central leaders of the Communist Party had been captured, that a number of killings had taken place, and that some cadres were already dead. So they decided to mobilize the masses and hold a huge demonstration in Halminuda, and if the Party leaders in Jakarta had truly been captured, they'd demand an unconditional release. But their information was a maze of contradictions—by some reports, DN Aidit had been executed, while others said he'd only been captured, and still others said he was just fine. There were equally confusing reports about what had befallen Nyoto and some others. But whatever had happened, they had to gather all the cadres, party sympathizers, fishermen, plantation workers, rail workers, farmers, and students. That day and the ones to follow were to be the stormiest days in the city's history, with the people facing giants in the streets.

Tasks were assigned and the comrades quickly dispersed to contact Party cells and prepare everything they'd need in the crisis. Posters were made, banners were raised. Meanwhile, Comrade Kliwon organized a secret meeting of five men, telling them to prepare weapons in case things got really bad. They conducted an inventory of what they had: there were still lots left over from the guerrilla revolutionaries, and a number of their men had fighting experience from the war for independence. Karmin was tasked with organizing this armed branch, so he quickly went off and Comrade Kliwon armed himself with a pistol—he was too valuable to the Party to take any chances.

At ten o'clock, a crowd of fishermen and plantation workers were already gathering along Jalan Belanda. The farmers, rail workers, dockworkers, and students were all still on their way.

"Let us take to the streets," said Comrade Yono.

"You go," said Comrade Kliwon. "I'm waiting for my newspapers."

Nobody protested. They saw his behavior as the depression of a

Party leader facing an extremely dire situation, and tried to understand. They left him on the veranda of the Party headquarters at the end of Jalan Belanda, waiting for newspapers that would never come, with only Adinda for company.

Those headquarters were comparatively new, stationed in a large two-storey house, the Party flag flying in the front yard beside the Red and White. A copper hammer and sickle hung from the front door and almost all the walls were painted a gleaming red. In the front room, the first thing one noticed was a large oil painting of Karl Marx and other Soviet socialist-realist paintings. Comrade Kliwon lived there with some guards. They did have a radio, but Comrade Kliwon preferred reading newspapers—though now the newsrooms were occupied by the army and the blood of communists had replaced all the newspaper ink.

Comrade Kliwon had now led the city Party for two years, and no longer went to sea at night because he was busier and busier. He had succeeded in organizing the plantation workers and the farmers into unions, and had directed more than ten glorious strikes. The city's Communist Party had one thousand and sixty-seven active and dues-paying members and thousands more sympathizers, half of whom contributed positively to every strike, showed up for every rally held in the soccer field, and attended the Party's courses.

Is wasn't as if there had never been clashes; Comrade Kliwon had reactivated the veteran guerrilla revolutionaries from the war, and they had weapons and an enthusiasm for military training. Of course there weren't enough of them to fight an army, but they'd defended strikers from strong-arming by the railway and plantation companies, landowners, and boat captains.

He'd let two members go during that time because they'd left their wives for other women—that was strongly forbidden under his watch—and three others were thought to be Trotskyites. With this strict leadership, Comrade Kliwon had reached the height of his reputation and people would always remember him as the most charismatic Communist Party leader that city had ever seen.

"It's the rainy season," Comrade Kliwon said all of a sudden.

Adinda agreed, looking up at the bright sky: the morning was fair, but who knew, it had been known to rain in October. "But they won't retreat because of the rain. I think we're being deceived by the troops in Jakarta."

"Maybe the newspaper trucks have been caught in a flood."

"No newspapers have been published today, Comrade," said Adinda. "And I'm willing to bet there won't be any newspapers for at least a week. Maybe there won't be any newspapers ever again."

"We'll go back to the Stone Age without newspapers!"

"I'll make you some coffee, maybe that will help you return to your senses."

Adinda went to the kitchen and made two cups of coffee, and when she returned, she saw Comrade Kliwon standing at the gate peering down the street. It looked as though he was still hoping the paperboy would appear on his bike. Adinda placed the cups of coffee on the table and sat back down in her chair.

"Come back to your seat," she said to Comrade Kliwon, "if you've come back to your senses."

"What makes no sense is a day without newspapers."

"Forget the fucking newspapers, Comrade! Your Party is in crisis, and they need a clearheaded leader."

Whatever the case, it was truly unbelievable that the Communist Party—by far the strongest faction in Halimunda—could be facing a coup d'état. At that time, the Party had the most gleaming reputation in the entire history of the city. Had there had been an election, the Communist Party would have won hands-down. The city was decorated all in red, and even the mayor and the military let them do whatever they wanted.

The Communists pressured the schools, even the kindergartens and the schools for the disabled, to teach the *Internationale* to their students. And of course they plastered pictures of Marx and Lenin on the classroom walls, all in one line with the portraits of national heroes. And on Independence Day—and please remember that in Halimunda that meant the 23rd of September—they held the most cheerful carnival and parade, with the communists shouting out their revolutionary cheers. The city folk would spill out in a crowd along the road and listen to verses from the "Sama Rata Sama Rasa" treatise that Marco Kartodikromo had written many years ago, proclaiming that everyone should be treated equally no matter their rank or occupation.

Adinda was thinking the mass demonstrations about to be carried out by the communists on the streets of Halimunda would be like that. Years later, she would realize that after the Communist Party was outlawed she never again saw such cavalcades, with all the decorated cars driving by on all the roadways. Usually Comrade Kliwon would be right smack in the middle, riding in a convertible wearing the cap that he had gotten from Comrade Salim, waving his hands at the young girls who screamed hysterically by the side of the road.

The opposing parties were amazed by his incredible popularity, and prayed that public elections wouldn't be held anytime soon. Other parties claimed to be fellow revolutionaries and waited for the communists to drop their guard so they could stab them in the back. Still, none of this had been achieved effortlessly, but through two years of exhausting work. It was even said that Comrade Kliwon had been the victim of two mysterious attempted assassinations. One night he was knifed by an attacker who suddenly appeared and then just as suddenly vanished without a trace. Someone else tossed a hand grenade through his bedroom window. But he remained quite healthy, and said in a public rally that he forgave the attempted murderers, whoever they were. He said people like that simply didn't understand the communist mission, which was to eradicate the abuse of man against man—this made his reputation, and the Party's, rise even higher in the people's esteem, until even little children praised them.

All of this frenzied political activity worried his mother Mina terribly. She still remembered her husband, executed by the Japanese, and saw all the propaganda and carnivals as ridiculous and pointless commotion. Mina sometimes watched her son giving a speech in front of a mass of thousands, shouting slogans, like "Crush the landlords!" that would be enthusiastically echoed by the crowd. And he cursed not only the landlords, but also money lenders, factory owners, boat captains, plantation officials, and the railway company. Of course, he also cursed America and the Netherlands and neocolonialism, all with such eloquence it was as if God himself was whispering the words into his ear

Every time Comrade Kliwon went home for a visit, Mina would tell him that it wasn't good to make too many enemies. "One friend is way too few, but one enemy is way too many. You are making a lot of people hate you," she said worriedly. Comrade Kliwon would reassure her that what had happened to his father was not going to happen to him, then he'd smile and drink the tea that she had made for him before going to lie down.

One day, at the urging of the Communist Party, a group of young kids was thrown into the military prison. They had been having a party at school and all they did wrong was take the stage and sing some rock and roll songs, but Shodancho complied with the communists. Hearing this, Mina's worry turned into anger and she marched to the Party headquarters and blew up at her son. "I can't let this happen!" she screamed in the middle his crowded office. "Didn't you used to play those songs on your guitar in the old days, didn't *all* of you?" she said to the people gathered around. "And now you are ordering those kids into military custody for singing them?"

But party discipline had made Comrade Kliwon inflexible and

his attitude toward his mother was cold. He just placated the woman, walked her out to the side of the main road, and asked a *becak* rickshaw driver to take her home.

He didn't stop there, but started putting pressure on the city council, the military, and the police to confiscate those brain-rotting Western pop records and throw whoever listened to them—even in the privacy of their homes—into jail. "Crush America and may its false culture be cursed!" he shouted every time. In exchange, the Party began to generously support folk art, providing the usual snacks and some Party propaganda too, so that all the folk art that had been subversive in feudal and colonial times now began to jazz up the Halimunda scene. For the Party's anniversary they performed *sintren*, with a pretty girl who disappeared inside a chicken coop and reappeared holding a hammer and sickle, looking even more beautiful in full makeup (and the audience clapped). The *kuda lumping* trance dancers didn't just eat glass and coconut shells, but now also swallowed the American flag. The forbidden rock and roll records were also smashed and swallowed.

After his success building up the Party so rapidly, the Party members in the capital fixed their sights on Comrade Kliwon. It was heard that he had been asked to join the Politburo and that he was a strong candidate for the Central Committee of the Indonesian Communist Party. His political career was dazzling, but Comrade Kliwon refused all honors with an attitude of incomprehensible defiance, even one crazy offer that would have made him a member of the Comintern. He was not working for his own luminous career, he said. He was working so that communism might blossom on Halimunda soil, and so he didn't want to leave the city.

Men began to return, reporting on the demonstrations in the streets. The military was prepared on all sides—the city forces had taken to the streets and had gained, led by Shodancho, who was motivated by his personal hatred for Comrade Kliwon.

"DN Aidit has been captured," someone reported.

"Nyoto has been executed," another report came in.

"DN Aidit met with the president."

All reports were convoluted and the only information that could be gleaned was from the radio, which couldn't be trusted. All morning it had been reporting the same exact thing over and over again, as if the news had been prerecorded: *The Communist Party attempted a coup d'état, which failed because the army acted quickly. The army has temporarily taken power in order to rescue the nation.* Another report arrived: *The president was under house arrest.* Everything was completely confusing.

"Do something!" said Adinda.

"What can I do?" asked Comrade Kliwon. "There is no word from the Soviet Union or China."

The comrades planned to extend the demonstrations and protests into the night, and then indefinitely, but while everyone was busy preparing public soup kitchens, and the People's Army veterans were preparing to make war against the regular soldiers, Comrade Kliwon still didn't go down into the streets. Adinda left him there, on that very same veranda, waiting for his newspapers.

The next morning, as usual she prepared breakfast for her mother, who hadn't yet returned home from Mama Kalong's, and then she went to watch the protest. She next went to the Party headquarters, carrying some breakfast on a tray, and found Comrade Kliwon sitting on the veranda with a cup of coffee.

"How are you, Comrade?"

"Terrible," he replied.

"Eat something, you didn't eat anything all day yesterday." Adinda placed the breakfast tray on the table between them.

"I can't eat until my newspapers come."

"I swear to you, they won't come," said Adinda. "The army has forbidden the newspapers to publish anything."

"But the newspapers don't belong to the army."

"But the army has weapons," said Adinda. "Tell me, when did you become such an idiot?"

"Then they'll appear from underground," Comrade Kliwon insisted. "That's what usually happens."

That morning the emergency meetings continued. Anti-communists had arrived in the streets and the two groups clustered in opposition. It seemed as if the war that the people had previously feared would break out between the soldiers and the local thugs was now going to happen with a new cast of characters: the communists against the anti-communists. The army and the police hovered around, but they couldn't prevent small skirmishes and the throwing of a few Molotov cocktails. People also began throwing stones, and more emergency meetings were held.

"All this chaos started with the disappearance of my newspapers," Comrade Kliwon complained.

"Don't be ridiculous," said Karmin. "Seven generals were murdered two days ago."

"Why," Comrade Yono couldn't stop himself from asking, "do you care so much about those newspapers?"

"Because the Russian Revolution would never have succeeded if the Bolsheviks hadn't had their newspaper."

That explanation made more sense than anything else up until this point, and so they left him on the veranda with Adinda to wait.

As morning turned into midday, the waves of anti-communists grew larger and they were echoing the previous day's radio report, that the communists had attempted a coup d'état.

Comrade Kliwon, who had not yet lost his sense of humor, commented, "They attempted a coup and censored their own newspapers."

The first clash finally came at one o'clock. Stone throwing escalated into intense battles, where people used whatever they had to maim or kill. The hospital was soon overwhelmed. The Party opened a field hospital, and Adinda busied herself with the emergency paramedics, but Comrade Kliwon didn't budge.

Wounded men started to arrive at the Party headquarters, and the place became seriously frenetic. Nobody had died in Halimunda yet, neither communist nor anti-communist, but a massacre in Jakarta was reported. One hundred communists had been killed there, and the rest were being captured, and hundreds of other communists had been murdered in East Java, and the massacres were beginning in Central Java. Everyone began to have a bad feeling that all this would spread to Halimunda.

In the end, someone *was* killed that afternoon. The first communist to die in Halimunda was a veteran revolutionary guerrilla named Mualimin. He was one of the Party's most faithful members, a master of its ideology in both theory and practice, a true fighter who had struggled for the cause from the colonial times up until the neoliberal era. That was what Comrade Kliwon said in the short eulogy he gave at the funeral, which was held that very same day. A Muslim communist, Mualimin had always wanted to die for the cause, his *jihad*. Years ago he had already written in his will that if he died in battle he wanted to be buried as a martyr. So he wasn't bathed, only prayed over and buried straightaway with his clothes still covered in blood. He had been shot by the army in an armed clash on the beach, the only man to die that afternoon. Mualimin left behind only one child, a girl of twenty-one named Farida. They'd been very close ever since the death of the girl's mother many years before, so when the crowd started to leave the cemetery, Farida stayed by her father's grave even though everyone tried to convince her to return home. In the end, they left her there alone.

Now here is a little romance: a love story in a city gripped in the crisis of war.

The gravedigger *cum*-watchman of the fishermen's district public cemetery was Kamino, a young man of thirty-two. He had been the gravedigger and watchman of the Budi Dharma cemetery since he was sixteen, when his father had died of malaria. Without any brothers or sisters, he had inherited his father's post—an occupation that had been the family business, all the way back to his grandfather's grandfather maybe, because nobody else wanted to do it, and his family was already quite familiar with the world of the dead. Accustomed to the silence of that place since he was a little boy, Kamino had no difficulty learning his trade. He could dig a grave as fast as a cat could dig a hole to take a crap. But the work presented him with a grave difficulty: no girls to marry, because nobody wanted to live in the middle of the cemetery.

The fact was, most of the people of Halimunda were superstitious. They still believed that demons, spooks, and all kinds of supernatural beings ran wild in the cemetery, living among the spirits of the dead. And they also believed that the gravedigger lived in close communion with all of these supernatural beings. Aware of his difficult situation, Kamino had never even tried proposing to anyone. His only interactions with other people happened in the course of his business. He usually just stayed at home, a humid house made out of moldy old concrete shaded by big banyan trees. The sole entertainment in his lonely life was playing *jailangkung*—calling the spirits of the dead using a little effigy doll—another skill that had been passed down through the generations of his family, good for invoking the spirits to chat with them about all kinds of things.

But now, for the first time, his heart pounded to see a kneeling girl refusing to budge from her father's graveside: Farida. He had already tried to cajole her to leave after everyone else had failed, saying that the air there was the coldest in the city when night fell, that it would be better if she returned home. The girl didn't look in the least bit afraid of a little cold air. So Kamino tried to tell her about the *jin* spirits and spooks, but saw that the girl was not at all swayed. That made his heart bubble over, and Kamino prayed silently that the girl was truly hardheaded and that she would never go home, and that after all these years he had finally found someone to keep him company in that place.

The Budi Dharma public cemetery was about ten square hectares, spreading out along the edge of the beach, and separated from human habitations by the cocoa plantation. Built in the colonial era, plenty of the cemetery's plots were empty and overgrown with weeds, and a strong wind blew in from the ocean. When night came, Kamino once again approached the girl with a shining lantern, which he placed on top of the grave marker.

"If you really don't want to go home," said Kamino, without daring to look at the girl's face, "you can stay at my house as a guest."

"Thanks, but I'd never go to anyone's house late at night all by myself."

So as the night grew colder the girl stayed where she was, without any blanket or cushion, sitting directly on the sandy dirt. Feeling that his presence was disturbing her, Kamino finally left, going back into his house and preparing dinner. He reappeared with a portion of food for Farida.

"You're too kind," she said.

"Oh, it's just a side job for gravediggers."

"I bet not that many people sit by a grave until you give them some dinner."

"True enough, but many souls of the dead are starving."

"You *socialize* with dead people?"

Kamino saw a small crack through which he could slip into the girl's life. "Yeah. I could even call your father's spirit if you wanted." And that was what happened. By playing *jailangkung* as he'd learned to do from his ancestors, Kamino called back the soul of Mualimin and let that old veteran possess his body. Now he became Mualimin, speaking with Mualimin's voice, on behalf of Mualimin, who came face-to-face with his daughter, Farida. The girl was overjoyed to hear her father's voice again, as if it was just like any other night, talking for a while after eating dinner before going into their own rooms to sleep. Now, after finishing the dinner that Kamino had given her, Farida found herself once again chatting with her dad, as if death didn't exist, until she remembered and said:

"But you are dead, Daddy!"

"Well don't be too jealous of me," said her father, "you'll get your turn someday."

The conversation tired her out, especially because she'd been there since the early afternoon, and she fell asleep beside the grave. Kamino ended his *jailangkung* session, and went to get a blanket. He covered the girl, with the attentive gentle movements of a man intoxicated by love, and then stood gazing at her face which appeared, and then was swallowed by the darkness, and then appeared again in the quivering light of the lantern, tossing in the wind. After making sure the girl was safe inside her blanket and that the lantern would last until morning, Kamino went back to his house and tried to sleep, but he thought about the girl all night long, dozing only when the first morning light broke through the frangipani leaves.

At half past ten he woke to the aroma of spices. Not yet fully alert, he stumbled out of bed and walked to the back of the house. His vision was still a little blurry, but he saw a girl carrying a steaming bowl, which she placed on the dining table.

"I cooked for you."

He immediately recognized Farida. He was amazed.

"Bathe first," said Farida, "or wash your face. We'll eat together."

Like a hypnotized man, he walked only half-conscious to the bathroom, almost forgetting to take his towel, and bathed as quickly as he could. He found the girl sitting at the dining table waiting for him. The rice was still warm. The bowl was filled with cabbage and carrot and macaroni soup. On one plate he saw fried tempeh, and on another plate he saw flying fish that had been chopped up into small pieces and fried nice and crispy.

"I found it all in the kitchen."

Kamino nodded. It felt miraculous—he hadn't eaten with another person for years, not since his mother and father were still alive. Now here he was with a young woman, the one he had secretly fallen in love with the previous afternoon. His heart raced uncontrollably, and he still didn't dare to look at the girl's face as he ate. They only peeked at each other every once in a while, and if their eyes met they would smile shyly, like two sinners caught in the act. They sat across the dining table from one another, looking exactly like a pair of happy newlyweds.

This love story was slightly disrupted by a busy afternoon. Five people had been killed in a clash between communists and anti-communists. There were four communists and one anti-communist and Kamino had to bury them all. He soon realized that more and more corpses were going to arrive at that cemetery, and that these days would mark the inevitable downfall of the Communist Party. He knew this from the numbers of dead. He dug five new graves, four in one corner for the communists, and one in another corner where the regular folks were buried. Five dead people, each with their kinsmen crying over their graves, and short speeches from the Party leaders, consumed all his time until the afternoon. But while he was busy, Farida didn't go anywhere. She sat all day beside her father's grave, just as she had done the day before.

"I am willing to bet," said Kamino to Farida after his work was done and he was walking back to the house to wash up, "that tomorrow ten more communists will die."

"If it gets to be too much," said Farida, "bury them in one mass grave. On the seventh day there might be as many as nine hundred dead communists—there's no way you can dig that many graves."

"I just hope their children aren't as foolish as you," said Kamino. "Because to feed them I'd have to throw a banquet."

"Tonight, may I be your guest?"

That question took Kamino off guard, so he could only respond with a nod. Farida prepared their dinner, and after eating they once again called a spirit: none other than Mualimin, of course, and Farida could once again have a nice chat with her dad. This continued until nine o'clock at night, when it was time to go to bed. Farida got the room that used to belong to Kamino's mother and father, while he slept in the same room he had slept in since he was a child.

The next day, Kamino and Farida's predictions came true—early in the morning twelve communists died. This time there were no eulogies by Party leaders, because the situation was dire. There was talk that DN Aidit and the leaders of the Communist Party had in fact been executed. The twelve communist corpses were thrown into the cemetery without ceremony. He didn't know their names. And even though he only dug one big grave for twelve corpses, it was a busy day for Kamino because at noon the military truck reappeared and tossed out eight more corpses. Then in the afternoon he got seven more.

Farida sat at her father's grave, and when night fell she was Kamino's guest, while he was still busy with the onslaught of corpses. And that's how it went until the seventh day.

While most Communist Party sympathizers had gone running, more than one thousand communists still held out against the mob of soldiers and anti-communists at the end of Jalan Meredeka. Some of them shouldered old weapons, with severely limited ammunition. Besieged for one day and one night, they were very hungry but not willing to surrender. The stores in the area had already been destroyed and all the inhabitants had fled. Heavily armed soldiers surrounded them from all directions, and their commander had ordered the communists to disperse, telling them with a shrill voice that the Party had been finished from the moment their coup failed. But one thousand or more communists still held out.

As dusk approached, a few of them took shots at the soldiers. But their bullets wounded no one. The commander finally lost his patience and ordered his men to shoot. Hit from all sides, communists collapsed in the street. Those who had not yet been killed ran about in a blind panic, knocking one another down, before the bullets killed them off one by one. That afternoon, in one quick massacre, one thousand two hundred and thirty-two communists died, bringing an end to the history of the Communist Party in that city, and the entire country.

The corpses were heaved onto trucks, more and more, packed like stacks in a slaughterhouse transport, and a convoy of those corpse-filled trucks headed for Kamino's house. That day was the man's busiest day of all. He had to dig an extremely large pit—by the middle of the night he still wasn't done, only finishing up with the help of some soldiers as dawn broke. He kept hoping that the communists would surrender, so that no more corpses would appear and he could finally rest. Through all this, Farida stayed with him, waiting for him, preparing his food, and sitting beside her father's grave.

That morning, after the troops and their trucks had gone and one thousand two hundred and thirty-two communist corpses had been buried in one mass grave, Kamino, who hadn't slept but still looked full of energy, approached Farida, who'd been there for almost an entire week, and asked:

"My lady, would you like to come live with me and be my wife?"

Farida knew that it was her destiny to accept that man. So that morning, after they'd bathed and put on their finest clothes, they went to the village headman and asked to be married. They became husband and wife and went on their honeymoon to Farida's old house.

This meant there was no gravedigger on duty that day, but that was no problem, because the army troops had grown tired of bringing all the communist corpses to the graveyard and having to help the gravedigger dig mass graves. After all, some of those communists had been killed by regular army troops but most of them had been killed by anti-communists—carrying machetes and swords and sickles and whatever else could be used to kill—who had left their corpses at the side of the road to rot. The city of Halimunda was now filled with corpses sprawled out in the irrigation channels and on the outskirts of the city, in the foothills and on the riverbanks, in the middle of bridges and under bushes. Most of them had been killed as they tried to escape.

Not everyone had been killed, however. Some had surrendered and had been thrown into local jails and the military prisons before being brought to Bloedenkamp, the delta's most terrifying prison. Interrogations lasted for hours, ending with the promise that they'd be continued the following day. Some would die there, starved or beaten to death. Communists still on the loose were savagely hunted down, even deep into the jungle.

And Comrade Kliwon remained the most wanted man of all.

Shodancho formed a special unit to capture him, dead or alive.

Comrade Kliwon had in fact been sitting on the veranda with Adinda, patiently waiting for his newspapers, at the Communist Party headquarters when the special forces arrived. But swear to God, they didn't see those two. They charged in and tore the place apart, ripping down the painting of Karl Marx and burning it on the side of the road along with the Party flag, the hammer and sickle, and all the books from the library, except for the books about *silat*, Indonesian martial arts, which Shodancho rescued for his own enjoyment. He'd led the attack himself, and he got two whole boxes of those *silat* books, which he immediately stashed in his jeep. All this happened right in front of Comrade Kliwon and Adinda's eyes, who were in shock that nobody noticed them.

The troops went off to look in the public cemetery, because someone had reported he was hiding there, but it was abandoned—not even the gravedigger was there. Next they went swiftly to Mina's house, following another tip, but she insisted throughout the long interrogation that she hadn't seen Comrade Kliwon since the week before.

When the forces had gone, Mina said to herself, "That stupid kid should have known—all communists end up in front of a firing squad."

A man hurried up to Shodancho, saying he'd seen Comrade Kliwon escaping out to sea with a young woman. In his growing annoyance and with his abiding and unsated desire for revenge, Shodancho ordered a search of the open sea. His soldiers chased Kliwon on motorboats, but all they found was an empty floating skiff tossing in the waves, without a trace of him. Hoping that they could find his corpse, Shodancho ordered three soldiers to go diving, but they came home deeply disappointed.

To vent his anger, Shodancho reinterrogated the few important Party men they'd been able to capture. Each man said that the last time he'd seen Comrade Kliwon he'd been sitting on the veranda waiting for his newspapers. Shodancho took their tale as a mocking joke and he brought those men out behind the military prison and executed each one with his very own pistol.

Rumors flew that Comrade Kliwon had mystical powers, that he could disguise himself as someone else, or split and multiply himself so that he could appear in many different places at once. But in the end, he was finally captured. Shodancho retraced his footsteps, led his troops back to the Party headquarters at the end of Jalan Belanda, and then suddenly he saw him, still sitting on the veranda with Shodancho's own sister-in-law, exactly as the people he'd just executed had said. It was afternoon and a drizzly mist filled the city. Shodancho felt too embarrassed to ask where he'd been all day, because it seemed apparent, from the way Comrade Kliwon was sitting, that he had in fact been right there all along.

"You are captured, Comrade," said Shodancho, "and my dear Adinda, you'd better go home."

"What am I being arrested for?" asked Comrade Kliwon.

"Waiting for newspapers that will never come," said Shodancho, with bitter humor.

Kliwon held out his hands and Shodancho handcuffed him.

"Shodancho," said Adinda, standing there with tears streaming down her cheeks. "Allow me to say goodbye, because I'm afraid you'll execute him as soon as he gets to prison."

Shodancho nodded, and her farewell was simply a long kiss on Comrade Kliwon's lips.

The news of his capture was quickly known and almost everyone in the city, some with their hands still caked with blood, quickly gathered and lined the street from the Communist Party headquarters to the military prison. Each person had special fond memories of Comrade Kliwon, and waited patiently for that man to pass by.

Comrade Kliwon had refused to climb up onto the military jeep, and walked with what remained of his dignity, escorted by soldiers. Adinda was in the jeep with Shodancho, moving very slowly behind that small procession, while the people crowded on the left and right sides of the street in a solemn silence. They looked with mixed emotions at the man who, even then, was still wearing his beloved cap. Many of the spectators had been his friends ever since their school days, and they wondered how it could be that the cleverest and handsomest man in the city had chosen to live as a misguided communist. Some were women who'd gone out with him, or had dreamed of going out with him, and they watched with teary eyes as if their one true love was leaving them.

The people's anger vaporized as soon as they saw him. He walked straight and tall, still full of resolve, not at all like a conquered man. He walked like a commander certain he'd soon win the wars still yet to come. And the people who saw him remembered all the good he had done in the past, and forgot all the bad. He was a clever, smart, diligent, and polite young man, and suddenly no one remembered that he used to be a rabble-rouser who'd stiffed prostitutes, or that he had burned down ships.

On his cap there was now embroidered a small red star. He was wearing a shirt his mother had sewn for him, and slacks from his brief time studying in the capital, and borrowed leather shoes.

He turned his head hoping to catch a glimpse of Adinda, but he couldn't see her inside the jeep. He also looked for Alamanda in the crowd, but she wasn't there. Thinking that there wasn't anyone of importance in the crowd, he walked calmly to the prison behind the military headquarters, where without a trial Shodancho pronounced that he was to be executed the next morning at five o'clock.

Adinda reappeared not long afterward and since visitors were forbidden, she just left one change of clothes that she asked Shodancho to pass on with a tray full of food.

"Promise me, Shodancho," said Adinda, "that you make sure he eats it. Ever since he didn't get his newspapers he hasn't eaten anything."

Shodancho delivered all these things himself and found Comrade Kliwon lying down on a cot, his two hands folded beneath his head and looking up at the ceiling.

"I guess you still have a good reputation with the ladies, Comrade," said Shodancho. "One of them sent you a set of clothes and a tray of food."

"And I know which lady—your very own sister-in-law."

After that Comrade Kliwon fell silent, his body language unchanged. But in the dim light of the room, Shodancho smiled, enjoying his little revenge. This is the man who robbed me of my beautiful wife, he told himself, and cursed my two children.

"Tomorrow I will see you executed."

He didn't plan for the execution to be as simple or fast as a bullet. He wanted to see Kliwon die slowly—his fingernails yanked off one by one, his scalp peeled off, his eyes gouged out, his tongue hacked off. Shodancho smiled a cruel acrid smile in anticipation.

But Comrade Kliwon did not react. Incredibly, he didn't seem to care, and that really got under Shodancho's skin. Lying in his cot, this living corpse looked full of authority, full of self-satisfaction as if he was dying as a martyr, full of wonder at the life that he had chosen and would never regret, even though it had brought him to this unfortunate end. There was a huge gulf between them, between a man with the authority to order executions, and a man counting the hours until his death. The first made uneasy by his power, the second made calm by his fate.

In fact, Comrade Kliwon was not thinking about Shodancho at all, instead swept away by nostalgia back to all of his memories of the city he would soon be leaving. How exhausting revolution was, he thought to himself, and the one thing that made him happy was that *I can leave this all behind without having to become a reactionary or a counterrevolutionary.*

So Comrade Kliwon felt like he should thank whoever had carried out the coup. Because the following day he was going to die and would leave all this exhausting business behind. He wasn't too worried about his mother, she was strong and could take care of herself, and that made him all the more ready to die, even happy. A little smile played across his lips, which made Shodancho all the more annoyed.

"You are going to be collected at ten to five, and at five o'clock sharp your execution will begin. So tell me your last request," Shodancho ordered.

"This is my last request: Workers of the world, unite!" replied Comrade Kliwon.

Shodancho left and the door slammed shut.

{13}

LOTS OF PEOPLE get married in the months of the rainy season. Crowds of villagers attend ceremony after ceremony for weeks on end and the golden *janur kuning* poles marking the houses holding wedding parties stick out of fences at almost every single intersection, arching over the street to dangle their festive decorations. Meanwhile, those men who aren't married yet go off to the whorehouse, lovers meet more often to get it on in secret, long-married couples seem to relive their honeymoons in the months of the rainy season, and God creates many tiny little embryos.

Even during the massacre of the communists, people still made love whenever they had the chance, especially during the heavier downpours. But this kind of thing, at least for the moment, was not happening with Shodancho and Alamanda. Nor was it happening with Maman Gendeng and Maya Dewi, who were still acting out the same drama they'd been acting out ever since their wedding night almost five years ago.

But one thing was making Maman Gendeng very happy: he now had what could be called a home, something he'd long dreamed about, ever since he first fell in love with Nasiah and saw the girl's glowing love for her sweetheart. For years he had fantasized about a loving gaze like hers, about a family and a house—years full of despair doubting he would ever have anything even close to his dream, mostly because everyone thought of him as a troublemaking scoundrel.

Now when he came home from the bus terminal, after hanging out and chatting the whole afternoon, or playing cards with Shodancho, his wife would be waiting for him at the dining table and would hasten to prepare his bath. He spent every night floating in an indescribable joy and now felt quite civilized, because he had clean clothes just like his neighbors, ate at a dining room table just like his neighbors, and slept on a mattress covered by a blanket, just like his neighbors.

As well as completing her household tasks and doing her homework, Maya Dewi diligently took care of her husband. Just as he had promised Dewi Ayu, Maman Gendeng never touched another woman, even though he hadn't touched his own wife yet either. Year after year passed, and the little girl began to grow into an adolescent. She was already much taller, her body had filled out and her breasts were developing perfectly. But Maman Gendeng still saw her as the same little schoolgirl she had always been. He kept her company, smoked his cigarettes while she did her homework, and he tucked her in at night, but they never even slept in the same bed.

He was carrying out a truly amazing feat of sexual abstinence. When his lust appeared from time to time, he would conduct some experiments in the bathroom to try to calm himself down and, with regards to this issue, Shodancho was the best friend Maman Gendeng could have had. Even though their backgrounds were so different, fate had united them in a deepening friendship and Shodancho didn't just bemoan the possibility that his wife might still love Comrade Kliwon, he also began to discuss all his family problems with his most trustworthy friend.

After they'd played trump, and the other players had made themselves scarce, and any city issues had all been taken care of, they usually began to discuss their personal problems. And then they no longer seemed like friends, but more like a pair of brothers moaning and sighing to one another. One day, Shodancho spoke frankly about Alamanda's iron underwear.

"And the key to unlock them is a mantra that nobody except my wife knows."

"But I heard she was pregnant?"

Then, Shodancho suddenly burst into tears, sobbing, "She's been pregnant twice. I named both those babies Nurul Aini, but they both vanished from her womb!"

"There's no woman who can get pregnant without getting fucked, unless you believe in the Virgin Mary."

Shodancho gasped for breath and explained, "Well, I raped her when she was careless with that crotch protector."

Maman Gendeng comforted him by saying that even he himself hadn't yet touched his wife. "And I vowed, Shodancho, that I would never go to the whorehouse again, so I only entertain myself in the bathroom. It's pretty effective for relieving crankiness and preventing tantrums. You really do have to routinely purge the contents of your balls."

"But I already do stuff like that," complained Shodancho.

They then agreed that the key to their happy marriages would be found in time, even though it seemed to move so slowly, and in their patient acceptance. Maman Gendeng would have to live in anticipation until his wife was old enough to be made love to. "I don't know when that will be, Shodancho. And really what you need is time too, isn't it, time to grovel, because sooner or later, with enough persistence, a woman can be brought round." At least that was what the wise men who had been with many women always said. "So, if you are patient, your patience will bear fruit. Just like drops of water can wear away a hole in a rock, your wife will finally let go of her stubbornness and maybe even begin to fall in love with you. You won't need to cajole or convince or seduce her into opening her crotch protector, because one night she'll open it for you herself. Believe that this will happen, Shodancho, because there is no woman—or man—who can stay stubborn to the death."

These strange and wise words from Maman Gendeng, who he partly and secretly hated still, truly comforted Shodancho so that for just a moment he could stop obsessing about how delicious it would be to sleep with his own wife (although he still couldn't forget that one persistently sweet memory of when he raped her in the guerrilla hut).

Unlike Shodancho, Maman Gendeng had absolutely no thought of raping his own wife. Maybe if he asked, Maya Dewi would take off her clothes and lie down on the bed and wait for him to spring upon her naked. But no, he couldn't treat that young girl, whose eyes were still so innocent, so cruelly. Sweet youngest daughter, that was what he used to call Maya Dewi back when he was still Dewi Ayu's lover. He thought the most important task for a husband was to ensure his wife's happiness, and let her learn for herself how to become a good partner. "And look how proud I am of my little wife," he always said to his friends. "At twelve years old when I married her she was already good at cooking and sewing and straightening up and flower arranging. Now, as soon as she gets home from school she is even busier fulfilling all her cookie orders."

The baking business was so successful that Maya Dewi had hired two employees: two young orphan girls, each about twelve years old, whom she had taken in. They kept busy all day with the dough and the oven and the cookie decorating.

But school and business never made her negligent of her husband, and that was what made Maman Gendeng so very happy. But he still didn't touch her—he didn't want to plunder the happiness of her childhood, because even though she'd lived with the most famous whore in the city, maybe she herself had never thought about having sex or anything of that nature. And, especially after he heard what had happened to Shodancho's first two children, he felt sure that it wasn't right to force a woman in any way. Even if that woman was your wife.

And Maman Gendeng grew very proud of his own patience, for years not making love to anyone, except his own hand in the bathroom. His physical contact with his wife was limited to a kiss on her forehead before she went to sleep or when she was leaving for school, and sometimes they sat with their arms around each other at the movie theater, and he would carry her to bed if she fell asleep on the sofa. He had never even seen her naked. He held out with the mysterious patience of a man who'd been a warrior nomad, watching one season turn into the next with a peaceful anticipation.

Then one day when she was almost seventeen years old, Maya Dewi surprised Maman Gendeng by saying, "I am going to quit school." She gave her reason quite firmly, saying she wanted to take better care of her house and her husband.

Even though Maman Gendeng could have protested that up until now he and his house had been taken care of quite well, in fact probably way better than any other husband in the entire city, considering how many husbands ran away to Mama Kalong's whorehouse, Maman Gendeng accepted whatever his wife had decided—he saw the unshakable conviction in her eyes.

Later that night, Maman Gendeng went into his wife's room to kiss her good night and tuck her in just as usual. He found her lying naked on the bed, on pink sheets, under a dimly glowing lamp, smiling at him, with the fragrance of roses wafting about. Maya Dewi said:

"My darling, I am your wife and I am now grown up enough to receive you in this bed. Hold me and make love to me tonight. This will be the most beautiful night that we will ever experience, our first night together, the night we have been waiting five years for."

She was truly gorgeous, having inherited her mother's beauty, with her hair spread out on the pillow, her pert breasts and her lovely strong hips. Maman Gendeng lost his breath for a moment. Swear to God he had never realized that his five-year wait would reward him with such an extraordinary blessing, as if he had traveled a long way and finally found the most precious jewel in the world.

Then, as if pushed by an invisible force, he approached her, reaching out to explore his wife's body with caresses so gentle she arched and twisted with whispering sighs. With an unhurried calm forged by years of anticipation, Maman Gendeng climbed up on the bed and affectionately sniffed his wife's forehead before covering her cheeks and her lips in long smoldering kisses. Maya Dewi took off the man's clothes with such delicate gestures that he didn't immediately realize that now they both were naked.

They melted into a glorious wedding night that went on for weeks. Like a pair of true newlyweds they almost never left the house, making love from nightfall until morning and then from morning until afternoon. They only left their bed to eat and drink and go to the bathroom and breath in the fresh air. They were still in the middle of their extraordinary honeymoon in the early days of that rainy and bloody October in Halimunda, so they had no idea what had come to pass.

Alamanda was the last person to hear the news of Comrade Kliwon's capture and the plans for his execution at five in the morning. That news was carried by the wind that blew in through the window as she was lying in her room waiting for her husband to come home. She almost never left the house ever since Shodancho had become so preoccupied with the early October business that was so sudden and so strange. Alamanda shivered to think that the man she still secretly loved would die at dawn, maybe in front of a firing squad, maybe hung, maybe drowned, or maybe pitted against *ajak*.

She sat on the edge of her bed wrapped in a blanket, her eyes glued to the wall clock, watching the minute hand move slowly but surely toward the moment her old lover's life would end, on the orders of her husband. Maybe even Shodancho himself would carry out the execution. Feeling isolated and alienated and all alone, she began to weep, suddenly yearning for a man's embrace. She was abandoned by the man she'd married to his preoccupation with all the recent mayhem, and powerless to help the man she would have far preferred to have in her bed.

She wasn't the only one unwilling to accept Comrade Kliwon's execution: to her and many other people it didn't matter that he had burned three of her husband's fishing ships and thrown teenagers in jail for being obsessed with rock and roll—that man *was* Halimunda and vice versa. He had built a positive image for the city, supplanting its old reputation as a den of prostitutes, bandits, and old guerrillas.

Every girl in Halimunda, including Alamanda, would picture that man every time they thought of the city, but at dawn he would die, and prayers began to float up in the air above the city, rising from the mouths of people powerless to prevent his punishment. It was only Alamanda who might be able to stay the man's execution: she held the key.

At quarter to five in the early morning, Shodancho finally appeared at home, wanting to rest for a moment before witnessing the execution of his most infuriating enemy, tossed the revolver he would use to shoot that crazy communist onto the bed and then, exhausted, laid himself down next to the gun before he realized that Alamanda was sitting on a corner of the mattress, shivering.

"Tell me, Shodancho, he is scheduled to die at five o'clock this morning, right?" Alamanda asked from the darkness.

"Yes."

"I will recite the mantra and I will give you my love, if you will guarantee that the man will live." Alamanda's voice rang out with conviction.

Shodancho got up and sat facing his wife in the dim room for a moment, entering into the strangest transaction ever to take place between a husband and wife.

"I'm serious, Shodancho."

"It's a fair deal," said Shodancho, "even though it fills me with jealousy."

He didn't say another word. He just stood, picked up his revolver and walked out of the room with hearty steps. He went to the military headquarters and found the firing squad polishing their rifles with pride, because in a half hour they would kill the biggest catch of their careers.

Shodancho found the squad leader and gave his orders. No one was allowed to kill Comrade Kliwon and no one was allowed to ask the reason why. He said that all things which fell under the jurisdiction of the generals in the central command were his responsibility, and if anyone dared to kill that man, he would not hesitate to kill that killer with his very own revolver (he said brandishing the weapon), along with his children, wife, parents and in-laws, older siblings, nieces and nephews, cousins, uncles, and aunts.

His order was so emphatic that no one dared argue, even though they were all wracking their brains trying to figure out what had happened. But then as Shodancho was heading home, he turned at the gate and gazed back at the soldiers, who hadn't slept all night long, anticipating this execution, saying:

"You can rough him up a bit, but I repeat, do not kill him. At seven o'clock this morning he must be set free."

And then he quickly went home.

Upon his arrival he found his wife lying naked atop their bed, exactly how Maman Gendeng had discovered Maya Dewi. The air in the room felt warm and refreshing even though the rainy season had frozen everything outside. In the glow of the night-light he saw the shape of the body he knew so well, every arc and dimple and curve. The woman was now twenty-one years old, ripe and tempting.

And then Shodancho realized that the room had been decorated like a bridal chamber. Everything was a golden color, as was Alamanda's liking, from the sheets, to the blanket, to the mosquito netting. There were orchids and tuberose in a vase on the corner table to delight his nose. This was like the wondrous offering of a wedding night, that was five years late.

Shodancho assumed the shy attitude of a new groom, not rushing like he usually did, but taking off his clothes slowly. Then that delayed wedding night began, followed by an extraordinarily romantic and warm honeymoon. The love they made that night was formidable and wild, moving to the floor when they rolled off the golden bed without noticing, then continuing in the bathroom, before they did it on the sofa as sunbeams began to pierce through the window.

They closed all the doors of the house, locked the servants in the kitchen, and did it again in the front parlor while reading aloud to each other from pornographic novels. Then they returned to the bathroom, and it was all a surprise for the servants in the kitchen and the neighbors listening to Alamanda's short yelps and Shodancho's low grunts. He came three times that evening, but satisfaction only arrived after they did it eleven more times the next day: truly, a pair of opponents who'd been starving for five years.

Just like Maman Gendeng and Maya Dewi, they didn't emerge from their house for weeks after that. They no longer cared about anything happening outside their own home.

Then, months later, Shodancho heard the news that Maman

Gendeng's wife was pregnant. A small party was held and the *preman* all got drunk in the backyard, paying no heed to Maman Gendeng's shouts forbidding anyone from getting wasted under his roof—they even began to pass out and Maman Gendeng was forced to drag them out to the street one by one.

Maman Gendeng sat on a veranda chair looking out at those friends of his, some lying on the side of the road and others staggering back to their benches at the bus station, from the giddy perspective of a man who is ready to live the normal life of all the other family men that he'd ever seen, and yet a man who'd for years lived in solidarity with his friends in the open air.

He was still a man filled with that ambiguity—a bad guy in the outside world, but such a good man at home—when their child finally was born. Just as he had sworn to do, he named the baby Rengganis. But most people ended up calling her Rengganis the Beautiful because of her extraordinary beauty.

That was when Shodancho appeared, saying with sincerity that he was truly overjoyed to see his friend have a little girl who was just as beautiful as her mother and her grandmother. Of course he also teased him, congratulating him that his equipment still functioned after its forced rest for five long years, not counting a few ridiculous bathroom episodes. At this, Maman Gendeng, usually so crude and ruthless, blushed shyly and cautiously asked how Shodancho himself was doing.

Shodancho revealed a wide grin: "Take a look at me my dear friend. We've both been graced with good fortune and all of our patience has finally born fruit. My wife is also pregnant and her belly is round and full. Oh my friend, don't look at me like that, I didn't do it the way I did for her first two pregnancies. It's true that those two sweet little baby girls were lost, but I hope that now my grief will finally disappear. I believe my wife will give birth to an honest-to goodness real child, and I swear that our baby will be no less beautiful than your little daughter here. Because this time I did it right, not by raping my own wife. We had sex like other newlyweds, a little bit shy at first but warm and passionate and sincere and full of love."

He continued, "You must be surprised to hear this. I was just as surprised when one night, as dawn was about to break, I found my wife naked and offering herself to me, saying that she was ready and willing to be ravished and would not put up a fight, and for weeks after that we enjoyed the exquisitely beautiful nights of our honeymoon. My story is not so different from yours, my friend, because maybe the universe destined us to the same fate."

Both men chuckled.

Shodancho did not mention—feeling there was no need for Maman Gendeng to know—that he had earned his wife's love by sparing the life of Comrade Kliwon.

Overflowing with joy, they toasted each other in the backyard near Maman Gendeng's fish ponds. They chatted about many things, including trump strategy, and promised that they would soon meet again at the card table after the long absences caused by their never-ending honeymoons.

Six months after Rengganis was born, when he heard that Alamanda was going into labor, Maman Gendeng brought his wife and daughter to Shodancho's house. They arrived just as the infant let out its first cries, and right at that moment Maman Gendeng clasped Shodancho's hand. The new father was ecstatic to see his baby, actual flesh and blood, bone and skin, just perfect, like almost every other baby in the world. The baby was a girl, and it turned out that she was in fact no less beautiful than the daughter of his dear friend and his enemy.

Maman Gendeng said, "Congratulations, Shodancho, I hope that these cousins will become best friends. Have you already thought of a name?"

"Just like her two older sisters who disappeared," said Shodancho, "I will name her Nurul Aini." But later people preferred to use her nickname, Ai.

And so that is the tale of two fathers who each had to wait for years to get their bundles of joy, both men who loved their daughters dearly, so that when they reunited at the trump table with the sardine seller and the butcher they sometimes brought those little girls along. And so it was that the kids grew up together. The men would let the children shuffle the cards in the middle of a game and toss them their betting coins, and their friendship grew closer with the presence of those two girls.

Meanwhile, twelve days after the birth of Nurul Aini, a third cousin was also born—a baby boy, Adinda's child, and his father named him Krisan. But that's another story, another family, another destiny which began the day Comrade Kliwon was scheduled to be executed at dawn but was spared because Alamanda bought his life with her surrender to Shodancho. At the time, no one knew that the birth of those three cousins, Dewi Ayu's grandchildren, would lead to the most harrowing tragedy in the years to come.

Meanwhile, in the cemetery, Kamino and Farida passed their quiet life together full of joy. Kamino, happy that he had finally found a girl willing to be a gravedigger's wife, didn't even mind when she told him repeatedly that the only reason she'd married him was because he lived close to her father's grave.

"It's pointless to be jealous of a dead man," said Kamino.

They still often played that *jailangkung* game, calling up Mualimin's spirit. The dead man seemed happy that Farida had landed a gravedigger husband.

"There's no one kinder than gravediggers," said the dead man. "They graciously serve people who no longer need to be served."

Their marriage grew even happier when Farida got pregnant.

"If it's a boy, then the next generation of gravediggers will have arrived," said Farida to her husband, "but if it turns out to be a girl, then this city might not have anyone to bury their dead."

That was their life together. They passed the time talking mostly to each other, and to the spirits of the dead, and occasionally talking with mourners accompanying the corpses, and they also enjoyed rare opportunities to visit their neighbors across the cocoa and coconut plantations.

Their life could be considered prosperous. They had the house the city had given them, and their family was never short on money because almost every day there were mourners who each slipped one or two bills into Kamino's hand. People made a pilgrimage to the grave on the seventh day after someone's death, and another pilgrimage on the fortieth day, and again on the one hundredth day, and then another on the thousandth day. Early in the fasting month of Ramadan they made a pilgrimage, and after Eid sometimes people made another pilgrimage too. Because so many people were buried in the cemetery, it wasn't surprising if every day someone came there on a pilgrimage, and Farida and Kamino enjoyed the entertainment of all those visitors.

The only slightly bothersome thing were all the disturbances from the ghosts. They weren't evil, but they were mischievous. They often teased people forced to walk past the cemetery, making spooky noises or appearing as headless sweet potato sellers. Everyone avoided the place at night but Kamino and Farida were quite used to the ghosts, and simply chased them away like other people shoo out a chicken that has wandered into the kitchen. Every once in a while the couple even teased the ghosts right back.

At midday, if there wasn't much to be done, Farida still often sat alone beside her father's grave. She had put a chair there, but once her pregnancy was farther along sitting became tiring, so she rolled out a woven mat and lay down under the shade of the frangipani leaves, but the sea breeze would set the sand flying along the ground. Kamino made her a rope hammock that he tied from one frangipani tree to the other so his wife could lie there lulled by the wind, closing her eyes with her body swaying gently.

But one day this led to disaster. When her pregnancy had reached six months, Farina fell asleep in that hammock and had a terrifying nightmare. In shock, she startled awake and bounced up out of the hammock and fell to the ground. She hemorrhaged, and before Kamino, who had heard her body thud onto the dirt, could reach her, she was dead.

How sad that man was: he had lost both his wife and his unborn child. He would now return to the same loneliness that he'd endured for so many years, except this new loneliness would be much more depressing, because now he had tasted happiness.

He took care of his wife's burial himself, only telling one or two neighbors what had happened, too overwhelmed to tell anybody else. He lovingly bathed his wife's body, lacerated by grief, and blaming himself for that hammock. He prayed over her body himself, and since his house was well stocked with burial shrouds, he even wrapped his wife's body in her shroud himself. In the afternoon he began to dig his wife's grave, right beside Mualimin's grave, because he knew that was exactly what Farina would have wanted. When night fell, the digging was finished. With tears streaming down his face, he carried his wife's corpse and placed it in the small recess at the bottom of the pit. He covered it with small planks of wood. As he began to fill in the hole with dirt, his sobs broke out into wrenching convulsions.

He didn't sleep that night. Like Farida had done when she was grieving the death of her father, Kamino just sat next to the grave of his wife without moving a muscle. His body was still stained with earth from her grave and the shovel still stood at his side. Suddenly he heard small whimpers. They were the cries of a child—no, a baby. He looked this way and that, but he saw no one. He began to think that maybe it was some cemetery ghosts making mischief, but as those cries became louder and more distinct, he knew that they were coming from his wife's grave.

Like a man possessed, he dug up his wife's burial plot. He pulled out the protective wooden planks. The corpse was still lying stiffly covered in the burial shroud, but near its crotch he saw something moving. Kamino quickly unwrapped the shroud, and saw a half-emerged baby, pinched by the corpse's two thighs. He pulled on the baby, who was clearly very much alive and crying loudly, and cut the umbilical cord with a bite.

That was his son. Born in a grave, premature, but seemingly quite healthy. The little one was a blessing in Kamino's time of sorrow, like a love token sent from his sweetheart. He raised that child himself, doted on him, and gave him the name Kinkin.

On the morning of the day he was supposed to be put to death, Comrade Kliwon was found battered and bruised in the field behind the military headquarters by Adinda, who had come to find out whether he was dead. As Adinda had hoped he would be, he was wearing the clean and proper clothes that she had sent for him (though now they were decorated with blood splatters), because at half-past four that morning he had calmly bathed, and then had sized himself up in front of a mirror, hoping that the angel of death would like how he looked.

"Are you afraid, Comrade?" asked one of the guards a moment before the time for his execution arrived.

"It's only soldiers who are filled with fear," said Comrade Kliwon. "If they weren't, they wouldn't need any weapons."

At the stroke of five o'clock a group of soldiers came to get him, soldiers who were pissed off because their mission to shoot him dead had been canceled at Shodancho's orders. And their anger boiled all the hotter to see the man's calm demeanor in facing death.

"I can walk to my grave by myself," said Comrade Kliwon.

"Please permit us to go through the trouble of taking you there," they answered, hauling him across the floor with his legs dragging outstretched behind. The soldiers kicked him as they pulled him down the corridor, without giving him the chance to utter even one word in protest. Then they threw him in the middle of the small field where he was supposed to have been executed and a spotlight illuminated the grass, which made Comrade Kliwon, who was trying to get up, blink. His body hurt everywhere from being kicked the whole way. Even facing death, he still hoped that he had no broken bones.

He stood, feeling blood dripping down his back as he walked, staggering a little toward the wall where he would have to stand to be shot. But those soldiers hit him with ferocious and practiced blows, kicked him again with their boots, and struck him with the butts of their rifles.

"You will never kill me this way," said Comrade Kliwon.

One more kick and he lost consciousness. That stopped all the torture. The soldiers just rolled him over with the toes of their boots. No one dared hit him again in his unconscious state, afraid that he would die. Shodancho had permitted them to torture him, but not to kill him, and so they dragged his unconscious body to a yard outside headquarters. If he died torn to shreds by dogs, that wasn't their responsibility.

When he came to, Comrade Kliwon found himself in a hospital bed, with his stiff body wrapped in bandages crisscrossing everywhere. Next to him, Adinda sat waiting, her face so lovely with such a heartfelt smile, overjoyed to see him conscious and alive.

"This young lady dragged you to the main street before bringing you here in a *becak*. You were unconscious for two days and two nights, and she's been waiting here the whole time," said the doctor standing next to him.

Comrade Kliwon murmured an inaudible thank you—even his

mouth was wrapped in a bandage—but Adinda could see from the look in his eyes that he was saying it, and she nodded, saying that she hoped he would get well as soon as possible.

This was the man who had led so many strikes, who had led more than a thousand communists in Halimunda, and he had lost it all: his friends, and even his own hometown, which was moving toward a new world, a world without communists.

He lay in isolation for a week, Adinda by his side and Mina checking in on him every morning. Sometimes, as he was still floating in and out of consciousness, he deliriously called out the names of his friends, but of course almost all of them were dead, and maybe had all already gone to hell. Other times he asked about his newspapers, still convinced that all this chaos had begun with their failure to appear. If his delirium began to intensify, Adinda quickly put a cold compress on his forehead burning up with fever, and he'd slip back into sleep.

"Do I need to recommend he be taken to the mental hospital?" the doctor asked Adinda.

"That won't be necessary," Adinda replied. "He is in fact remarkably sane, what's crazy is the world he'll be facing."

After leaving the hospital, physically already more or less recovered, Comrade Kliwon returned to Mina's house. He became antisocial, taking on his mother's work sewing clothes and avoiding interaction with other people. He lost touch with the reality of his city, his sunken eyes gazing down at the movement of the needle. Even when there were no customers, he would sew something else, from handkerchiefs to pillowcases, and when there was no more big pieces of cloth he began to collect torn fabric remnants and turned them into patchwork.

Because he didn't want to speak to anyone, and never left the house anymore, people began to act like he wasn't even there, ignoring him, and sometimes someone would mutter, "It would have been better if he'd been truly put to death."

"It's like you died without being executed," said Adinda, who tried a number of times to bring him back to life. "Maybe you *should* be sent to a mental hospital." He didn't respond, and the girl gave up hope of ever getting him back again.

But one morning he came out from the house neatly dressed, surprising his mother as he went through the doorway and walked toward the street. Hearing the news that *the* Comrade Kliwon had once again showed his face in the city, the people immediately filled the streets as fast as a flood. They watched him traverse Jalan Pramuka, Jalan Rengganis, Jalan Kidang, Jalan Belanda, Jalan Merdeka, and many other streets, just as they had watched him being brought to prison surrounded by soldiers. And just as he had walked then, he went on his way with an extraordinary indifference. He thought of those growing number of onlookers crowding around him as a carnival he was cutting through.

"Might I ask where you are going?" someone said.

"To the end of the road."

That was the first sentence he had uttered since emerging from the hospital, and for the people who heard him it was as sensational as if an orangutan had spoken. Many of them were thinking he would head for the old Party headquarters, which was now just a heap of debris, and would proclaim the return of the Communist Party. Others guessed that he would commit suicide by throwing himself into the sea. But nobody was really sure, so they continued to follow him like an honest-to-God circus convoy.

People were riveted when, as he passed through the city square, he suddenly plucked a rose and serenely inhaled its aroma, making the girls practically keel over. After one month of caging himself in his house, he looked plumper than when he'd been leading the Communist Party, and when they saw him smell that rose, they glimpsed a hint of the old glint in his eye that had made so many women lovesick. Each woman began to hope that he was heading for her house in a spirit of reconciliation or nostalgia or whatever you wanted to call it, to relive a love story that had once blossomed, or that hadn't yet had the chance to blossom.

"Might I ask who that flower is for, Comrade?" asked a young girl, her lips quivering.

"For a dog."

And he threw the rose to a feral dog who just happened to be passing by.

Many women grew even more heartbroken when it turned out that he was going to see Adinda, now twenty years old, with all the beauty she'd inherited from her mother. Dewi Ayu, who was surprised at Comrade Kliwon's appearance, invited the man in, while the hundreds of curious people huddled in her front yard, squeezed together at the windowpanes to eavesdrop and find out what was going to happen. Even Shodancho and Alamanda, who hadn't seen Dewi Ayu for five years, came and squeezed in with the others, for a moment forgetting their warm and passionate honeymoon. People were wondering whether he had come for Adinda or Dewi Ayu—apparently he was still the same man who had always been so popular, and everyone was waiting for whatever drama he would star in next. He had already played the role of the man most beloved in the city, and also the most despised.

"Good afternoon, Madam," said Comrade Kliwon.

"Good afternoon. I've been wondering why you weren't executed," said Dewi Ayu.

"Because they knew that death would bring me too much pleasure."

Dewi Ayu chuckled at his irony.

"Would you like a cup of coffee made by my daughter, Comrade? I've heard you two have grown quite close in recent years."

"Which daughter, Madam?"

"There's only one left: Adinda."

"Yes, thank you Madam. I have come to ask for her hand."

A thunderous uproar rose from the people gathered there, shocked by that proposal, and of course now the girls were even more heartbroken. Even Alamanda was brought to tears to hear it, feeling touched as if she herself had just been proposed to but also jealous that her younger sister had received such a blessing. Adinda, who had been eavesdropping from behind the wall, was more surprised than anyone to hear Comrade Kliwon's sudden proposal. She had been carrying two cups of coffee on a tray, but was brought to a halt behind that wall, lucky that the glasses didn't crash to the floor.

She stayed there, confused in her joy and surprise. Dewi Ayu, whose bitter life had accustomed her to keeping herself under control, smiled with sweet composure.

"Well, I will have to ask my daughter how she feels."

Then Dewi Ayu went to the back. Adinda was too shy to show her face, especially because of the crowd of people surrounding the house. But she nodded to her mother, full of certainty. Dewi Ayu returned to Comrade Kliwon and sat in front of him, bringing the tray.

"She nodded," she told Comrade Kliwon, and continued with a chuckle, "so you are going to be my son-in-law. The only son-in-law who has never slept with me."

"Well at one point I did want to, Madam," he said with a small shy look.

"I guessed as much."

Comrade Kliwon finally married Adinda at the end of the month of November of that year in a festive wedding celebration, everything paid for by Dewi Ayu. They slaughtered two fat cows, four goats, and hundreds of chickens; there was who-knows-how-many kilos of rice, potatoes, beans, noodles, and eggs. At first, Comrade Kliwon had hoped to have the simplest and most modest wedding possible since he didn't have very much money, just the small savings he'd tucked away from his fishing days. But Dewi Ayu wanted a festive wedding because Adinda was her last remaining child.

For a dowry Comrade Kliwon gave Adinda a ring that he had bought when he was in Jakarta, paid for with his earnings as a roving photographer, that in all honesty he had intended for Alamanda. Adinda knew the backstory to that dowry, but she wasn't the jealous girl her sister Alamanda used to accuse her of being. She even displayed it with a genuine pride. They spent their honeymoon in a hotel on the gulf that Dewi Ayu had arranged for them.

Dewi Ayu even bought the newlyweds a house in the same complex where Shodancho lived, just one house apart. Meanwhile Comrade Kliwon bought a plot of land and began to till the earth all by himself. He made a pond at the far end of the field, and sprinkled it with tadpoles, giving them chaff and cassava and papaya leaves every morning. In the paddies he planted rice just like everyone else. Adinda had a lot to learn to live as a farmer's wife, because she had never even so much as touched rice-paddy mud, but of course she was deeply content.

Comrade Kliwon would leave very early in the morning to go, just like any farmer, to his fields. He checked on the water drainage, plucked weeds, gave the fish food, and planted nuts and beans. Adinda took care of all the household duties, and by the time midday was approaching, after all those tasks were done, she would follow him to the fields carrying a basked filled with breakfast. They would eat together in the little open-air hut that Comrade Kliwon had built at the edge of the rice field, and when they went home the basket would be filled with young cassava leaves and sweet potatoes.

In January, Adinda took herself to the hospital to confirm that she was indeed pregnant. Everyone who knew them shared in their joy. Alamanda was the first to offer congratulations. At that time she herself was pregnant, and Nurul Aini had not yet been born. She arrived when the couple was relaxing on their veranda, looking out at the beautifully blooming flowers that Adinda had planted.

They were both a bit surprised by her arrival, because even though they were neighbors, Alamanda had never stopped by to say hello and vice versa.

Comrade Kliwon became slightly embarrassed, but Adinda immediately embraced her older sister and they kissed each other's cheeks.

"What did the doctor say?" asked Alamanda.

"He said, if it's a girl I hope she doesn't become a whore like her grandmother, or if it's a boy, a communist like his father."

Alamanda laughed.

"And what did the doctor say about your stomach?" asked Adinda.

"You know, my stomach has already fooled us twice, so I can't be certain."

"Alamanda," Comrade Kliwon said suddenly, making both women turn to look in his direction. They found him staring at Alamanda's stomach. Alamanda's face drained of color, remembering how Comrade Kliwon had twice said that her stomach was only filled with air and wind, like an empty pot. "I swear that this is not an empty pot like it was before," he proclaimed.

Alamanda looked at him, wanting to hear him repeat his words, and Comrade Kliwon nodded reassuringly. "It's a beautiful little girl, maybe even more beautiful than her mother, perfect, with jet-black hair, and piercing eyes that she got from her father. She will be born twelve days before my child. You can name her Nurul Aini just like her older sisters, but believe you me that she will live to grow up into a young woman."

"Dear God, if it is as the Comrade said, I will give her the name Nurul Aini," said Shodancho that evening. He and Alamanda began to understand that their two previous children were lost not because of a curse, but because of the absence of love. But just as she had promised when she begged for Comrade Kliwon's life, Alamanda had given her sincere and true love to Shodancho, and that love had now born fruit, and it now seemed that love could give them what they wanted.

Meanwhile Comrade Kliwon, who realized that his responsibility was growing along with the little one in his wife's stomach, began to think about work other than in the fields and rice paddies. When he had still been leading the Communist Party, he had gathered books for the children who were in Sunday school to read in addition to the Party literature. Most of the books had been destroyed, burned by Shodancho's men and the anti-communists who had set fire to their headquarters. But Shodancho had saved the martial arts novels and some pulp fiction clean of communist ideology, and brought them to the military headquarters for himself and his soldiers. One day not long after Alamanda's visit, Shodancho returned two cardboard boxes full of those books. Now Comrade Kliwon began his first small business, opening a small library in front of his house. Its customers were mostly schoolchildren, but it gave Adinda something to do and made them all quite happy.

Then, finally, Nurul Aini was born. Shodancho was impressed when Maman Gendeng said, "Congratulations, Shodancho, I hope the cousins will become good friends."

That was an honest-to-goodness original idea, to let those two children grow up in friendship as a way to placate the secret hostility that had began so long ago between their fathers. Shodancho agreed, saying they should enroll those two girls, Rengganis the Beautiful and Nurul Aini, in the same kindergarten once the time had come.

And then, influenced by that idea, when Adinda finally gave birth to her son twelve days after the birth of Nurul Aini as Comrade Kliwon had predicted, Shodancho echoed Maman Gendeng's sentiment of peace and hope in slightly different words: "Congratulations, Comrade, I hope that unlike us, your child and my child can be good friends—perhaps even a love match."

His father named the boy Krisan. And maybe he had indeed been destined for Nurul Aini, but life always has something else to say: Rengganis the Beautiful came between them.

{14}

IN THE YEAR 1976 Halimunda was filled with rancor, with vengeful ghosts trapped in limbo and unable to rest. All the city folk could feel it, as could the two Dutch tourists who had just disembarked from their train. They appeared to be a husband and wife in their seventies. Even at such an age, the man was still able to shoulder a huge backpack crammed full of stuff, while his wife carried a small bag and an umbrella. As they descended from the station platform, they jerked back at the soupy air, thick with a rancid stench and full of shadows that flickered with a reddish glow.

"It's like entering a haunted house," the wife commented, shaking her head.

"No," said her husband, "it's like there was a massacre in this city."

The *becak* rickshaw driver who took them to their hotel told them about the ghosts. They are very powerful, he said, so pray that they don't overturn this *becak* in the middle of the street. "Do things like that happen often?" asked the husband. "It's incredibly rare that it *doesn't* happen," replied the driver. He told them about a car that had crashed through the street divider and gone flying into the ocean. The passengers all died and everyone in the city believed this was the work of ghosts who couldn't rest. He also told them about the huge market fire two years before—everyone was sure those ghosts must have started it.

"How many ghosts are there?" asked the wife.

"You know, Madam, there has never been anyone fool enough to try to count how many."

They then learned that a number of years ago more than a thousand communists had died in that city in a most terrifying massacre. Even though they hated those communists, people said there had never been a more horrific slaughter in their city, and hopefully there never would be another ever again. Yes, more than a thousand people died. Most of them were buried in a mass grave in the Budi Dharma public cemetery. The others had been left to rot on the side of the road, until those who couldn't stand it anymore finally buried them, but even then it was more like burying some shit after defecating in the banana orchard.

Those two Dutch tourists had gotten a pretty good hotel on the bay. The wife whispered to her husband, "We made love here once and Papa caught us, and that was the last time we saw him." Her husband nodded. They walked toward the receptionist's desk and were greeted by a young man in a white uniform with such a perfectly symmetrical bow tie that he looked stiff and unnatural, smiling and thrusting forward the guest book. The man wrote their names there, in elegant old-fashioned cursive: Henri and Aneu Stammler.

That whole day they rested in their hotel room, which Aneu Stammler remarked had changed a lot since the colonial era: "I'm even willing to bet the present owner is a native." They were planning a small excursion for the following day but they didn't seem at all hurried, as if they planned to stay in the city for quite some time, maybe months or maybe years. Many Dutch tourists did that kind of thing, getting all nostalgic for the past when they had lived here, before being driven out by war.

A bellhop came, bringing them room service as well as the message, "While you are here, Sir and Madam, please do be careful of the communist ghosts."

"Karl Marx already warned us about that in the first paragraph of his *Manifesto*," said Henri Stammler laughing, and then they ate a dinner that brought back all the tropical tastes they had practically forgotten.

But before they ate, and before the bellhop left, Henri asked:

"Do you know a woman named Dewi Ayu? She's maybe about fifty-two years old."

"Of course," said the kid, "there's not a single person in Halimunda who doesn't know her."

Henri Stammler and his wife jumped with a feeling of untold delight. They had flown almost halfway across the world just to get to this city and find their daughter, whom they had left on her grandfather's doorstep. They both looked at the kid with a dumbfounded stare, as if they didn't believe that they could find her so easily.

"Is she half white?"

"Yeah, there's no other Dewi Ayu in this city."

"So she is still alive?" asked Aneu Stammler with her eyes welling up.

"No, Madam," said the kid. "She died not too long ago."

"Why did she die?"

"Because she wanted to." The kid prepared to take his leave, but before vanishing through the doorway he added, "But there are lots of other whores, if you're still looking for one."

So now they knew that Dewi Ayu had lived as a prostitute. The kid said that Dewi Ayu was a local legend, the most highly praised whore in the city, although that didn't impress Henri or Aneu Stammler that much. "All of the men wanted to sleep with her. Even two of her three son-in-laws took her to bed. She was an incredible whore."

"So she has three daughters?" asked Aneu Stammler.

"Four. The youngest was born twelve days before Dewi Ayu died."

The kid told them the address where they could find their youngest granddaughter, that she lived with and was taken care of by a mute servant named Rosinah, and that Dewi Ayu had named her Beauty.

"But she is hideous, like a monster," warned the kid.

They found out for themselves when they visited the house the next day. They both almost fainted, incredulous that they had a granddaughter like that. "Like a burnt cake," said Aneu Stammler, sinking down into a chair.

Rosinah lay the baby Beauty down in a cloth cradle-swing that was hung in the doorway, and gave the guests two glasses of cold lemonade. "Dewi Ayu was bored of having pretty children, so she asked for an ugly one, and this was the result," she said in sign language.

Henri and Aneu Stammler didn't understand her at all, and nothing made Rosinah crankier than having to communicate with people who didn't understand her sign language. But she was a kind woman, so she went and got a notebook, and wrote down what she had just said to them.

"What about her other children?" asked Henri.

"They have never set foot back here, ever since they discovered men's dicks," wrote Rosinah, repeating what Dewi Ayu had once said to her.

The couple took a little tour around the house, looking at the photographs hanging on the wall. There was a photo of Ted and Marietje Stammler that made them burst into tears, which in turn made Rosinah shake her head at these maudlin old folks. And after crying, now they were laughing to see a photo of themselves when they were still teenagers hanging in the front room. "I am willing to bet they've just been released from a mental hospital," Rosinah signed to the baby in her swing. Henri and Aneu Stammler were fascinated to see the photos of Dewi Ayu. There was one from when she was still small, and one when she was a teen. There were none from her twenties because of the war, but there were more pictures of her once she had grown up, even one from when she was already about fifty years old. They were struck by the fact that at any age, their daughter displayed an equally captivating beauty. It wasn't that surprising that she had been a prostitute, the idol of many men.

There were photographs of other beautiful young women too. "The one with the white face and tiny eyes like a Japanese is named Alamanda," Rosinah explained, playing her role as a tour guide. "She's married to Shodancho, a soldier, and has a child named Nurul Aini. The girl who looks most like Dewi Ayu is Adinda, her second daughter," Rosinah wrote in the notebook. "She is married to a communist veteran named Comrade Kliwon and has a son named Krisan. The third daughter, who looks more Indo than native, the most beautiful of all, is Maya Dewi. When she was twelve she married the most hated criminal in this city, Maman Gendeng, and now, after five years as a virgin bride, she finally has a daughter, Rengganis the Beautiful." Rosinah had never met any of the three children, but Dewi Ayu had told her all this.

Suddenly an incredible force hit them, as if the air had suddenly been sucked out of the room, or had congealed on their skin, and the hair on the back of their necks stood up.

"Oh my God," said Henri. "What sort of evil power is this?"

"I don't know, but this house *is* haunted. It's not a terribly evil ghost, but it is definitely holding a grudge."

"Is it a communist ghost?" asked Aneu Stammler, cowering against her husband.

"Those ghosts are out in the streets, not in this house."

The photographs on the wall began to sway slightly as if blown by a breeze. The book in Rosinah's hand opened and closed. Little

Beauty's swing rocked back and forth gently. Then there was the sound of a plate breaking in the kitchen and a pan went rattling across the floor.

"Is it Dewi Ayu's ghost?" asked Aneu.

"I'm not sure," wrote Rosinah. "Dewi Ayu once said that the ghost of Ma Gedik followed her wherever she went, and she was afraid of him, but so far he hasn't done anything to hurt us."

"Who is Ma Gedik?" asked Henri.

"Dewi Ayu said he was her ex-husband."

Once that supernatural disturbance had come to an end and the photographs were once again hanging stiff and straight on their nails Henri Stammler said, "This city has too many ghosts." Then he gulped down his cold lemonade, trying to calm himself down. "I don't see any pictures of a man who might be Ma Gedik."

"I have never seen him either," replied Rosinah.

Before Beauty was born, the two of them, Rosinah and Dewi Ayu, would often sit on a small bench in front of the kitchen hearth telling each other stories. Once, Dewi Ayu had told her the story of Ma Gedik. She had married him, forcing him to become her husband, because she loved him so much. She had never loved another man as much as she loved that old guy. "Even though it was clear that my love was completely unrequited. In fact, he thought I was an evil witch," Dewi Ayu had said, laughing. She had loved him before she'd ever seen him, because her mother's mother had loved him so much. "That poor pair of sweethearts, Ma Gedik and my grandmother Ma Iyang. Their love was destroyed, just as their lives were destroyed, because of the unbridled greed and lust of a Dutchman," Dewi Ayu had said. "And what's even more tragic is that the greedy and lustful Dutchman was my own grandfather." Dewi Ayu had loved Ma Gedik ever since she'd heard that tale. Maybe the houseboys or the neighbors had told her. She'd claimed that she'd kill herself if she couldn't marry that man, and so she'd had him kidnapped, and then she married him against his will, though in truth they'd never consummated their union. "He ran to the top of a hill and threw himself off." And ever since then, his ghost had followed her wherever she went.

The Stammlers of course knew the story of Ma Iyang and Ma Gedik, but they didn't know that Dewi Ayu had married *that* Ma Gedik.

"And so that's how Dewi Ayu lived, with his ghost for company, until she was fifty-two years old," wrote Rosinah.

"But why did she become a prostitute?" asked Aneu.

Rosinah told them what had happened to Dewi Ayu during the war, and how she'd once said to Rosinah that after the war had ended, she had stayed a prostitute not just to pay back her debts to Mama Kalong but also because she didn't want what had happened to Ma Iyang and Ma Gedik to ever happen to other loving couples. "If a man goes to see prostitutes, it means that he doesn't have to take a concubine," Dewi Ayu explained. "Every time a man takes a concubine, he's probably breaking the heart of that concubine's beloved. So a love is destroyed and lives are torn apart. But if he visits a prostitute, he only hurts a wife, who is clearly already married and who clearly has already done something wrong to make her husband go to a whorehouse in the first place."

"And that's why she became a prostitute," wrote Rosinah. "I feel like I'm writing my mistress's biography." And she chuckled.

"How could our daughter have such a vile way of thinking?" Aneu asked her husband.

"Don't think badly of the child," said Henri. "We're no better, a brother and sister who decided to marry—you mustn't forget that."

No one had forgotten it, not even Rosinah, who had only heard their story from Dewi Ayu.

Then the ghost came again, this time overturning the table and their cold glasses of lemonade with it.

❧

But no one suffered more terribly from ghosts than Shodancho. For years after the massacre he experienced terrible insomnia, and then when he did finally fall asleep, he suffered from sleepwalking. Communist ghosts were out to get him all the time, even sabotaging him at the trump table and making him lose again and again. Their constant annoyances were driving him insane—he'd often put his clothes on backward, or walk out of the house in his underwear, or go home to the wrong house. Or he'd think that he was making love to his wife but it turned out that he was fucking the toilet hole. The water in his bathtub would turn into a sticky pool of blood, and upon investigation he'd discover that all of the water in the house, even the water in the teapot and the thermos, had also suddenly thickened into dark red blood.

Everyone in the city sensed those ghosts and were terrified by them, but the most terrorized of all was Shodancho.

Ghosts sometimes appeared at his bedroom window, blood pouring endlessly out of holes in their foreheads, moaning as if they were trying to say something but had lost all powers of speech. If Shodancho saw them, he would scream and cower with a pale face, and Alamanda would come and try to calm him down.

"Think about it, it's just the ghost of some communist," Alamanda would say, but Shodancho could not be comforted, so she'd have to chase those ghosts away. Sometimes the ghosts didn't want to leave, and if they kept on moaning as if they were asking for something, Alamanda would give them things to eat or drink, and they would drink as though they had crossed a vast desert, and eat as if they'd been fasting for three years, and then they would disappear and Shodancho could be placated.

At first he really wasn't very scared as all that. If a communist ghost appeared with his gunshot wounds, mouthing some verses from the *Internationale*, he would just take out his pistol and shoot it. At first the ghosts would disappear with one shot, but after a while they became immune. Shodancho had shot so many ghosts in so many corners of the city that they turned bulletproof. They wouldn't vanish, but the shots would leave behind more bullet holes in their bodies, squirting out blood. They would still just stand there, and then they would try to come closer, finally making Shodancho run away, and that was when he began to feel truly afraid.

With all he was suffering, Shodancho seemed crazy, but he wasn't hallucinating. Other people could see what he saw, and other people feared what he feared. The difference was that he was more violently afraid than anyone else, especially compared to his wife, who after a while had grown accustomed to the ghosts and thought that at some point they'd probably get tired of bothering them.

Shodancho had to admit that he had killed a lot of communists, so he couldn't be surprised if they were plotting their revenge. He had to be careful around them but even when the ghosts didn't appear he was still constantly hounded by fear, which was turning his life into a chaotic mess.

Worst of all, his daughter, now ten years old, also seemed troubled. Ai, or Nurul Aini, was always complaining that an ambarella seed was stuck in her throat. She would chase after her father, asking him to help take it out. Shodancho told her the ghosts were responsible, and Ai believed him. Only her mother understood that the girl was just seeking attention from her father, who had grown so distant, caught up in his own fear.

Also, Shodancho's fear drove him to all kinds of irrational behavior. He once saw a crazy homeless guy striking a dog. Everyone knew that Shodancho really liked dogs, that he raised dogs, and that during his guerrilla years he had bred *ajak*. When he saw that crazy homeless guy hitting the dog he went on a rampage, beating him senseless and then throwing him into prison. Of course a crazy homeless person being thrown into military prison without a proper trial, just because he'd hit a dog, confused everyone. Even Alamanda was taken aback, and asked her husband:

"What really happened?"

"That homeless guy was possessed by a communist ghost."

Then a drunk fisherman was singing loudly in the middle of the night, waking everyone, including Shodancho, who'd finally just been able to fall asleep, for a moment overcoming his feverish insomnia. He immediately went out carrying his pistol and shot that drunk in the leg and then dragged him to the jailhouse.

"Are you crazy," asked Alamanda, "throwing someone in prison just because he got drunk?"

"He was possessed by a communist ghost."

Again and again, he accused everyone who did something that didn't please him of being possessed, and the last remnants of the old calm Shodancho, who loved to meditate, were completely gone.

Finally, in the year 1976, Alamanda brought him to Jakarta since there wasn't yet a mental hospital in Halimunda, and returned after a week, fully entrusting Shodancho to the care of the nurses, because no matter what was going on she still had a daughter to take care of.

Shodancho was gone from Halimunda for a while. The ghosts didn't disappear after Shodancho's departure but they were no longer displaying their damaged bodies or unleashing their cries of pain. And Shodancho, who could accuse whoever he didn't like of being possessed by communist ghosts with impunity and torture them or throw them in prison indefinitely, suddenly seemed more frightening to the city folk than the ghosts themselves, and so his absence brought everyone a sense of relief.

But Shodancho soon returned.

"Damn it!" was the first thing he said. "Those doctors thought I was crazy, so I shot one of them and I came home."

"You certainly aren't crazy," said Alamanda, "you're just a little bit not sane."

"There's an ambarella seed in my throat, Papa," said Ai.

"Open your mouth and I'll shoot that little communist."

"Do that and I'll kill you," threatened Alamanda.

Shodancho never shot at the ambarella seed, even though Ai opened her mouth as wide as she could.

Coming home to Halimunda meant returning to the source of all his fear. He tried to raise more dogs to chase away any ghosts that might approach, and this seemed to be somewhat successful in cutting down on their attacks, but a number of ghosts outsmarted the dogs by flying up onto the roof and appearing through the ceiling. Shodancho would yell and scream in his bed and Alamanda would serve the ghosts food or drink, which was all they ever seemed to want.

"Only Comrade Kliwon would ever be able to get them in line," Shodancho complained.

"Well, too bad then that you sent him to Buru Island not long after Krisan was born," replied Alamanda tartly.

This was true, and Shodancho deeply regretted it. Not because his wife had been furious at him for breaking his promise, because, from his point of view, he hadn't done so: his promise to Alamanda had only been to let Comrade Kliwon live, and the man's life had in fact been spared, and besides Shodancho was powerless to influence the commanding generals who had decided that Comrade Kliwon was one of die-hard the communists and that they all had to be exiled to Buru. Shodancho only regretted that Comrade Kliwon wasn't there to control the communist ghosts. He needed that man and thought that he would have to somehow get him home, or else be forced into exile himself.

He chose the latter.

Reports of a military occupation in East Timor had been coming in: guerrilla fighters were giving the National Armed Forces a bit of trouble, and Shodancho enlisted. He would say sayonara to the ghosts and go to East Timor, even if it meant leaving his wife and daughter. All of the generals knew his reputation and knew that his guerrilla knowledge was precisely what was needed in the occupied regions.

Shodancho's plans to leave soon became the topic of public conversation. At a farewell celebration at Independence Field on the day of his departure, a military marching band played. Then Shodancho traversed the city in an open jeep, dressed in full military attire, waving at all of the city folk and smiling derisively at all the restless, tortured ghosts. He and his retinue passed the city limits and gradually disappeared.

He had forgotten to say goodbye to his wife and child.

"He didn't even take out the ambarella seed," Ai complained.

"Trust me, he won't last long there," Alamanda comforted her. "He was an amazing guerrilla in Halimunda, but East Timor is not Halimunda."

And she was right. Within six months Shodancho was sent home with a bullet lodged in his shin. It seemed the city folk would never truly be rid of him.

He complained to his wife about how hard it was to make war in that shitty place, trying to make himself feel better about his swift return. "I don't know what they are looking for in that barren battlefield." She tried to get him to go to the hospital to remove the bullet, but Shodancho refused. He said that it didn't hurt anymore, just made him limp a little. He wanted it stuck there as a bitter souvenir: "Because the man who shot me aimed his rifle while singing the *Internationale*. It turns out those communist scoundrels are everywhere."

After a while, Comrade Kliwon's library had to close. A vicious rumor spread that he was poisoning the minds of schoolchildren by having them read noneducational trash, connecting this to his past activities as a legendary communist. Comrade Kliwon was enraged by that hogwash, but Adinda was able to calm him down. He finally closed the library, storing away the books and vowing that when his child grew up he would instruct him or her to read all of them, and people could see whether or not that child's morals were destroyed.

"It's not that I don't want to offer them trashy noneducational books, the problem is that they already burned all the trashy noneducational books I had," he said.

Shodancho had just opened an ice factory, using some joint capital from a shadow partner. Knowing that Comrade Kliwon was having difficulty after being forced to close his library, he proposed that the man help run this factory, practically as a full partner. Of course this was a very promising business. There were the ordinary fishermen but please note, since the collapse of the Communist Party (which meant the disbandment of the Fishermen's Union) there were also more big ships operating in the Halimunda seas, and they all needed ice. Comrade Kliwon was not at all interested in that proposal. He didn't state his reasons—maybe they were ideological, or maybe he felt uncomfortable taking any more help from Shodancho and his wife after the morning of his scheduled execution—but chose to become a bird's nest hunter instead. The nests could be sold at very high prices to Chinese merchants, who then would resell them in big cities and abroad. Comrade Kliwon didn't care who was going to eat the bird's nests, which according to him tasted no more delicious than plain macaroni—it was said the nests were made from the birds' saliva, but Comrade Kliwon couldn't have cared less if the nests were made from their shit—all he thought about was getting the things and selling them to the Chinese middlemen, and he joined a hunting team of four new friends.

There were walls of steep cliffs all along the jungle on the cape, and in those cliffs there were caves, big and small, high and low, the lowest ones visible only when the tide went out, and there in those caves the pretty black birds made their nests, coming in and out of the mouths of the caves, swooping across the foaming waves.

The team usually went out at night, armed with cages, a little bit of food, flashlights, and emergency antivenom medicine, because the birds shared their caves with serpents. The four men approached the cliffs silently, on a rowboat without a motor. They had to be very patient navigating the fickle waves that sometimes cooperated and sometimes closed off the mouths of the caves, and they had to constantly be on the lookout for the turning tide that could come rushing in without warning, trapping them inside a cavern. Sometimes they would drop an anchor at a jutting reef, take out their safety ropes and climb up the cliff, risking their lives to reach the higher caves. This work was incredibly exhausting, and sometimes they'd be kept waiting for days by unforgiving weather. But the hunts' earnings made the four of them quite prosperous. The money was way better than what Comrade Kliwon could get in the fields and rice paddies or from the library.

And he led his life as a nest hunter for about a month, while Adinda waited for him anxiously back at home, with the little newborn Krisan, but then one night one of the men slipped and fell, sliding down a cliff and slamming into a coral reef. He died instantly, not needing any help or even a hospital. They had already gathered lots of swallow nests that night, which suddenly all seemed worthless because they were also bringing home their friend's corpse. Everything they earned from selling those nests was given to the dead man's family, and then Comrade Kliwon and his two other friends stopped their hunting. Of course there would be other hunters, and other dead men, because the birds would keep on making their nests, but Comrade Kliwon had decided to forget that frightening business—he realized that if he died, he would leave behind a wife and a newborn child. He didn't want to do that.

He wracked his brains looking for a way to break into another business. By that time, Halimunda had become a beach resort. In truth the city had been a favored location since the colonial era because of the two beautiful bays formed by the jungle cape, but in the early years of the new government the city started promoting itself as a beach resort. There were new hotels tucked into a number of side streets, and new souvenir kiosks. Simple food stalls had turned into seafood restaurants, and the ruts in the road had been patched with new asphalt. The tourists arrived from every far-flung place, both domestic and abroad, and most of them came to swim at that beautiful beach. The western bay was their favorite spot, while the eastern bay became the port and the fish market. Comrade Kliwon thought hard about what the tourists who came to swim most needed, and tried to combine that with what he might be able to do. He found his answer.

"I'm going to make swim trunks," he said to Adinda.

That idea seemed silly, even to Adinda. But he didn't care. Comrade Kliwon bought a Singer sewing machine. He wanted to sell his shorts as cheaply as possible, because the tourists would probably only use them for swimming a few days before throwing them away. For that, he had to find the cheapest possible cloth. And for that, he went to ask his mother.

"Flour and rice sacks," said Mina. "I usually use them to line pant pockets."

Comrade Kliwon first studied bleaching techniques so that the merchant stamp could be erased from the sacks, and then he had plain fabric ready to be cut into the pattern of a pair of shorts. In truth, his shorts were not all that different from the shorts that farmers wore in the fields, but he distinguished them by silk-screening images onto the fabric before sewing the swim trunks. He designed these images himself, with the skill of a mediocre painter—brightly colored fish that he didn't even know the name for, or coconut trees whose leaves curved randomly against the background of an orange-colored setting sun. And at the bottom every image, he wrote the word "Halimunda" in big letters. If they wanted to, the tourists could then bring them home as a souvenir to remind them of the city.

He distributed the shorts to the simple bamboo and tarp kiosks lining the beach and it turned out the tourists liked those shorts. Maybe because they were cheap, maybe because of the interesting designs, but definitely because they needed them to go swimming. The kiosks asked for more shorts, and Comrade Kliwon had to work harder. Adinda could sew a little, but she usually just helped out with the bookkeeping, because she had to take care of little Krisan. When it seemed that there were too many orders to fill, Comrade Kliwon would throw some of the work his mother's way. Within a month, Mina was also overwhelmed and he bought three new sewing machines and hired three seamstresses and a silk-screen printer while still making all of the patterns and designs himself. Business was great, and he found that he didn't mind that he had become a small-time capitalist.

Perhaps he was forgetting his past, but in any case Comrade Kliwon enjoyed his pleasant days, with his work that was going well, his beautiful wife, and his healthy baby boy. Competitors of course began to spring up, especially the Chinese and Padang workers from overseas, but Comrade Kliwon's shorts were still the favorite shorts in Halimunda, and he was the latest business success.

But that happy life was soon destroyed by the mayor's plan. Comrade Kliwon returned to being *that* Comrade Kliwon, the *old* Comrade Kliwon.

Halimunda was thriving as a beach resort and the greedy mayor began to hope that he could sell the land along the coast to developers to build big hotels and restaurants and bars and discos and casinos and maybe even brothels better than Mama Kalong's. Most of that land belonged to the fishermen. Along the beach that abutted the street there was some more land that had no official deed holder, but that was filled with the humble souvenir kiosks. At first the local government approached the fishermen, asking politely if they would sell the land, and they gently tried to persuade the kiosk owners to move their kiosks to the new art market that would soon be built. But most of the fishermen refused to move off their ancestral land—their families had lived there for generations. They would never move inland, because they needed to smell the salty sea air. The kiosk owners didn't want to move either, because the promised art market would be located too far from the bustling beach.

And so, the soldiers came, backed up by the *preman*, to intimidate the people. But don't think that the fishermen scared easily—they faced death every night, out on the open ocean—and seeing the fishermen's resolve, the kiosk owners held out too. After intimidation failed, there came force and coercion. The land between the ocean and the street was not unclaimed territory but in fact belonged to the state, said the mayor who came to the beach and gave a speech, and the bulldozers would soon come to knock down all the kiosks.

Comrade Kliwon couldn't have such a thing happen before his eyes without turning back into the *old* Comrade Kliwon, though in fact no one knew whether he was acting out of solidarity or because his own business was being threatened. He organized a mass demonstration of fishermen and kiosk owners and many others sympathetic to their fate, the biggest demonstration since the collapse of the Communist Party. They blocked the roads against the bulldozers sent to flatten their flimsy kiosks until finally the army came. Comrade Kliwon still stood, leading at the front.

Intelligence agents sent to sniff out any communists amid the crowd of dissidents quickly recognized Comrade Kliwon. Reports were cross-checked, and it was soon confirmed that that man was truly an *authentic* communist. At the urging of the generals, Shodancho had to arrest Comrade Kliwon, and he laid into him, asking why he was doing such a foolish thing.

"I'm a communist, and any communist would do the same," said Comrade Kliwon.

He was finally sent to Bloedenkamp and found that some of his old friends were still being held there indefinitely. They were surprised that Kliwon wasn't dead, and even more surprised that he had come to Bloedenkamp after all this time. He was comforted to see so many people that he knew there, even though they were all living in heartbreaking conditions—starving, naked, and without any visitors. Their days were filled with interrogations and torture at the hands of the soldiers and guards. Given Comrade Kliwon's reputation, he experienced the same thing, doled out in an even more harsh and sadistic manner.

"Trust me, he'll survive," said Shodancho, calming his furious wife. "And even if he does die, communists always come back to life as ghosts, as you and I know very well."

"Tell that to Adinda and his child," said Alamanda.

Not long after that, the entire group of communist political prisoners at Bloedenkamp was moved to Buru Island. All of them, without exception. Nobody knew what would happen to them there. Maybe it was a kind of Boven-Digoel from colonial times, or maybe it was like a Nazi concentration camp. All of the prisoners anticipated excruciating forced labor and even more horrific punishments than the ones they'd already experienced. Comrade Kliwon wasn't able to say goodbye to his mother, his wife, or his child. He only said goodbye to Shodancho, who managed to visit him for a moment before the military ship carried all the prisoners to an island far out in the easternmost reaches of the Indonesian archipelago.

"I will look after your wife and child," Shodancho told him.

"And look, now he has been sent to Buru Island," said Alamanda when he got home, "where they will order him to chop wood and starve him to death."

"Think about it, he brought all of this chaos upon himself. A communist is always a communist, hotheaded and violent. I'm not the president, who can pardon someone, and I'm not a commander in chief, I'm just the *shodancho* of one small military command headquarters."

"And you still haven't gone and said as much to Adinda and her child."

So Shodancho finally went to see Adinda and said that he wholeheartedly regretted what had happened but he was powerless to prevent Comrade Kliwon from being sent first to Bloedenkamp, and then to Buru Island. This was a complicated political case.

"At the very least, tell me, Shodancho, how long will he be held there?"

"I don't know," replied Shodancho. "Maybe until there is another coup."

So Krisan never truly knew his father, because when Comrade Kliwon was sent to Bloedenkamp, and then Buru Island, he was still just a baby. He only knew about Comrade Kliwon through what his mother told him, or through Alamanda and Shodancho's stories. In 1979 his father returned, part of the last group of Buru Island prisoners to be sent home. Adinda was overjoyed at the man's return, but Krisan couldn't share in her happiness. By then the boy was already thirteen years old and felt like his father was a stranger who had suddenly moved into their house.

He paid very close attention to the man, especially when sitting across from him at the dining table. The figure he saw was way skinnier than the one in the old photographs that his mother had shown him. Before his face had been clean shaven, but now he'd let his mustache and sideburns and beard grow, and waves of long hair covered his neck. Krisan was quite surprised that the first thing his father looked for when he arrived was his threadbare cap still lying in the cupboard, its color so faded it was no longer clear whether it was black, brown, or grey. He patted it, but he never put it on and always returned it to its place inside the cupboard.

Comrade Kliwon didn't speak much after returning from exile. Krisan wondered whether it was really true that the man had once been an eloquent speaker at giant rallies. Maybe he talked more to his mother when night fell and they were lying together in bed, but he didn't talk to Krisan very much. He just said, "How are you, my son?" Or, "How old are you now?" He asked these questions over and over so frequently that Krisan was afraid his father had lost his senses. Maybe he was already senile, even though he wasn't yet fifty years old. He didn't know how old his father was. Maybe forty. But he looked old, frail, and forlorn, and he always dressed in tatters. It depressed Krisan.

Maybe Comrade Kliwon felt strange, too, because just as Krisan was studying him, he would often gaze at his son for a long time, as if he wanted to know what he was thinking.

For a number of days Comrade Kliwon didn't leave the house, and no one came to visit him because he had arrived surreptitiously and Adinda and Krisan hadn't told anyone. They wanted to protect the man's peace, and let him remain undiscovered until he was ready. Not even Shodancho or his wife knew yet. Nor did Mina.

"What is it like there?" Krisan asked once at dinner. "At Buru Island."

"The best food there is what you would usually find in the toilet," he replied.

With that, the atmosphere grew uncomfortable. Adinda gave Krisan a sign, and after that there'd been no discussion at all. Comrade Kliwon never wanted to say anything about Buru Island, and Adinda and Krisan no longer dared ask any questions.

Without any conversation, and without ever leaving the house,

Comrade Kliwon seemed to grow even more gloomy. Maybe he felt alienated from the place he had left behind for so many years, or maybe he could sense the many communist ghosts in the city and they made him sad. Once someone knocked on the door and Krisan opened it. In front of him stood a man in shabby clothes, with a bullet wound in his chest and a steady stream of blood pouring out of it. Krisan almost screamed, but his father appeared and said:

"How are you, Karmin?"

"Terrible, Comrade," replied the wounded man, "I'm dead."

White in the face, Krisan shrunk backward and pressed himself against the wall. After getting a bucket full of water and a washcloth, Comrade Kliwon approached the ghost and cleaned his wound, with loving care and attention, until the blood stopped flowing.

"Can I offer you a cup of coffee?" asked Comrade Kliwon. "Though there's no newspaper."

They drank coffee together while Krisan looked on, incredulous that his father could be so close with such a terrifying ghost. They talked about the lost years, laughing quietly. When the coffee was finished, the ghost took his leave.

"Where are you going?" asked Comrade Kliwon.

"To the place of the dead."

When the ghost disappeared, Krisan dropped to the floor.

Every time another communist ghost visited, Comrade Kliwon grew more forlorn. Maybe he was sad for them, or maybe it was something else. Krisan, who'd already lost out on thirteen years of knowing his father, was jealous of the ghosts. He wanted his father talk to him instead, but he didn't dare ask him anything after the incident at the dining table.

One day Comrade Kliwon asked Adinda, "How is Shodancho?"

"He's practically insane because of all those communist ghosts."

"I want to pay him a visit."

"You should," said Adinda. "Maybe it will be good for you."

It was a warm afternoon, with a gentle wind blowing from the hills. He went on foot and a number of neighbors caught sight of him, stunned that the man had returned. Shodancho's house was visible from his house, so it only took him a minute to reach the front door. Alamanda was the one who opened it and, just like the neighbors, she was flabbergasted.

"You are not a ghost, are you?" was what Alamanda asked.

"Well, I am a terrifying creature if you are afraid of living communists."

"So you have come home."

"They sent me home."

"Come in."

Comrade Kliwon sat on a chair in the front room while Alamanda went to bring him a drink. When she returned, Comrade Kliwon asked after Shodancho.

"He either went to some far-off corner of the city to shoot communist ghosts," said Alamanda, "or he's playing cards at the market."

After that they didn't say anything else. Comrade Kliwon wondered about Nurul Aini, but Alamanda was gazing at him so gently, with a look of pity or something else, and he wasn't sure when or where, but he had seen that look before, and it made him forget all about the little girl. Maybe Ai had gone to play somewhere, or maybe she was at Rengganis the Beautiful's house, but that didn't matter now, all he wanted to do was gaze back into the eyes of the woman before him, eyes that he had come to know so well so many years ago.

His brain had been damaged during his long exile and was now slow to understand anything. But then he remembered, and understood. Yes it was true, he knew that look, it was the same loving look that only Alamanda with her small eyes had, a look she'd given him so many years ago. That look was as gentle as a woman's smooth caress along a kitten's back, full of tenderness and now with a flame of longing. He recognized it and recognized he was a fool to have ever forgotten it. So he returned that look, a gaze full of passion, and was suddenly transformed from a morose old guy into a man who had rediscovered his long-lost love.

And that was how the following came to pass:

The two stood up and without a word they leapt into each other's arms and embraced, weeping, but not for long because they had already plunged into long and fervent kisses, just as underneath the almond tree, kisses that brought them down onto the sofa, where they quickly took off each other's clothes, and made wild and crazy love.

When it was over, they didn't regret it, not even one little bit.

But when he went home, Comrade Kliwon's wife was waiting at the front door. He tried to hide his radiating joy, and return to his morose face, but Adinda was not fooled in the slightest.

"The ghosts told me," said Adinda, "so I know what you did at Shodancho's house. But it's alright with me, as long as it made you happy."

That unnerved him. He didn't regret what he had done, but he was ashamed all of a sudden, feeling so dirty facing a wife who said, *It's alright with me, as long it made you happy*. A wife who had waited for him for years, and then after he'd suddenly arrived, had been just as suddenly betrayed.

Comrade Kliwon said nothing and went straight into the guest bedroom, locked himself inside, and didn't come out the next day even though Adinda and Krisan knocked on the door over and over inviting him to come eat dinner. When morning came and breakfast was ready, Adinda and Krisan took turns knocking on the door, but Comrade Kliwon didn't make a sound, so with growing worry and suspicion they pounded on the door harder, but still there was no answer.

Finally, Krisan went to the kitchen and got the hatchet that he used to split wood to make cages for his doves and as Adinda looked on used it to smash down the door. It split down the center, and then with a few more blows, he finally had a hole big enough to put his hand through and unlock the door. They found Comrade Kliwon hanging from a sheet that he had rolled up and tied to a crossbeam, dead. Krisan grabbed hold of his mother as she lost consciousness.

The news of Comrade Kliwon's appearance, which had been witnessed by his neighbors, had spread quickly. But everyone was too late. All they could see now was the convoy surrounding the man's coffin heading toward the graveyard. They were too late, just like Krisan, who had never had and now would never have the opportunity to know his father. They had only met for such a brief period of time, hardly even a week, and that was not nearly enough time to truly get to know one another as father and son. Out of everyone, Krisan was the most dismayed by the death of Comrade Kliwon. He claimed the inheritance of the threadbare cap that he'd seen his father wearing in old photographs and he often put it on, to comfort himself and to feel close to his father.

Now there was one more communist ghost in that city, but thankfully he never showed himself to anyone.

{15}

ONE MORNING, WHEN Rengganis the Beautiful gave birth to a baby boy, the people of Halimunda abandoned all their morning rituals and came crowding to her house to see. There were many reasons for them to shirk their responsibilities of feeding the chickens their bran porridge or filling their washtubs to clean the dirty dishes. First, Rengganis the Beautiful was famous in Halimunda, especially after being selected as Beach Princess of the Year. Second, she was the child of Maman Gendeng, who was also quite well known even though he was also quite detested by the city folk. Third, and this was the most important, in the city's long history it had never before come to pass that a young girl gave birth after having been raped by a dog.

When the midwife announced that what had emerged from the Beautiful's womb was truly a human baby, people turned over the old piece of gossip that she had been raped by a brown dog with a black snout, the kind of dog you see wherever you look in Halimunda, just like whenever you look up at the night sky you see stars. It had happened in a school bathroom, more or less nine months ago, not long after the recess bell rang.

The whole thing started with the Beautiful's bad habit of wagering, which she had inherited from her father. Her naughty friends had challenged her to drink five bottles of lemonade, saying she could have the drinks for free if she could finish them all without a drop left over. She did it, but when the entrance bell rang she paid the price, suddenly feeling like she was about to pee in her pants. It was bad timing, because lots of other schoolchildren were also going to the toilet, stretching out recess and cutting down on study time in a tradition that had been passed down from generation to generation. It was a cutthroat queue, and by the time your turn came, your pants or your skirt might already be soaking wet, but to go into class and risk peeing in your seat was also not a wise course of action, and even simpleminded Rengganis the Beautiful knew that, so she ran away from her snickering and giggling friends in the cafeteria, and headed quickly for that evil line.

There were fourteen toilets lined up behind the school building, and thirteen of them already had schoolkids waiting outside them, more likely planning to puff shared cigarettes than pee or take a shit, hidden from the eyes of the principal. The last toilet hadn't been in use for years. One rumor had it that a girl had killed herself in there, and another that a girl had given birth in there and then strangled her bastard baby. Nothing could be proven, the only reliable fact was that the toilet seemed more like a cage for evil spirits than anything else.

Built in colonial times next to a cocoa and coconut plantation, the school had previously been a Franciscan school. After the Dutch had gone, it next belonged to the national government, and the most reasonable story about the fourteenth toilet was that at some point a coconut or tree branch had fallen through its roof and the school hadn't had the money to repair it right away. As time passed, cocoa leaves had fallen through the hole into the toilet and gotten wet and moldy, and then lizards had made their nests beneath the detritus, and spiders had spun their webs. The water in the tub had filled with mosquito eggs and algae and weeds, and perhaps some people had taken a piss in there without ever flushing, but in any case that toilet became a place full of horror and now no one even dared stand in front of its door.

It hadn't been touched for years, not until Rengganis the Beautiful went inside. The five bottles of lemonade in her bladder began to mutiny, and with no other choice, she approached that accursed toilet, looked inside and saw a dog busy sniffing at the cocoa leaves, looking for traces of a cat who'd slipped out through the hole in the roof. It was a neighborhood dog crossbred with an *ajak*, with brown fur and a black snout, and Rengganis the Beautiful had no time to chase it away, but just went in, closed the door, locked it, and then—trapped in the small space with this dog—all she could do was stand stock-still as her urine, seemingly more than the five bottles of lemonade in liquid volume, began to spill out before she even had the chance to pull down her underwear. The warmth flowed down her thighs and her calves, soaking her socks and her shoes.

Next she caused yet another uproar—one of the many uproars that she'd already caused during her sixteen years of simpleton existence—when she appeared in class as naked as the day she was born. All of the children stopped in their tracks, dropping books and tripping over chairs, and even the old math teacher, who was about to start complaining about his dirty chalkboard, suddenly realized that the impotence he had been suffering from for years was miraculously cured, and his weapon was standing stiff and strong. Everyone knew that she was the most beautiful girl in the city, the true descendant of Princess Rengganis, Halimunda's goddess of beauty, but to see her body, that was just as beautiful as her face but usually hidden, dumbstruck everyone inside the classroom.

"I was raped by a dog in the school toilet!"

It's all true, if you believe what she said about what happened when she peed in her pants, stuck in that toilet with this dog—for the first five minutes she stood stock-still, helplessly staring at her skirt, socks, and shoes, all wet and stinking of piss. Even when she could no longer hear the sounds of the other children outside the toilet, she was still inside there bemoaning her misfortune. Her brain, which still had the logic of a little girl, ordered her to take off all of her wet clothes, as well as her shirt and her brassiere, and in a bizarre trance-like state, she did so. She hung them all up on the rusted nails, hoping that the rays of sunlight breaking through the perforated roof would quickly dry the remaining urine, and like travelers who wait at the laundromat, she stood naked in front of this dog, who was instantly aroused. It was then, the Beautiful would say, that the dog raped her.

"And he even took all of my clothes away with him after."

In any case, it was true that her mysterious beauty combined with her innocence gave her a look of sensuality. It's pretty certain that any man who might have stumbled upon her naked or found himself stuck with her inside a school toilet would have forced himself upon her. She had the kind of allure that made people want to have relations her, whether in a nice and proper way or not. It was only because everyone living in that city knew full well that her father was vicious and evil and scary that she had remained a virgin until the morning the dog raped her.

And Maman Gendeng wouldn't have hesitated to murder any man who dared touch his only child, despite the fact that the girl's beauty was a poisonous provocation wherever she went. Sometimes, while standing at the side of the road waiting for the bus, her childlike purity led her to absently lift her skirt and bite its hem. And if a mercilessly hot wind blew, she might undo a few of the buttons on her shirt. You could see the smooth skin that covered her calves and her thighs, the kind that only belongs to a nymph, and the curves of her beautiful breasts, the kind that only belong to sixteen-year-old girls. But you'd better not savor this provocation for too long, because if you did, sooner or later Maman Gendeng—stronger than any *dukun* or black magic sorcerer—would find out that you had been looking at his daughter with lust, and leave you lying in a heap in a hospital ward for six months.

At times like that, another young girl from another beauty, Nurul Aini, who had been the Beautiful's friend ever since they were babies in their cradles, would act as the protector of the perfect Beautiful. She would quickly pull down the Beautiful's skirt, and she would rebutton the girl's shirt: "Don't do that, sweetheart," she would say. "It's not proper."

And when Rengganis the Beautiful stood naked in front of the class—four and a half feet tall and eighty-eight pounds, with her natural calm, her gleaming ripe body, and her long hair as black as a river of ink, the most beautiful Indo in Halimunda, heir to her mother's beauty with captivating traces of Dutch ancestry, her blue eyes glittering as she looked out at the whole silent class sadly, wondering why all of a sudden everyone's mouth was wide open like a crocodile that had been waiting for its prey for weeks—Ai with her instinct to always be ready to deal with the bizarre things that the Beautiful did, rose from her chair, ran down the aisle of school benches, and yanked the tablecloth from the teacher's desk (sending a glass flying to shatter on the floor, as the teacher's black leather bag collided with the blackboard, spewing out its contents, and a flower vase and books went spinning). She wrapped that tablecloth around the Beautiful's body, making her look like a young girl in her towel after a bath.

Maybe Ai had inherited her resolute character from her father, Shodancho, but now, without her having to say a word, with just a look in their direction, the boys and the old math teacher promptly exited the classroom. As they went, their words of regret and grunts of disappointment could be heard passing between them.

"Damn it, a dog?! As if none of us could have raped Rengganis the Beautiful."

A few girls went to the gymnasium to look for a school soccer uniform to replace the tablecloth wrapped around the Beautiful's body.

At more or less the same time Maya Dewi, mother of the Beautiful and wife of Maman Gendeng, had a small but gravely worrisome household incident. She was cleaning when a lizard perched on the ceiling lampshade defecated and its scat fell down onto her shoulder. She wasn't worried about the smell or the filth, but she knew falling lizard scat always foreshadows catastrophe—it was a sign.

Unlike her husband, Maya Dewi was highly respected by the city folk, who didn't care that she was the daughter of Dewi Ayu, that notable whore. She was calm, and friendly, and even pious, and when they saw this woman people forgave the troubling childish character of her young daughter and her husband's frightening evil instincts. Maya Dewi went to the women's Thursday night prayer meetings and to the *arisan* on Sunday afternoons, socializing and contributing money to the women's lottery pool. She made her family seem just a little bit civilized, in part by earning a living from her daily work of making cookies with her two mountain-girl helpers.

Moments after she had cleaned off the lizard shit and ordered one of the girls to take over her work sweeping the middle room, her face, which still showed its Dutch roots, was as pale as a two-day-old corpse. She sat on the veranda and worried whether something had happened to her husband or her daughter. Of course lots of little things happened to them so often that she didn't think about those anymore, but she had always felt that sooner or later something big was going to happen, she just didn't know what. All she could do was worry. That damn lizard shit.

At a time like this of course Maman Gendeng would be at the bus terminal, as usual. He'd killed to get that chair, and Maya Dewi always worried that someone might murder him to get it, too, and no matter how bad that man was, she loved him as much as they both loved their daughter, and Maya Dewi did not want that to happen. She hoped that her husband was in fact invincible to weapons, as the Halimunda rumors always claimed.

Her thoughts were interrupted by a *becak* stopping in front of their gate. Two young girls got out and she recognized Shodancho's daughter, and then her own. She wondered why they were coming home so early, and why Rengganis the Beautiful was wearing a soccer uniform and not her school clothes. She stood up with the worry of a mother hen as the two young girls entered the yard and came to stand before her. Wanting to ask what had happened, Maya Dewi looked at Nurul Aini, but her face seemed as pale as a three-day-old corpse. Ai was on the verge of tears and Maya Dewi hadn't had the chance to ask anything when the Beautiful spoke.

"Mama, I was raped by a dog in the school toilet," she said, calm and purposeful. "And maybe I'm gonna get pregnant."

Maya Dewi collapsed back down onto her chair, with a face as pale as a four-day-old corpse. The kind of mother who never got mad, she just looked at the Beautiful helplessly, and then she asked, "What kind of dog?"

Soon after, the bad news came to the city that there'd be a total eclipse of the sun the following year. Soothsayers predicted it would be a year full of misfortune, and if it was in fact true that Rengganis the Beautiful had been raped by a dog, then the catastrophes had already begun. The news spread like a plague until everyone in Halimunda had heard it, except for the Beautiful's father, poor Maman Gendeng. For the very first time, people looked at that thug with gazes of pity and woe.

For a whole month, no one had the guts to tell him, until one day a slobby, chunky, awkward, and ridiculous-looking schoolboy around his daughter's age appeared, named Kinkin. He was wearing a sweater that was way too small for him, faded brown corduroys, dingy white keds, and round glasses that made him look like a comic book character. The fact that he dared approach the thug, who was nodding off in his sacred banged-up old mahogany rocking chair after drinking a glass of beer that had tasted like horse shit, caused a little bit of a stir. A number of people knew him to be Kamino the gravedigger's only son, but they were too late to prevent him from disturbing the *preman*.

Maman Gendeng, awakened from his snooze, reluctantly set down his beer glass and glanced with some annoyance at this kid who just stood there stiffly, rolling and unrolling the bottom of his shirt, until Maman Gendeng lost his patience.

"Tell me what you want and then get out of here!" he roared.

After a whole minute passed, the boy still hadn't said a thing and the thug, exasperated, grabbed his glass and poured out all the beer over the kid's head.

"Speak, or I'll dunk you in a cow wallow!"

"I am willing to marry your daughter, Rengganis the Beautiful," Kinkin finally said.

"She would never marry *you*," said Maman Gendeng, more amused than upset: "She can marry anyone she wants, but I'm sure it won't be you. Plus, you're way too young to talk about getting married."

Kinkin and Rengganis the Beautiful were in the same class at school, and he explained that he'd been in love with her ever since he first met her: he trembled every time he saw her, and kept on trembling with longing when he didn't see her. He was suffering from fever, insomnia, and shortness of breath, and all because of love. He'd secretly slipped some love poetry into the Beautiful's notebook, as well as a letter written on perfumed paper, but no response ever came—he was practically dead inside. He assured the thug that he loved the Beautiful the way that Romeo loved Juliet and Rama loved Shinta.

"She's going to finish school and become a dentist, like that rich woman down the street, so even if you two love each other, there's no reason to get married right now."

"Your daughter is pregnant and someone has to marry her," said the kid.

Maman Gendeng smiled a condescending little smirk. "Someone would have to rape her for her to get pregnant, and that would only happen over my dead body."

"A dog raped her in the school bathroom."

That amused Maman Gendeng even more, and he sent that pesky love-drunk kid away saying that if Kinkin truly loved his daughter, he shouldn't give up.

When afternoon came and he went home, he quickly forgot all about it. Rengganis the Beautiful hadn't said anything, nor had his wife, so he thought everything was just fine and took his usual nap. When his wife woke him up for dinner at seven and lit the incense coil to keep away the bugs, he remembered Kinkin and wondered to his wife whether he actually had been approached by a kid who'd said that the Beautiful had been raped by a dog in the school bathroom or whether it had just been a dream.

"She told me the same thing a few weeks ago," said Maya Dewi.

"Why didn't you say anything to me?"

"A dog would have had to kill us both before he dared to rape her."

For the next few weeks they were both preoccupied with this rumor. The reality was that not one person believed what she said—either thinking that she was just looking for attention or imagining what it would have been like to be that lucky dog—but because of her pitiful condition the pious women put their hands to their hearts and prayed for her well being.

"No one will lay a hand on her," the *preman* said tersely. "Not as long as we are still alive."

He had named his daughter after the city's goddess of beauty, but now he remembered that according to the legend, Princess Renggannis had married a dog.

"She is not pregnant," he said with certainty. "But if it turns out to be true, I will kill every dog in this city."

The family fell back into their daily routine, trying to ignore all the rumors. After all, it was not so unusual for the Beautiful to cause a stir. She had once dropped a cute little kitten into a pot of boiling oil, and once disrupted a circus when, out of curiosity, she had gotten out of her seat and pulled off the clown's mask. Maya Dewi returned to overseeing the two village girls and Maman Gendeng returned to his post, playing cards with Shodancho in the afternoon.

For many years he had eased his boredom by playing trump with Shodancho and a rotating assortment of sardine and vegetable sellers, market coolies and rickshaw drivers. Only when Shodancho went to East Timor to make war for six months did they skip cards, but most days he would ride over on a moped without a muffler, at around three in the afternoon, and the sound of his scooter, like a rice thresher's engine, was so familiar that if the thug was napping he would immediately awaken. Shodancho was skinnier and shorter than most soldiers, but his impressive military uniform—the dappled green camouflage uniform with hard alligator boots, and the pistol and wooden club swinging at his hip—hid his slight stature. His skin was dark and his mustache showed a few gray hairs. Most people had forgotten his real name, only remembering that he used to be a *shodan* commander in the revolution against the Japanese.

One Thursday afternoon, at their card table with the cow butcher's apprentice and a fish merchant, the ritual began with Shodancho tossing a pack of white American cigarettes onto the table. Before the cards were shuffled all four had already pounced on them, the tobacco smoke chasing away the tangy smell of salted fish and rotting vegetables.

"Ah, here's the joker," said Shodancho, "what's new with yours?"

The pair's fragile amity had solidified thanks to the friendship that had blossomed between their two daughters—and back when Rengganis the Beautiful and Nurul Aini were little girls who still peed in their pants, their fathers would give each girl a joker to hold in her pudgy little hand so she'd feel included but wouldn't bother the game, since the joker is never used in trump, and jokers now signified their daughters.

"A snot-nosed kid came to me to ask for her hand in marriage," replied Maman Gendeng.

Halimunda was filled with loudmouths and gossip, so Shodancho already knew about this, just as he had already heard about the hullabaloo in class. But he seemed hesitant to respond.

"I can't imagine her getting married and having a child and me becoming a grandfather." Maman Gendeng looked at his three card-playing friends, especially Shodancho, to gauge their reaction. "She's barely sixteen."

"Just like my joker."

People had already heard about Shodancho's plans to retire the following year. The injury that he'd gotten in East Timor had never completely healed, and the bullet was still lodged in his shin. Retiring with the rank of colonel would quickly put an end to the controversy about him holding on to his post for too long and hoarding control over the city military district—a post that had always been way below him, having led the revolution of the Halimunda *daidan* and destroyed the Japanese barracks six months before independence, when he'd been the first in line to become the great commander. But he never left Halimunda and never led the National Army. He made colonel when he chased out the Allied army during the period of military aggression, but after that he never aspired to rise further in rank. After he'd finished off all the communists, he declined the offer to become the aide to the president of the republic. Now, with a wife and a child he loved so very much, there was no reason to leave the city, and he was ready to retire.

"I heard that Rengganis the Beautiful was raped by a dog?" he asked.

"There are way too many dogs in Halimunda," muttered Maman Gendeng.

This surprised Shodancho—there were a lot of dogs in the city, but he had never heard anyone complain about it.

"And if it's true, what happened in the school bathroom, well I have plenty of dog poison," the thug continued coldly, "ever since that whore died of rabies two years ago. And no matter what might have happened with my daughter, there are more than enough reasons to send those curs to those dog-eating Batak kitchens."

Even though he seem to address anyone in particular, his friends at the card table knew all this was meant for Shodancho. Most of the dogs in Halimunda were *ajak* half-breeds, domesticated and bred ever since Shodancho began hunting pigs. Long ago, when Princess Rengganis had first come to the misty jungle that then grew into Halimunda, everyone knew she'd been accompanied by a dog. But no one had ever bred dogs until Shodancho.

"I hope it's just gossip," said Shodancho finally.

"Or just another bit of my daughter's foolishness," the thug replied dryly. He reminisced about all the *dukun* they'd visited to make his daughter more like other girls. Some said she was possessed by an evil spirit, while others suggested that her spirit was just refusing to grow up: she was a six-year-old child inside the body of a sixteen-year-old young woman. But whatever they said, they couldn't *do* anything about it. "And you know, just to make them allow her in school I had to punch out three different teachers." Growing a little mawkish losing his taste for the card game, he asked, "Are you all going to laugh at her as well?"

"Well, we always laugh at jokers," said Shodancho.

Maman Gendeng left and as he walked home the wind began blowing down from the hills and he could hear the sea thrashing. A group of bats flew clumsily against the wind, like drunkards, in a sky as orange as the fruit. The fishermen were stepping out of their houses with oars and nets and vats of ice, while from the opposite direction, the field laborers were coming home with their sickles and empty sacks. The overcast weather made him uneasy.

But seeing the starfruit tree, flowering verbena, and the shady sapodilla growing in the front of their house lifted his spirits. His home almost always rescued him from any storms of gloom, but this time he found his wife sitting in front of a tub full of laundry, crying.

"I'm worried that she's pregnant," said Maya Dewi, this mild-mannered woman, in a tone of fury. "A month has passed and I still haven't come across any bloodstained underwear." And, with that, she hurled that laundry tub, spilling the contents out across the floor.

The thug mulled it over. "If that turns out to be true, then it couldn't have been a dog," he said with certainty. "And in any case, if anybody is going to rape anybody, it should be my daughter who rapes a dog."

After his failed proposal in the bus terminal, Kinkin threw himself into his new hobby of hunting dogs lost in the graveyard and shooting them dead with his pellet gun. He was the only person who believed that Rengganis the Beautiful had been raped by a dog and, burning with a blind jealousy, he would not let even one dog under his dominion survive. If no dogs appeared, then he would buy posters of dogs that were sold in front of the market and hang them from the branches of a frangipani tree before shooting them to shreds. His father was the only one who knew about this odd behavior, and grew concerned.

"What's wrong with you, child?" his father asked. "The only sin dogs are guilty of is barking too much."

"Dogs are dogs, Dad," he replied coldly without turning his head, still aiming at the poster swinging from his last bullet. "And one of them raped the woman I love."

"I have never heard of a dog raping a woman. Or maybe you have fallen in love with a female dog?"

"Enough bullshit," said Kinkin. "Go home, Dad, this final bullet is intended for a dog and not for you."

Falling in love had totally destroyed any air of mystery that had surrounded him, or at least that was how his classmates saw it. No one had ever wanted to play with him, just as he had never wanted to play with anyone. His close friends were a gang that no other kids would like: *jailangkung* creatures. He had never even had a deskmate, because his uniform stunk of incense, and the teachers never called on him because sometimes he answered in the voice of a dead person. And even though the other children knew that he cheated during recitation by asking his *jailangkung* for the correct answers, no one dared tell on him nor ask for his help. He was like a bellybutton: everyone knew he was there, but they didn't pay any attention to him. That was before he saw the Beautiful.

The first time he saw her was the first day she entered her new school: after nine boring academic years, a scuffle had broken out in the office and the children came running to see what had happened. Kinkin was maybe the last person to see it, a man pounding to the ground three teachers who had refused to accept his daughter at the school and had suggested a special school for retarded, idiot, and insane children, an idea the man rejected, saying that his daughter was just fine.

"The only thing that makes my daughter different is the fact that she is the most beautiful girl in this entire city, if not in the entire universe," the man declared, glaring at the three teachers sprawled on the floor and at the principal quivering behind his desk.

The girl stood behind her father, wearing a brand new white and grey school uniform, still smelling of sewing machine grease, with sharp pleats in her skirt. She had tied her long hair in two braids that hung past the left and right sides of her waist, accented with red and white ribbons, in respect for the colors of the national flag. She wore the required black shoes, and short white socks with small lace flowers encircling the rims, her bare calves more captivating than anything that she was wearing. She clearly was not an idiot, anyone could see that, even Kinkin who was watching her from behind the glass window in the teacher's office. She was nothing less than an angel, lost in this vicious world, and ever since his first glorious glimpse, Kinkin had been swept away in an uncontrollable fever of love. Although he had never talked to anyone at school, he approached the girl and, struck by Cupid's arrow, asked her name. The girl, seeming confused, pointed to the small emblem that had been embroidered onto her shirt on top of her right breast, "You can read it right here: Rengganis."

All the children had name tags stuck to the chest of their uniforms, but Kinkin couldn't focus when the girl pointed to hers with the tip of her slender finger, instead staring at her breasts. He trembled for the rest of the first day of school, suffering alone in a corner of the classroom.

He suffered all the more, feeling the stares of his classmates, shocked to hear him speak up for the very first time since elementary school. They didn't dare make fun of him, though, because they were paranoid that the weird kid might hurt them with witchcraft or black magic. Only one girl, seemingly put in the class as Rengganis the Beautiful's guardian, had the guts to approach him.

"Listen to me, Jailangkung Boy," the girl threatened, "if you bother my little friend here, I will slice your dick into pieces like a carrot."

Ai quickly went and sat back down next to the Beautiful, leaving Kinkin almost in tears, imagining all the obstacles he would have to overcome in order to obtain the love that he so desired. To him, Ai was the most annoying creature on the planet. Everyday he hoped he could escort the Beautiful home from school, since walking next to her was of course the most rapturous thing that a schoolboy in love could ever imagine, but Ai always beat him. He was so pissed off, he once said to the girl, "Someone should murder you."

"You'd do it yourself if you weren't such a faggot."

But he didn't dare. So he missed every opportunity to walk the Beautiful home from school and his only happiness came in class, when he could turn his head and gaze at that beautiful face for as long as he wanted. He became the dumbest kid in school, because he no longer paid attention to any of the lessons. The only thing that helped his grades was the *jailangkung*, whom he consulted during exams. He also grew tragically skinny from not eating or sleeping enough, assaulted by love.

"You look worse off than me," the Beautiful even commented, "like a *real* idiot."

They brought her to the hospital, and the doctor said with complete certainty that the girl was in fact pregnant, seven weeks along. Both Maman Gendeng and Maya Dewi tried not to believe him, but five other doctors who examined her said the same thing. So did a *dukun*.

With this new certainty, the first course of action taken by her father was to lock the girl in her room, to prevent the spread of any more rumors. Maya Dewi had tried to escape the shadow of her past, with a whore for a mother who had given birth to multiple children without ever getting married, but now it was as if what had happened to Rengganis the Beautiful only confirmed that the curse still lived on in their bloodline. People would say that a depraved family would forever give birth to children just as depraved. So the couple agreed that the girl had to be locked up, hoping that sooner or later people would forget they had a pregnant teenage daughter.

Her room was on the second floor, too high to jump from, and the door was locked tightly from the outside. Her only companions were a teddy bear, a pile of trashy novels, and the radio. Maya Dewi herself took care of all of her needs, bringing her breakfast, lunch, and dinner, a chamber pot, and buckets full of water to bathe. Even though the girl whined that she wanted to go back to school, her mother firmly said no. "I promise I'll be more careful around dogs," said the Beautiful miserably. Maya Dewi burst into tears and choked out between her sobs, "No, sweetheart, not unless you can say who raped you in the school bathroom!"

They had asked her this again and again, but it led nowhere because the girl, with an amazing stubbornness, would reply over and over: a dog with brown skin and a black snout. Dogs like that could be found in every corner of Halimunda, and there was no way they were going to ask about each of them one by one. After failing to obtain any sensible explanation from the Beautiful, Maya Dewi would lock her up again and leave her, and then the Beautiful would scream and shout, asking to be let out and allowed to go back to school. Her cries were quite heartbreaking, and of course deafeningly loud, like the cries of an uncomfortable baby whose wet diaper hasn't been changed. Hearing her shrill voice, the neighbors came outside and looked up at the second-storey window, and pedestrians stopped in their tracks and whispered to one another. Maman Gendeng advised they send her away, but Maya Dewi opposed that idea and insisted on continuing to hold her in her own room, saying, "It's better to live in shame than to lose my daughter."

Finally they gave up and sent her back to school. Hers wasn't an easy case, because pregnant girls are never allowed in school. The school administration argued that such a thing would negatively influence the other young girls. For the second time, Maman Gendeng appeared at the school, and once again went into the principal's office without knocking on the door, to ensure that his daughter would not be expelled. The unfortunate principal was truly cornered. On the one hand he had to deal with the parents of the other students, who were worried about their daughters, because what had happened to Rengganis the Beautiful proved that the school wasn't safe. On the other hand, he had to deal with this thug who no one was brave enough to cross. The principal wiped away the cold sweat that was streaming down his forehead and neck.

"Alright my good friend, as long as she has not yet graduated she can be a student here," he said. "But please help me out, you have to find whoever did this to your daughter so that I can placate all the other parents. And one more thing, please get her some baggier clothes to wear."

That reminded Maman Gendeng of the kid named Kinkin. In the afternoon, sneaking off from the trump table, he went to Kamino the gravedigger's house to look for the boy. Just as in previous days, Kinkin was busy viciously shooting at posters of dogs. For a moment Maman Gendeng admired his marksmanship, even though he wondered why the kid had developed such an odd habit. After Kinkin had fired a number of rounds and the picture of the dog was thrown to the ground, he turned and approached the *preman* without any evident surprise.

"You can see for yourself what I'm doing, can't you?" he asked proudly. The *preman* didn't understand at all and just nodded until the kid explained, "I am shooting all dogs and even all pictures of dogs. I hate them and I envy them, because a dog raped your daughter and you know how incredibly much I love her."

Kamino watched them from the side of the house. Something wasn't right about the most frightening criminal in the city coming to look for his son, but he approached and tried in his most cordial way to invite the man in for a cup of coffee. Maman Gendeng and the kid Kinkin sat in the front room that was filled with a weird assortment of stuff left behind by dead people. After the coffee was ready and old Kamino left them alone, he asked the kid, "Tell me, who raped Rengganis the Beautiful?"

The kid looked back at him in confusion. "I think you already know: a dog, in the school bathroom," he said with conviction. That was not the answer that Maman Gendeng was hoping for, and in fact it pissed him off a little, but it was clear to him that the kid didn't know any more than anyone else, and only Rengganis the Beautiful and God knew what had happened in that school bathroom. He chugged his cup of coffee, just to calm himself down.

It seemed as though he was stuck with an unsolved mystery. He would have vastly preferred to have been facing an enemy in mortal combat than an unknown daughter rapist. He sat in front of the kid without saying another word until he realized that it was getting late. Although he wished he could postpone going home until he had a satisfying answer, he stood to leave, breaking the silence between them with a husky voice.

"Well, I guess it turns out that is all we know. If indeed it was a dog that raped her, then she will marry a dog."

Hearing that, Kinkin couldn't sleep, even worse than the previous evenings. He kept his father awake all night long and the ghosts in the cemetery couldn't relax either. When morning came, he quickly bathed and left for school early, ran to the house of Rengganis the Beautiful, and found her father who seemed cranky to be woken up so early in the morning.

"There's no way she is going to marry a dog!" he gasped with a voice that sounded like it was coming from the mouth of a dying man. "I will marry her."

This was way better, and the thug knew it. He looked at the kid, and remembered their first meeting in the bus terminal. He regretted that he hadn't accepted the kid's proposal then, before the problem had dragged on. He nodded and asked why.

"It wasn't a dog who raped her, but me."

That reason was enough to have the kid dragged out into the backyard and beat mercilessly, even though the very first punch alone sent him slamming into the corner of the fence with a bloody face. The child did not fight back and indeed would have been powerless to resist even if he had tried. Maya Dewi came rushing to stop her husband's brutality before the boy was killed. She had to struggle tooth and nail to get a hold of her husband, who was still hounding the boy, even though Kinkin had collapsed in a heap on the edge of a small fish pond. He wasn't dead yet, but he was suffering severely and moaning in pain.

"Of course I am not going to kill you," said Maman Gendeng, after his wife managed to drag him a short distance away. "Because you have to stay alive and marry my daughter."

In the afternoon, after hearing Kinkin's prattle all morning at school about his plans to marry Rengganis the Beautiful once she had given birth to her child, Ai went to the graveyard to meet with Kinkin, riding on the back of a minibike steered by her cousin Krisan.

"I know you weren't in the toilet that day," she said angrily.

The kid, smiling at their visit, didn't deny it but instead invited them in, and gave thanks because this was the first time a classmate had ever come to see him. His house was not a pleasant place—it was old and without a woman's touch, rarely swept, and the objects left behind by the dead were piled up in creepy, dusty heaps, like an excavation of a mummy's tomb.

After bringing them two glasses of cold lemonade from the kitchen, he said that his mother had passed away long ago, having died the moment he was born, to apologize for the house's unkempt condition, if not to change the topic of conversation. But the girl's face did not seem the least bit relaxed, as she waited for the next opportunity to harangue him some more.

"You sly faggot, there's no way you raped her," Ai said.

"Of course, I could never be so cruel," said Kinkin calmly. "If you love someone, you would never do that, not even if the opportunity arose. I proposed to her properly and I am going to marry her because I love her."

He would inherit his father's line of work and the house in the graveyard. Such things were always passed down through the generations and the reason why was clear: nobody else would want the job. Everyone in the city believed that the graveyard was filled with evil spirits and ghouls, and only a gravedigger's family could stand to live there year after year. The family also passed down their secret magical knowledge about how to carry on relationships with the spirits of the dead through the use of *jailangkung*. Kinkin was the last and only available heir, without brothers and sisters. But if his peers were afraid of him, it was not just because he was a gravedigger's son and could play *jailangkung*, but because of his cold face and the humid stench that emanated from his body, as if he carried an evil spirit on his shoulder wherever he went. It was enough to make the hair on the napes of their necks stand up, so Krisan stayed mostly silent. He truly had not wanted to come, and had done it just because his cousin had forced him.

"Don't think that just because you know black magic you can do whatever you want," the girl continued.

"Black magic is not useful at all," Kinkin said, waving his hands in protest. "It gives you a pseudopower that is false, artificial, and of course evil. My own personal experience has taught me that love is more powerful than anything."

Apparently love had made him quite stubborn and the girl Ai knew it. She didn't really want to prevent him from loving Rengganis, she just wanted to protect the Beautiful, and she could sense that there was something not right about these marriage plans. She stood and reached for Krisan's hand, but before leaving she looked at Kinkin and blurted out, "Love the Beautiful with all your heart," sounding exactly like a mother giving her son-in-law advice on his wedding day.

Kinkin nodded confidently. "Of course."

"But if it turns out that your love is just like one-hand clapping and my beautiful cousin doesn't want you in return, I will never let anyone marry you two," Ai threatened. "I am destined to protect her, so that she can always be happy."

The assertiveness of her voice often made people unable to meet her gaze, and Kinkin also bowed his head. "Yes but," said Kinkin, "her own father has already accepted my marriage proposal."

"Even so."

Ai didn't give the kid the chance to say another word. She yanked on Krisan's hand, and that boy quickly walked toward his minibike. With the girl riding behind him, they left and went to the Beautiful's house, where they found a household in chaos and the sound of her howls coming from the second floor. In the room below, they found Maya Dewi crying silently on the corner of the sofa, with the two mountain girls standing awkwardly in the kitchen doorway. Krisan sat down in front of the woman while Ai sat beside her, reaching for her hand with a confused, worried expression: "What's wrong, Auntie?"

Maya Dewi wiped away her tears with her sleeve. She tried to smile at her niece and nephew as if to say that it was nothing serious before explaining, "She went on a rampage the moment she knew that she was to be married to that Kinkin."

"He has been running his mouth off at school," said Ai.

"The poor kid, wanting to marry a girl who is pregnant by somebody else," said Maya Dewi. "He loves her so much."

"I don't care whether he loves her or not," said Ai. "Rengganis will not marry someone she does not love."

The Beautiful's howls suddenly fell silent. They were alarmed, but then she came hurrying down the stairs with a face that was as red and swollen as if it had been submerged in ice water, wearing nothing but her nap-time pajamas. She sat right down next to her mother without even trying to wipe away her tears.

"If you don't love the gravedigger's son and don't want to marry him, then tell me," her poor mother said, "tell me, who is the man you care for and wish to make your husband?"

"I don't like anyone," said the Beautiful. "If I have to get married, I want to marry my rapist."

"Tell me who he is."

"I will marry a dog."

Her pregnancy was already clearly showing, and just like all pregnant women, her beauty had grown even more radiant. It was as if her black hair came from a deep mysterious darkness, falling straight past her hips, not having been cut for years. She had skin like the crust of a freshly baked loaf of bread still warm from the oven. Ever since she was born, people had known that she was the most beautiful girl in the city. Both her parents were quite proud of such a blessing, but they had always been concerned about the price to be paid for it: her simplemindedness. They helped her to always look her best, struggling to braid her hair every morning before going to school. At the annual Beach Princess competition, her father brought the Beautiful even though it was quite evident that she couldn't dance very well and sang with a heartbreakingly bad voice, but her beauty had intoxicated every member of the jury so that she was chosen as the princess.

"Do you know which dog?" asked Ai.

Rengganis shook her head, full of regret. "Every dog looks the same to me," she said. "Maybe he will come once his baby is born."

"How will he know that it's been born?"

"My child will bark and he'll hear it."

Nobody knew where she had gotten such a far-fetched fantasy, but she looked so happy imagining it, with her cheeks now glowing, that the others stayed silent. Without forcing her to say anything more, her mother embraced the girl and stroked her long hair, saying, "You know, your Mama got pregnant with you at the same age you are now."

When night fell, she told her husband everything that had happened that day, while pointing out the remnants of the commotion the Beautiful had created. Maman Gendeng sat on the stairs with a tragic face.

"Everyone knows that Kinkin wasn't in the toilet that day," she said. "And Rengganis doesn't want to marry him."

"Well if that's how it is, then we have to force our daughter to tell us who did it."

"And if she stays mum?"

"If she stays mum, then I will marry that girl to whoever wants to be her husband," her husband said. "As long as he isn't a dog."

As it turned out, she kept mum. Of course lots of men wanted to marry her, but only one had the guts to propose to her, and that was Kinkin. So despite Rengganis the Beautiful's refusal, they began to prepare for the wedding, as her time to give birth grew ever closer. It wasn't that Rengganis the Beautiful didn't know about these plans, but now, unexpectedly, she was facing them calmly, saying that it was the kid who would end up feeling resentment and regret.

The girl Ai was caught in the middle of that messy situation. "If we force her, she will do something terrible," she said. She knew what Rengganis the Beautiful was like. Her mother and father did too, but apparently they no longer cared. For them it was enough that Maya Dewi was the illegitimate, fatherless child of Dewi Ayu, just like her older sisters, and they did not want the Beautiful to share a similar fate. Even Maman Gendeng, who had never lived virtuously, was deeply saddened—someone had raped his daughter, and he, the most feared man in the city, didn't know anything about what had happened. He felt he was facing the most formidable enemy of his entire life.

"I gave her the name Rengganis," he said sadly. "And as everyone knows, Princess Rengganis married a dog."

As the day of the wedding drew closer, he contacted a rental business to reserve some chairs for a festive party. He would present an *orkes melayu* on the street in front of his house. He did all this because he didn't know what else to do.

"This is not right, Uncle," said Ai. "She doesn't want this wedding. Tell me, why does a pregnant girl always have to get married?"

He didn't want to deal with her shrewish fretting and continued to prepare for the wedding as if it was his own. The doctor had confirmed the due date of the child growing in the Beautiful's stomach, and they planned to marry her on the very next day after that. But when the baby was born with the help of a midwife, Rengganis the Beautiful once again insisted it was the offspring of a dog while her parents insisted she was to sit on the wedding dais. In response, the night before the wedding, she disappeared with her baby.

"She must have gone to Ai's house," said her father. The people looked for her there, but even that girl didn't know what had happened. Panic began to spread. They returned, hoping they would find her back at the house, but what they found instead was a short message written on a slip of paper: "I've gone to marry a dog."

{16}

CONFESSION: IT WAS Krisan who dug up Ai's grave and hid her corpse under his bed.

In the old days, every morning he'd stand at his bedroom window looking out at the back veranda of Shodancho's house. Of course Ai was still alive then, and he stood at his window just to watch her emerge, sleepily heading to wash her face at the water tap that poured down into the fishpond. He'd stand in the same spot every afternoon too, looking out at Ai chatting with her mother while chopping a chicken or some water spinach for dinner, but on this particular afternoon Ai wasn't there, because Ai was dead and now her corpse was lying under Krisan's bed.

He imagined people already knew about the violated grave and he pictured Shodancho, who was now really starting to show his age, but still kept his post as the head of the Halimunda military district, hearing that it had been dug up by a dog. He of course would not believe that the grave of his third daughter had been excavated by a dog, because that grave had been dug quite deep, and was protected by strong wooden planks.

"Only a human being could do it, and maybe the only one who

would do it is Maman Gendeng." Maybe that's what Shodancho would say.

Krisan was happy to think he could outsmart people. He knew Shodancho still harbored an old grudge against the *preman*, Maman Gendeng, who would never have dug up Ai's grave—all he thought about was being reunited with his daughter, Rengganis the Beautiful, who had run away. To repeat: it was Krisan who had dug up that grave, and now the corpse was carefully stored underneath his bed, and he was amazed that nobody suspected him of being the one who did it.

Indeed, he had done it just how he thought a dog would have done it, thinking that way Ai wouldn't be angry, and in fact might be pleased. Krisan dug up Ai's grave with his own hands and feet, raking through the pile of dirt that was still soft even though she'd already been buried for a week. He dug all night long, without taking a break. To make Ai happy, he had even brought a stray dog along, though the animal just watched silently, chained to a trunk of a frangipani tree. The dog's tracks would trick people into thinking that a dog had done it, and Krisan neatly erased his own footprints.

It was hard to dig up a grave with one's hands and feet, but wasn't that how a dog would do it? Pretending he was a dog, Krisan even stuck out his tongue, and moved it in and out as he worked, believing Ai would be happy watching him from heaven. And when he became parched with thirst in the middle of his crazy task, he moved on all fours to the canal at the edge of the graveyard, and lapped the water. Working like that, he finally reached the wood planks at three in the morning after digging since seven-thirty in the evening.

The planks had been laid out in sloped row. Krisan only had to dismantle a few of the planks before he could lift up Ai's body, wrapped in a burial shroud, from its crevice of earth. Her body was light, and Krisan's heart jumped with a mysterious joy. He could finally hold her as tightly as he wanted, so he practically didn't care that she was dead. From the burial shroud there wafted a strange fragrance, as if from a flower garden. Of course it wasn't the smell of blossoms, but the aroma of the girl's own body.

After freeing the stray dog, Krisan heaved Ai's corpse onto his shoulder. He hastened home with cautious steps because at that hour people were usually already awake getting ready to go to the mosque. Some vegetable sellers would be heading to market to open their kiosks, and maybe a few people would be going to take a shit in one of the ponds lining the edges of the city not far from the graveyard.

He arrived at his house safely, without anyone spotting him, not even his mother or his grandmother (after the death of his father, his grandmother Mina had lived with them, taking care of all the sewing), who were both morning people. He entered through the kitchen door, tiptoed into his room, and hid Ai's corpse under his bed. Then he retraced his steps to wipe up any mud that he might have dragged in—he cleaned up as efficiently as a school janitor, and then it was time for him to check on the corpse. He pulled Ai's body out from under the bed and unwrapped her burial shroud.

Immediately, that fragrant scent burst forth even stronger and Krisan could see Ai's body, which looked so fresh. The girl seemed to be merely lying on the floor, just sleeping for a moment. Krisan was not surprised, convinced that Ai's body would never rot, not even if she were buried for years, or even centuries, and he gazed at her cheeks that were still slightly flushed, just as they'd been when she was still alive.

All of a sudden he felt embarrassed to be looking at her nakedness. He quickly covered her body once more with the burial shroud, leaving only her face exposed so he could continue to admire her beauty. And then he was weeping, this sappy kid, sad because she was dead and now he was all alone in a desolate world.

But then the tone of his weeping changed, into cries of gratitude, thanking Ai because even though she was dead she hadn't let herself rot. She remained in a state of eternal beauty, and he believed that she was doing it for him. Before he knew it, he was kissing the cheeks of that girl's corpse.

Krisan had fallen in love with Ai long ago, and he was sure the girl had fallen in love with him long ago as well, maybe when they were still sleeping in the same cradle. She was his cousin, just as Rengganis the Beautiful was. Ai was born twelve days before Krisan, and hers was the very first face he saw the moment he was born, lying in her mother's arms, as Alamanda and Shodancho and his own father stood waiting for his arrival. Who knows, maybe love at first sight can happen to babies too. And, what's more, then Shodancho said something like "I hope our children will be a love match." Krisan probably heard that just as he appeared on earth, and so he believed that they had been destined for each other. And they had been together ever since, crying together, peeing their pants together, going to the same kindergarten, and attending the same schools, until Krisan realized that he had always been in love with Ai.

But it wasn't an easy matter to tell her that he loved her, because Ai was his cousin and they were such close friends. Such a confession could destroy their sweet relationship, but if he didn't say anything, maybe the girl would never realize that he would love her for as long as she lived, and he would regret it if she was taken by another. That was the thing he was most afraid of: he would rather hang himself than endure that heartbreak.

There was another serious problem: Krisan had no friends other than Rengganis the Beautiful and Ai to talk to. There was no way he was going to talk about it to his grandmother or his mother, much less his two uncles or aunts. And he couldn't write about it in a diary, because Ai would certainly find it and read it no matter where he hid it. That wouldn't be a problem if he knew that Ai loved him too, but he only suspected that she might, and he was afraid that he was hoping for too much. It would be awful if Ai found out that he loved her but it turned out that she didn't love him. The whole thing was quite troublesome. He often cursed his own fate and wondered why he had to be born as the girl's cousin. When that *jailangkung* boy had asked Maman Gendeng for Rengganis the Beautiful's hand in the bus terminal, terror had swept over Krisan. Someone had announced to the world that he loved Rengganis the Beautiful, and soon someone else would certainly come to Shodancho to propose to Nurul Aini. Krisan was determined to get that girl before someone else did.

He planned his declaration of love for weeks, weeks filled with excruciating pain.

Krisan began to write love letters, and every time he had to write the word Ai, he would purposefully leave the space blank by *not* writing those two letters, just in case. He wrote ten long love letters, each like a short story, but he never sent any of them, just stashed them under a pile of underwear in his closet. That's not because he was perverted, but because it was the safest place. Ai came over all the time and got into everything, taking whatever she liked, especially Comrade Kliwon's martial arts novels. There was an unwritten agreement between the three of them—Krisan, Ai, and Rengganis the Beautiful—that what belonged to one belonged to all. Except his underwear. Ai had never wanted to touch those, so the proof of his unspoken passion was safe underneath them.

Then the boy decided it was stupid to write letters. He would just plainly say that he loved her, more than as just a cousin, but the way a man loves a woman. He was consumed with the feeling that even though they were so close and their friendship was so warm, and even though fate had already determined that one day they would marry, life would be flat and flavorless until he could voice his true feelings.

He spent days practicing his declaration, standing in front of his mirror imagining the girl was standing next to him—maybe they would be looking at a seagull swooping down over the surface of the ocean during a trip to the beach—and he would say, "Ai," and then he'd pause on purpose, assuming that he would need a moment for Ai to look at him, or at the very least to perk up her ears. Then he would continue with a strong voice that would be heard clearly over the cacophony of pounding waves and the wind shaking the leaves of the coconut trees and the pandan bushes. "Do you know that I love you?"

Just one line, one short sentence. Krisan believed that he could say it, and he could imagine the girl then blushing—it would be like that even though she had known for a long time that Krisan was secretly in love with her. Of course maybe Ai would not look at him, Ai tended to be shy, and so maybe she would bow her head, afraid of seeming too overjoyed. But then, without looking at him, she would confess that she loved him too.

What would happen next was way easier for Krisan to imagine. He would take the girl's hand and then everything would be happy ever after as they'd get married, have children, see their grandchildren, and die together many decades later. But all that was so beautiful it would make Krisan unsure of himself all over again, so he'd practice even harder, repeating that short one-line sentence over and over: in the bathroom, lying in bed, wherever he went.

One afternoon he even tried to turn his grandmother into his lab rat. As Mina was sewing on the front veranda and he was sitting next to her he suddenly said, "Grandma ..." And just as he had practiced, he stopped right there.

Mina stopped working and turned her head to look at him with a questioning glance from behind her thick glasses, figuring that the kid wanted to borrow some money to buy some silly thing he didn't need, as usual. But how shocked Mina was when Krisan continued:

"Grandma, do you know that I love you very much?"

Mina's eyes welled up and she immediately put down her sewing, scooted her chair over and embraced Krisan, with her tears flowing faster and faster, saying, "How sweet you are. Even that crazy Comrade, my very own son, never said anything like that to me."

But every time Krisan was with Ai, even if it was just the two of them alone without Rengganis the Beautiful, which almost never happened, everything he had memorized evaporated. He would vow to tell her at another opportunity, and then the words would again disappear. Ai always struck him dumb. It was like she pierced him to the heart, left him lost in a storm of unspeakable love.

Until one day this happened: Rengganis the Beautiful gave birth to a baby and disappeared from her house. The person most upset, maybe even more upset than Rengganis the Beautiful's parents Maya Dewi and Maman Gendeng, was Ai. Everyone knew Ai thought of herself as Rengganis the Beautiful's protector, and now that the girl had gotten pregnant without knowing who had impregnated her (even though Rengganis had confessed: a dog), and then had given birth to a baby, Ai was devastated. She fell ill on that same day, stricken with a high fever and calling out Rengganis's name in her sleep. It made sense, even though it still made Krisan quite jealous. Krisan knew the two girls were extremely close, way closer than either of them had ever been to him, maybe because they were girls.

Her fever continued for days, and no doctor could figure out what kind of sickness it was. All the tests showed she was in perfect health.

"She's possessed by the ghost of a communist," Shodancho said.

"Shut your mouth!" screamed Alamanda.

In the afternoon, after coming home from school, Krisan was her most faithful attendant, sitting at her bedside and looking at her lying there weakly with an empty gaze, her feverish body shivering.

Clearly this was not the right time to tell her that he loved her the way a man loves a woman: at this point they were both seventeen years old.

Ai often suddenly appeared in Krisan's room. Sometimes through the door, but just as often she would jump right in through the open window, even right before she got sick. One night, around seven o'clock, she appeared again, jumping through the window with a mischievous smile as if she had a naughty plan. She looked so beautiful, so sweet, and so healthy. She was dressed all in white frilly lace, so clean and pure, as if she was wearing a set of new clothes to celebrate Eid. Her face and body were radiant, and her dark straight hair fell loose down her back. Her piercing eyes were shining, her pink cheeks were adorable, and that naughty smile of hers displayed her beautiful tempting lips. Krisan had just lay down after eating dinner, and was startled by the sudden visit.

"You!" he exclaimed, sitting up on the edge of his bed. "You're all better?"

"As healthy as a female olympian," said Ai, chuckling and raising up both her arms to flex like a bodybuilder.

Then, as if being lassoed by a powerful longing, the two moved closer and held each other tightly, even tighter than Adinda had held Comrade Kliwon after being chased by a dog so long ago. And without knowing who started it, they were kissing, with kisses hotter than the ones Alamanda and Comrade Kliwon shared under the almond tree, and then the two fell onto the bed.

"Ai," Krisan said finally, "do you know that I love you?"

Ai replied with a captivating smile, which made Krisan all the more head over heels intoxicated with love, and he kissed her again. Not long after that they'd stripped off their clothes with the urgency of uncontrollable adolescent lust—making love more wildly than Alamanda and Shodancho had on the morning they didn't execute Comrade Kliwon, more wildly than Maman Gendeng and Maya Dewi had after waiting five years—dedicating the entire night to the game of love, which they played with the shining enthusiasm and the extraordinary spirit of inquiry that only a pair of teenage kids can have.

Afterward, Ai put on her all-white clothes, jumped back out through the window, and waved her hand.

"I have to go home," she said, " ... go home ... go home."

That last part was already growing hazy when Krisan was rocked by a jolting shock in his groin and awoke without Ai. His bedroom window was closed tight. It had only been a dream. It wasn't his first wet dream, but it was certainly the most beautiful, and the first one with Ai, which made him ecstatically happy.

When the rays of the sun could be seen dimly breaking through the window lattice, he opened it and looked out at the back veranda of Shodancho's house. There were hordes of people milling about, even his own mother was there. Something snapped in his heart. He jumped through the window and, without even washing his face or putting on his shoes, he ran toward Shodancho's house and broke through the crowd. He entered the room where Ai had been lying, and saw Alamanda sitting atop her bed weeping. At seeing Krisan appear, Alamanda quickly stood and hugged the boy without ceasing her weeping, tearing at her hair, and before Krisan asked what had happened, Alamanda said:

"Your sweetheart is gone."

Now, after he had dug up her grave and brought her body to his house, Krisan cried beside her body, remembering the dream. Perhaps he was grieving the fact that up until her death he had never actually professed his love to her. Or maybe he was crying because he was touched that before she left, the girl had taken the time to come to him, if only in a dream. The girl had come to hear his words of love, had come to give him her virginity, had come to make love to him, before she went home to never come again. Maybe he was crying at all his loss and longing, half-dead with suffering, because no matter how beautiful a corpse is, it can never be the same as a living girl.

A second confession: it was Krisan who murdered Rengganis the Beautiful and threw her body into the ocean.

One week after Krisan dug up Ai's grave, someone knocked softly on the shutter of his bedroom window. Krisan got up and opened the window and there stood Rengganis the Beautiful, looking bedraggled. Her hair was disheveled and her clothes were wet, but none of that could mask her amazing beauty. Even Krisan admitted it, Rengganis the Beautiful was indeed prettier than Ai, just as Ai herself had always said.

"Oh my God, what are you doing?" asked Krisan.

"I'm freezing."

"You idiot, that's obvious."

Krisan leaned out over the sill hoping that nobody had seen them, and yanked on Rengganis the Beautiful's hand to help her jump in through the window. She looked as if she had fallen into a muddy ditch or something, and clearly she was also starving.

"Change your clothes," said Krisan while checking that his bedroom door was locked.

Rengganis the Beautiful opened Krisan's wardrobe, taking out a t-shirt and jeans and a pair of Krisan's underwear. Then, in front of that boy, without embarrassment, she took off all her clothes, piece by piece, until nothing was left. Her body, glittering wet in the lamp light, made Krisan practically choke. He sat cross-legged on his bed, that kid, erect, but even though he wanted to ravage the girl standing in front of him, so fuckable and so spectacular, he didn't move. He was still on his bed while Rengganis the Beautiful, in her marvelous nonchalance, dried her body with a small towel that she found hanging on the back of the door.

Her breasts were as perfect as a full-grown woman's and Krisan looked at them for quite a while, imagining that he was caressing them, kissing them, and teasing their nipples with a naughty touch. There was a beautiful curve leading from her breasts to her hips, as if drawn with a compass, perfectly symmetrical on the left and right. And in the middle of her crotch, behind the luxurious thicket of her hair, there was something slightly protuberant, like the fruit of a young coconut, but certainly soft. Krisan got even harder, wanted all the more to jump up and drag that girl cousin onto his bed and ravage her. But he didn't do it. Not with Ai's corpse underneath his bed.

The torture slowly came to an end. Rengganis the Beautiful put on Krisan's underwear, not caring that it was men's underwear. Then she put on his jeans, and her breasts quickly disappeared behind his t-shirt. But Krisan stayed hard because he could still see the outline of her nipples through that t-shirt.

"How do I look, Dog?" asked Rengganis the Beautiful.

"Don't call me Dog, my name is Krisan."

"Okay, Krisan," and Rengganis the Beautiful sat at the edge of the bed next to the boy. "I'm hungry."

Krisan went to the kitchen and got a plate of rice, with cooked spinach and a piece of fried fish. That was all he found in the cupboard. He brought it to the girl with a glass of water, and the girl ate it ravenously, and when she was finished she asked for more. Krisan went back to the kitchen, taking another similar portion of food, and the girl ate it with the same voraciousness, as if she had never been taught proper manners. Krisan was thankful that after that second portion the girl didn't ask for any more, because the next morning his mother would not have believed him if he said that he'd eaten three entire portions during the night.

"And now," said Krisan, as Rengganis the Beautiful began to dry her hair, "where is your baby?"

"It got eaten by an *ajak* and died."

"Shit!" said Krisan. "But thank God. Tell me what happened."

Rengganis the Beautiful told him. The night she left her house with the baby she headed for the guerrilla hut that Shodancho had built in the middle of the jungle. For a long time the place had been a secret clubhouse for Rengganis the Beautiful, Ai, and Krisan. They had heard about that hut, searched for it, found it, and visited it on fun little excursions. That night Rengganis the Beautiful went there with her baby, knowing that it was the best possible hideout, and that even Ai herself would never guess she'd gone there. The baby was really fussy, she said, and she tried to nurse, but it still fussed. It wasn't wearing anything, that baby, swaddled only in a blanket and warmed only by its mother's embrace.

Normally the guerrilla hut could be reached in an eight-hour walk. But Rengganis the Beautiful took a whole day and a night. She got a little lost, wandering here and there, and was walking very slowly, carrying the baby, and had stupidly forgot to bring any provisions. So they arrived at the guerrilla hut already quite famished.

"There was nothing to eat there," said Rengganis the Beautiful.

Anyhow, she was a city kid, and didn't know what there was in the jungle that might be edible, but after a while she was forced to scavenge for whatever she could find. Some walnuts had fallen from the trees, and amazed by their hard shell, she broke them open with a rock, sampling the insides. When it turned out they tasted pretty good, she gathered lots of walnuts and that was what she had for dinner the first night. Drinking wasn't too much of a problem, because a little stream with clear water flowed next to the guerrilla hut.

The big problem was the baby. It kept on fussing. For the entire journey she had stuffed its mouth with the corner of its blanket, so that they wouldn't be discovered. She had avoided public streets and instead ran under the cover of the shadows of trees, cutting through the banana orchards and cassava fields. Even then she still had to be very careful because lots of farmers roamed about at night to check on their land, and there were watchmen, and people out hunting eels and grasshoppers. The blanket worked pretty well to muffle the baby's cries, but also almost killed it. When she entered the jungle on the promontory, she finally dared to take out the gag, thinking that no one else would be wandering there in the middle of the night, and ran into the thicket with that baby wailing on and on.

In the guerrilla hut the baby still fussed, even though its mother had at last nursed it, but then, in its final days, it refused to nurse. It had urinated and the swaddling blanket was wet, but Rengganis the Beautiful had no other blanket, so she just turned it a little bit so the wet parts were on the outside. But the baby still cried, with a voice that grew weaker and weaker as time passed. Only then did Rengganis the Beautiful realize the baby was sick with fever. A hot air came rising off its body, and yet it shivered. She didn't know what should be done, so she just watched that baby suffer.

"Then on the third day it died," she said.

And she still didn't know what she should do. After unwrapping it from the blanket, she brought the baby out of the guerrilla hut, placing it on a rock that many years ago had been used by Shodancho and his men as a dining table, and for the entire day she just looked at her baby's corpse, unable to think. It was already afternoon by the time she had the idea of throwing it into the ocean, but just then a pack of *ajak* came and encircled her and her baby, summoned by the smell of the corpse. Rengganis the Beautiful looked at those *ajak*, and saw how eager they were to get at that baby's body, so she hurled the infant in their direction. They immediately fought over it, and then one dragged the baby deep into the forest, as the others trailed behind.

"You're more gruesome than Satan," said Krisan, shuddering.

"But that was easier than digging a grave."

They both fell silent, maybe both imagining how those dogs must have torn apart that little poor baby's corpse. Krisan didn't know what Maman Gendeng would do if he knew this was his grandchild's fate. Maybe he would go crazy and burn the entire city down, killing all the *ajak* and most probably killing all the people too. But now it would be pointless to search for its remains. Those *ajak* probably hadn't left anything behind, because even its little bones were still tender enough to eat. Krisan almost puked imagining a dog swallowing the baby's head whole.

"And you didn't come," said Rengganis the Beautiful, looking at Krisan with an expression torn between anger and disappointment. "I waited until yesterday afternoon, eating nothing but those hard nuts."

"I couldn't come."

"You're mean."

"I couldn't come," said Krisan, gesturing to Rengganis the Beautiful not to talk so loud, worried that his mother and grandmother would catch them. "Because Ai got sick and then she died."

"What?"

"Ai got sick and then she died."

"That's impossible."

Krisan jumped up from the bed, groped for the corpse beneath his bed, dragged it out and showed it to Rengganis the Beautiful. Ai's body was now lying on the floor wrapped in a burial shroud, still in the same condition as the first time Krisan had held her—so fresh, and so pretty.

"She's just sleeping," said Rengganis the Beautiful, coming down off the bed to inspect Ai's face. She tried to rouse Ai. "Get up!" She shook her, forced the corpse's eyes open, pinched her nose, and finally she sat with her own sobs, weeping over the death of the girl who had been her closest friend her entire life, who had been there whenever she needed her. Rengganis the Beautiful suddenly regretted not including Ai in her plans to run away, not inviting her to the guerrilla hut. She would have been even more distraught if she had known the girl had died from grief and worry over her disappearance. Meanwhile Krisan stayed completely still, mostly worried that the Beautiful's ever-louder sobs would wake his mother and grandmother, until finally the girl asked:

"Why is she here?"

"I dug up her grave," said Krisan.

"Why did you dig up her grave?"

He didn't know what to say to her. He just looked at the girl silently, a little bit embarrassed, before a glorious idea appeared in his mind right at the moment he most needed it. "So that she could watch us get married."

That explanation seemed to please Rengganis the Beautiful.

"And when are we getting married?"

The question annoyed Krisan. He sat at the edge of the bed and glanced at Rengganis the Beautiful, peered down at the face of Ai's corpse below him, stared at the clothes hanging on the back of the door, considered the piles of his martial arts novels, examined his pillow, and then looked back. The girl was gazing at him expectantly.

"Tonight," said Krisan.

"Where?"

"I'm thinking about that right now."

And when the idea appeared, he immediately told Rengganis the Beautiful. They quickly removed the burial shroud wrapped around Ai's body and gave her some clothes from Krisan's closet, men's clothes like the Beautiful was wearing—men's underwear, jeans, and a t-shirt. Once the corpse looked just like an ordinary casually dressed girl who happened to be lying down, Krisan opened his bedroom door, checking his mother and his grandmother's rooms to make sure they were still asleep. He quietly walked his mini-bike out through the back door, without making a sound. Then he went back and heaved Ai's corpse onto his shoulder, walking out of the room followed by Rengganis the Beautiful, and locking the bedroom door. They tiptoed through the kitchen to the backyard. Rengganis the Beautiful rode on the back behind Ai's corpse, which she hugged as tightly as she could, and Krisan sat in front. With one push of the pedal the bike had left the backyard and was speeding toward the ocean, in the middle of the night, underneath the street lamps.

They were lucky that not many people saw them. Even if one or two people were passing by, they weren't that suspicious to see a seventeen-year-old guy with two young girls riding on the back of his bike, thinking the three were coming home late from a party.

Krisan stopped at a concrete seawall marking the division between the ocean and the shore. It was almost dawn, and he could see that some boats had already docked. A pinkish color was beginning to appear in the eastern sky. A very auspicious time, he thought.

"Wait here, I'm going to steal a boat," said Krisan.

Still embracing Ai's corpse so that it didn't collapse, Rengganis the Beautiful sat against the wall, next to the bike, waiting for Krisan.

The kid reappeared, rowing someone's boat. Or maybe it didn't belong to anyone anymore, because it was in really bad shape, even though it didn't have any holes in it. Krisan slid up close against the seawall where Rengganis the Beautiful was waiting. "Throw me the corpse," he said. Rengganis the Beautiful threw Ai's body into the hull of the boat, making it rock back and forth a bit, and now the corpse was lying there. Rengganis the Beautiful jumped to one end of the boat and sat down, while at the other end Krisan began to row away from the beach, toward the open ocean, the place where he had promised to marry her.

Krisan tried not to cross paths with the fishing boats that were returning to the beach, and didn't worry about the larger vessels that were farther out. Morning was breaking behind Ma Iyang Hill, its rays like strong straight lines that penetrated the surface of the ocean, glittering with phosphorescence. The reddish color on the horizon began to fade; seagulls, and swallows, began to fly overhead. The light made it easier for Krisan to see where the fishing boats were going, and he could turn if he thought they were going to pass by too close.

For a long time he rowed in widening circles, looking for a quiet area of the ocean, that he thought no other ship would visit. Then he found it, in a dark blue part of the water. He knew for certain that the spot would be very deep, and that was why it was deserted, because there weren't a lot of fish in such a place. Of course neither Rengganis the Beautiful nor Krisan knew that many years ago Comrade Kliwon had kidnapped Alamanda and had brought her to this very same spot.

Morning came in all its perfection.

"So when are we going to get married?"

"Don't rush, soak up the sun for a moment first," replied Krisan.

Krisan lay down at his end of that boat, looking at the sky. Rengganis the Beautiful tried to do the same at the other end. Krisan's forehead was wrinkled and his face looked gloomy, not at all enjoying the perfectly clear day. Meanwhile Rengganis the Beautiful was growing restless, waiting for their wedding. Finally she sat up again, now truly impatient, and asked:

"How are we to be married?"

"I'm making it a surprise."

Krisan approached the girl, stepping over Ai's corpse.

"Turn around," he said.

Rengganis the Beautiful turned around, looking out at the horizon, her back to Krisan. She waited until she saw Krisan's hands making a fast circle, and before she realized what was happening, she was being strangled. A handkerchief was wound around her neck and Krisan's hands were tightly pulling its corners. Rengganis the Beautiful struggled to get free, her legs kicked everywhere, and her hands tried to pry that handkerchief loose. But Krisan was way stronger. They fought for about five minutes, before Rengganis the Beautiful lost the fight and lay sprawled out on the bottom of the boat, dead, right next to the corpse of her cousin.

Krisan looked down at her, and his eyes welled over. His breath came in ragged gasps and wheezes. With his hands shaking violently, he lifted Rengganis the Beautiful's body and heaved it into the ocean, letting her sink. Then he cried at the gunwale, crying like sentimental teenage girls cry, crying like newborn babies cry, crying with a deluge of heartbroken tears. And in between sobs he spoke aloud, although there was no one there to hear him.

"I killed you," he said, sobbing again, "because I only loved Ai." He cried for a full half an hour after that.

A third confession: it was Krisan who raped Rengganis the Beautiful in the school bathroom and didn't take responsibility for what he had done.

This is the hardest part of the story to tell, but it is the truth.

One day, when he and Ai were visiting Rengganis the Beautiful's house after school, he was sitting on the sofa reading an old magazine. The two girls were upstairs in Rengganis the Beautiful's room. But all of a sudden he heard footsteps coming down the stairs. Krisan put down the magazine, and Rengganis the Beautiful appeared before him, wearing nothing but a bra and underwear. He might have seen her like that before, he might have even seen her totally naked, but that was when they were still little kids. Now they were both fifteen, and Krisan had been having wet dreams for quite some time.

Just like most men, Krisan was in awe of Rengganis the Beautiful's body, which was both beautiful and provocative. Delicious, that was the only word for it. He often imagined her firm round breasts and her softly curving waist, and now he could see almost everything. The bra that she was wearing didn't really cover all of her breasts, so Krisan could appreciate their gleam, and her low-cut panties that covered a small soft mound. It made his dick come alive, and turn hard as steel. He had to grope at his pants to adjust it, because it was slanting up and getting pinched. Meanwhile, Rengganis the Beautiful didn't seem to mind that Krisan was there and looking in her direction, in fact she seemed pleased that that boy was looking at her. She came down the stairs with perfectly calm steps, approached the ironing table, picked out some clothes, and put them on, and that lustful moment passed, but Krisan never forgot it.

There are two kinds of women that a man can love: the first kind of woman he loves in order to dote upon and cherish her, and the second kind he loves in order to fuck. Krisan felt he now had both kinds: Ai was the first kind of girl, and Rengganis was the second. He wanted to marry Ai, but he always dreamed of one day having sex with Rengganis the Beautiful, despite the fact that he had never succeeded in declaring his love to Ai and he had no idea how to have sex with Rengganis the Beautiful without getting in terrible trouble.

When the three were small they had a nice hideout: the field that Comrade Kliwon had bought. Shodancho built them a tree house on a branch of an old banyan tree at the edge of the orchard. Their mothers and fathers never worried about the three of them roaming about in the fields, because they could all watch out for one another. They played together, just as they had always done since before the tree house, and just as they continued to do long after. But in the days when they were going to the tree house all the time, the game they played most often was the wedding game. Rengganis the Beautiful always wanted to be the bride, and because Krisan was the only boy, he always played the groom. Ai would play the same roles every time too: the witness, the village headman, and the invited guest. They always enjoyed this game, even though Krisan felt forced into playing his role; he really wanted to be the groom for Ai.

Rengganis the Beautiful would be adorned with a crown made from a wreath of jackfruit leaves, as would Krisan. They would sit under the banyan tree, next to each other, while Ai kneeled with her knees on the ground before them and said:

"Are you two ready to marry one another?"

"Yes," Krisan and Rengganis the Beautiful always said.

"And so you are married," said Ai. "Now kiss."

Rengganis the Beautiful would kiss Krisan's lips for a few seconds, and that was the moment Krisan liked the best.

But beyond that—outside of the game—Rengganis the Beautiful always still thought of Krisan as her fiancée.

That annoyed Krisan, but he couldn't do anything about it, because just like Ai, he knew what Rengganis the Beautiful was like: spoiled, willful, childish, simple, fragile, unstable, and a whole series of other words that explained how pointless it would be to get mad at her. What was even more annoying was Ai's attitude. Krisan in fact wanted them to gang up on Rengganis the Beautiful a little bit, just to make her come to her senses, but instead Ai faithfully defended every scandalous thing the Beautiful did.

At that time Krisan wasn't yet quite so hot for Rengganis the Beautiful, even though he knew the girl was very pretty and quite provocative, because he liked quiet girls with serious faces, girls who were calm but could also be quite fierce, and a girl like that was Ai. Forget lusting after her, he often thought of the Beautiful as a third wheel. And Ai's tendency to protect her made him jealous.

However, there was something else that made him even more jealous: dogs. Shodancho's child had been infected by his obsession with dogs. Krisan used to always hope that if Ai wasn't with Rengganis the Beautiful, then he could be alone with her, but if Ai wasn't with her cousin, then it could be sure that she was playing with dogs, and she would keep playing with them even if Krisan tried to spend time with her.

"Do I have to be a dog for you to pay attention to me?" Krisan asked once, at the height of his irritation.

"Not necessarily," said Ai. "Be a real man, and I will like you just fine."

Those enigmatic words were difficult to analyze, so Krisan complained to Rengganis the Beautiful: "I wish I was a dog."

"That's good," said Rengganis the Beautiful. "I have often imagined a dog without a tail."

It was impossible to have a serious conversation with Rengganis the Beautiful.

He started acting like a dog to get Ai's attention. If the three of them were walking together, maybe coming home from school or just out strolling in the afternoon, and he saw a dog in the distance, Krisan would bark, "Woof, woof, woof!" Or sometimes he became a little wounded puppy, "Yip, yip, yip," and other times he would be a wild dog howling in the middle of the night, "Ow-ow-owwwwwwww!!"

"At least your voice sounds like a dog," Rengganis the Beautiful commented. "That *ajak* howl gives me goose bumps."

"But it won't make a bitch fall in love," said Ai.

She seemed to be mocking his childish behavior, but Krisan didn't care and continued to play the role of a dog, quite well in fact, whether or not the girl was there. He would piss in the bathroom lifting up one leg, and he began to loll out his tongue all the time.

"Even if you walk around on all fours, your body will never turn into the body of a dog," said Ai, who thought Krisan was being completely ridiculous. "But watch out for your brain."

Maybe it was true: it was his brain that had turned into the brain of a dog. When Ai died, he dug up her grave just like a dog would have dug up the treasure of a bone he had hidden. Because Ai liked dogs, he had become a dog—or at least, he barked, stuck out his tongue, lapped up water from the ditch, and dug up the dirt of her grave with his hands.

And before that, he had also been a dog when he raped Rengganis the Beautiful in the school toilet.

The incident where he was sitting on the sofa and saw Rengganis the Beautiful come down the stairs wearing nothing but a bra and underwear was the first time he thought about having sex with her. He began to lust after Rengganis the Beautiful, and forgot about all the problems caused by her childish personality. He would stand still if she suddenly hugged him from behind and covered his eyes, asking him to guess who. He always knew that it was Rengganis the Beautiful, because no one else would cling so close to him. He could feel the pressure of what was definitely her breasts against his back, and he would stay like that for quite some time, pretending to try to guess who had covered his eyes, just to enjoy the smooth touch of the skin on her hands.

If the three of them were walking together, Rengganis the Beautiful almost always walked in the middle. Ai would definitely be holding the girl's hand. And bringing up the rear, Krisan would hold Rengganis the Beautiful's other hand, to feel how soft it was.

Ai and Krisan always took Rengganis the Beautiful home first, because their houses were close together. As her way of saying goodbye, Rengganis the Beautiful always kissed Ai's cheek and Ai kissed her back. At first Krisan hung back, because he thought it looked childish, but after the case of the sofa and the stairs he really enjoyed feeling the warmth of the girl's lips pressed against his cheek, and kissing the girl's warm cheek with his own lips.

And if night fell, he didn't just fantasize about his future marriage to Ai anymore, but also fantasized about an extraordinary fuck with the Beautiful.

All he needed was an opportunity to do it.

Once, when Ai let her guard down and only Krisan and Rengganis the Beautiful were sitting in the front yard of Shodancho's house, Krisan embraced the girl and the girl hugged him back. No one would have been bothered to see something like that, not even Ai. The three of them were like siblings, more like triplets than cousins, really. What's more, Rengganis the Beautiful was always happy to hug and be hugged. Then Krisan started to seduce her:

"Do you want to marry me for real some day?" he asked in a joking tone.

But Rengganis the Beautiful replied to him seriously. "Yes," she said. "There is no other man in my life besides you, Krisan, so you *have* to marry me."

"Married people have to have sex."

"So then we will."

"We'll do it some day."

"Yeah, some day."

Krisan let go of Rengganis the Beautiful, who was left with her arm still around his shoulder when Ai appeared with a small basket full of guavas, a knife, and a mortar filled with *sambal lutis*. They had a picnic and heated their tongues with that chili pepper paste, and Krisan felt the heat all the way to his heart, imagining the opportunity for screwing that would someday come.

And it did come, on the day Rengganis the Beautiful won the bet of drinking five lemonades. Krisan was smoking a cigarette near the toilets when he spotted the girl. As Rengganis the Beautiful went into the far toilet that had become a nest of ghouls and demons, Krisan suddenly realized this was his chance. He quickly left his friends, and in one quiet corner of the schoolyard he jumped the two-meter-high rampart of the cocoa plantations. He knew the roof of the bathroom was filled with holes, so he quickly headed for that toilet, climbing back onto the rampart across a cocoa tree branch, and peered through the perforated roof, spying on Rengganis the Beautiful, who was squatting and peeing.

"Hey-ey," he called out to her softly.

Rengganis the Beautiful looked up and was shocked to see Krisan up on the roof. "What are you doing up there?" she asked. "Be careful, you could fall and die."

"I'm waiting for you."

"Waiting for me to climb up?"

"No. Aren't we going to screw?"

"Can you even get down?" Rengganis the Beautiful asked again.

"Of course I'm going to come down."

Holding onto a rotted beam, Krisan swung down into the bathroom. Now they were both trapped inside, Rengganis the Beautiful with her underwear still sagging around her knees. The toilet stank, and obviously the place wasn't very nice. But Krisan didn't care, because he was at the peak of desire.

"C'mon, let's screw," he whispered.

"I don't know how," Rengganis the Beautiful whispered back.

"I can teach you."

Slowly Krisan began to pull down the girl's panties from her knees, and hung them on a rusty nail that was hammered into the wall. Then with the same composure he unfastened the buttons of Rengganis the Beautiful's school uniform, button by button, so that he could enjoy the sensation of seeing her body slowly being exposed. The shirt was also hung on the rusty nail. He then took off her skirt, and was spellbound to see the black at the girl's crotch. It made his hands tremble slightly, and he hurried a little bit as he removed the girl's brassiere. But the moment he found the breasts that he had so longed for, he relaxed again. Now he took off his own clothes. His shirt was off, then his pants, then his underwear. His shame was outstretched, hard and pointing up, and he held it and showed it to Rengganis the Beautiful. The girl laughed a little at its shape.

After that there was no more calm. He seized those breasts, caressing and squeezing them full of desire, making the girl writhe and gasp. Rengganis the Beautiful held the boy's body tight. Krisan pushed the girl against the wall of the bathroom, and pressed against her body with his body. He began to kiss her lips, which he had coveted for so long but hadn't felt since the wedding game. His hands were playing between their chests, while the girl's hands softly clawed at his back. His shame urgently began to advance, trying to penetrate her, but the way they were standing he could only bump it against the soft skin of the girl's thigh, making it buckle. All he could do was rub it in the space between her thighs. "Lift your leg up onto that small basin," Krisan whispered. Rengganis the Beautiful did it, and her vagina opened wide. Krisan took her quite freely, because the place was already sopping wet, and warm, and their repetitive rocking movements made a loud noise, as if they were walking across a path filled with stones. They enjoyed it very much, even though like all beginners, they finished quickly.

That is what really happened.

❧

"But what if I'm pregnant?" asked Rengganis the Beautiful after their brief lovemaking.

Krisan was a little surprised that the girl even knew having sex could get you pregnant. All of a sudden it frightened him too, and a crazy idea appeared in his brain.

"You can just say that you were raped by a dog."

"I wasn't raped by a dog."

"Well, aren't I a dog?" asked Krisan. "You have often seen me bark and stick out my tongue, haven't you?"

"I have."

"So say that you were raped by a dog. A brown dog with a black snout."

"A brown dog with a black snout."

"And don't mention my name in this business, not even once."

"But you are going to marry me, right?"

"Yeah. If it turns out you really are pregnant, we can start making plans."

Krisan quickly got dressed, climbed up out of the same hole in the roof that he had entered through, and had the idea to take Rengganis the Beautiful's clothes and dispose of them somewhere they would never be found. Meanwhile Rengganis the Beautiful, stark naked, not even wearing her shoes or socks, came out of the toilet and returned to her classroom. Krisan never saw the uproar caused by her appearance, because he wasn't in the same class.

Then, when it turned out she was actually pregnant, they made their plans for escape. They would hide out in the guerrilla hut and have a *real* wedding celebration there. But it didn't turn out like that. Instead, for nine months Krisan was paralyzed with the fear that people, especially Maman Gendeng and Maya Dewi and also his own mother, would find out that he was the one who had had sex with the Beautiful. Krisan had planned to kill the girl in the guerrilla hut, to bury the truth, but it turned out he killed her in a boat, and threw her corpse into the ocean.

{17}

MAMAN GENDENG ROSE again on the third day after he vanished into heaven in *moksa*. He came to say goodbye, of course. To Maya Dewi, who else.

This was despite the fact that, just three days before, Maya Dewi had buried his corpse, which was almost completely unrecognizable after having been torn to shreds by *ajak*, gnawed on by maggots, and so swarmed with flies that as his body was being carried home, those insects still followed behind like the tail of a shooting star. "That was not me," said Maman Gendeng reassuringly. Maya Dewi had been in mourning for those three days, profound mourning, because she had lost Maman Gendeng after they had both lost their daughter, Rengganis the Beautiful. But even though she was wearing all black, for those three days she had also been lying to herself, telling herself that her loved ones were still alive.

She tried to remind herself that a similar fate had befallen her two older sisters. Alamanda had lost Ai, and Shodancho had disappeared to go look for his daughter's corpse, which had been stolen from its grave. Adinda had lost Comrade Kliwon, who had killed himself, though she still had Krisan.

But still Maya Dewi could not be comforted. Every morning she still prepared breakfast, plates of rice and vegetables and side dishes, for herself and Maman Gendeng and Rengganis the Beautiful, just as she used to do. Of course it was only she herself who ate, and so at the end of this ritual she threw out the two portions of food that remained completely untouched. She did this at dinner too, for three days.

When Maman Gendeng was still alive, before he left, they had played out this lie together, tricking themselves into thinking that Rengganis the Beautiful was still with them. They would meet at the dining table, with a portion prepared for their daughter as usual, and throw it out when their meal was done. Now Maya Dewi had to do this all alone.

All alone.

But on the third day after Maman Gendeng's death, she was not alone. She had someone to eat with. Just like the two nights and three mornings before, she sat down at the table in those dark clothes with two other portions of food, for her husband and her daughter. She hadn't yet swallowed her first bite of rice when the door to their bedroom opened and the man appeared, and sat right down in his chair like usual. Maya Dewi continued to eat her rice with her right hand and the man began to stir his sauce. They both ate as hungrily as usual, without talking to one another. Only one portion of rice remained untouched, because only one chair was empty, but Maya Dewi was still imagining that Rengganis the Beautiful was in her spot, just as she thought she was imagining Maman Gendeng sitting in his chair and eating. She only realized that the man was truly present when dinner was finally over. She found her husband's plate empty and the Beautiful's plate still filled with the rice. She looked at Maman Gendeng in disbelief. They gazed at one another for a long time before that woman asked in an almost inaudible whisper, "Is it you?"

"I came to say goodbye."

Maya Dewi approached her husband, touching him with extreme care as if he was made of wax and might easily melt away. Her fingers crept to touch the man's forehead, then moved down to his nose, lips, and chin, and after this tentative caress she stared at him with the curiosity of a child. When she felt the heat emanating from his body, felt that he was alive, she moved closer and held him. Maman Gendeng embraced her in return, letting that woman cry on his shoulder, stroked her hair, and lovingly sniffed the crown of her head.

"You came to say goodbye?" the woman asked suddenly, looking up into Maman Gendeng's face.

"I came to say goodbye."

"You are leaving again?"

"Because I'm already dead. I already rose up into the heavens."

"What about *her*?"

"I am going to watch over her. There."

After stroking one of his wife's cheeks and kissing the other, Maman Gendeng walked into the room that he had come from, closing the door behind him. Maya Dewi looked at the door in confusion, then looked at Maman Gendeng's empty plate, then looked at the plate that was still filled with the rice that should have been eaten by Rengganis the Beautiful, then again looked at the closed bedroom door. In a panic, she ran to the door, opening it but finding no one there.

She kept looking for him. She made sure that the bedroom window was locked, as it had been since afternoon. She peered under the bed but all she saw was the remainder of an incense coil and the house slippers she usually wore before prayers. There was no other place the man could be. It would be impossible for him to hide inside the closet with its big mirror, which was divided into sections and filled with their clothes, but Maya Dewi opened that door too and then closed it again right away. She checked the surface of the bed and her dressing table, hoping to find some sort of a clue, but her search was very much in vain. She left the room and once again stood looking at the dining table.

Then she returned to her work. She neatened up the table and put the leftover rice and vegetables and side dishes into the pantry. Later the two mountain girls who helped her make cookies would eat it for their meal. She took the dirty plates to the washtub, and threw the rice that Rengganis the Beautiful hadn't eaten into the garbage. She only washed her hands, not feeling like washing the dishes as she usually did, and returned to her bedroom, looking out into the empty space, then asked a question as if Maman Gendeng was still there.

"If you rose to heaven in *moksa*," she said, "then who did I bury three days ago?"

This was a tale of betrayal, which began long ago, when they still were newlyweds, before their wedding night that came five years too late, and before Rengganis the Beautiful was born.

A stocky man with a bald head and one of his ears chewed off came to the bus terminal on a sweltering Sunday afternoon, pushing his way through the crowd, most of whom were tourists scrambling for their buses after spending their weekend in the city. He slammed into whoever got in his way, making the cigarette sellers spill all their wares, going to claim the battered old mahogany rocking chair that belonged to Maman Gendeng, who had in turn claimed it by killing Edi Idiot.

Since he had taken power, Maman Gendeng had faced many men who wanted that battered chair, the emblem of his rule, and had defeated all of them, but new men were always showing up and now, once again, a stranger was approaching. A number of Maman Gendeng's cronies had been watching the stranger ever since he had entered the terminal, and they knew what he wanted without having to ask. Maman Gendeng also knew, but he remained silent, with his legs crossed, rocking himself back and forth, smoking a cigarette. Nobody yet knew the man's name, where he came from, or how he knew that Maman Gendeng was in charge there, but clearly he wasn't from Halimunda, because if he had been a local with ambitions, he would have challenged Maman Gendeng for that chair a long time ago.

At that time Maman Gendeng still kept his money stuffed into earthen jars stored by an ugly woman named Moyang, whom he trusted almost as much as his own wife. He was saving up his money to buy a surprise gift for his wife, although he wasn't sure what exactly. Every day Moyang was at the bus terminal, as was he. She sold drinks and cigarettes during the day, and at night she would get fucked by men who didn't care about her ugly face (because what's the difference between a pretty face and an ugly face when you are behind some dark bushes?) and didn't want to spend their money at the whorehouse, because Moyang never asked for any payment. Maman Gendeng had never screwed her, and he did not want to, but he did save his money in her jars, which were stored under her bed in the hut where she lived. All of Maman Gendeng's friends knew where it was, but no one dared steal it, nor even dared look at it.

There were often scuffles at the bus terminal, since the schoolkids used the place for their fights, but Maman Gendeng was rarely the one fighting. Now, as that bald man approached the criminal to challenge him, everyone was waiting to see what would unfold, and how it would unfold. Nobody was sure the stranger would get what he wanted. After all these years, the people in the bus terminal had come to believe that no one could defeat Maman Gendeng, unless all the soldiers in the republic attacked him at once, and even then there were doubts, if what people said about him being impervious to weapons was true. Despite this, people were always waiting for his fights.

Very early that morning, when she was setting out a fresh set of clean and neatly ironed clothes for Maman Gendeng on top of the bed before leaving for school, Maya Dewi had requested that he not come home covered in filth as he often did. Sometimes it was because of oil or grease splatters from helping the bus conductors repair their protesting vehicles, other times it was the soot that stuck to the walls of the terminal. It wasn't that such things made the clothes harder for her to clean, Maya Dewi explained, but that her husband just didn't look as handsome in dirty clothes. That day he was wearing a cream-colored shirt, on which the dirt would immediately show, so he had promised that he would not get his clothes dirty, no matter what happened.

He was relaxing in that infamous chair on that sweltering Sunday afternoon, slowly inhaling the smoke from his cigarette and then slowly exhaling it, when he saw the man enter the terminal. Like everyone else, he knew they would come face-to-face. Now the bald man was right in front of him, and before he could speak, Maman Gendeng said, standing up, "If you want this chair, please feel free to take a seat, or feel free to just take it with you." No one could believe it—even Baldy didn't believe it, and stayed silent for a moment, looking at the empty chair.

"It's not that simple," said Baldy. "I want that chair and everything that goes along with it."

"I understand perfectly, so please sit down and you'll get everything." Maman Gendeng nodded, tossing his cigarette butt.

"A *preman* who has never been defeated in a single fight suddenly surrenders his power without protest," said Baldy. "There is no reasonable explanation for it except that he wants to quit the life and become a good husband."

Maman Gendeng nodded his head smiling, and gestured for the

guy to sit. The bald man wasted no time approaching that chair, the symbol of great power, daring, and victory, but right before his butt touched the seat, Maman Gendeng struck him on the nape of his neck with his fist, so hard the people thought they could hear the man's very bones breaking as he collapsed next to the chair. In any case, Maman Gendeng did not get his clothes dirty. Someone dragged the bald guy out to the sidewalk while Maman Gendeng sat back down on his chair, smoking.

Since that day, Baldy had roamed about the terminal, becoming one of the thug's best men. He called himself Romeo. Maybe he had read Shakespeare, maybe not, but he called himself Romeo, and everyone called him Romeo, even though they felt it was a weird name for a big bald guy with half an ear ripped off and its remaining stub all torn to shreds. Romeo became a part of the community, living among them and respecting Maman Gendeng's power. People still didn't know anything about his history or where he had come from, but the rest of them weren't exactly transparent about their backgrounds either. Just like the rest, Romeo would have a screw with Moyang once in a while, until one day he said to Maman Gendeng, "I want to marry her."

"So go ask her yourself," said the criminal, "whether or not she wants to be your wife."

Moyang wanted to marry him, so they had the ceremony and a small party paid for by Maman Gendeng, one month later. They both lived in the hut that Moyang had been living in alone up until now.

"I swear to God," said Maman Gendeng, "Romeo married a woman who loves to sleep around."

They had a honeymoon that made many people jealous. They came late to the bus terminal after making love all night long, and at midday they sometimes disappeared from Moyang's kiosk and made love behind the bushes not far from the terminal, near the cocoa plantations. But after a while, it was clear that what Maman Gendeng had said was true. At night, if her husband was out and she had just closed her kiosk, Moyang would make love to other men—sometimes with a *becak* driver, other times with a bus conductor, and one time with both of them fucking her at once.

"We can not prevent a woman from doing what makes her happy," said Romeo, "even if she is our wife."

"You should have become a philosopher," said Maman Gendeng, "that is, if you are not completely insane."

"Well she herself gives me money," Romeo continued, sitting next to that mahogany rocking chair that he had once coveted, "to try out the women at the whorehouse."

The bus terminal had been the pride of their community for years, from the time Edi Idiot was still controlling the city until Maman Gendeng took his place. It wasn't too big, because there was only one route leading away from the city to the east and to the north, while to the west there was only a small road that came to a dead end after passing through two other small cities. Not every *preman* gathered at the bus terminal, in fact it really might have been just a minority, but because Maman Gendeng was always there, watching the people passing by from that mahogany rocking chair, the terminal was an important place for them. Everyone in their community seemed happy; even though Moyang had married Romeo, they could still sleep with her for free whenever they wanted without having to pay, as long as she was in the mood.

But that happiness was disturbed one peaceful day that should have passed without incident. Moyang opened her kiosk but didn't sell anything, instead just waited for Maman Gendeng, who hadn't showed up there yet. When he did finally appear, looking practically dapper—a new look his friends had grown familiar with since his wedding—Moyang approached him straightaway and sobbed before him. Cries like that were the cries of an abandoned wife, so

Maman Gendeng assumed that Romeo had left Moyang. But Maman Gendeng wasn't convinced of the woman's love or faithfulness toward Romeo, so he asked her:

"What's going on?"

"Romeo left."

"I thought you didn't really love him that much."

After wiping away her tears with the edge of her shirt, revealing her stomach with its many rolls of fat, she said, "The problem is, he left with all your jars of money."

There was no way that Romeo would try to escape through the bus terminal, and that early in the morning no train would have left the city yet. So he'd probably run into the jungle, or someone must have helped him escape in some kind of vehicle. Whatever had happened, Maman Gendeng was furious and intended to catch him, dead or alive. So he gathered every last one of his men, and he ordered them to spread out in every direction, even to neighboring cities, and to touch base with the local thugs there. No one was allowed to return before Romeo was caught, unless he wanted a beating. So all the *preman* in the city left, and Halimunda was the most peaceful it had ever been. Only Maman Gendeng stayed behind, restless with fury. He had long dreamed of a peaceful family life, of being able to survive on honest money. He wanted a family just like other families and he had been saving his money to make this beautiful dream come true. He would buy something, maybe a fishing boat, and he would become a fisherman. Or a truck, and he would become a vegetable hauler. Or a few hectares of land, and he would become a farmer. He hadn't even decided what he wanted to buy yet, and now someone had stolen all that money. He was truly enraged. For three days he waited impatiently, not explaining anything to his wife, who was dumfounded by his anxiety, and becoming an extraordinary grump at the bus terminal, so that all the conductors and bus drivers avoided him as best they could.

But on the fourth day, two of his men brought Romeo back. He had been found in a small and distant city, at the edge of the massive jungle to the west of Halimunda, where the most violent guerrilla warfare had once taken place. Luckily, Maman Gendeng's money was still safe—less only what it cost to buy a mug of *tuak* alcohol, a lemonade, and a pack of cigarettes. His two men had caught Romeo before he had the chance to buy anything else, but Maman Gendeng's rage was a whole other issue.

By the time he arrived, Romeo had already been beaten black and blue by Maman Gendeng's men, but Maman Gendeng was so irate that he beat him again, while people gathered around them in a circle as if they were watching a cockfight. Romeo howled pitifully, begging for mercy and swearing that he would never do such a horrible thing again, but experience had taught Maman Gendeng to never trust a traitor. More and more people gathered. The ones closest to the action in front sat down and the ones furthest in the back were standing, unable to do anything except watch the brutality. Even the policemen who were patrolling back and forth in front of the terminal closed their eyes and stayed at their posts.

The carrion-eating buzzards began to circle as the smell of the man's imminent death began to rise and disperse, carried by the ocean wind. But Romeo wasn't dead yet; not because he was all that strong, but because Maman Gendeng was purposefully drawing it out, making his death really torturous, as a valuable lesson to everyone that *this* was the fate of a traitor. And he really felt sorry for those carrion-eating buzzards, not because the victim's death was so long in coming as he knocked out his teeth slowly, broke two or three of his fingers, tore off his fingernails, stripped him naked and started to pluck out his pubic hairs one by one, and adorned his entire body, which was already battered and bruised, with the butts of still-lit cigarettes—no, he felt sorry for those buzzards because he didn't plan to share any of his happiness with them. He wasn't going to give the corpse away, instead intending to burn him alive as the final manifestation of his fury.

But just when he was preparing the gas and the cigarette lighter, suddenly that hideous woman burst into the middle of the crowd and stood before him. Moyang begged for mercy for her husband, saying that if Maman Gendeng let him live, she promised to take care of him and turn him into a trustworthy man.

"Please give me this chance, my friend," said Moyang, "because whatever else he may be, he is my husband."

Maman Gendeng was deeply moved and suddenly his heart melted. He threw the can of gasoline into the garbage and announced to everyone present that he was giving that man his second chance, but there would be no such second chance for any other man who might try to betray him. And that was how Romeo, who was married to Moyang, did not become food for the fire or the buzzards, and instead lived to become the best friend and most faithful follower of all of Maman Gendeng's men. Meanwhile Maman Gendeng gave all his money to Maya Dewi, who soon after turned it into the startup money for her cookie business.

"That's the man you buried," said Maman Gendeng, "Romeo."

Of course Maya Dewi didn't know anything about that.

She hadn't known about Romeo or the specifics of any of her husband's troubles at the terminal—all her trouble started when Rengganis the Beautiful ran away from home with the baby she had just given birth to, "to marry a dog."

It was early December, a month of often unpredictable weather, and the city was full of tourists spending the end of the year holidays there, so it was easy to get lost in the crowds. At this time of year the city became quite hectic and people stopped paying close attention to one another, because business was bustling. The souvenir kiosks were still going strong, ever since Comrade Kliwon had protected them from eviction. There were always lots of lost kids, lost old folks, and young women who disappeared in the middle of the bustling throng, and so workers stuck missing-person posters up everywhere and also made announcements though loudspeakers that reverberated along the length of the beach.

But Rengganis the Beautiful was not lost like that. Tourists who disappeared were only temporarily lost, and after a moment of inquiry would surely be reunited with their group. Rengganis the Beautiful had run away from home and her entire family was looking for her. Maman Gendeng and Maya Dewi asked everywhere, and their men spread out just as they had before when they were looking for Romeo, but they didn't find the girl. Shodancho—who was especially worried about his daughter, Ai, who had fallen sick with a spiking fever at the loss of Rengganis the Beautiful—deployed rescue parties to look for her, but he forgot about the guerrilla hut, because he had never realized the children knew about it.

The search continued, day and night, while the preparations for the wedding that had been planned were halted, the decorations taken down, and all the rented furniture returned. That kid Kinkin became slightly insane because of what had happened, and went out all alone to search in every corner, carrying his rifle and killing all the dogs he met along the way. He asked the spirits of the dead about it with his *jailangkung*, but not one of them knew where she was.

"The power of some evil spirit is protecting her," he said to himself.

"She will die in a few days time," said Maya Dewi, weeping. "She's not going to know what she can eat on such a journey, and she didn't bring any money, not even one penny."

"I don't see any reason that she should die," said Maman Gendeng, trying to comfort his wife. "If she gets too hungry, she can eat the baby."

The members of the search party began to return one by one without any success. No one had seen a trace of her, not even one clue. "There's no way she was taken up into the heavens, body and soul," said Maman Gendeng. "She can't have reached *moksa,* because she has never even tried practicing meditation." So the search parties went out again, tracking her bush by bush, looking in the city alleyways and the slums, but they still didn't find her. Maya Dewi tried visiting each of her daughter's girlfriends from school, but only Ai and Krisan had been her close playmates. Maya Dewi was a nervous wreck, and regretted that she hadn't stayed by her daughter's side the night she disappeared.

After the new year, the city grew even more crowded with tourists. A number of people drowned, as announced by the workers, and Maman Gendeng and Maya Dewi examined every corpse, one by one. Most of them were tourists who had disobeyed the signs indicating where it was forbidden to swim, but finally they found her. She was immediately recognizable, since not even the seawater could ravage her beauty. Although no one knew how long ago she had drowned before the waves carried her to shore, Maman Gendeng and Maya Dewi were immediately informed about the discovery. She was lying on her back with her clothes almost completely disintegrated. Her face was still that alluring face, with her hair floating on the surface of the water, played with by waves. They quickly realized that her stomach wasn't bloated, like most people who drown, and there were blackish bruises on her neck. Someone had killed her before throwing her into the ocean. Maya Dewi broke out into wracking sobs.

"Whatever has happened, she must be buried," said Maman Gendeng, holding back his fury, "and then we will find that bastard murderer."

"There's no way a dog strangled her," said Maya Dewi, leaning against her husband's shoulder, practically unconscious.

Maman Gendeng himself carried home Rengganis the Beautiful's corpse, which had been found at the farthest point of Halimunda beach almost one month after she disappeared from her home. Maya Dewi followed behind, with swollen eyes and unstoppable tears, and sympathetic onlookers trailed behind.

That afternoon, after all the funerary rituals had been performed, Rengganis the Beautiful's casket cut across the city toward the Budi Dharma cemetery. Kinkin, who almost fainted when he discovered the burial that day would be that of the girl he loved, joined his father in digging her grave, lost in an inconsolable grief. He even helped lower the body, with Maman Gendeng and Kamino. And after Maman Gendeng scattered the first handful of earth on top of her burial shroud, Kinkin joined him in covering up the grave of his beloved, lovingly placing her wooden grave marker in the dirt.

"I will find out who killed her," said Kinkin with a voice full of hate, "and I will avenge her death."

"Do it," said Maman Gendeng, "and if you catch him, I will let you kill him."

That night the two met at Rengganis the Beautiful's grave. Kinkin called her spirit while Maman Gendeng looked on. The game of *jailangkung* was begun, but the spirit of Rengganis the Beautiful did not appear. Kinkin tried to call another spirit, to ask who had killed the girl, but none of them knew the answer, just as before they hadn't known where she had run to.

"We can't do it," said Kinkin giving up and ending the *jailangkung* session. "A mighty evil spirit has been thwarting all my efforts from the beginning."

"If it's necessary, I will meditate myself into the spirit world in order to combat it in the afterlife," said Maman Gendeng. "I still want to know who killed her."

That was when he and his wife began to lie to themselves by

imagining that Rengganis the Beautiful was still alive. They prepared a seat for her at breakfast and dinner, and dished out a portion of food for her, even though Maya Dewi just had to throw it out after. Meanwhile the police dug up Rengganis the Beautiful's grave to conduct an investigation before burying her again. Maman Gendeng tried to believe the police would find her killer, but for a week, and then a month, there was no explanation, not even one clue. They did interrogate lots of people though: everyone was called to the police station and questioned, Maman Gendeng and Maya Dewi each went five times, and other people just as many, but everything seemed to take them farther away from the discovery of Rengganis the Beautiful's killer. The whole thing was exhausting, and Maman Gendeng no longer trusted the police. He rebuked the last cop who came to his house to conduct an investigation.

"You are never going to find the killer in this house," he said annoyed, "and you were stupid to have ever thought that you would."

At that moment, as if receiving a divine revelation, the *preman* understood very clearly what he had to do.

"If no one knows who killed her," he said full of certainty, "then that must mean the entire city is responsible for her death."

On the following Monday, with about thirty of his men, he took action. It was brutal, and the people of the city would remember it as a horrifying time. The men began by going to the police station, destroying whatever they found there, and challenging any policemen who tried to stop them. Maman Gendeng brought the visit to a close by burning the place down, to vent some of his rage over their incompetence.

The city was stunned. The smoke rose high into the sky and even the fire brigade was unable to put out the blaze. No one dared to come to watch that station burn the way they usually did with other fires, once they heard that Maman Gendeng and his scoundrel friends were in the throes of an uncontrollable rage. The people stayed quiet, passing the news by word of mouth, while trembling to imagine what that terrifying man might do next.

Despite the fact that Maman Gendeng was now an old man who had already lived more than a half century, everyone knew that his strength wasn't the least bit diminished. And now he had lost his beloved daughter in the most bitter way possible: someone had murdered her and thrown her corpse into the ocean, and he didn't know who. He regretted that he hadn't done something as soon as the girl had said that she had been raped by a dog in the school bathroom. Why hadn't he looked for that dog from the very start, or why hadn't he butchered all the city dogs just as that kid Kinkin had tried in his quite amateur way?

"*Mijn hond is weggelopen*," he said. My dog ran away. But it wasn't clear what he meant by that.

After burning down the police station, he found his first dog, a stray dog scavenging through the trash, and he captured and killed it, twisting the dog's neck until it broke and the animal sprawled out dead.

"What's the use of me having power if I can't even protect my own daughter from a dog?" he said. "Let's kill every dog in this city."

His thugs began to spread out in large groups, carrying their deadly weapons. A number of them carried pellet guns, others had machetes and unsheathed swords.

"I'm going to do it, even if it brings me no peace," Maman Gendeng said with a sigh.

"Can't you just make another child?" That was Romeo's stupid question.

"Even if I have ten other kids, someone has already killed this one and because of that there is no way I can rest." His eyes stared down the cobblestone alleyways hoping to find another dog, and he added sadly, "She was only seventeen years old."

"Shodancho's child is also dead," said Romeo.

"That doesn't make me feel any better."

And so the most horrifying dog massacre began, almost like the massacre of communists that had taken place eighteen years before. Who knows what would have happened if Shodancho had found out, because those dogs were the crossbreeds of the *ajak* that he had trained, but he was away searching for his daughter's body. The thugs easily slashed open the dogs that were roaming in the streets, hacking them to pieces as if they were going to turn them into satay meat. Their heads were hung at street corners with blood still dripping from the napes of their necks, like a warning to all other dogs to steer clear of that city. After the strays were killed, the thugs began to eye pet dogs, knocking down house fences and killing the dogs in their cages, powerless against their killers. They also went into houses, smashing windows and attacking the pets lying peacefully in their dog beds, killing them where they lay and then throwing them into kitchen woks.

People protested, but Maman Gendeng didn't care. "If it is true that a dog raped my daughter," he said, "then dogs have truly inherited the evil ways of men." He even ordered his underlings to destroy all dog owners' property.

"We will come face-to-face with the army if you continue to wreak havoc like this," said Romeo in a tone of undeniable fear.

"We have faced those soldiers before."

Romeo looked at him in disbelief.

"What else do you think can be done by a man who is enraged by his daughter's murder?" asked Maman Gendeng. "I know those people are completely without sin, but I'm upset."

He was indeed truly furious at everyone in the city, except for his cronies, but his daughter was also sort of like an excuse. He had in fact held a grudge against the people for quite a long time, knowing for sure that they all looked down on him and his friends as unemployed goons who passed their time doing nothing but drinking beer and fighting. He also held a grudge against them for thinking of Rengganis the Beautiful as an idiot, and for having stared at her with lustful and depraved looks. He had a reason to be angry.

"They believe that we are the garbage of society," Maman Gendeng summarized. "This is true, but many of us never got enough education to make anything of ourselves, and they closed the doors on us. What can be done if we finally became robbers, became pickpockets, and only bided our time until we could get revenge on the people who made us jealous? I was jealous when I saw good people with happy families. I wanted something like that. I finally got everything I wanted, and now, after I have tasted happiness, someone has stolen that joy from me. All my old grudges have been ripped open like a half-healed wound."

What Romeo had been afraid of truly came to pass. Riots spread throughout the city. Some dog owners fought back, and the thugs grew all the more violent, now ruining whatever they could get their hands on in addition to dogs. Cars were demolished and signposts were uprooted and hurled, as were the shade trees lining the streets. Shop windows were broken into smithereens. A number of police posts were burned, and a number of people were injured. An extraordinary terror swept over the city, until the order for military rule was sent from the central command to the city military authority, which nominated Shodancho to straighten out the goons, and if they couldn't be straightened out, to slaughter them.

"I have already thought for quite a while that those scoundrels should be finished off just like the communists," said Shodancho to his wife, after coming home from another fruitless search for his daughter Ai's body.

"After banishing Comrade Kliwon now you are going to kill Maman Gendeng?" asked his wife (she had never told him about her affair with the Comrade the day before he was found having committed suicide). "Are you going to turn all my younger sisters into widows?"

Shodancho looked at his wife, surprised.

"If he is not killed, he is going to kill everyone in this city, so what do you want me to do?" asked Shodancho. "What's more, think about this: he failed to properly protect his own daughter, so she got knocked up, and then he forced her to marry a kid that she didn't want to marry, so she ran away on the night she gave birth to the baby. And because she ran away, our daughter, who had been her dear friend for so long, fell sick and died. And then after she died, someone snatched her from her grave. Don't you get it? The leader of that goon squad killed our child, our Ai—Nurul Aini the third."

"Why don't you also blame Eve for seducing Adam into eating the apple and forcing us to live in this accursed world," said his wife crankily.

As it turned out Shodancho didn't pay any attention to his wife. In addition to the chaos those thugs were causing, and the order from the central military command, Shodancho was furious over Ai's death and was still smarting from his old grudge ever since Maman Gendeng had barged into his office and threatened him after he slept with Dewi Ayu. No one had ever threatened Shodancho to his face, not a Japanese and not a Dutchman, but this one hoodlum had dared. Even though he had seen proof of Maman Gendeng's power with his very own eyes, Shodancho believed there were still one or two ways to kill the man, and he would use whatever means necessary. He may have been Maman Gendeng's friend, especially at the card table, but all the same he had always longed to kill him someday. Now the time had come, so he closed his ears against whatever Alamanda had to say.

"Do it and you need not return," Alamanda said finally, "so all three of us will become widows and everything will be fair."

"Adinda still has Krisan."

"So kill the boy if you are jealous."

Shodancho himself led the operation of eradicating those thugs. He gathered all his soldiers, and pulled in some extra troops from the nearest military posts. He held an emergency meeting and made a map of where the thugs had committed acts of violence and a plan for how they would be finished off. Shodancho himself was really getting too old for a field operation, in fact he was waiting for his retirement papers, but he appeared quite energetic, and even a little bit wise. "We are not going to do it like when we slaughtered the communists," he said. "This time, everyone who is killed must be put into a sack."

So one truck came filled with empty sacks.

The operation was carried out at night, so as not to induce a mass panic. The soldiers spread out, carrying weapons but dressed in civilian clothes, and so did the snipers, heading for the groups of thugs. They identified as thugs anyone who was tattooed, drinking alcohol, caught making trouble, or killing dogs, and all thugs were shot right where they stood, before being stuffed into a sack and thrown into the irrigation ditch or simply left lying by the side of the road. The people who found them would bury them in their sacks: that was way more practical than wrapping them in burial shrouds.

"They are too accursed for burial shrouds," said Shodancho, "let alone cemetery plots."

As soon as morning came on the first day, half the city's criminals had already disappeared, swallowed by those sacks that were tied with plastic cords. They were found along the roadways, bobbing in the river, lapped by the waves on the shore, in heaps under the bushes, and lying in the irrigation ditches. Some of them were getting pawed at by dogs, and others were being visited by flies. Not one person touched them before the afternoon. The people were overjoyed that help had come, from who knows where, to finish off each and every last one of those troublemakers. Of course they still remembered the massacre of the communists, and how they had been terrorized by their ghosts for years. But no matter, those thugs were better off turning into ghosts than living and causing trouble for so many people. So they left the corpses just as they were in their sacks, hoping the maggots and buzzards would finish them off, right down to the marrow of their bones. But when the offensive rotting stench began to ambush them and they couldn't take it anymore, the people finally dealt with the corpses closest to their settlements, burying them in their sacks.

But it wasn't like burying a corpse—it was more like burying a turd after taking a shit in the banana orchard.

The massacre continued into a second night, and a third, and then a fourth night, a fifth, and a sixth and seventh. The operation was carried out swiftly, almost finishing off the entire supply of thugs in Halimunda. But Shodancho was not in the least bit satisfied, because Maman Gendeng was not among the corpses.

For that entire week, Maman Gendeng did not return home. Maya Dewi was very worried about him, especially after she heard that the city thugs were being killed off one by one, for seven nights straight, all shot to death, in the head or the chest. Although no one knew for sure, everyone could guess who had done it, because only certain people carried weapons. So Maya Dewi went to find Shodancho.

"Have you murdered my husband?"

"Not yet," Shodancho replied sadly, "ask those soldiers."

She asked them one by one, almost every single soldier, and they replied just as Shodancho had replied:

"Not yet."

But she didn't really believe them. Shodancho had banished Comrade Kliwon to Buru Island, so he could certainly kill her husband Maman Gendeng. She hoped that her husband truly was invincible, but seeing so many corpses in the street, she could not stop herself from keeping up her search, because maybe one of the bodies was his.

So that beautiful woman, with a red headscarf protecting her from the bright sunlight, began to go from one sack to the next, and one by one she loosened their cords—unmoved by the rotting stench that violated her nose, not caring that she was competing with the flies—and examined the corpses inside, comparing their faces to her beloved memory of her husband's face. Not one of the corpses was Maman Gendeng, but she recognized most of them as her husband's loyal friends, and so she felt sure that her husband had died as well. Maybe all that talk of invincibility had just been hot air. She had to find him, and if indeed he was already dead, she would have to bury him in an honorable manner.

In order to find out about those corpses that had already been buried by the people who couldn't stand their smell, she approached a group of amateur gravediggers and asked whether they had buried her husband.

"From the smell we don't think so."

"What do you think my husband smells like?"

"Well, he must smell much worse than all these other thugs, because he was the biggest thug of them all." Maya Dewi acknowledged the truth in those words, and continued her search. She chased after a couple of corpses that were floating in the river and getting swept away by the current, but after she had worn herself out catching them, it turned out that neither one was her husband. She also examined the corpses scattered along the beach, a sight that had scared all the tourists away from Halimunda. But after a whole day, her hard work was still in vain and she returned home as night fell, hoping there would be no more slaughter that evening, and that her husband would return. Her wish was not granted, and when morning came she began her search again, opening all the sacks she hadn't tried yet.

She kept on this way until finally a couple of people told her that they had seen Romeo and her husband escape into the jungle on the cape on the seventh day of the massacre. But the soldiers had heard about this too, so she was in a race against time, hoping that they had not been able to shoot him yet. She went into the jungle alone, wearing only flip-flops on her feet, and protected by the same red headscarf she had been wearing the day before, stumbling along a footpath that was grown over with shrub brush. That jungle had been a protected forest since the colonial era, and it wasn't inhabited just by monkeys and wild pigs, but also by wild buffalo and even jaguars, but Maya Dewi was not afraid of anything. All she wanted was to find her husband, dead or alive.

She passed by a group of four soldiers, and she stopped them.

"Have you killed my husband?"

"This time yes we have, Madam," said their leader, "and we extend our condolences."

"Where did you put his corpse?"

"Go straight for about a hundred meters, and there you will find his body, already surrounded by flies. We crucified him on a mango tree first."

"Is he in a sack?"

"In a sack," replied the soldier, "curled up like a baby."

"See you later."

"Later."

Maya Dewi continued on her way, walking straight for a hundred meters, just as the soldier had told her to do, and there she did in fact see a sack, already lined with flies. The carrion-eating buzzards were already pecking at it, and two *ajak* had been tearing at its corners. Maya Dewi chased them all away, opened the cord around the sack, and made sure the person "curled up like a baby" inside was that man, her husband, and even though his face was almost unrecognizable, it was indeed him. She didn't cry, not then in any case. With impressive composure, she tied the sack back up with its plastic cord. And because she was not strong enough to carry him on her back, she dragged the sack the whole way from where she had found him to the Budi Dharma public cemetery, where she asked that her husband be buried in an honorable manner. The flies besieged his sack for the entire journey, stretching out behind her like a comet's tail.

The insects only dispersed once Kamino had bathed and perfumed the man. Now the corpse was lying stiffly, with bullet wounds visible in his forehead and his chest, just two shots that must have killed him instantly. The wound on his chest was right at his heart. It was only when she saw this that Maya Dewi wept, and to spare her further grief, Kamino quickly wrapped him up in a burial shroud. He recited the prayer for the dead, along with Kinkin, who paid his respects to the man who should have been his father-in-law. Maman Gendeng's body was buried right next to the grave of his daughter, and Maya Dewi knelt for almost an hour there in between those two graves, feeling abandoned, alienated, and alone. She began her days of mourning, and on the third day Maman Gendeng returned from the afterlife.

As had already been proven, that man truly was invincible. He wasn't afraid of the massacre. But he couldn't stand to see his friends lying dead in the streets and said to Romeo, who was faithfully following him:

"Let's run away into the jungle."

They went on the seventh day of the massacre, after moving from one hiding place to the next. It was true: that city no longer pleased the *preman*. He couldn't bear to remember all of his pride over his strength and invulnerability while his friends lay dead at his feet.

"Soon they will become ghosts, and if we survive, we will suffer to see their suffering," he said during their escape, remembering the last days of Comrade Kliwon's life, when that man had been beaten down by an ever-deepening grief to see the ghosts of his friends in a condition of such grave suffering. Living like that was much too painful, and Maman Gendeng wanted to avoid it.

"There's no way we can run from ghosts," said Romeo.

"That's true, unless we join them, just as Comrade Kliwon finally chose to kill himself."

"I'm not brave enough to kill myself," said Romeo.

"I don't want to either," said the criminal. "I'm still trying to think of some other solution."

He chose to escape to the jungle on the cape because it was almost completely deserted. It was a protected forest, and because of that there were no farmers working the land, just a few lazy forestry officers. He hoped that by escaping there, he could buy some time before being discovered by the soldiers, who might not be able to kill him, but would nevertheless be deeply annoying. He was trying to make a decision.

"There is no way I am going to stay alive when I know that all of my friends have been killed in a massacre," he said in a heartbroken tone.

"There is no way I am going to die while many people are still enjoying their beautiful lives," said Romeo dryly.

"But I am also still thinking of my wife. She will be so sad, especially since we have already lost our daughter."

"I don't care about my wife. She can still find lots of guys to have sex with who won't care how ugly she is," said Romeo. "But I still prefer to live."

They arrived at a small hill with a cave that the Japanese had carved into one of its slopes for defense during the war. They both rested at the top of the hill, as Maman Gendeng continued to weigh his desire to put this life behind him against his reluctance to leave

Maya Dewi all alone on this earth. He looked at that Japanese cave, so dark and humid, with its boxlike walls, looking more like a prison cell than a fort. But a place like that was quite fitting for meditation. Maman Gendeng wanted to meditate until he achieved liberation and left this earth in *moksa*, but he continued to think about his wife until he said finally:

"Whatever the case, sooner or later, death will come. And she is the strongest woman I know."

He decided to meditate in the Japanese cave, and went inside. He ordered Romeo to stand guard at the top of the hill in case the soldiers had sniffed them out and chased them to that spot. "Come get me if those soldiers arrive," he said.

"I will kill them dead before they even have the chance to arrive," said Romeo.

"Your voice doesn't sound that reassuring," said Maman Gendeng, "but I trust you."

Maman Gendeng went down into the cave, sat on the moist floor, and began to meditate. Not long after, he attained *moksa*: disappeared and dissolved into little orbs of light. He didn't kill himself, but he left this world by shedding his body, abandoning all the material that shackled his soul, and now he was one with all light, sparkling like crystal and rising up toward the sky. But before he reached heaven he saw four soldiers pointing their weapons at that guy Romeo on top of the hill. He wanted to help the man by blurring the soldiers' vision, but before he could, he heard Romeo say:

"Don't kill me! I'll tell you where Maman Gendeng is hiding."

"Okay, tell us," said one of the soldiers.

"He's meditating in that Japanese cave."

The four soldiers went down and searched the Japanese cave. But of course they weren't going to find Mamang Gendeng. Romeo was going to take the opportunity to run away, but Maman Gendeng wasn't going to let that happen and held him back, so that Romeo found himself running and yet unable to move from his spot.

"A traitor is always a traitor," said Maman Gendeng, and Romeo, who couldn't see him, could still hear his booming voice.

Maman Gendeng then transformed Romeo's face into his own face, exactly at the moment those four furious soldiers returned.

"So finally we find you, Maman Gendeng," they said, aiming their weapons at where he stood on the crest of the hill.

"I'm Romeo," said the man, "not Maman Gendeng!"

But two shots of a rifle had already ended his life. One bullet in his head and another in his chest. It was that corpse Maya Dewi found, while Maman Gendeng rose up to heaven and visited her on the third day after he attained *moksa*.

{18}

THAT MIGHTY EVIL spirit was now overjoyed to see all its victories, to see all its rancor and hatred avenged, even though it had been forced to wait for so long.

"I have separated them from the people they love," he said to Dewi Ayu, "just as he separated me from the person I loved."

I have separated them from the people they love, just as he separated me from the person I loved, its voice echoed.

"But I loved you," said Dewi Ayu, "with a love that came from deep in my guts."

"Yes and so I ran from you, granddaughter of Stammler!"

Yes and so I ran from you, granddaughter of Stammler!

Dewi Ayu couldn't believe how firmly that evil spirit's longing for revenge had been rooted. He had always seemed just like an ordinary ghost. She had known that he had evil plans for some point in the future, but she had never imagined that he could do so much harm, never guessed how deeply his bitterness had been planted in his heart.

❧

"Look at your children," said that evil spirit, "they have now all become pathetic widows, and the fourth is a spinster who has never been married!"

Look at your children, they have now all become pathetic widows, and the fourth is a spinster who has never been married!

This was after the ghost had killed Shodancho in his guerrilla hut, the place where he used to hold dominion. When Shodancho appeared out of the blue early in the morning and squatted before the hearth, Dewi Ayu, who had been dead for years and even when she had been alive hadn't had any contact with him for a very long time, had truly forgotten that he was her son-in-law. The man said that he had been combing the cities and the jungles for years, ever since he had massacred the city thugs, searching for his daughter's stolen body. He was exhausted and had returned to the city a failure. He didn't dare go home to his wife, Alamanda, so he had come to the house of his mother-in-law, Dewi Ayu.

"I didn't have a character suitable to play the role of Shodancho's killer," said the evil spirit, "So I did it myself."

I didn't have a character suitable to play the role of Shodancho's killer, so I did it myself.

"I knew from early on," said Dewi Ayu, "that you were an amateur comedian."

No, he didn't really do it himself, not with his own hands. But indeed, no human being killed Shodancho. In the forlorn solitude of his old age, without the courage to face his wife, who had sent him away after he turned her younger sisters into widows, and having lost his beloved daughter, Shodancho frequently tried to make himself feel better by going to his guerrilla hut in the middle of the jungle on the cape. The hut was just as it had always been, not quite as sturdy as before, but still strong enough to carry him back to a comforting nostalgia.

He also tried to keep himself busy by once again raising wild *ajak* around the guerrilla hut. He was already quite old and feeble, but he still took the pups from their dens. Then one day, their mother came looking for them.

He was lying down on the rock that he used to eat on with his men, the same rock that Rengganis the Beautiful had lain the corpse of her baby on before throwing it to the dogs, when that female *ajak* came with her pack. This bitch didn't wait too long when she saw her enemy in such a vulnerable state, lunging right for him and tearing into the muscle of his thigh. To repeat, Shodancho was now quite old, his reflexes were slow, and his resistance was weak. He hadn't yet been able to fight back when other *ajak* began arriving, one pouncing on his arm and the other snatching at his calf. Gaping wounds opened up across his body and his old man's blood flooded out over the rock. Shodancho was still able to twitch and kick this way and that, hoping to shake off those *ajak*, but his wounds were quite severe, and he exhausted himself. He began to quiet, looking up at the sky, realizing that his death was imminent and that it had come at the hands of the *ajak* he had cared for his entire life. He died with his body torn to shreds, eaten alive. Please do realize though, that in truth *ajak* are lazy creatures who usually only eat carrion. Shodancho is perhaps one of the only people to have ever been eaten alive. His death was destined to be just that tragic.

Dewi Ayu began to worry about Shodancho when he hadn't returned from the guerrilla hut after a week's time, because he usually didn't stay for quite so long. With the help of two retired soldiers who had once been Shodancho's men, she hacked through the jungle on the cape looking for him. They found an appalling and pathetic corpse. His face was almost completely destroyed, so the only part of him they could immediately recognize was the remnants of his uniform. The *ajak* hadn't dragged him away, they had eaten him on the spot, while he was still warm, and the buzzards were pecking at what few pieces of muscle and meat still clung to his bones. Dewi Ayu had arrived right before these began to rot.

They brought him back to Alamanda in a black plastic bag, the kind firefighters use to carry the corpses of burn victims to the morgue, and to her, after placing the black plastic bag at her feet, Dewi Ayu said:

"Child, I am bringing you the bones of your man. He was killed and eaten by *ajak*."

"I had a feeling that might happen, Mama, ever since he came to town with those ninety-six *ajak* to hunt pigs," said Alamanda, not looking in the least bit forlorn.

"Be a little sad," her mother said. "At the very least because he didn't leave you anything in his will."

Alamanda buried those bones with the bits of torn flesh stuck on them, looking like beef bones that are chopped up and sold for soup. Shodancho was buried in the memorial cemetery for war heroes and they held a military ceremony for him. At least Alamanda gave thanks for that, because if he had been buried in the public cemetery, she would have worried that his ghost would fight with the ghost of Comrade Kliwon. He would be peaceful in the memorial cemetery for war heroes, with a casket and the national flag wrapped around him. They shot off the cannons to pay him his final respects, but Alamanda imagined that her husband's ghost was being catapulted, so that he would be as dead as dead could be, and that made her a little bit happy too.

Now she was truly a widow, just like her two younger sisters.

❧

"I first realized you were on a quest for revenge when they massacred the communists and that Comrade had to face the firing squad," said Dewi Ayu, returning her attention to the evil spirit.

"He should have died then, an excruciating death."

He should have died then, an excruciating death.

"But love showed its true strength," said Dewi Ayu. "Alamanda intervened right at the moment he was to die."

The evil spirit laughed mockingly, "And then she fucked him more than ten years later, right before he killed himself. Killed himself. Killed himself!!! He died! Ha. Ha. Ha."

And then she fucked him more than ten years later, right before he killed himself. Killed himself. Killed himself!!! He died! Ha. Ha. Ha.

"But I finally realized what was going on."

It was true. Dewi Ayu had realized that the evil spirit was plotting its revenge. She had guessed that he would try to destroy the love of her family, the remaining descendants of Ted Stammler, just as Ted Stammler had destroyed the love he had with Ma Iyang, although she didn't think the revenge would be this cruel. Even when that evil spirit was still alive, still just a man, Dewi Ayu had felt his bottomless sorrow deep in her own heart, even before she had met him. This led her to blind love, and drove her to marriage. She wanted to give him the love he had never gotten from her grandmother Ma Iyang after she had been stolen by her grandfather Ted Stammler, but the man had refused to accept her love, a love that was completely pure, that came from deep within her guts. That was when Dewi Ayu had realized that his love for Ma Iyang was irreplaceable, and she felt how he suffered more and more, after his one and only true love had been ripped out at the root. So when he died, Dewi Ayu knew that he was sure to become a vexed and vengeful and tragic ghost who would never rest in peace in the world of the dead. And it was true. That ghost followed her wherever she went. She had sensed its presence at Bloedenkamp, in the whorehouse, and in both her homes. But she hadn't known that it had been plotting its evil revenge until the morning she heard that Comrade Kliwon, the man beloved by both Alamanda and Adinda, was to be executed.

"He wasn't even married at that time, and I would not let him die before he married one of your children. Ha. Ha. Ha."

He wasn't even married at that time, and I would not let him die before he married one of your children. Ha. Ha. Ha.

Not long after Shodancho's death, with her conviction undeterred, Dewi Ayu had finally summoned the evil spirit with the help of that *jailangkung* kid Kinkin. And now the evil spirit stood in front of her, laughing uncontrollably, showing his bottomless and malicious joy.

"This is the evil spirit who time and time again prevented me from finding out who killed Rengganis the Beautiful," said Kinkin.

"Yes, I even separated *you* from the one *you* loved. Ha. Ha. Ha."

Yes, I even separated you *from the one* you *loved. Ha. Ha. Ha.*

When she had learned, from the whispering winds and the howls of the *ajak* deep in the jungle, that at Alamanda's request Comrade Kliwon had not been executed, Dewi Ayu believed that love still might be able to vanquish the vengeful curse of her husband's ghost, but she wasn't sure. For almost her entire adult life she had been thinking about this, thinking about how to save her daughters and guard their happiness, keep them free from the resentful curse of the evil ghost who would be her companion and her adversary for the rest of her life and beyond. So when her children married their husbands, she chased those couples away and told them never to return to her home. She didn't chase away Maman Gendeng and Maya Dewi, but instead chose to move herself to a new house. She wanted to distance her children from the ghost, even though she hadn't yet realized that he would exact such an evil revenge.

Her concerns again surfaced when, about ten years after her last daughter was married, Dewi Ayu got pregnant. Now, she was growing fresh prey inside her womb for the evil spirit. Dewi Ayu had to save the child, however she could. She tried to abort her baby in a number of different ways, so that it would never have to be born into this world, and would be free from all curses, from all revenge. But that child was so strong Dewi Ayu couldn't kill it, and the baby kept growing in her womb. If it was a girl, she would be as beautiful as her older sisters, and if it was a boy, it would be the most handsome man on the face of the earth. A creature like that would be showered with love, and would have a lot of love to give, but all the while Dewi Ayu still felt the evil spirit lurking, waiting to target that love. He would destroy it, however possible, just as Ted Stammler had destroyed his love with Ma Iyang.

So she said to Rosinah, "I'm bored of having beautiful children."

"If that's how you feel, pray for an ugly baby."

She had to give thanks to that mute woman, because her prayers were answered and for the first time she had an ugly daughter, uglier than any woman you would ever meet, even though ironically she was named Beauty. With a face and body like that, no one would ever love her, neither man nor woman. She would be free from the curse of the evil spirit. She had to give thanks to Rosinah.

"But now she's pregnant!" bellowed the evil spirit. "Doesn't that prove that someone loved her?"

But now she's pregnant! Doesn't that prove that someone loved her?

The evil spirit was right.

"But you have not yet killed him."
"I haven't killed him yet."
I haven't killed him yet.

One night, when she once again heard a strange commotion, like the grunting and groaning of people making love, Dewi Ayu finally broke down the bedroom door with a mighty heave of an axe. She was disappointed, to say the least, to discover that someone was making love to that ugly Beauty. Somebody loved her, and that was exactly what Dewi Ayu hadn't wanted since before the girl had even been born. Overcome with resentment, she wanted to know what kind of stupid man would love a girl like that. But she didn't see anyone in the bedroom except Beauty, who had been startled and was huddling stark naked in a corner of the room.

"Who were you making love to?!" Dewi Ayu demanded in anger, disappointment, and panic.

"I'll never tell. He is my prince."

But Dewi Ayu saw something, little more than a blur, moving as if coming down off the bed. Then as she walked around toward the bedside table, she could barely make out some footsteps on the floor, a little damp as if from sweat, faint under the light of the bedroom lamp. The invisible figure parted the curtain in quite a hurry, opened the window, and of course then he jumped out. At that time Dewi Ayu thought the ghost had come to make love to Beauty, although she couldn't guess why.

"No, it wasn't me," said the evil spirit, offended.
No, it wasn't me.
"You prevented me from seeing who it was."
"That's true. Ha. Ha. Ha."
That's true. Ha. Ha. Ha.

❦

It's as if his revenge had been carried out perfectly, almost without a hitch, and his curse continued to destroy whatever what was left of her family. Alamanda had lost Shodancho, and despite the fact that she had never really loved him all that much, and actually mostly hated him, there had still been a few moments when she did sincerely care for him. And after losing her first two children, she had lost Nurul Aini the third, Ai, who died at such an early age. And Maya Dewi had lost Rengganis the Beautiful even more tragically: someone had killed her and threw her into the ocean, and no one knew who. Then her husband vanished through *moksa*, after having seen almost all his friends slaughtered. Dewi Ayu's second child, Adinda, had seen her husband, Comrade Kliwon, dead after hanging himself in his bedroom. But she still had Krisan. And it turned out that Beauty had a lover. Dewi Ayu had to save whoever was left from that evil spirit. She would not let Krisan be taken from Adinda, nor let Beauty's lover be taken from her, whoever he was. Dewi Ayu would stake anything to fight the evil spirit before her.

"I must stop you," she said then.

"From what?" asked the evil spirit.

From what?

"From destroying my family."

"Ha. Ha. Ha. Your family's ruin was fated long ago. Nothing can stop my revenge now."

Ha. Ha. Ha. Your family's ruin was fated long ago. Nothing can stop my revenge now.

"You were unable to tear Henri and Aneu Stammler apart," said Dewi Ayu.

"Because one of them is the flesh and blood of my beloved."

Because one of them is the flesh and blood of my beloved.

"And I'm Ma Iyang's granddaughter."

"That's already too far removed."

That's already too far removed.

Dewi Ayu slowly slid a dagger out from the pocket of the gown she was wearing. The blade was the kind used by soldiers, shining and sturdy. "I found it in Shodancho's room," she announced. Kinkin watched in horror (an angry woman holding a dagger!) but the evil spirit only smiled in disdain. "I am going to kill you with this blade."

"Ha. Ha. Ha. No human being can kill me," said the evil spirit.

Ha. Ha. Ha. No human being can kill me.

"Might I at least try?" asked Dewi Ayu.

"Go ahead, be my guest."

Go ahead, be my guest.

Dewi Ayu approached as the evil spirit smiled a way more disgusting, contemptuous, and self-assured smile. Kinkin, unable to bear being a witness to the murder, hid his face. After glaring at the evil spirit for a few seconds as he glared back, Dewi Ayu, with all the power of a woman carrying a profound rage, maybe in the end with a power and force as strong as that of an evil spirit, stabbed her ex-husband with all her might. Blood spurted out, and she stabbed him again, and blood spurted out again, and she stabbed him again, five stabs with a strength that grew from one stab to the next.

The evil spirit collapsed on the floor, moaning and holding his chest.

"How is it possible," he said, "That you were able to kill me?"

How is it possible that you were able to kill me?

"I died when I was fifty-two years old, from the strength of my own will, in the hopes that I could someday resist and contain the strength of your evil soul," said Dewi Ayu. "And today I have come. Do you believe that a mere human could rise from the grave after being dead for twenty-one years? I am no longer human, and so I can kill you."

"You may have succeeded in killing me, but my curse will live on."

You may have succeeded in killing me, but my curse will live on.

Then that evil spirit died, turning into a dense cloud of black smoke and disappearing, swallowed up by the atmosphere. Dewi Ayu looked at the kid Kinkin.

"My duty is done, and now I will return to the world of the dead," she said. "Goodbye, child. Thank you for all your help."

Then she vanished too, changing into a beautiful butterfly who flew away through the open window and disappeared into the yard.

The man often appeared out of the blue, but because it happened so often, Beauty was no longer surprised by his presence. He had been showing up like that ever since she was young, inviting her to talk. Rosinah was often by her side, but Rosinah could never see him, even though Beauty could. Rosinah never heard the man's voice either, even though Beauty could hear it. She learned how to speak from that man. He was old, so old his eyebrows were already all white. His dark skin had been burned by the sun, and he had lean muscles that had been forged from years of hard work. She learned everything she knew from him. When Rosinah had tried to enroll her in school and the principal didn't want to accept her, and she herself didn't even want to go to school, the man had said:

"I will teach you to write, even though I never learned how to write."

I will teach you to write, even though I never learned how to write.

He continued:

"And I will teach you to read, even though I never learned how to read."

And I will teach you to read, even though I never learned how to read.

✣

She had everything she wanted, it seemed, and never needed anything else because she was so happy to be friends with him. Other people didn't want to associate with her, because she was ugly. But that man was friends with her and didn't care that she was hideous. Other people didn't even want to cross her path, but he spent time with her. They often played together, and Rosinah was frequently startled by the little girl's joyful outbursts that seemed to come suddenly and without apparent reason.

Little Beauty was so happy to be able to read and write. She found all the books that her mother had left behind, and read almost all of them with an overflowing joy, copying over parts of them in her efforts to learn to write and finding a similar delight. But Rosinah looked at her with a gaze full of confusion.

"It's like an angel is teaching you," Rosinah wrote to Beauty.

"Yes, an angel *is* teaching me."

The angel didn't necessarily come every single day, but Beauty was sure he would always come at certain times, whenever he felt like it, to teach her something. She didn't need any other friends, who didn't want her because she was ugly. She didn't need to leave her house to play, because she could play inside the house. She didn't want to bother anyone by showing her disgusting self, so she was never bothered by anyone showing up to see her. It was the house that made her happy and content, because a kind angel lived there and had become her dear companion.

"I can even teach you how to cook, even though I never learned how to cook."

I can even teach you how to cook, even though I never learned how to cook.

❧

So she learned how to cook and was soon an expert at mixing spices. It didn't stop there, she also began to knit, sew, and embroider, and maybe she would have even been able to do some auto repair and plow the fields if she had been given the opportunity. She learned everything she knew from that kind angel, who taught her with such patience and diligence.

"If you never learned how to do any of this, then how do you know how to do it, and how can you teach me?" asked Beauty.

"I steal from the people who know how."

I steal from the people who know how.

"What do you know how to do without having to steal it from anyone else?"

"Pull a cart."

Pull a cart.

And that was how she grew up in that house with Rosinah, who soon grew accustomed to all the strange and supernatural qualities the girl exhibited. Beauty had been given a quite adequate inheritance from her mother, all Rosinah had to do was figure out how it could sustain their life together. She went to market every day to shop for their daily needs, while Beauty stayed at home. There was a ghost in this house, just as Dewi Ayu had once said, but he didn't seem to bother anyone. If in fact it was true that he had taught Beauty everything she knew, then you could say that the ghost was a good ghost. So Rosinah didn't need to worry about anything when she left Beauty alone.

Even the kids who sometimes grew curious and peeked in from behind the fence in fear didn't need to worry. Beauty would never show herself to them, because she was a kind girl and she knew it would frighten them half to death. She only showed herself to Rosinah, who had known her since the day she was born. She was so kind that she sacrificed herself and her desire to have the kind of life most people enjoyed. Her life was limited to the house: her bedroom, the dining room, the bathroom, the kitchen, and sometimes she went out into the yard in the dark of night. She was so kind to sacrifice herself, or punish herself, by leading a monotonous and terribly boring existence, but she seemed to be quite content with it.

"Now I am going to give you a prince," said the good angel.
Now I am going to give you a prince.

She had grown into a young lady and so of course longed for a man who would fall in love with her, and whom she would fall in love with. This began to depress her, because she was certain that no man would ever want to love her. She wasn't made to be loved. She was a hideous girl with nostrils that looked like an electrical outlet, with skin like jet-black soot. She was a frightening girl who made people feel nauseous and puke all over, faint from terror, piss in their pants, and run away as if possessed, but didn't make people fall in love.

"That isn't true. You will get your very own prince."
That isn't true. You will get your very own prince.

That was impossible. No one had ever even seen her, so no one even knew her, and there was no way that someone could fall in love with her without knowing her.

"Have I ever lied to you?"
Have I ever lied to you?
No.

"Wait on the veranda at dusk, and your prince will come."
Wait on the veranda at dusk, and your prince will come.

She would often sit out on the veranda once night had fallen, to breath in the fresh air without having to worry that her monster face would bother people. In the dark she felt quite safe, and the nighttime was like her best friend. Sometimes she even got up early in the morning, before the sun set everything ablaze, in order to sit outside and look up at the pinkish star the angel called Venus. She loved it because of its beauty. Just like her name.

Now she sat on the veranda in order to wait for the prince who had been promised her. She didn't know how he would arrive. Maybe he would be riding a dragon that came from Venus, or maybe he would appear from underground, popping out of the earth in some astonishing fashion. She didn't know he would come, but she would wait for him. That first night passed without any prince walking by her house. Not even a beggar walked by.

But she believed the angel wouldn't lie, so she waited again for a second night. There was one funeral procession that passed by, but no prince. There was also a *bajigur* seller who passed by, but he didn't stop to say hello or even turn his head to look at her. There was no prince, until finally she fell asleep exhausted in her chair and Rosinah came and picked her up, carried her inside, and put her to bed.

On the third night, still nobody came. Rosinah would ask her why she was sitting out on the veranda every night and Beauty would reply, "I am waiting for my prince to come." Rosinah began to understand that the girl had entered puberty. She knew that the girl was already menstruating, and now she wanted a lover. She was sitting on the veranda hoping that someone would see her and fall in love with her. Rosinah felt sad to think about this and went into her room, weeping over the misfortune of ugly Beauty, who hadn't even realized that no one would ever love her, maybe for as long as she lived. There was no prince for her.

But Beauty was still waiting on the fourth night, and the fifth, and the sixth. On the seventh night a man appeared from behind the bushes on the edge of the yard, startling her. He was quite handsome and she immediately felt sure that this was her prince. He was about thirty years old, with a gentle gaze, his hair neatly combed back, wearing clothes that were dark and sombre. He was holding a single rose, walking toward her, and then he handed her that rose hesitantly, as if afraid of being rejected.

"For you," said that man, "Beauty."

Beauty accepted it with a flowering heart, and then the man disappeared. He appeared again the following night, with another rose to give her, and then disappeared again. Only on the third night, after he had given her another rose, and Beauty had accepted it, did the man say:

"Tomorrow night I am going to knock on your bedroom window."

That whole day she waited for night to come and for her prince to appear at her bedroom window, like a girl eager for her first date. She wondered what dress to wear, and fussed over her outfit in front of the mirror. She forgot about her hideous face and tried to adorn herself with everything that was on her mother's old dressing table, even borrowing some things from Rosinah's vanity. Rosinah herself didn't know about the man's visits, and every time Beauty came in with a rose she simply thought the girl had picked it herself. But Rosinah grew perplexed, or saddened, when she saw Beauty making herself up in a fuss all day.

"Like a frog trying to dress herself up like a princess," she thought to herself while rubbing her wet eyes.

Beauty hoped to meet that old man, that kind angel who liked to appear out of nowhere, but he never visited her anymore, not since the prince had come, despite the fact that she had a lot of questions, like what a girl was supposed to do to prepare for her first date, what she should say or do if the prince seduced her, what she should do when he knocked on her window and she opened it, and, if they had to talk, what should they talk about. She wanted to discuss everything with the kind angel, but the old guy never appeared.

In the end she just wore an ordinary everyday dress and began to wait in earnest once night finally fell. Not on the veranda, but in her own room. She sat on the edge of the bed, obviously quite nervous, her ears perked up, like a job applicant who waits nervously for her name to be called, anxious that she would miss the sound of the knock, that might be gentle and quiet. Every once in a while she would stand up and peek out the window curtain, but there was nothing but the view of the yard with its plants all black in the dark, and she sat down again on the edge of the bed, just as anxious as before.

Then she heard the knock, so soft that she had to strain her ears, and then she heard the knock again, three times. With mixed emotions, half-running, Beauty went toward the window and opened it.

There stood her prince, with a rose just as usual.

"May I come in?" asked the prince.

Beauty nodded shyly.

After handing the rose to Beauty, the prince jumped through the window into the bedroom. He stood for a moment, looking around, slowly walking back and forth from one corner of the room to another, and then turned to look at Beauty, who had just closed the window without locking it. The prince sat on the edge of the bed, and gestured for Beauty to sit beside him. The girl obeyed, and for a moment they both were silent.

"I have been wanting to meet you for so long," said the prince.

Beauty was quite flattered so she didn't ask where he knew her from.

"For so long, I have been wanting to get to know you," the prince continued, "and for so long I have been wanting to touch you."

That made Beauty's heart race. She didn't dare look at the man, and her whole body suddenly felt cold as the man touched her hand, and held it so gently.

"Might I kiss the back of your hand?" asked the prince. Beauty hadn't even responded, or maybe she was unable to reply, when the prince kissed the back of her right hand.

Their first date was dominated by the words of the prince, while Beauty mostly stayed mute, embarrassed and shy, occasionally nodding or shaking her head, and then turning embarrassed and shy once again. They spent an hour and a half like that, until it was time for the prince to go home. He left the house the same way he had come: jumping through the window. But before he left, he made plans for their next date.

"Wait for me, just as you were waiting for me, this weekend."

In any case, that weekend Beauty vowed to speak. She would not stay dumb, nor just nod and shake her head, embarrassed and shy. She had to speak and do whatever was necessary so that the prince would not get bored with her. The old man never came again, but Beauty stopped caring. She had found his replacement, who was better looking, and kinder, who flattered her, who often seduced her, and who maybe even loved her. Her heart pounded waiting for the weekend to come.

Just as he had promised, the prince came that weekend, still carrying yet another a rose. He came in through the window and sat at the edge of the bed with Beauty. Then, taking the initiative, Beauty asked in an unwaveringly timid voice:

"Where did you get that rose?"

"From your yard."

"Oh really?"

"I'm short on cash."

They chuckled.

Then the prince once again took Beauty's hand, and this time Beauty returned his grasp. Without asking if he might, the prince kissed the back of her hand, making Beauty return to her old habit. All embarrassed and shy. She felt him begin to gently stroke her hand, with a touch that was so soft and lulling it made her float, just like someone who was slowly drifting off to sleep. Then suddenly she had the man right in front of her, his face was right in front of her face, and it made her heart pound harder and harder. Before realizing what was happening, that face was approaching, and she felt her lips touched by the lips of the prince, then felt the prince crush her lips, making them quite wet. She tried to return his kisses, and began to feel that it wasn't only their lips, but now their tongues that began to play roughly. They kissed for a long time, almost half an hour, until it was time for the prince to take his leave and go home.

"I'll wait for you next weekend." This time it was Beauty who spoke, and the prince nodded with his enchanting smile.

Those kisses were quite impressive to Beauty, and she hoped the weekend would come as quickly as a flitting fly, which comes and goes and comes back again. She was still feeling their heat the next day, and she was still feeling it the day after that. She remembered, step by step, how they had arrived at the moment of the kiss, and it made her heart tremble every time she thought about it.

And so it was, at their next meeting, that kisses were the first thing they said to one another. They started practically at the windowsill, with Beauty standing in her bedroom and the prince still standing outside. Finally the prince climbed through the window into her room and Beauty closed the shutters, but the whole time they never unlocked their lips. The kisses continued inside the bedroom, with Beauty pressed to the wall and the prince pressed up against her body, wild and full of desire.

Slowly but surely the prince's naughty hands began to slide under Beauty's dress, and the atmosphere in the room grew hot. They took off their clothes piece by piece, dropping them to the floor, until they were bare and the prince embraced Beauty and carried her to the bed.

"I am going to teach you to make love," said the prince.

"Yes, teach me," Beauty replied.

So they began. Beauty was still a virgin so she moaned, caught between her feelings of pain and pleasure, causing a ruckus and making Rosinah stand outside the bedroom door, confused. She opened the door (that Beauty had forgotten to lock) and saw only Beauty's naked body bouncing up and down on top of her bed. She just shook her head in a sad and solemn manner, closed the door gently, and left her. Meanwhile the prince continued to destroy Beauty's crotch, making her bleed but also making her scream in exquisite joy.

Her prince always came in through the window but Beauty always waited for him on the veranda, because she wanted to witness the moment of his arrival, driven by her uncontrollable longing. They made love every time they met, sometimes twice, and felt like the happiest couple in the world. Beauty didn't wonder why Rosinah couldn't see the prince, or why when Dewi Ayu rose from the grave and returned to the house and forced down the door, she couldn't see the prince either. They had been feeding on a regular diet of miracles in that household, and so she didn't feel amazed. After all, Rosinah had never even seen the old man angel either, even though Beauty could see him.

Then Beauty got pregnant.

But even after she realized that she was pregnant, Beauty still waited for the prince to come, and they made love. She never told the prince about her pregnancy, because she was afraid it would ruin all their happiness.

Until one night, not long after Dewi Ayu had once again vanished into the world of the dead, as Beauty was lying naked with the prince in her bed, resting after making love, a man broke down the door with an air rifle in his hand. He was a man of short and chubby stature, with a sad air about him. He shivered a little in terror when he saw Beauty's face, but his gaze quickly shifted to the prince, filled with rage.

"You!" he said. "Murderer of Rengganis the Beautiful, I have come to avenge her death!"

The prince wasn't able to save himself when the rifle fired and its expertly aimed bullet lodged in the center of his forehead. He fell back onto the bed, dying. The man with the gun pumped the air again, loaded another bullet, and shot the prince again. He shot as many as five times, full of hatred, as Beauty screamed and screamed.

All anybody knew was that he was shot to death while visiting his grandmother's house.

Krisan's burial was attended by the entire family, with Adinda looking full of grief. Now it was complete: Alamanda had lost Shodancho and Ai, Maya Dewi had lost Maman Gendeng and Rengganis the Beautiful, and Adinda had now lost Krisan after having lost Comrade Kliwon. They had all lost everyone they loved.

The three of them followed Krisan's coffin, heading toward the Budi Dharma cemetery, and along the road Alamanda and Maya Dewi tried to comfort Adinda.

"We are like a cursed family," Adinda sobbed.

"We are not *like* a cursed family," corrected Alamanda. "We are truly and completely cursed."

Old Kamino was digging a grave for Krisan right next to his father's grave, as Adinda had requested. She had already reserved the next plot over for herself.

Usually, women didn't go to the graveyard. Only in special cases did a woman go, when she truly couldn't bear to be separated from the dead, as had happened with Farida many years ago. But for

Krisan's burial, the attendants were the three sisters, plus six neighborhood men who served as pallbearers and the mosque imam, who would pray for the dead man.

There was no one else besides them, standing in their dark clothes under the parasols that protected them from who knows what, because the sun never shone very brightly in the afternoon and no rain was falling. There was only those three, until after a long while two dark spots appeared in the distance. They grew closer and closer and then those spots turned into figures, and when they were even closer it turned out they were two other women, also dressed in mourning clothes.

What was even more surprising was that those two women had also came to bid Krisan farewell, just as his corpse was being lowered and the earth began to swallow him up. Those three sisters were shocked, not just by their presence, but also by the hideous face that one of them had, which at first they thought must be the face of a graveyard ghost. But they soon remembered the gossip about Dewi Ayu's fourth daughter, whom they had never met, but who was said to be as ugly as a monster. That woman, the ugly one, seemed to be quite distraught over Krisan's death. She cried and looked desperately at the body wrapped in a burial shroud which began to disappear under the earth as if she wasn't willing to let him go. She seemed even more upset than Adinda herself.

It was Alamanda who emboldened herself to ask, "Are you Beauty?"

Beauty nodded. "And I know that you are Alamanda, Adinda, and Maya Dewi."

"We are all Dewi Ayu's daughters," said Alamanda. She embraced Beauty without a care for her monster face.

Beauty spoke again. "Please accept my condolences at the death of the only one that you all had left."

When the funeral ceremony was finished they all went to Dewi

Ayu's house, where Beauty lived with Rosinah. They circled through the house, looking at the photos of themselves from when they were still small, looking at the photos of Dewi Ayu, and crying to remember their difficult past. They had become a gang of abandoned orphans. All they had now was each other, and their effort to try to truly belong to one another once again.

"Mama came back but she didn't stay for very long, and left again before Krisan died," said Beauty.

"That's just how dead people are," said Maya Dewi. "My husband came again too, on the third day after his death."

After that, they each still lived in their own houses, continuing on with their quiet lives. To entertain themselves, they visited one another. After her first appearance at the funeral, even Beauty began to venture out of the house to visit her older sisters. She no longer cared about people's stares. She wore long dresses and a veil that almost covered her entire face. The women took a deep pleasure in their new lives, trying to forget all the misfortune that had befallen them, loving each other, and satisfied with that love.

And it was that way until they grew old, to the point that people often gossiped about them, calling them "the gang of widows" when they all got together.

But they were so happy, and loved each other so much.

During the sixth month of her pregnancy, Beauty went into premature labor and her baby died without ever getting the chance to cry or shout. Her older sisters buried the baby in the garden behind the house, with the help of the mute Rosinah.

"Didn't you give it a name before you buried it?" asked Alamanda.

"A name would only hurt me more."

"If I might ask, whose child was that baby, in fact?" asked Adinda.

"Mine and my prince's."

Of course much still remained unsaid between them. So they didn't force Beauty to say who he was, that man she called her prince.

The baby was buried and they went on with their lives, loving each other and guarding each other's secrets.

When Rengganis the Beautiful's corpse was found, Krisan suffered from a profound terror that people would finally discover that it was he who had murdered that girl. The fear grew worse because he had also hidden Ai's corpse under his bed, and Shodancho was furiously looking for Ai everywhere.

He considered returning the corpse to the cemetery but was afraid someone would catch him at it, because ever since Shodancho found out that someone had dug up the grave and taken his child's body, the cemetery had been guarded. Returning Ai to her grave was not a wise move at all, and he practically lost his mind trying to think how he could make that body disappear from underneath his bed before somebody discovered it.

He practically caged himself inside his room, with the door always locked, worried that his mother or his grandmother would enter and investigate the fragrant aroma that wafted up faintly from the space under the bed. He even swept his own room himself, so that his mother or grandmother wouldn't try to come in and clean up the place.

Krisan had even tried to chop up the body of the girl he loved into small pieces so that he could easily dispose of them. Maybe making her into food for the dogs was safer than returning her to the grave, since that way she would never be found. But to see that beautiful face, that face that didn't rot even in death, that face that looked just as if she was sleeping and at some point would wake up and rub her eyes, Krisan couldn't do it. He loved her so much, and it made him cry to imagine himself chopping her up to bits, so that he no longer had the strength to lift the cleaver that he had ready, and he returned Nurul Aini, still wrapped in her burial shroud, to her place back under his bed.

He was at the point of desperation, about to confess all of his sins, when he thought of a brilliant idea. He would do it, and say goodbye to Ai.

Just as when he had gone to the ocean with Rengganis the Beautiful and Ai's corpse, he dressed the body up in his own clothes. At night, as dawn was approaching, he lifted that corpse onto his back and rode his bicycle to the shore. He stole the same boat he had stolen before. He brought Ai's corpse to the middle of the ocean. And not just her corpse, but also two large stones, almost twice as big as her head.

He reached the spot where he had killed Rengganis the Beautiful as the new day dawned. That part of the ocean was very deep, even the sharks wouldn't find her there. He tied the girl's body—with tears streaming down his face, but he had to do it—to the two stones, so tightly that bites from sail fish wouldn't break the cords apart. With such heavy stones, when he threw her in, Ai's dead body quickly sank to the depths of the ocean and disappeared without a trace. Shodancho would never find her, even if he sought her for a hundred years.

Krisan headed for home with a heavy heart, but he was finally at peace. He passed by a fisherman who was out boating all alone, and that fisherman questioned him.

"What are you doing alone out on the ocean, without even one fish in your boat?"

What are you doing alone out on the ocean, without even one fish in your boat?

"Getting rid of a corpse," said Krisan, shivering to hear that man's voice echo, reverberating against who knows what.

"Heartbroken over a beautiful lover? Ha. Ha. Ha. Let me give you some advice, kid, look for an ugly lover. They will never hurt you."

Heartbroken over a beautiful lover? Ha. Ha. Ha. Let me give you some advice, kid, look for an ugly lover. They will never hurt you.

Then the fisherman left, heading off in the opposite direction, but Krisan kept thinking about his advice. And when he arrived at the place where he had parked his minibike, he said to himself, "Maybe it's true, I should look for an ugly lover. The ugliest in the world."

Not long after Dewi Ayu was able to kill that mighty evil spirit, Kinkin played with his *jailangkung* at Rengganis the Beautiful's grave. He was certain that this time he would succeed, because that evildoer who had always thwarted him had now been defeated. He planted an effigy in the shape of a wooden doll into the dirt on top of the grave, which would become the medium for Rengganis the Beautiful's spirit, and then he began reciting mantras. The doll began to tremble, a sign that the spirit had been called, but then it shook violently, a sign the spirit was angry, and then it almost collapsed. Kinkin tried to calm it down, but Rengganis the Beautiful's spirit rebuked him.

"You idiot, what are you doing?!"

"Calling your spirit."

"Yes, obviously," said Rengganis the Beautiful. "But listen up: no matter what, you will never be able to marry me."

"I just want to know who killed you. Please permit me to seek revenge for you, and avenge my love," said Kinkin while prostrating his body in front of that wooden doll, truly begging.

That wooden doll, Rengganis the Beautiful, said, "Even if you lived for a thousand years I would never tell you who killed me."

"Why not? Don't you want me to avenge your death?"

"No, because I still really love him."

"Ok, then I'll kill him and you two can meet in the world of the dead."

"That's bullshit. You're just trying to trick me." And Rengganis the Beautiful disappeared.

But finally he did find out the truth, not from the spirit of Rengganis the Beautiful but from another spirit, one he didn't recognize. He called spirits at random, believing that now no one would be preventing them from speaking truthfully, and believing that all the spirits knew what human beings didn't know. He called one of the spirits, who looked old and frail, but its voice was quite strong.

"Ha. Ha. Ha. I'm not as strong as before, but I'm back, kid."

Ha. Ha. Ha. I'm not as strong as before, but I'm back, kid.

"Do you know who killed Rengganis the Beautiful?" asked Kinkin.

"Yup. It was Krisan who killed Rengganis the Beautiful. Kill him, if you really love that girl, and if you have the balls. Ha. Ha. Ha."

Yup. It was Krisan who killed Rengganis the Beautiful. Kill him, if you really love that girl, and if you have the balls. Ha. Ha. Ha.

And that was how he killed Krisan, in Beauty's room, with five well-practiced shots from an air rifle.

For seven years after that he huddled in prison, at the mercy of all the bad guys there. He was sodomized about once a week, beaten almost every day, forced to share half of his allotment of food at every meal, and lost all of the possessions that he had given to Kamino for as long as he was locked up. But even amid all of that suffering in prison he was happy, because he was there on a mission of true love, avenging the death of the woman he had adored ever since the first moment he laid eyes on her.

He received one year's clemency for good behavior and was freed. He appeared in the outside world looking haggard and emaciated, with long unkempt hair and his face turned into skin and bone, his brow and jaw protruding. He was like a living skeleton, but he inhaled the air of his liberty with a sense of complete independence.

Even though he had been given some clothes and some money for food and transportation he walked on foot from the city jail, and didn't change his clothes, still wearing tattered rags like a city hobo. The clothes they had provided him were just folded in his hands, and the money he had been given was safe in his pocket. He didn't want to stop anywhere or waste any time. He wanted to go back home and make sure that that man had been buried.

Finally he found Krisan's grave, next to the grave of Comrade Kliwon. His name was clearly written on his grave marker, so there could be no mistake. Kinkin made a new grave marker. He threw away the old one bearing Krisan's name, and exchanging it with the new one he had made.

And so now there is written: DOG (1966–1997).

For years, Krisan had kept thinking about that idea, about having a hideous lover. "What's wrong with ugly women?" he asked himself. "They can be fucked just like beautiful women can." And he remembered the talk about Dewi Ayu's daughter who people said was ugly, maybe the most terrifying-looking person on the face of the earth, and even though he knew that Dewi Ayu was his grandmother, which meant that this ugly face who they said was named Beauty was his aunt, he didn't care. He had screwed his own cousin, so where was the harm in screwing his own aunt?

So one night he went to his grandmother's house, and saw that the girl was sitting on the veranda as if she was waiting for someone. He was a little bit unsure about how he could get to know her, so for a number of days he just watched her from the darkness before going home tired. Only on the seventh day did he dare push through the hedge at the side of the yard. He picked a rose that was growing there, approached Beauty, and gave her the flower.

"For you," he said, "Beauty."

After that it all went well, until they finally fucked. Fucked. Fucked. And kept on fucking. What was the difference now, everything felt the same. Sleeping with Rengganis the Beautiful and sleeping with hideous Beauty wasn't all that different. Everything was the same, everything made his genitals spew. He kept on having sex with that woman. "Fucking her," he explained. And then he found out that the girl was pregnant, but he didn't care "and kept on fucking her."

Until one day Beauty asked, "Why do you want me?"

He replied, not knowing whether he was being honest or not, "Because I love you."

"You love a hideous woman?"

"Yeah."

"Why?"

Because "why" is always difficult to answer, he didn't answer. He could only respond "how," and that was easy. To show his love, he kept on caressing her; he didn't care how ugly she was, how disgusting, how terrifying. Everything felt fine, he had discovered a joy almost unlike any other that he had ever experienced in his life. But Beauty kept on hounding him, every time they met and made love, with the question, "Why?" Krisan stayed mute. Even though he knew the answer, he didn't want to say it. But the night before he was killed, he finally replied.

His fourth confession: "Because beauty is a wound."

Because beauty is a wound.